Praise for Brooke Lea Foster's
Summer Darlings

"I was immediately seduced by *Summer Darlings*. Foster cleverly conceals her characters' deceits and betrayal beneath a stunning, sun-spangled surface, and Martha's Vineyard is portrayed with glamorous period detail. This is one terrific summer read."

—Elin Hilderbrand, *New York Times* bestselling author of
The Hotel Nantucket

"A perfect summer book, packed with posh people, glamor, mystery, and one clever, brave, young nanny. This book just might be the most fun you'll have all summer."

—Nancy Thayer, *New York Times* bestselling author of
Surfside Sisters

"Engrossing . . . Foster's musings on money and class, along with her believable depictions of over-the-top behavior, elevate this tale above typical summer fare."

—*Publishers Weekly*

"Innocent intrigue segues into a love triangle—and goes out with a blackmail-back-stabbing bang."

—*People*

"Beautifully written and richly detailed—it pulled me in from the very first page. Heddy is an unforgettable heroine, and I'll be recommending this book to everyone I know."

—Sarah Pekkanen, #1 *New York Times* bestselling author
of *You Are Not Alone*

"Foster has written a coming-of-age story that exposes the sparkling glamor and dark underbelly of the haves and have nots in the 1960s. *Summer Darlings* is utterly atmospheric and compelling."

—Julia Kelly, author of *The Last Garden in England* and *The Light Over London*

"I was swept away by *Summer Darlings* and its fiercely unforgettable heroine, Heddy Winsome. This perfect summer read blends it all: intrigue, romance, a gilded atmosphere, and gorgeous writing."

—*Entertainment Weekly*

"A fresh new voice in historical fiction! Filled with 1960s nostalgia and a host of deftly drawn characters, this is a novel that gives us an intimate look at the world of privilege, proving once again that money does not buy happiness."

—Renée Rosen, bestselling author of *Park Avenue Summer*

"The enchanting beaches, dazzling parties, and elusive social circles of Brooke Lea Foster's 1962 Martha's Vineyard carry secrets and twists that keep us breathless. A delicious read filled with an acute sense of place and unexpected discoveries about class, status, and ambition."

—Marjan Kamali, author of *The Stationery Shop*

"*Summer Darlings* has all the ingredients of a delightfully fizzy beach cocktail: A spunky, working-class Wellesley student determined to make her mark, the deceptively 'perfect' wealthy couple that employs her, two alluring suitors, and a bombshell movie star with a heart of gold. If you like your summer escapism with a nostalgic splash of *Mad Men*–era glamor, you'll love this surprisingly twisty debut."

—Karen Dukess, author of *The Last Book Party*

"A delicious romp through mid-century Martha's Vineyard replete with movie stars, sun-drenched beaches, and fancy outings to the club. *Summer Darlings* is about the human desire to strive toward something more, and the strength a woman will find within herself when she listens to her inner voice."

—Susie Orman Schnall, author of
We Came Here to Shine and *The Subway Girls*

"The romantic entanglements and the scandalous exploits of the rich and entitled makes this suitable for a quick beach read."

—*Booklist*

"This luminous novel feels like the summer you first fell in love. This unputdownable novel sparkles with wit and insight, captures the Vineyard's beauty, and, most of all, reveals Heddy with truth and tenderness."

—Luanne Rice, *New York Times* bestselling author of *Last Day*

"A taut portrait of money and social status, and of a young woman navigating her place in the world. Foster offers a glittering glimpse into the private lives of New England's elite families, while exposing the dark underbelly of privilege. I couldn't stop turning the pages until I had reached the breathless, satisfying conclusion."

—Meredith Jaeger, author of *Boardwalk Summer* and
The Dressmaker's Dowry

"A solid beach read."

—*Library Journal*

ALSO BY BROOKE LEA FOSTER

Summer Darlings

ON GIN LANE

Brooke Lea Foster

GALLERY BOOKS

New York   London   Toronto   Sydney   New Delhi

G

Gallery Books

An Imprint of Simon & Schuster, Inc.

1230 Avenue of the Americas

New York, NY 10020

First Gallery Books hardcover edition May 2022

GALLERY BOOKS and colophon are registered trademarks of Simon & Schuster, Inc.

For information about special discounts for bulk purchases, please contact Simon & Schuster Special Sales at 1-866-506-1949 or business@simonandschuster.com.

The Simon & Schuster Speakers Bureau can bring authors to your live event. For more information or to book an event, contact the Simon & Schuster Speakers Bureau at 1-866-248-3049 or visit our website at www.simonspeakers.com.

Interior design by Davina Mock-Maniscalco

Manufactured in the United States of America

10 9 8 7 6 5 4 3 2 1

Library of Congress Cataloging-in-Publication Data is available.

ISBN 978-1-9821-7443-9
ISBN 978-1-9821-7445-3 (ebook)

*To my mother, my grandmother, my sisters, my aunts,
and all of the other strong, smart, and passionate women
who have helped me find my way.*

May we all have a Starling in our lives.

ON GIN LANE

PROLOGUE

May 22, 1956
New York City

Everleigh invited herself inside the commanding foyer before the butler had fully opened the door, and now, even as he disappeared down the wood-paneled hall to announce her, his pace lacked the urgency she felt. She glanced down at her black pumps against the Persian rug, the peacock-green and mauve weave fading at the center. No doubt from a long line of women parading on top, a fidgety, well-dressed stream of society girls accompanied by their mothers or aunts or grandmothers holding crocodile-leather purses, waltzing in and out of Madame Dillard's sitting room. No one liked to think they were visiting Madame to talk to a matchmaker, no. Modern girls had more romantic notions about love, and yet, on their mothers' urging, everyone Everleigh knew had met with her. "She's been around for a generation, and she has a knack for connecting the right families," Everleigh's mother had assured her.

That was three years ago, when she and her mother were planning the guest list for Everleigh's debutante ball, before her friend Elsa's tragedy, before Everleigh's bad days outnumbered her good ones. Madame Dillard kept a blue book on two thousand wealthy gentlemen in New York, calling it "Madame Dillard's List," and there was a high premium for a peek inside her prudent dossiers that assessed a man's personality (aimless, spirited, Machiavellian) and his financial outlook (grim, growing, established). In the end, she'd provided Everleigh and her mother a list of shiny young men to invite to her ball at a ratio of two to one, each with a pedigree to match Everleigh's own.

And a year later, it had ended in an engagement. Now a canceled engagement.

Beyond a grand staircase, down a hall lined with knotty pine wall paneling, Everleigh heard the rustle of papers, an exchange of quiet words between the housekeeper and Madame herself. Everleigh pulled off her gloves, then tucked them into her demure kiss lock purse, the delicate gold chain link balanced against her wrist. Inside was a red lipstick, face powder, two rolls of film, an embroidered handkerchief, a checkbook, and a satin change purse as well as a gingham head scarf to protect her hair on those windy walks down Madison Avenue.

The petite cuckoo clock ticked to five after eleven, then ten.

"Hello, dear." Madame's cream Chanel suit was without wrinkle, but you could count the creases in her splotchy neck like pancakes on a plate. Everleigh followed her into the dim and moody parlor, with its pinch-pleated thick floral drapes and trendy hourglass brass fireplace sconces.

"Mother is indisposed. She apologizes." Everleigh hadn't spoken to her mother in two weeks; they wouldn't let anyone in to see her yet, believing it best to separate her entirely from her family during the most intense of her therapies.

"I heard about what happened. It's unfortunate." Madame sat near the crackling fireplace; spring's chill was holding firm into May. "Would you like to take care of the unpleasantries first?"

"Of course," Everleigh rushed to open her purse so she could write out her father's check for fifteen minutes of Madame's time. She needed to explain what happened with George and how since they broke up last year, men at parties would flirt with her but only briefly.

How they sometimes looked past her altogether while talking, indicating that the conversation had gone on too long. At last night's gala, not one person had asked her to dance.

What are we going to do with you? her father had been saying to Everleigh since she was sixteen, shaking his head and rolling his eyes, and he'd said it again last week over pastries at the Palm Court. As if the sight of her, twenty-three and without a ring on her finger, was a burden he didn't know how to be rid of. He'd always wanted a son— *Oh, how much easier it was to send a son into the world,* he'd bellow— and he and her mother had tried for another child, but then Everleigh's mother's mind had unspooled like thread, and she wasn't sure they tried much after that.

"Madame, thank you for seeing me." Everleigh's lips pressed inward, her hands folded in her lap. Truly, she wished she didn't have to sit here; truly, she wished she could spend the day browsing the aisles of Willoughby's camera store on Thirty-Second Street, where clerks placed picture finders on velvet cloths as if you were examining precious jewels, or pulling spines from the Art & Architecture Collection at the New York Public Library, where she read everything she could about photography. But a hobby was useful to her only in that it provided entertainment, an escape from the pressure to be exactly as she was expected to be; it certainly wasn't going to get her married. Which was why she was here. She needed to be practical. Plus, she was tired of living at a hotel with her parents. She wanted her own life.

"Madame. Can you tell me what is being whispered about me? I need to know what I'm up against. In meeting someone else." She'd asked her friends already, but she could tell they were being too kind in their assessment.

Madame flicked her eyes catlike, tilting her head to the side. "Some women find this a very long season in their lives."

Everleigh nodded. Mating season, as she and her best friend,

Whitney, called it, was endless. In the beginning, Everleigh had reveled in the daily champagne lunches, the monthly order of new dresses for upcoming engagements, the fun of prancing around gilded ballrooms under crystal tiered chandeliers for men to admire. But most of the women her age were already engaged, if not married, including Whitney. She was beginning to feel like an undesirable pair of pumps left on the clearance rack.

Madame poured her tea in a porcelain cup with violets on it, and after taking it, Everleigh spun a honey stick at the center, watching the tea leaves swirl like a whirlpool, then finding comfort when they settled on the bottom. How badly she wanted to be settled. Married. A mother. She would finally graduate from this strange purgatory she was living in, where she was no longer a college girl and not yet a young bride, but something purposeless in between.

Madame blew over the steam of her cup. "Sometimes a young woman figures out who she is during her coming out, performing with the grace of an Olympian, and sometimes she shuts down entirely, confuses herself, and her light grows dim. You're not the latter, are you?"

"You misunderstand," Everleigh pushed her shoulders back with pride, clearing her throat. "I'm not worn down. What happened with George was . . . necessary. It's that gentlemen in my extended circle aren't asking me out at all, like my name has been wiped clear from their memory."

What Everleigh had come for today was a list, a slip of paper where Madame would jot down the names of a few men who were new to the city. Men who didn't know what happened with George or judge her past. Men her parents would approve of, but ones, too, whom Everleigh might develop feelings for in due time.

The tailored armchair creaked under Madame's weight as she set down her teacup. "I might as well be blunt. Your dossier is slipping, dear. I'm sorry, but it's your mother. Those nervous conditions may be genetic, and men don't like knowing that you may carry some of those traits. Plus, I've been hearing whispers again about you and your friend Elsa Loring, and even if I know you weren't involved in that awful nightmare, people talk, and talk can lead to ruin."

The tea was now too bitter to sip, and Everleigh returned the cup to the table. "But I didn't, you know I had no part in that, and my sanity—I can provide the report of an analyst. Mother's conditions have skipped me entirely." She dropped her head in her hands. Everleigh knew her ex was spreading ugly rumors about her, but she wasn't certain how far they'd traveled. *You're as crazy as your mother,* he'd told her the night he'd walked out on her. And what if her mind did fail her someday? A psychologist couldn't guarantee she'd remain sane for her entire life. "Madame, please. You didn't blunder in your match with George. I blame myself for the breakup. But you must know those rumors are from the mouth of an angry ex-fiancé."

"Oh, Everleigh. You've always been a generous girl, and I won't soon forget the day you helped me home after I twisted my ankle on that patch of ice. I appreciate you, dear. I do, but . . ." Madame leaned back into the couch, patting her thighs with both palms, like she was done with the conversation. Perhaps she was done with Everleigh. "What about the eldest Lawlor son? Didn't you two have a spark?"

"Engaged." Everleigh's smile flickered with nerves. "Most of the men I know are, and the ones that aren't, I couldn't force an attraction with."

The woman's stout figure leaned forward onto her substantial knees. "You will find someone, dear. If you're sensible, if you choose wisely."

"But I want to fall in love, and my father, he's angry about—"

"Dear, all of you girls today want butterflies and roses, but times haven't changed as much as you will them to. It's more important to find a gentleman you can trust with your inheritance than someone that brings color to your cheeks. Accept that, and you'll see there are small choices, perhaps the better word is *allowances*, you can make to pick a partner."

Madame called to the butler to show her guest out, and Everleigh gathered her purse, rising to her feet. Without a slip of paper. Without a single name.

There was resignation in her goodbye as she followed the butler into the hallway. But Everleigh surprised herself when she stopped, doubling back to the parlor, where the doyenne was making notations in a black notebook. Everleigh waited for Madame to look up at her in the doorway.

"Not only did I help carry you home the day you twisted your ankle; I iced it and fetched pain reliever and made you tea, keeping you company until your staff returned from lunch." Everleigh smiled at her, her tone even and kind. "So, perhaps, maybe you can telephone me. With a single name or two?"

"My, my. Aren't you full of pleasant persistence?" Madame closed her black book in her lap, her sagging cheeks crinkling. "Okay. I will do some research and call you."

A bus whooshed by as she opened Madame's front door, stepping triumphantly into a chill that whipped her hair against her cheeks and stung the damp corners of her eyes. She was startled by the presence of a young gentleman facing her on the brownstone's steps. He was raising his finger to the doorbell but stopped when he saw her, grinning, the light growing slanted and sunny around him.

"Are you Madame Dillard?" he asked, using his hand instead to push his fingers through a handsome wave of blond hair.

"Goodness, no," Everleigh said, pulling the door shut. "I'm just visiting."

"Well, hopefully you're off to somewhere more fun." He stared up at the brownstone, then back at Everleigh. "I'm a bit nervous. A friend told me Madame was a required stop in my coming of age in New York."

"Aren't you a bit old to be coming of age?" She laughed, grateful to him for making her smile.

"Excuse me, but I just turned twenty-five." His eyes crinkled, blue rounds alight like Fourth of July sparklers.

She hesitated before going down the steps. "I'm going for a walk in Central Park." There was something about the dashing way he stood in his tweed blazer and collared shirt, how his smile was generous and forthcoming, how he was gazing at her like a new puppy, exuberant and ready to play, that made her curious. He hadn't landed on her doorstep, but he'd shown up here nonetheless, meaning he was an eligible man in Manhattan. Perhaps a worthwhile one.

"Now how would I get to that part of Central Park called the Ramble, if I were to leave from here?" He pivoted toward Lexington Avenue, then back in the direction of Park Avenue. "One month in, and this city still turns me around."

"But it's a—"

"It's a grid, I know. All of you New Yorkers are the same." He shook his head, unfolding a map he pulled from the back pocket of his trousers. "This is my bible these days."

Everleigh pointed to the large green rectangle at the center of the map, running her finger to the northern section. "The Ramble is my favorite part of the park. I bring my camera sometimes." She could lose herself climbing the enormous boulders, taking pictures of the sun setting over the city, the light bouncing off the lush sycamore trees.

"Maybe we can go for a walk there sometime. My name is Roland." He gripped her hand, leaving a warm imprint where his palm had pressed into hers. "Roland Whittaker."

"Everleigh Farrows," she said, waiting a beat before turning and descending the stairs. "Well, enjoy New York."

She adjusted her scarf about her head, moving in the direction of the park. She would lose herself in the paths straight away, wandering until she came up with a plan.

"Everleigh, wait."

She watched Roland hop down the steps toward the sidewalk. He seemed out of breath, or maybe he was just flustered, but he was in front of her now.

"You know," he said, rubbing the back of his head and holding her gaze, "if you don't mind, I think I'd rather go for a walk. With you."

Already, this man was confident and glossy, flirtatious but earnest. Clearly, not at all shy.

A taxi honked; two young children ran past them. Her mother would murder her if she knew she went to Central Park with a perfect stranger. He could be penniless. He could be a terrible bore. But at this point, what did she have to lose?

Because he might also be wonderful.

JUNE 1957

ONE

S unrise Highway opened up in front of the green MG roadster, and with her hands gripping the steering wheel perforated with tiny supple leather dots, Everleigh hollered to Roland, "Is this thing a car— or a rocket?"

He didn't hear over the roar of the roadway, and she zipped the convertible forward, racing by dry, dusty potato farms, charging for Southampton, that exclusive enclave of old money, a charmer of a town on the Atlantic Ocean that sat about thirty-three miles from the eastern tip of Long Island. She couldn't believe how the car could catch the horizon on these wide-open roads.

She glanced at Roland in the passenger seat, who was pretending to play guitar to the notes of Chuck Berry's "Roll Over Beethoven."

"Should I go faster?" she hollered, this time louder. Roland nodded her on with a mischievous grin, and she felt a jolt, some kind of electric shock in her reflexes, and she pushed down on the accelerator. The speedometer read eighty miles an hour.

Wisps of her dark hair blew out of the gingham headscarf she'd tied about her neck, and she gripped the steering wheel tighter, cursing her parents for forbidding her from learning how to drive, how they said it wasn't a proper pastime for well-bred Manhattan girls. Which was why, in a rare act of rebellion, Everleigh paid their Upper East Side building's doorman five dollars in secret to teach her anyway. They went out together once a week, and then she'd borrow his car sometimes, for an extra five. Later, after she'd been driving for a few years, she'd begged her father for one of those new two-toned pink-and-white Dodge La Femme models that came with a pink jacquard-printed shoulder bag and umbrella to match the car's interiors. But all two-hundred pounds of him shooed her out of his law office on the tenth floor of Thirty-First and Madison, exasperated that the family had a private car service and she didn't want to use it.

Well, now she had a fiancé's car to drive.

As the slick two-seater raced over the Shinnecock Canal, the water's color mimicking the blue of her favorite sapphire ring, the farms turned to forests then back to farms, and Roland began yelling at her to slow down. She had to turn right—"Right now," he yelled—and she managed the sudden angle, the car emitting a resounding screech, catching air and bouncing down on the shiny blacktop. All six feet of her fiancé slammed down alongside her in the passenger seat.

"Take it easy, Lee—I actually need this car. You know, to get around in." He stretched out his tanned arm and rubbed the back of her neck where her garnet necklace clasped. She imagined that as a boy his hands gripped the gear shifts of the cars at his parents' Detroit automotive factories as child's play and, later, when he was a teenager, how he must have stared out at the assembly line and dreamed of building a speedster of his own. Curious that he lost all interest in the family business at the age of twenty. He liked to tell people that he might be a Whittaker, but he was not a Sovereign, the company's fanciest sedan, which Everleigh had seen Princess Grace step out of in *Life* magazine.

"Roland Whittaker, I've done everything I'm supposed to do in this life of mine, from earning straight As and running the high school charity ball to landing one of Manhattan's most eligible bachelors.

Now please, let me have my fun." She noted his aviator sunglasses, how his slick of light hair was blowing up off his baby face. He wore a simple white T-shirt, sleeves rolled over his modest biceps. Just then, the speeding car hit a pothole, and it felt like one of their tires was swallowed whole.

"Your father will kill me if he finds out you've been driving my car without a license." He smirked, but she was forced to brake hard rather than return the gesture. A horse trailer pulled in front of them, the smell of manure so strong that Everleigh pinched her nose. They were truly in the country.

"Well, Daddy doesn't have to know." She wished they were back on the highway, where she didn't have to think much about details, surviving on instinct and adrenaline alone. "When are you going to tell me what we're doing out here?"

His mouth turned up, showing off his fresh shave—Roland was always meticulously groomed—and his whole face glowed like stars, the way it did whenever he had some big idea he wanted to spring on her. Already that afternoon, a week after their June engagement party, a year after they met, he'd surprised her with a telephone call, telling her to pack her bathing suit and several changes of clothes for the weekend. They'd pulled out of her parents' Upper East Side garage to the bleating horns of yellow cabs for a weekend in Southampton. "Souse-hampton," as Roland liked to joke, since residents at the fabled summer colony were known for their spirited parties. Everleigh loved Roland's impulses, the ones where they got in the car and just went, figuring out the details later. They gave her a sense of freedom she'd rarely felt as a debutante.

Roland scratched at his temple, acting perplexed. "Wasn't this drive all your idea?"

"Roland!" She glanced in the rearview mirror, relieved her lips were still the color of fire engines, and, out of the corner of her eye, saw him smiling. "We promised each other no secrets, and this is starting to feel like a secret." Everleigh always thought it a silly promise though; of course she had secrets. After a childhood dressed in stiff formal dresses and elephantine bows, her parents parading her through the Plaza's marble-and-crystal lobby to reach their three-bedroom suite (the apartment her parents snatched up two years after the war), Everleigh savored any night that she and Whitney changed into trousers and talked over martinis at a no-frills bar in the Village. A place where no one knew their names or their parents' names or where they attended school or what their addresses were. It was exhilarating to experience the city anonymously; she sometimes attended free photography lectures or slipped into the Paris Theater across from her apartment, eating a bucket of popcorn alone. These outings were her secrets to keep, and anyway, she knew Roland and her parents would judge them as unconventional, if not entirely improper.

The car began driving rough, like it was trudging through mud, and she and Roland met eyes with concern. He leaned his torso out the window to get a look. "We have a flat, Lee. Let's go as far as we can."

"I thought we didn't have a destination," she toyed.

She steered the car on to Southampton Village's Main Street. It was dusk, and fashionable couples strolled the bricked, tree-lined sidewalks, some eating outdoors at the Buttery, the biggest crowd at a place called Bowden Square. "The owner, Herb McCarthy, is a hoot, a former Brooklyn Law grad turned restaurateur," Roland told her. "You won't get a better steak or a better joke than at Herb's. I'll take you there." He kissed her cheek, and she blew him a kiss in return, her eyes wide with wonder at the sight of a clerk in a suit and pumps locking fancy Saks Fifth Avenue's double doors. Roland caught her surprise and chuckled. "It's not *really* the country out here."

Air hissed from the tire, and the car began to pull to one side. She drove slowly through a lovely neighborhood of imposing houses and parked where Roland told her to, in front of a shingled manse with a large portico out front.

"We can walk from here," he said. "I'll deal with the tire later."

"Walk where?" Everleigh unstuck the cotton of her white collared dress from the backs of her knees. She let Roland grab their suitcases, one leather handle in each of his hands.

"Come on. I want to show you something," Roland said.

A Ford Thunderbird with wood paneling on the side slowed to a stop, and inside, a gentleman about their age, wearing a stethoscope and a shine of dark hair, leaned toward the passenger window, unrolling it.

"Hi, buddy," the young man said, as if he knew them. "You need some help?" On the breast pocket of his white coat, embroidered in red thread, was his name: "Dr. Brightwell." Everleigh immediately blamed his friendliness (or was it nosiness?) on small-town life; as if anyone in the city would care if someone was stuck on the street.

Roland leaned into the open window. "Just a flat, Doc. We'll come back for it."

"You sure? I got a jack in the trunk." The doctor's car idled, puffing gray smoke from the tailpipe.

"It's okay—we live right around the corner."

Everleigh took a step back. "We do?"

The young doctor smiled. "It's going to be hard to get a mechanic out to the summer colony tonight. Unless you have one on staff . . ."

Roland put his hands on his hips, flipping his hair off his face. "Maybe I can borrow one from Mr. Ford. He's on Gin Lane, isn't he?"

"Well, his son is here, Henry Ford II," the doctor said. "A lovely man."

"The Fords live near here?" Everleigh had heard about Halcyon Lodge and its modernist cube-like addition, a glass box designed by Phillip Johnson, but she'd only seen a photo in the *Post*. Roland shushed her, and when the stranger drove off, Roland offered Everleigh his arm, hooking hers inside.

"Shall we," he said.

There was a long row of elm trees on either side of the gracious street, several driveways leading to several more summer "cottages," although it was a hoot to call them that when they probably had six or seven bedrooms, maybe more. She untied her headscarf, setting free her shoulder-length hair and tying the cravat into a fashionable knot at her neck. Her cherry-red flats clicked against the pavement.

Roland pointed to a pair of sparrows jumping branches in a bush. "All the other kids at grammar school went to Lake Michigan, but my mother insisted on Southampton—it's where she summered. There was barely a town then."

Everleigh remembered him mentioning this, but she'd only been here once or twice, to visit Whitney. "Did your family have a house here?" she said.

"Yes, just down the road. They let it go over the years, but I visited last August, and no one had been here in a decade, since Mom died. It was a mess, really. But I remembered how much I loved it. There's something about it. Something that keeps you coming back. It's the light, I think, how it reflects off the potato fields and all that ocean."

The sun shot through the trees, dappling the lush, tended lawns with bright speckles. It was a lovely time of day for a walk, the sun no longer beating directly overhead, and the air was cooler than even thirty minutes before.

"You came out to Southampton without me?" She didn't actually *expect* him to have secrets.

It was as though they'd landed in one exceptionally large and lush park, extravagant mansions tucked amid the flowering shrubs and tall privacy hedges, some with gray shingles and black shutters, others sporting green awnings over white-trimmed windows.

Roland set down the suitcases on the road, kissing her softly. "I was getting things ready for you."

A front door opened, and out of a grand, columned house came a uniformed maid shaking out a rug.

"Ready for me? What on earth are you talking about . . . Is that the ocean?" They walked on; the road ended at a dune, a hill of sand sloping down to the water. White caps crested on blue, like a painter was taking a brush and dotting the landscape with foamy waves. She could hear the surf colliding with the sand, the slow roll of the sea slipping back into the current—how the water could simply disappear, start over, emerge anew, and how appealing that was to her. To think that the very essence of life could begin again.

"See that hotel over there? That's where we're going." Roland was so handsome you wanted to dress him in the latest fashions, like a dashing young actor, and simply admire him. "Welcome to Gin Lane."

She paused in front of the dollhouse of a child's dreams, only it was life-size. "That's your beach house?"

"Not exactly." He started to run toward the expansive hotel in his white Keds despite their heavy suitcases, and Everleigh ran after him, both of them suddenly giddy. She wasn't entirely sure why, other than that they were on holiday. They paused at the hotel, which mimicked a New England–style colonial mansion with a grand porch and white-gravel circular driveway, staring up at its white shingles, emerald-green shutters, and matching double doors. It was only three stories high, but the building extended sideways from the wraparound front porch, with nearly a dozen windows on either side. *Those must be the guest rooms,* she thought.

Roland pointed at a long white sign nestled amid the rose bushes, like he'd built the best paper airplane of his life and needed her to watch him fly it. Everleigh was already reading the sign: "The Everleigh Beach Club Hotel." She said it aloud, taking in Roland's mile-long smile, then looked back at the words emblazoned before her. She noticed then that the shutters had cutouts of seahorses, and there was a large seahorse brass knocker to the side of the hotel's front doors; truly, it was her favorite animal, a fantasy of a creature that had always sparked her imagination in drawings and stories as a child. Had she told him that? Inside she could see a staff busily moving about—the women wearing crisp white pinafores, the men in khakis and white collared shirts with white ties.

Roland put his arm around the curve of her back. "I can't believe no one told you, pet. I was certain you'd find out. I had to hide the paper one day last week because they mentioned that 'this season's most anticipated hotel, the Everleigh,' was opening in Southampton this weekend."

Everleigh didn't fully understand what he meant. "Tell me what, Rolly?"

"That I built this hotel for you. The Everleigh Beach Club Hotel. For my lovely Lee. Happy early wedding present, pet."

Sometimes on the grass in Central Park, Roland's architectural degree inspired daydreams about building a skyscraper, designing a theater, opening a hotel. In return, she'd say she couldn't wait to live in the house her parents had purchased for them in Bronxville, a four-bedroom colonial with a fenced yard, and how soon, they'd hear the pitter-patter of little feet running about. How she'd catalogue their growth with her camera, giving them stacks of photographs to frame and hang through the house, a house where you didn't have to share an elevator with relative strangers to get to the front door.

"This hotel is for me?" She stared up at a large oval window with panes in it, a robin resting its delicate feet on the gingerbread trim.

"Didn't you wonder who I was talking to all those times when I took my calls in the lobby of my apartment building?" He had a look about him, smug and content, like a guy who took a risk on the trading floor and came out on top.

She had mentioned these secretive phone calls to Whitney, but her friend had reassured her that Roland was probably planning their honeymoon; Whitney had seen him visiting the Park Avenue Travel Agency just last week. "You said it was business."

"And when I went away those two weekends?" His eyebrows knitted with amusement.

Everleigh smiled at how obvious it was now and fingered the pearl buttons on her sleeve. "You said you were meeting with the carpenters, on the house in Bronxville."

"I was here!" He grinned. "My father signed the deed to the land over to me, Lee, and I built this. Now we can spend the summer and throw lavish parties at night, then nurse our hangovers the next morning in the waves."

Her heart fell. She supposed that was what they did in the city, but recently, she'd grown tired of all the socializing. Sometimes she just wanted to stay in and read beside him or take her camera out and fiddle with the dials while he played guitar. Maybe put an album on the turntable, listen to their favorite song, and write out the lyrics together. Since she and Roland were engaged in December, it was like they were perpetually getting off a roller coaster, a whirlwind of excitement with people greeting them and congratulating them about their nuptials.

"Spend the summer here? Roland, I couldn't possibly. My parents would never allow it."

"Your parents trust me, Lee, and besides, aren't you dying to escape them? You can go back and forth to the city whenever you need to. Your driver will fetch you, or you can ride the Long Island Railroad. It smells of sour pickles, but it's an easy ride all the same."

Her head kicked back with laughter. "Spending time with you at your apartment is one thing, Rolly, but living with you in a hotel all summer? Never. It's a miracle Daddy agreed to this weekend away."

"Will you trust that I've taken care of it?" he snapped playfully, pointing to the garden. To get to the hotel's double front doors, you traveled a herringbone-patterned brick walkway that curved along another garden with thick tangles of purple, blue, and white flowers on either side. "Now look. One hundred rose bushes planted because they're your favorite. The air in the lobby spritzed with honeysuckle since that's what you wore the day we met."

He tugged her softly backward. "And see that widow's walk? That's our private terrace. I'm having them put two chairs up there. I'll mix you a Paloma every night at sunset. Or heck, we'll drink champagne with strawberries floating in the glass. You can see everything from up there."

"It's incredibly romantic," she said. "You're incredibly romantic. But . . ." Everleigh willed the wrinkles in her forehead to smooth. Most women—every woman she knew actually—would have jumped into his arms by now, over the moon that this was happening. She was happy, but she couldn't live here. She vowed she'd never live in a hotel again.

Roland waited for her response, but she could only stare at the crisp white trim around the windows, the neat lines of the wood siding wrapping the looming building, dwarfing the two of them standing there.

"Oh, Rolly, how did you convince Daddy?"

He took her hand, twirling her into his arms. "I promised that you'd stay in your own hotel room."

Her mouth fell open. "Can you talk a snail out of its shell, too?" She'd seen Roland's silver tongue finagle them the best restaurant reservations, but her father? That meant that when she left for Long Island that second Friday in June, her father had known she was leaving for the summer. He'd barely said goodbye. Mother wasn't even home, playing cards with the bridge ladies. She supposed that they were so blinded by the Whittaker name, by this society wedding, that they were willing to allow Everleigh freedoms they wouldn't have normally.

They'd had to keep pace, too, since Roland's and her relationship had moved swiftly. After their all-day walk in Central Park last May, he'd called her the next day to join him for a picnic. Two nights later, they were dancing at El Morocco, and two weeks after that, they were snuggled up on his living room couch. Everleigh had cradled his head in her lap, stroking his hair, as he explained that he had a girlfriend, someone he wanted to break it off with.

Well, that was a problem she could understand. After that, it was easy to fall into each other, Everleigh secure in the fact that he had left someone *for her*.

A dish broke inside the hotel, and they looked toward the open front doors.

There was so much she wanted to say: how being raised in a hotel residence mostly by her nanny was the loneliest time in her life. That she'd learned to ride a bike in the endless hallways at the Plaza and had hung around the hotel lobby listening to strangers' conversations when her mother and father left her alone. She did her homework at the reception desk, sometimes asking the rotating staff to quiz her on her times tables, and for her reading and writing assignments, she'd employed the help of one of the aging (and rather legendary) widows who occupied the upper floors of the hotel but spent their days reading in the overstuffed armchairs in the lobby. And there were other things that happened in those years at the Plaza. Things no child should have to see.

He rested his chin at the top of her head. "Imagine us, Lee: Sand in our hair, sun on our face. We'll come down only when we feel like seeing people. And skinny-dip by moonlight. We'll kick everyone out some nights so we have the place to ourselves."

"You have it all planned," she said, charmed by how fabulous he made everything sound. She lowered her eyes to the ground. "I just wish you would have asked me—if I wanted to live here, that is."

He twirled her into his arms. "Oh, Lee, you're missing the point. It was a *surprise*. You're not so set in your ways that you can't appreciate a surprise, right?" He pivoted his arm like one of those girls from the game shows gesturing to a prize. "For my Everleigh, my outrageously entertaining, always tenderhearted, beautiful young wife."

"Not yet," she teased, wrapping her arms around his neck. She kissed him softly on the mouth. "Five months until the wedding."

"Listen, pet," Roland turned her around, pulling her backward against his chest, and they stared up at the glowing windows. "It's not just the people at the summer colony that want to be out East anymore. It's every clock puncher from Thirty-Third to Seventy-Second Street, and there's nowhere to put them. So I built a hotel for some of them, and maybe this hotel is just my first. Maybe I can grow an empire, just like my father did with his cars. I had this coveted parcel of land just waiting, prime real estate in a prime resort town, with a dilapidated cottage on it. I could have renovated it for us, but I thought to myself, *There are no zoning laws here. I can do anything!* Do you know how amazing that is, Lee? You can build anything out here if you can buy the land." He kissed the back of her head. "I can make a mark."

"And the house my father bought us in Bronxville? The one I've been furnishing with that interior decorator who has me swimming in swatch fabrics?"

"I told you, just tell her we'll take chintz everything." He laughed, and she did, too, but then his voice turned tender. "The house will be waiting for us the other nine months of the year." Everleigh thought of last night, how they'd seen a movie and then gone back to her parents' apartment, sneaking kisses in the hallway after the elevator doors closed. How happy her parents were when they met Roland. How everyone stopped looking at her with pity.

Everleigh turned around, her eyes crinkling. She had to support him in this, even if she hadn't chosen any of it. "Rolly, I thought you were only good at organizing our Saturday nights, but it turns out, you're more than a pretty face."

He touched a finger to her nose. "And no longer new to the Manhattan social order either. You gave me entrée. The hotel will seal my place."

She felt heat rise in her cheeks at the brazenness of his status seeking. Everleigh had been taught to fight for her place in the pecking order, and yet, she'd always been the woman who felt relieved rather than slighted if she didn't get a gala invitation.

"You have nothing to prove to anyone," she said, even though she knew that New York society judged newcomers with a critical eye. He'd reminded her of the same several months ago when she'd confessed what happened with George, addressing the cruel rumors about her mental state. Roland had shrugged it off. "Everyone makes at least one big mistake in their life," he'd consoled. "George was yours." Roland, who often remarked that Everleigh, who was five foot seven, looked like the young Joan Collins (because she, too, was long legged with wide-set eyes), had accepted her just as she was.

Everleigh hadn't told him the entire truth of what transpired with George, and only Whitney knew the whole story. That she and George had dinner while his parents were out, and after clearing their plates of chicken divan, they'd watched Jackie Gleason, and then he'd drunkenly forced himself upon her on the crushed-velvet sofa in the sitting room. It started innocently with kissing, but then he wanted more, and he'd pinned her, ignored her pleas to stop, and pushed himself between her legs. She wasn't against relations before marriage, but she'd rather her first time be memorable. Luckily, the front door clicked open. The housekeeper had returned to get the sweater she'd left behind, and Everleigh immediately gathered her belongings and raced away. Confusion rattled her as she walked Park Avenue toward the Plaza. They were engaged, so thrusting himself upon her wasn't entirely wrong, but she'd said no, and he'd done it anyway.

Whitney encouraged her to talk with him, and two nights later, they'd met at the Landmark Club. But when the main course arrived, Everleigh began to cry. "George, you were drunk, and this is sacred to me. I want it to feel right." He'd tossed his fork on his medium-rare steak, growling, and they went back and forth a bit, him accusing her of being a prude. She accused him of forcing himself on her. "If you think that there's anything wrong with what I did. If a man can't love his fiancée . . . then, well, then you're crazier than even your mother is," he'd said. When she tried to explain, to say she merely wanted him to move slower next time, he'd pushed out of his chair, rattling the glasses, his voice low and sharp. "I don't want this. It was all my father's slick idea for a family merger. But you're not even *attracted* to me, or I you."

Everleigh had raced to the wallpapered bathroom, crying in the gilded mirror, thinking that he was mistaken and not mistaken in his accusation, while the elderly attendant kept handing her tissues, and then breath perfume, those awful Sen-Sen candy squares that smelled of licorice. The next morning, their mothers tried to smooth things over, but a week later, George announced he was boarding a plane to study viticulture in southern France, leaving his parents furious, and Everleigh's future uncertain.

A year later, when Everleigh told her mother that Roland had proposed, she'd clasped her hands at her chest. "Heavens to Betsy. I declare he's going to save our family name."

Indeed, Roland had rescued Everleigh the moment they met on the sidewalk in front of Madame's brownstone, and best of all, everyone loved him. Well, everyone except her best friend, Whitney, who thought his ego rivaled a Pan Am pilot's. On the outside maybe, Everleigh thought, but Roland let his guard down with Everleigh enough that she knew he needed her for the comfort he could no longer get from his mother.

And now. Now they were here at the ocean, amid farms and wide-open roads. It was summer. Of course she would live in this beautiful place for three months. She would do it for him.

Everleigh felt the fullness of Roland's lips on hers, but then she pulled back and whispered, "The Everleigh Beach Club Hotel." She let the weight of it fill her up inside, the way those Tiffany boxes were supposed to when you popped one open to find a pendant. "Oh, my goodness, Rolly. You named a hotel for me. A hotel!"

She danced her fingers up his T-shirt, giddy and dreamy, like she *had* been missing the point until now. Because he'd whisked her away to this beautiful place, and in an instant, she had a new life. "Roland James Whittaker, did we just run away together?"

The gravel of the driveway crunched underfoot as Roland arranged his newsboy cap on her head, his eyes crinkling. "Let's run away together for the rest of our lives."

TWO

As soon as they stepped inside the bright hotel, the staff began rushing about like they couldn't be busy enough. Everleigh smiled politely at the first arriving guests checking in, while someone in a hotel uniform handed her a flute of champagne. A staffer, perhaps the manager, leaned in to Roland and said, "Mr. Whittaker, she's as beautiful as your hotel, sir."

Blushing, Everleigh held the champagne glass in her palm, cradled between her pointer and middle fingers, and turned 360 degrees to look around at the cushioned wicker chairs and settees. She strained for the right words, hoping to mask the anxiety she was feeling sitting in this unfamiliar lobby that had her name stamped on the entrance. "You might add a few colorful throw pillows to the couches, Rolly, like the Breakers in Palm Beach—I heard from our decorator that Jack Lenor Larsen fabrics are what everyone wants."

"Whatever you like, pet. There's a fabric shop on Jobs Lane." Stevie, a friend from the city, appeared from a back office and handed Roland documents, three different fire and flood insurance policies to review.

"You're here, too?" she said, laughing.

"A nice break from the city," said Stevie, his red hair gelled solid. "I'd be happy to drive you to the shops tomorrow."

"Thank you—how kind. But I prefer to explore new places on foot." Everleigh stretched out her arms, exhausted from the long journey, and smiled. It wasn't the best news that Stevie, who wore awful Hawaiian shirts and spoke with a lisp, was working with Roland on the hotel. Stevie was nice enough, the son of a tailor from the rough part of the Irish Bronx, but there was a hunger in him that, if Everleigh was being honest, sometimes bordered on desperate. She didn't mind when moments later he disappeared into an office behind reception, where a woman in a powder-blue suit was checking in, her brown bob clipped to one side, like her clipped smile. Her husband, dressed in a power suit, laughed with the receptionist.

Setting down the champagne flute on a mirrored side table where Roland stood, Everleigh's thoughts sailed to her girlhood self sitting in a very different hotel lobby. She'd always loved playing hide-and-seek amid the palms and sofas at the Plaza. She'd plead with the smartly dressed tourists not to reveal her hiding place to the concierge or doorman or whoever it was she could enlist to play with her. From her hiding places, she would spy on the women sipping cocktails and tourists who hailed from places as far as England and India, enthralled by their accents and attitudes and the seriousness with which they carried themselves. She wondered if those people ever felt the way Everleigh did now, like every hotel worker had their eyes trained on her. Growing up, the staff at the Plaza might as well have been a team of secret spies. One day the head of chambermaids, Miss Hemlock, actually phoned Everleigh's father to ask in her thick British accent if he knew his teenage daughter was leaving the building with bare shoulders.

Everleigh sprang up, nerves pushing her to move about the beach hotel, glancing in the mirror and fixing the mess of her hair, wishing her bulbous nose wasn't looking quite so rotund in this light. She traveled the long white shelves along the walls, each lined with large glass jars filled with sand and shells. On one wall, mounted wooden lattices appeared hand carved with oversized morning glories on each panel, giving the appearance of wallpaper. When Everleigh was once again beside Roland, a woman with auburn ringlets tied back with a black satin ribbon came instantly to refill her champagne.

"Don't you look pretty today, Sara?" Roland smiled, and without addressing either Everleigh or the woman in a pressed pinafore directly, he said, "Sara's parents run the feed store in Bridgehampton."

"I keep telling Mr. Whittaker if he installed a small chicken coop behind the tennis courts, he'd have eggs all summer." The woman locked eyes with Everleigh, then darted them away.

Roland elbowed the woman's curvy middle playfully. "And I keep telling Miss Sara that this isn't a farm."

"I won't be needing any more champagne, Sara, thank you," Everleigh said, turning away. Roland was handsome and rich; of course women would flirt with him, but she didn't need to be nice to them.

Stevie returned to the lobby, holding another document for Roland to review, and Roland breezed over it, nodding and signing it with a flourish, the *W* in Whittaker bold and imposing. How had he turned into a businessman overnight? It was like Everleigh announcing she was a Broadway actress and telling him he had to attend her starring performance that evening. Roland hadn't had a proper job since she'd met him and he was always attending meetings that seemed rather ambiguous to Lee.

He handed the clipboard back to Stevie, who once again disappeared behind reception, then motioned Everleigh to follow him through the lobby. "As a kid, we were always barefoot, running off the beach to have dinner on fine china. That's how I wanted this hotel."

"Beautiful, without being too fancy."

"Exactly," he said, threading his fingers in hers. "Just like you." He'd gotten her to smile. "There's something else I want you to see."

At either side of the shiny mahogany reception desk, there were potted palms, and a modern chandelier hung overhead with at least twenty small illuminated crystal balls shooting out from bronze spokes. She glanced at the young woman behind the front desk as they passed, a brunette with long shiny hair whose prominent dimples deepened at Roland as she answered the phone. "Everleigh Beach Club Hotel." A pause. "What room, please?" The receptionist pushed a wire plug into the corresponding slot.

"That's Vivienne. She just finished her secretarial training at Miss Tuthill's School for Girls in New York." Roland waved to her.

"Wonderful." Everleigh noted how nicely the perky woman's white uniform hugged her full B cup. She could tell he enjoyed striding through the hotel lobby, the mansion's former foyer now connected with the parlor and formal living room through large open archways, the staff growing quiet as he approached. They were nearly to a set of doors when he excused himself for a moment to use the lavatory. Everleigh stood to the side of the telephone booth, tucked under the stairwell, waiting for him.

A fair-skinned chambermaid in a pressed pinafore, her straight, dark hair tied at the nape of her neck, walked in giggling with the woman with the auburn ringlets, the housekeeper named Sara, who had poured Everleigh's champagne earlier. "Well, what do you expect of the idle rich? She can lounge around and throw out orders for fancy throw pillows because what else is she going to do? Scrub the bathtub?"

The one named Sara snorted. "Did you see how many times she gazed at herself in the mirror? She gets a hotel named after her and she thinks she's a princess."

Everleigh took a step backward, her throat burning with shame as they rounded the stairwell. The young women stopped short when they spotted Everleigh, who had buried her nose in her compact, wincing. This hotel wasn't her fantasy; it was Roland's, and now she'd be forced to spend the summer following him from room to room, with this awful staff hating her for no reason, writing her off as a spoiled brat.

Sara's mouth fell open. "I'm sorry, Miss, I didn't . . ."

Everleigh snapped the small silver mirror shut. There was always this assumption among outsiders that her life was peaches, that money took away the sharpest edges, that it could take away pain, but Everleigh knew the truth: No matter how deep her father's pockets were, his money couldn't fix Everleigh's mother. And it couldn't fix the tabloids' steady—and hurtful—interest in Everleigh either, even if gossipmonger Igor Cassini's Cholly Knickerbocker column had grown quiet as of late.

Everleigh reached out to shake the hand of the housekeeper she hadn't met, then looked the other square in the eye. "Mother always told me, 'Don't soil your own nest.' I think it's rather good advice."

The woman pulled her ringlets around her face. "Oh, yes, Miss, but I hope you don't think we were talking about you because we weren't."

Everleigh refrained from an eye roll. "Of course, you weren't." The women were only a little younger than her, which made the exchange sting more. She might have counted one as a friend, even if hotel staff didn't typically make the most trustworthy of pals. "Must be some other princess then."

Roland stepped out of the bathroom. "Back to work, ladies," he teased. "This isn't a sorority."

The two housekeepers parted instantly, their heads down.

Everleigh smiled as he tugged on her hand, the sour notes of the exchange lingering, and he gestured her to follow him to the back of the lobby, where the hotel's ceiling morphed into a conservatory greenhouse filled with botanicals of all varieties. The room was being set up for a party with three dozen tables covered in white tablecloths and gold-rimmed dishes. A shiny white baby grand piano stood at the center.

Everleigh sat down at the bench, the keys glossy and white and waiting. Her hands glided along them, and she played the haunting opening notes from Debussy's "Clair de Lune," the sound filling up the cavernous space. Roland leaned an elbow on the piano.

"Don't you know any happy songs, pet?"

She stopped suddenly, then banged out: *Oh, when the Saints go marching in, oh when the Saints go marching in.* He broke into a grin, tapping the piano with the flat of his palm. Before she'd met Roland, whenever Everleigh needed an emotional release, even just from her parents' suffocating apartment, she'd wander off into one of the Plaza's empty ballrooms at night and play melancholy songs on the piano. How endless that time in her life had felt.

She sighed with relief, grateful she was moving in the right direction now, her fingers flying breezily over the keys while Roland sang along.

Tomorrow night, she'd be the attentive fiancée she was required to be, laughing at all of Roland's jokes, making sure he was meeting who he needed to make connections with. She'd hold her "head high, shoulders back, walk around the party without treads touching the floor," as Madame Dillard reminded the debutantes before their coming out. "Float, girls. Float. Men make history, ladies—your job is to put them at ease," she'd said, the girls nodding along. At Everleigh's ball at the Waldorf-Astoria, she'd been so nervous that her hands and ankles swelled from their normal size, and still, she danced all night with different men, a lovely smile plastered on her face. An image of her in the arms of that awful George Sheetz had appeared in the pages of *Life* magazine that January, along with those from other cotillions, titled "The Debutante's Big Moment."

Everleigh closed the piano, following Roland outside, the air brisk and windy off the ocean. They walked the cool slate patio to the edge of the rectangular limestone pool surrounded by loungers, each one striped green and white. She dipped her toe into the crystalline water, surprised that the pool was heated.

"I could spend an entire day at this pool," she said.

"You mean, we will spend many days together at this pool." He smiled, and she smiled back, but she wished he would stop telling her what she was going to do, even if it was in innocence. He walked to the end of the diving board, bouncing a couple of times, nearly teetering into the water, his jazz hands waving in the air.

Her laugh ricocheted around the pool's concrete edges. "Can you remind me why you're not in theater?"

He pretended to dance with a cane. "Just because you like going to the theater doesn't mean you should *be* in the theater."

"Right." Her mouth turned up.

Croquet was set up on a large, lush lawn, and a sign pointed toward tennis courts behind a stand of trees. At the back of the property was a true cottage, one story and cedar shingled, the kind that turned gray after years of being pummeled by storms and sea air. It had a gabled roof to match the hotel's and a small driveway, where two bikes were tucked under a striped retractable awning. A skinny cat sat upright by the back door. "Here, kitty," she called, crouching down, but the cat skittered away.

"Who lives there?" she asked.

"That would be our caretaker Gordon's house—I regret not including it in the renovation. It's a bit of an eyesore." Roland pressed his hands on top of her shoulders, pivoting her back toward the doors to the conservatory. "Anyway, if you think this view is good, wait until you see ours."

They climbed the velvety carpeted staircase to the third floor, and she glanced out the oval window where she'd seen the robin perched outside. Roland unlocked the door to a penthouse suite. It wasn't what they were used to in the city with its compact living room, but Roland was careful to point out that there were two bedrooms; he'd already reassured her parents of this, he said. It was decorated with white and wicker, and they were up so high that they had unobstructed views of the ocean. Without leaving the room, Everleigh could tell if seas were rough or calm, and what color the sailboats were when they crossed the horizon. She thought her reaction outside silly now; she was surrounded by beautiful things. And she loved beautiful things.

She tossed her white Chanel purse on the sofa, sat, and put her feet up on the glass coffee table. "What shall we do now?"

Roland flounced down beside her, mistaking her flirtation for worry. "Be assured. There's plenty to do, and you'll find a rhythm out here. Our days will always start with tennis at the Meadow Club—the grass courts will improve your backhand entirely." Roland raised an eyebrow. "I imagine you're quite good with a racquet."

"Of course." She curled into him. "It's sweet, how excited you are."

He grinned at her, flicking his blond hair off his forehead. "After the Meadow Club, we'll rinse off, then head for lunch at the Bathing Corp—take a swim and eat their 'embellished' hot dog with bacon and American cheese—well, as long as they let us in. We'll languish in the hot sun like lizards and drink plenty of 'Southsides,' this refreshing mix of vodka, rum, lime juice, and mint, and then we'll return to the hotel and rest before attending dinner at the golf club. You'll start seeing the same people, and in no time, we'll fit right in, just like in the city."

"Three clubs? Oh, Rolly, how will we keep up?" Other than the sunbathing, it sounded taxing. If the clubs were anything like the one her parents attended, everyone would drink at night and talk viciously about each other the next morning.

He shrugged. "It's what *everybody* does in Southampton."

Her mouth fell. "We'll be louts."

"We can schedule plenty of naps."

She climbed into his lap and planted a kiss on his lips. "This will be fun, won't it?"

He seemed pleased at the show of affection, kissing her back. "I'll have them ship your belongings from the city, but I brought your camera. I didn't think you could live without it."

That act alone, that he'd brought her camera, meant more to her than the building of the hotel. He pinned her backward onto the couch, and she gave in to him, wrapping her legs around the warm middle of his body. They'd never been quite so alone, even if she'd given in to his advances a few times. Mostly because he'd let her choose how far things went and when they would stop, giving her a sense of control, even if it was a false one.

"Oh, this man I'm marrying." She laughed. "He's smart and funny and handsome and full of surprises. I had no idea you had this in you, Rolly." She said it because she sensed that he needed to hear this, that he needed her to reinforce the idea that he was worth something. That this hotel made him remarkable. Since arriving in the city, he'd had a few meetings at architecture firms, but the Whittaker name didn't carry in those circles, and nothing came of them. He'd cursed his lacking portfolio, but Everleigh had been worried that something else was lacking in him, too; she rarely saw him design anything. No pencil to paper, no rulers on architectural plans. Everleigh began to worry that he might languish if an opportunity didn't present itself soon, and she was on the verge of speaking with her father about helping him find a position when he'd planned this weekend away. And now here he was, determined to make it on his own, a relief to Everleigh. This hotel, she could already see, would be his everything. "I like Roland the businessman."

"You're only going to see more of him." His eyes crinkled.

"I hope so." She closed her eyes as his tongue traveled up her neck, thinking of her camera. Of all the pictures she would capture in this glittery light. Because she realized then how lucky she was to be young and in love and on the beach in summer.

THREE

With the party in full swing and the live band playing Elvis Presley's "All Shook Up," Everleigh stood at Roland's side at the entrance to the hotel's conservatory greenhouse at a quarter after seven the following night, shaking hands with so many people that she lost count, her palms growing warm inside her long gloves. She was the epitome of style in her shiny satin tube dress with its mermaid skirt and large bow in the back, a dress she'd found at Saks earlier that day. The heels the dress seller had chosen made her nearly as tall as Roland, and taller than many of the people coming to greet her under strands of twinkling lights, which tented the twenty-foot glass ceilings like a circus big top.

"I hope my father comes tonight," Roland said, a steady stream of partygoers already mingling in the conservatory. "You'd think he'd want to see what I did with our land."

"He'll be here, don't worry." She rested her palm on his shoulder, and it felt firm and solid, the same two words she'd use if asked to describe why he brought her comfort.

"Well, I'm not counting on it. Remember, my father makes yours look like a pussycat." Roland smiled broadly, reaching for a fashionable couple's tanned hands, Everleigh nodding along with the introductions while not paying attention to them at all. Roland didn't like to discuss his father, an executive in the family business who could board his private plane at a moment's notice if he was so inclined. She knew his mother had passed away when he was fourteen, and she knew this had been hard on him, but even though he was an extrovert and would tell you anything, he was cagey about his teenage years. She didn't press him because she hadn't wanted to break him open, worried at the sadness she'd find there. There was only so much room in someone's heart for sorrow, and she had enough of her own locked away.

Three couples arrived at once after that, each woman on the arm of a man, all of them greeting Everleigh gaily. She knew them from the city; they made the rounds in the party scene, but how they'd ended up at this particular gala she had no idea.

"Alice Anna? Is that you?" Everleigh said, kissing the tall actress's sculpted cheekbones.

She waved her off. "Oh dear. You sound like Mommy. I'm just Alice now." Alice liked to brag about the Broadway shows she performed in, although she'd never played a lead.

Everleigh found Alice conniving, one of those women who'd tell you they like your dress only to turn around and whisper about how garish the pattern was. "I haven't seen you since last year, at Ruby's twenty-second birthday party."

The actress snorted. "Ernest had to pick me up from some beatnik's house in the Village that night. Beads hanging in the doorway. Dried fish on a paper plate. Frightening." Alice's boyfriend, Ernest, introduced himself as a horse trainer at his family stables in Wainscott, a rural pocket of green that bordered Southampton. He had a pair of finely arched cheeks, his eyes glossy with booze.

"You have such beautiful friends, Alice," Ernest said, his English accent catching Everleigh's attention. She turned her head to escape his sour breath. "Where's the big band? I want to swing." He held Alice's dainty arm up like he was about to spin her toward him, but she rather elegantly ducked out of his grip.

"He's such an old soul, my Ernest—loves organized dances."

"Are you two engaged?" Everleigh eyed the size of Alice's ring; it was twice as big as her own. She got mad at herself for looking. Why did she let herself get wrapped up in this strange competition with other women about who was more powerful based on something that gave them no power at all? Well, unless she considered divorce, in which case she *could* sell the ring for a tidy sum. But that wouldn't happen. It was Everleigh's job to keep Roland happy, and she would do just that.

Alice and her fiancé purred at each other. "Yes, we're engaged; the wedding is in September."

"Oh! I'm getting married in October." Everleigh pointed at Roland, returning from the bar with two fresh drinks. She felt her ego rising in her chest. "This is my fiancé, Roland"—she waited a beat—"Whittaker."

Alice clicked her tongue, the hemline of her organza slip dress at least two inches shorter than what was considered acceptable. "Oh, yes, I know Mr. Whittaker. My cousin, Birdie, ran in the same crowd as him in Detroit."

"Hello, Alice." Roland smiled but didn't meet Alice's eye, instead gulping his martini and handing Everleigh hers, slipping a hand around the small of her back. "How is Birdie?"

"About as well as she could be, considering *everything*." Alice's eyes took on the look of a cat's, narrowed and mischievous. "Roland is quite trouble, if you want to know. I don't know how you even got this hotel built, Rolly. It's quite the controversy."

With a showy gesture of his hands, he motioned to the room. "It's wonderful, isn't it?"

Alice snorted. "Well, you know the summer colony doesn't like change. My parents are talking like it's the end of the world, the hotel bringing too many people to Gin Lane."

"Tell them they need to learn to share." Roland snapped his fingers to the rock and roll beat, the conversation failing to penetrate his upbeat mood. "Everyone can get used to new things, don't you think? Even the stalest of money." The way he said it reminded Everleigh of her father putting an unscrupulous client in his place.

Alice turned her glossy lips into a frown. "Their memory is long, Rolly. They won't forget what you did."

Roland coughed into his fist. "Oh, Alice. This is a party, not a courtroom."

"What you did?" Everleigh searched Roland's face for a clue.

Alice looked off toward the dance floor, her arms folded.

"I apologize," Ernest slurred. "She can be a bit overdramatic after her nightly vodka."

Everleigh shot her eyebrows up, looking at Roland, making clear she wanted an answer. He whispered in her ear, "Later."

Conversation about the hotel carried on, and Everleigh considered the other fact she'd learned, that the hotel was unwelcome. Rather than gush about its interiors to loose-lipped Igor Cassini for Monday's papers, would the residents of the summer colony find fault in the grand structure instead?

Across the room she spotted the gossip columnist mingling in the crowd in a suit. If he turned left, she'd move right.

The band's guitar riff grew faster and louder, the bass making everyone rock in place. "I wish I didn't leave my guitar in the car."

"Roland is my hidden performer," said Everleigh. "He's dying to be onstage even if he's never set foot on one." A round of polite laughter arose from the friends.

"Then get your guitar, Rolly," challenged Alice, his nickname giving their relationship an intimacy not lost on Everleigh. She eyed the actress suspiciously; why was she acting as though she and Roland shared some sort of past?

"We'd better greet the other guests," Everleigh said, rather abruptly. She tucked herself under Roland's arm, waiting to feel him squeeze her against his side. "It's been a pleasure to see you all."

Ernest stumbled away toward the dance floor, remarking that he needed a drink, and the friends pushed into the crowd. Alice followed, her twiggy limbs rushing to catch up with her fiancé, until she turned back to address Everleigh. "I'll be in town on and off this summer in between performances at summer stock," she said. "My parents' place is number 232, just past Gin Beach. Maybe we can lunch at the Beach Club?" It's what everyone called the Bathing Corp, Everleigh had learned.

"Of course." Everleigh smiled.

A waiter appeared with a platter of shrimp cocktail and tried to hand her and Roland each a napkin, but they gestured him away. Roland turned to face her, traveling his finger down the tension in Everleigh's neck, tracing a path from her ear to her clavicle. "It's not what you think with Alice—I dated her cousin a while back and she's had it out for me ever since I broke things off. I didn't think she'd even come tonight, and anyway, this was all long ago, before I laid eyes on this stunning woman named Everleigh Farrows."

She pressed her lips inward, wondering if the bitter memory that Alice's parents carried of Roland would make its way into the newspapers in one way or another. Then Everleigh would have to learn things about Roland's past along with café society, which would anger her. "What do you mean, you broke it off with her cousin? You broke up with her to be with me?"

Roland waved to Igor Cassini, who seemed to be approaching, making Everleigh pull her fiancé toward the back wall. Everleigh wasn't sure if she was jealous that Alice knew Roland intimately or worried that they'd have to sidestep her comings and goings all summer. Suddenly, Everleigh wished she and Roland could slip upstairs to watch TV and eat pizza out of a box.

"No, this was years ago. I was young and stupid, Lee. We were in a boating accident, her cousin and I, on the night we broke up, and the boat crashed right into the town dock. My father paid to fix it, and I apologized, and still, Alice's parents act like it happened yesterday. It's rather frustrating." He gazed ruefully into her eyes.

"They are rather dreadful." She leaned her forehead against his chin, knowing she could trust him. Everleigh's parents disliked Alice's mother and father just as much as Roland did, calling the wife a stiff neck and the husband a twit. "And what of the fact that they oppose the hotel?"

"Oh, Lee. Her parents are one of a few people with very loud voices who are upset, and besides, the hotel is built. It's done."

She kissed him, like they'd won a prize. "It's true. What can they do now?"

The wrinkles in Roland's forehead smoothed, and he kissed the shine of her espresso-colored hair. A new song by the band broke their embrace, and they turned back to the hotel entrance, hand in hand, Everleigh overcome with a possessiveness that hadn't been there before seeing Alice. A black sedan pulled up outside, and Roland craned his neck to see who stepped out of the backseat. He bit the insides of his cheeks when a woman with coiffed white hair emerged.

"Let's go mingle," Everleigh said, hoping it would distract Roland from thoughts of his father's uncertain arrival. "I think that supermarket executive might know Conrad Hilton. Maybe you could get a meeting with him and become an owner of a string of hotels." She twirled around in his arms, and he grinned, eyeing the whiskered gentleman they'd met earlier. Everleigh didn't mention that she actually knew Conrad Hilton. Her parents had forced her to dance with the elderly gentleman at her debutante ball, just because they were in his hotel, his old-man hands on the small of her back.

Shiny silver candelabras alight with fat white candles cast a honey glow among the sea of faces. She recognized one immediately, a cherub-cheeked heiress of Standard Oil whom she'd met only recently at a luncheon. Then her eyes landed on Whitney, who must have arrived after she and Roland left their post at the front door.

"Whitney!"

Her friend turned, her expression lifting into a smile. Whitney was freckly and golden-blond to the eyelashes—her facial features as delicate as a bird's.

"I saw you when I came in, but you had quite a group around you. Was that Alice?"

To most people, Whitney was a New York socialite regularly appearing in gossip columns and photos from charity balls, but to Everleigh, who'd seen her at her highest and lowest moments, she was just Whitney, her best friend since the fifth grade. They both attended Spence, and they became close after their mothers had forced them to join a French club, where in between lessons, they traded barbs about the rather rotund size of Madame Perrot's oversized ass. It was filthy of them, and they went on to further misbehave, telling their parents they were sleeping over at each other's houses only to stay at another friend's house with a looser curfew.

Whitney took Everleigh's hands, swinging her arms like they were children. "I can't believe you're really out here. In all these years, you've been to our house in East Hampton—what?—once?"

"Well, you know Albert and Eleanor, they only take me to lakes Upstate."

"Oh how your parents love to torture you with those leeches." A waiter handed Whitney a Moscow mule, and her slender fingers wrapped around the bronze mug. She leaned in to examine Everleigh's diamond drop earrings. "Lovely little things, aren't they? When did you get those?"

She and her friend didn't see each other quite as much as they used to; with all the fundraising luncheons Whitney ran these days, they didn't get much one-on-one time together. Whitney decided the minute she graduated from college and married Truman that she wanted to be at the pinnacle of New York society, while still being everybody's favorite guest. And she somehow managed to be a bulldog, a social climber, and a lovely person. Still, Everleigh and Whitney could frustrate each other like siblings. Lately, Whitney had frowned upon Everleigh's "feckless" days with Roland, always pushing Everleigh to join yet another committee or subcommittee at the Upper East Side Women's Club. Meanwhile, Everleigh resented her friend's methodical series of checklists, always ticking off tasks on her thick monogrammed stationery. Still, they knew all the same people and found fault in them in quite the same ways. After a cocktail or two, they could be quite the she-devils, as her mother affectionately called them.

"I told Roland that two carats is a bit much, but I'll admit I really love them."

Whitney tilted her Waspy chin. "Don't dare tell him that. You want him to feel like he must top the last gift he gave you—every single year. You remember how I got this?" She ran her finger over her pendant necklace, which didn't hang from a chain but a circle of large emerald-cut diamonds.

"Oh, yes, you're Miss Subtle. Leaving love notes around, pictures of the necklace with the jeweler's address stapled to the back."

Whitney shrugged. "But you have to get what you want somehow. Have you been dodging Cassini? Because you don't have to worry; there are much bigger names here tonight."

Everleigh smacked her friend playfully. "Well, then I'm grateful to be chopped liver."

Whitney spoke at a clip. "Anyway, about your wedding. . . . What is this I hear about three hundred invitations? I thought you wanted something small."

In the center of the dance floor, Alice twirled into Ernest's embrace. Everleigh sighed. "Well, Mommy wants something big, and we know that her happiness depends on whether or not my bouquet is white roses or red." Everleigh had wanted the invitation on a single ivory card with simple script announcing the wedding, but her mother had selected a three-page booklet that looked like something you'd get at church on Palm Sunday.

"Well, you know, it's her big day, not yours." Whitney rolled her eyes, lightly poking her friend's bare shoulder. "Can I call your mother and politely make it clear that I need to help pick my maid-of-honor dress? I don't want her to put me in some frumpy pouf with too much crinoline."

The two friends turned to stand with their satin hips touching, taking in the couples dancing, the music ratcheting up in volume. *Mommy.* Whitney was right. Everleigh was going along with all her tastes in planning because she needed to appease her. It gave her mother reason to get out of bed, arrange lunch with a friend, move manically through the apartment rather than stare blankly out the windows. The wedding made her happy, and if she was well, then Everleigh was, too.

Whitney tapped her foot to the beat. "Make sure she swallows her meds, and then you can start making decisions."

"I'm going to start fishing those pills out myself. I'll sell you one."

They laughed, even though it wasn't funny that her mother's nervous condition had landed her in the hospital most recently because she'd been flushing her "mother's little helper" tranquilizer pills down the toilet. But laughter was the only way Everleigh had learned to survive the ups and downs of her mother's emotions, and she certainly preferred it to the days when her own mood grew dark and her thoughts slipped into fear. Because Everleigh knew her mind could betray her still. What if her hands began to tremble, like her mother's did, or her eyes settled into a blank stare, like Mother's, and she too was wheeled into a hospital too weak to tell them her name? They were questions that left Everleigh feeling pinched in the knees. She was too afraid to ask anyone, even Whitney, if feeling sad *sometimes* meant she was at the beginning of her own spell. After a thorough emotional evaluation at the age of seventeen, doctors had reassured her father that his daughter hadn't inherited his wife's condition. But it didn't mean Everleigh wouldn't develop her mother's exhaustion and sad spells as she grew older, they'd said. And that lurking worry, that her mother's unreliable heart might live deep inside of her own, ran through the family's Manhattan apartment like the plumbing, a coursing that no one could see but was ever present, behind walls, under floorboards, flooding their thoughts at the earliest sign that something was amiss.

Whitney slid her arm around Everleigh's shoulder, tilting her friend's head to meet her own. "Will you come to Summerfield this week? We can lie by the pool and catch up. Truman heated it for me."

From here, Everleigh could look up through the windows to see the penthouse, the widow's walk aglow at the rooftop. "Only if you promise you'll explain why I'm full of nerves staying upstairs with Roland."

"Because you've never lived with a man before!" Her friend began to giggle. "Rule number one. Get dressed in the bathroom after a shower because he won't be able to take the sight of you in a towel."

Everleigh felt her stomach flutter, thinking about how she'd woken at daybreak to brush her hair and teeth and apply blush, returning to bed before Roland opened his eyes. She'd been overcome with some irrational fear that if he saw what she *really* looked like in the morning—puffy eyes, blotchy cheeks, her hair unruly like a wildebeest's—he might change his mind about her. About them.

The band launched into another fast-paced song, the pianist hitting all the right notes, and a few couples broke out into the bop on the dance floor; the footwork looked like the Charleston if you danced it twice as fast. *I want to dance*, she thought, and Everleigh glanced around the room for Roland. Someone nudged her from the back, taking hold of her hand and sweeping her out to the dance floor. She put her cocktail on a table, thrilled that Roland had found her.

But then she registered the size of the man's palm, how much smaller her hand felt in his than in Roland's. She spun around and turned up her eyes, finding herself facing a striking gentleman with short windswept hair gelled to one side, both wild and polished, the look of a leading man on a movie poster. He grinned, appeared to be a few years older, and challenged her to dance with a cock of his chin. Everleigh threw her head back with laughter, in part because she was nervous, and in part because she allowed him to pull her in toward him then jettison her out, their feet keeping the beat.

"What's your name?" he asked, somehow able to talk and dance at once.

She didn't answer, trying to keep count with her high heels.

"I said, what's your name?" He pulled her close to him, as part of the dance, and for a moment it seemed like he couldn't unglue his eyes from hers. Her breath caught in her chest, and she blushed. She recognized him then; he was the one who had slowed his car to see if she and Roland needed help with their flat tire. The young doctor.

"Everleigh Farrows," she hollered, willing her attention back to her dance steps. "Yours?"

"Curtis Brightwell," he said. "You know, there's something about this dance. I always have this stupid grin when I do it, and I'm not one for giving out the stupid grin. I'm not really a big-band guy."

She liked the way his face came together, his expression content, like the pieces were meant to be put on his face that way. "You live in town?"

"Just moved back from Boston. I'm here to take over an old friend's medical practice," he said, swinging her away from him, then back in. His tuxedo smelled of vanilla and wood fire, like he was dressed entirely wrong and should be in denim and chambray.

She met his eyes, smiling. "Welcome back, good doctor."

Curtis was a shade darker than the other men at the party, with an olive complexion and dark eyebrows that marked him different. He took her hands, pulling her in and pushing her back out right as the chorus repeated, making the move feel like a burst.

"How do you know I'm any good?" he said, smiling with his eyes, his face bright like he was on the verge of happy laughter.

She wished she were in flats; her feet would keep the beat better. "If your bedside manner is anything like your dancing, then the people of Southampton are in good hands."

He chuckled, rocking back and forth on his heels. "Well, some residents at the summer colony think a local doctor is too provincial."

They stepped together to the left, then the right, keeping beat with the snare drum. "You have the same medical degree as everyone else, don't you?"

He laughed, and something inside her leaped. She realized then she was flirting, the way that she'd flirted with Roland on the day they met. Speaking of Roland, she glanced around the room and spotted him in conversation with a Southampton official she'd met earlier. The stout man's eyebrows were furrowed, his forehead creased. They seemed to be arguing.

"I'm still trying to figure out how I got an invite to this party." Curtis reached for her hand again, then swung her out once more.

"Well, this is my hotel, and if I'd had anything to do with the invitations, I would have sent you one, too," she found herself saying, then decided it was a little much. "My fiancé built it. You met him the other day when you offered to change our flat tire."

The song was ending, and he slowed her twirl. "Now that's too bad, Everleigh."

Over the microphone, an announcer instructed the dance floor to do the Madison, the jazzy music getting louder. Everleigh dropped her hands from his, but they paused a minute, catching their breath.

"What's too bad?" she said. Her diamond ring caught the light.

Curtis took her martini off the table where she'd set it down and handed it back to her. "I would have liked to ask you to dance again," he said, a bit apologetic when he met her eye.

She shook her head. "Oh, you didn't offend."

"I only intend to charm." His eyes crinkled as he pushed his hands into his pockets, the corners of his mouth turning up.

The vodka went down smooth when she swallowed, and she tilted her head to the side to study him, thinking him sweet. "In another lifetime, maybe."

He said, "In another lifetime then."

Everleigh watched him turn to the crowd, his sturdy back disappearing into a group of onlookers.

Whitney arrived back at her side, the fruity notes of her Femme Rochas perfume traveling with her. "What was that about?"

She worried then what people would say, having seen her dance with him. "Just some local doctor thinking he can spin any girl he wants out on the dance floor. I better find Roland."

Whitney faked a cough. "I'm suddenly feeling quite ill. Oh, Doctor, wait up." The women broke into laughter, a silliness fueled by the fact they were on their second or third drink.

It was later reported in papers from Boston to Washington that there were five hundred flutes of champagne poured that night, one thousand shrimp peeled, thirty-five pineapples cubed, and forty-five pounds of beef skewered and marinated in something called teriyaki, but Everleigh guessed it was triple that. Guests continued to arrive from Further Lane in East Hampton and Dune Road in Westhampton, and there were scores of weekenders visiting friends or staying in summer shares, too: young men and women looking for a party and hearing about this one, their cars parked down all of Gin Lane, many not even making use of the valets, the same men who worked the lifeguard stations by day. Roland was thrilled, like he'd thrown the most exclusive house party in high school. He welcomed everyone with a pat on the back. "Get a drink, new friend," he'd say, putting on like he was twice his age, a fixture at a long-established hotel. Roland once told Everleigh he had been an actor in high school (he starred in a production of *The Little Foxes*), and it was at moments like this that she could see it.

By now, it was after ten, and Everleigh ran to the hotel front desk, where she'd left her camera. She positioned the brown leather strap around her delicate neck and snapped on the flash so she could shoot at night. There was Roland talking to Anne Ford, her neck strung with strands of pearls (*click, snap*). Near the bar, Everleigh blew kisses to the always-elegant and perhaps best-known New York socialite C. Z. Guest, Whitney's idol, who was engrossed in conversation with Jacqueline Bouvier Kennedy, who had brought along her husband, the senator from Massachusetts who had just won the Pulitzer Prize (*focus, zoom, snap*). When Everleigh came face-to-face with the artist Willem de Kooning, his saddle shoes speckled with paint, she asked how his work was coming, and he invited her to his barn in a thick Dutch accent (*snap, snap, snap*).

Everleigh found herself enjoying the party now, like holding her camera marked her different from everyone else, and she didn't mean that in a snobby way. She simply preferred to exist on the periphery, watching people, knowing them, but avoiding the distinction of being one of them, even if that's exactly what she was. A gentleman with a mustache and beaten-down suit was roving the party with his own camera, and after seeing hers, he introduced himself as Dean Simmers, the photographer for the *Hamptonite*, a weekly insert in the local paper that printed pictures of society parties. "You realize you can get prints of any of my pictures," he said, a line of slick sweat around the collar of his shirt.

Everleigh smiled politely. "I enjoy taking my own." He tipped his hat, took a picture of her mugging for him, and went on his way. He wasn't the only one unnerved by the sight of her with a camera. Whitney had already scolded her to put it away. "You're the host. Smile, don't tell others to."

"It's fun is all," she told Whitney, who mumbled something about being demure and walked away with an eye roll.

The night beat on, and in between bits of conversation and three rolls of film, she nibbled pineapple chicken skewers near Roland, who was entertaining a group of smug Wall Street types, the greedy and enterprising former jocks who built nothing but bank accounts and were enamored of Whittaker auto money. It was eleven now, and she was using a white cloth napkin to clean pineapple sauce off her finger when she heard an audible murmur sweep over the crowd, a collective gasp, even though everyone kept talking. She craned her neck to see the spot where everyone else was trying not to look. At the back corner of the conservatory, near the French doors that led to the pool, a buxom blonde in a simple powder blue tank dress had entered. *It couldn't be her.* Everleigh hunted the woman's face for the signature mole that marked the space above her famously pouty lips.

She tugged on Roland, pulling him away from the money guys and the cloud of cigar smoke around them. "Is that who I think it is?" she whispered.

"Oh. My. God." He turned to Everleigh, then looked back at the curvy woman near the doors. "It's not. It can't be."

"I think it's her," she said, both of them giddy in each other's arms.

At the sight of Whitney approaching, Roland pulled away and cleared his throat. "Whitney," he said.

"Roland," Whitney said, equally curt. They both took a step away from each other. Last month, they'd attempted a double date with the two couples, but Whitney and Roland had sparred across the table before the main course even arrived, leaving Everleigh and Truman to exchange weary glances.

"Can you believe Marilyn Monroe is here?" Everleigh said, looping her arm in Whitney's; they used to walk to and from Spence this way.

"How did you get her to come?" Whitney seemed impressed. "Truman says they've been fairly reclusive."

"We dropped an invitation in the mail. She and Miller are living in some house that looks like a witch hat, over in East Hampton." Roland downed a shot of something strong, gagging from the burn. He handed Everleigh one, but she put it on the bar's white marble countertop and straightened his black silk bow tie.

"Don't drink too much, Rolly—we still have guests."

"One more won't put me over, pet," he said, pecking her cheek. But he was already past his prime, his eyes bloodshot, his hands loose on her body as he spoke. It was her one complaint about him: he didn't always hold his liquor.

Everleigh found the potted date palm where the actress—the one and only Marilyn Monroe—was standing with her husband, playwright Arthur Miller. There were few people at the party who weren't used to spending time in A-list crowds, so while the actress's arrival sent a bolt of energy through the party, no one crowded them.

"We need to thank them for coming," said Everleigh, reapplying her red lipstick in a compact pulled from her silk clutch.

"Yes, of course." Roland took her hand. "And bring your camera. We can give a picture to the papers. Old Igor Cassini will eat this up . . ."

"I will not give *him* my picture. But I will take a picture and give it to someone else, if you'd like."

"Everleigh, everyone reads his column . . ."

"Absolutely not."

Whitney excused herself, and Everleigh watched her rejoin Truman.

"But, Everleigh, items in his column are picked up all around the country. What if it appeared in the *Detroit Free Press*? Father will see it, or at the very least he'll hear about it." She remembered then that his father wasn't here, that he hadn't shown up.

"Your father has to know what you've been up to by now," she said, but this only made Roland seem disappointed.

"Maybe," he said.

She squeezed his hand. "Okay, okay. You can give it to Cassini, but we have to get him to agree to stop writing about me and my family in exchange."

He squeezed her hand back as a familiar guitar riff broke through the room, the band launching into Buddy Holly's "That'll Be the Day," as platters of chocolate-covered strawberries and slices of coconut cake crisscrossed the room on silver trays.

"It's my favorite song," Roland yelled to Everleigh as they pushed through the smoky crowd, his face aglow with drink. "What are the odds that such a grand moment would have a soundtrack?" She threw her head back, feeling exuberant, and then there they were, next to the tall date palm where the famous couple stood.

Roland tapped Mr. Miller on his shoulder—the playwright was taller than Roland by at least a few inches—and introduced himself.

"I was wondering who was behind this place," Mr. Miller said. His black, shiny, thick-rimmed glasses overtook his whole face, even his prominent nose. "Art Miller. Nice to meet you."

"I'll have you know that I think Congress was being heavy-handed in convicting you of your un-American activities," Roland said, and Everleigh smiled through her cocktail, wondering why Roland would choose to bring up something so utterly awkward; he always said the right thing. He must have been nervous. "I mean, your work stands on its own, whether you're a communist or not."

"Well, I'm not a communist." Mr. Miller chuckled, pushing a hand into his pocket. "I'm an easy target with this brilliant girl on my arm. But thank you." Art was one of the few men not wearing a tux, donning instead a white collared shirt, the sleeves rolled up to his elbows. She admired that he was dressed as he wanted to be, not as he was expected to be—the dress code didn't apply to everyone, she supposed—and that he spoke honestly and not in those clever one-line barbs some famous men used to try to sound sharper than they were.

Everleigh tried to change the subject. "I went to see *The Crucible* when it was at the Martin Beck Theatre on Broadway a few years ago—it was very powerful." She glanced at the actress, who was petite and unassuming up close, other than her curves, and Everleigh tried to acknowledge her with a sideways smile.

Marilyn sipped champagne. "You know that Art vowed that if it wasn't a commercial success he'd stop writing forever. Then he won the Pulitzer."

"Actually, love, that was for *Death of a Salesman*," he said quietly, only to her, like he was afraid his words might break his famous wife.

"I'm Everleigh Farrows," she said in her perkiest tone, reaching out to shake Marilyn's hand. "Roland and I are delighted you came by tonight. Are you here all summer?"

"Yes, sorry, this is my fiancée, Everleigh." Roland laughed, his cheeks red.

"Oh! You're the lucky girl that inspired this place. I read something of that in the Cholly Knickerbocker column this morning." Marilyn took in the tall glass ceilings of the conservatory; her cheeks were flush, and she seemed a bit drunk. "Did you have a hand in it?"

Everleigh shook her head, leaning back on her heels, suddenly feeling proud. "The hotel was an early wedding present. A surprise."

Art's tone turned sarcastic. "Apparently, I'm in the wrong field."

Marilyn pointed at Everleigh's camera. "You take photographs?"

Everleigh examined the lens, smiling. "It's a hobby."

"Maybe it should be a passion." The actress said it with a glimmer in her eye. "Every woman should have something that keeps them getting up in the morning." Marilyn leaned in to her ear. "It could be a baby, I suppose. But it shouldn't be your husband, no matter what other women try to tell you. Make yourself a living, and no one can boss you around."

"As if I could tell this one to do anything she didn't want to do." Art laughed.

Everleigh got a vision of her younger self at Barnard, her time at the campus newspaper, when she held a notebook against her palm. How her favorite part was when she'd pull out her camera and capture whoever was in the frame. How much satisfaction she got when she saw her photograph printed alongside a story in the paper. It wasn't that she *lacked* ambition; it was that her ambition was treated like child's play. Her parents expected her to get married, establish a household, build a life around being a couple. She was to ease her husband's strain, not distract from it with her own desires. And she accepted that.

"My goal, really, is to be a good wife." She smiled at Roland, who put his arm around her.

"And mine, a swell husband," said Roland, and she was glad Whitney wasn't there to witness this blind devotion. She would have stuck a finger in her mouth and gagged.

Marilyn laughed. "Aren't you two adorable?" The crowd pulsed closer, one gentleman with broad shoulders stepping in to introduce himself, and even as they all shook his hand, then his wife's, Everleigh clicked through a slideshow in her mind. She pictured herself after the wedding, the wife of Roland Whittaker, standing in the foyer holding a leather planner, the keeper of the golden appointment book, curating a list of interesting social engagements. There she was dabbing her mouth twice after each bite and eating escargot to impress Roland with her exotic palate, sitting at a table with a white tablecloth, with the same haircut as the woman next to her, and the woman next to her, all of them with some variation of the same makeup, all of them wearing a frost of jewels around their moisturized wrists. All of them members of some strange species of woman whose money afforded them the great privilege of being exactly the same.

She'd never thought of her life the way she just had. As something that was so predictable. As the same life her mother had lived. That everyone she knew would live.

A senator Everleigh recognized from the papers called the famous couple over, and Art waved goodbye while cupping Marilyn's back, saying, "You know, Starling Meade is based at the Sag Harbor artist colony this summer. It's a little nutty over there—they're all sleeping on raised platform tents or some nonsense—but her work is interesting. Her gallery showing in East Hampton in August is the most anticipated of the summer."

"At Guild Hall?" Everleigh raised her camera up to her eye; Starling Meade was one of the most famous women photographers, maybe the only famous woman photographer. Everleigh had recently read an article about her in *U.S. Camera* magazine.

He smiled. "A private gallery. The *New Yorker* plans to send a reviewer out. There will be a party, too, I'm sure. Artists know how to throw a good one."

Even as the couple moved on, Everleigh focused, zoomed, snapped. Later, long after the party was over and the film was developed,

Everleigh found she had two workable images of the celebrity couple. The first was fairly posed: two attractive people smiling side by side at a party, one of them happening to be Marilyn Monroe. But the second, a candid shot, showed Marilyn reaching toward the camera, a large emerald-cut diamond ring over her blue satin glove, her face furrowed with directive. It seemed like she was speaking directly to Everleigh, telling her something she needed to know, and when she looked at it later, Everleigh heard Marilyn's unexpected words all over again: *Make yourself a living, and no one can boss you around.*

FOUR

oland walked her upstairs to bed that night at one-thirty, with
most guests having picked up their cars from the valet, their headlights shining through the dunes as they made their way home. She
and Roland were undressed and under the thin white bedspread within
minutes, Roland falling asleep instantly, snoring and sweaty with drink.
Everleigh put her hands behind her head, staring at the moonglow
streaked across the ceiling, while recounting the events of the night.
How Roland slid his hand down the small of her back to show they
were a couple, how he presented them as the lord and lady of the hotel.
The pleasure and simultaneous torture of mingling, the disappoint-
ment of seeing Alice, and the wonder of talking to Marilyn.

Everleigh turned on her side, staring out the window in the direction of the ocean, and considered what she'd do now that she was here
for the summer. She could attach herself to Whitney, who could introduce her to her friends and help her maintain a busy social calendar. It
might be more interesting to help Roland with the hotel when he
needed it—maybe she could try her hand at the front desk. That
would really give people reason to talk. But if her parents found out
she was working an hourly job, they would demand her return home.

She tossed and turned, her mind busy and scattered. She sat up, then got out of bed entirely.

Striding out to the balcony in her champagne-colored satin night-gown, her hair loose at her shoulders, Everleigh sank into one of the white Adirondack chairs to smoke. She puffed the cigarette, blowing circles with her mouth, listening to the American flag on the lawn flapping against the flagpole. It was too early in the summer to hear the crickets, the days so long she'd been waking to blinding sun. She pictured herself on the beach, her camera hanging around her neck. How powerful she'd felt at the party capturing the faces of guests—some pinched, some radiating, some leaning over another but catching her eye before she snapped, all while looking back at her through the lens of her camera.

There were voices below. Leaning back from the balcony's edge, she strained to hear—it was someone in the pool area. Someone with a high-pitched voice. She peeked over the edge and recognized the woman's leggy silhouette. It was Alice.

"You can't even walk, you fool," Alice said, trying to push Ernest off the lounger. "I won't carry you to the car."

From her perch, Everleigh could see that the lights were still on in the conservatory. She recognized members of the staff, some sweeping and vacuuming, others wiping spilled drinks and crumbs of food, stuffing the soiled linen tablecloths into cloth laundry bags. Her eyes traveled to the lights in the lobby, then over to the narrow telephone booth, where two people were kissing in full light, the woman's bare back visible against the glass. When the man came up for air, Everleigh saw Roland's friend Stevie's unmistakable copper-colored hair and shrank back from the moonlight, uncertain if he could see her, since he seemed to have angled his face up to where she was sitting. A car started in the distance, the rev of an engine. Perhaps Alice, finally leaving.

Everleigh took one last drag of the cigarette and tossed it over the balcony, returning inside. She quietly closed the glass door and crawled into bed next to Roland, her eyes softly closing, then woke almost immediately with a frightful dream about her mother, who somehow didn't have a face. Everleigh sat up and shook off the nightmare, a lingering creeping sensation that made her check for the contours of her own eyes, nose, and mouth, before falling back into her pillow.

At some point later, when the only light was the moon outside, her body jolted awake to the kind of incessant ringing that brought you back to a primary-school fire drill. Everleigh reached out for her alarm clock and banged her hand against the nightstand table, hunting for a way to stop the overwhelming dinging. It was at that point that she smelled smoke. She sat up, realizing it was still mostly dark outside. Too early for her alarm to ever go off. She sniffed and smacked Roland to wake him up. He mumbled something and put a pillow over his head.

Stumbling out of bed, her bare feet thankful for the soft carpeting underfoot, Everleigh felt her way into the living room of their suite. The smell of smoke was stronger—a hint of it mingling with the salt air—and when she opened the door that led to the hall, she could hear shrieks below. The slamming of doors, harried footsteps moving down the stairs. She sprang back to the bedroom, fumbling in the dark for her pink satin kimono, jumping onto the bed and shaking Roland.

"Rolly, it's an alarm." When he didn't respond, she vigorously patted his hairless chest, leaning into his ear. "Roland, I need you to wake up right now. The fire alarms are going off, and I smell smoke."

He sat straight up, his eyes slits of sleep, rubbing his forehead and yawning.

"The fire alarm?" He looked at the alarm clock on the nightstand, registering that it wasn't trembling, and he heard then that the screeching was emanating from the red metal box on the wall. Jumping up, his foot catching in the sheet, tips of his honeyed hair spiking like a cactus, Roland pulled on the tuxedo pants he'd draped over the armchair. Together, they dashed down the carpeted steps, finding a chaotic tangle of people, disoriented guests, many of the women with hair still in rollers.

Someone was yelling, "Keep the doors closed. It will keep it from spreading."

There was smoke on the second floor, gray clouds of it drifting up, and they pushed past the people coming toward them to find the central staircase. Her heart was beating fast and hard, and she rested her hand across her chest, trying to quiet the palpitations.

"Everleigh, go outside, and be sure the fire station has been called. I'm going to get everyone out." She nodded and took the steps two at a time toward the lobby before remembering her camera and turning back. She dashed back upstairs in the dark to their penthouse suite, reaching for the black rotary phone in the living room and frantically dialing the operator.

"Please, please," she pleaded into the phone, "call the fire department. Yes, the Everleigh Beach Club Hotel. There's a fire. I don't know where it's coming from. Just get here."

The operator punched off the line, and Everleigh coughed on the rising smoke. She grabbed her camera off the desk and stuffed whatever else she could into her pocketbook—her ruby pendant and the diamond earrings Roland had given her, her makeup, her flats, a shirt, Roland's wallet. *Get out. Get out. Get out.* But she ignored the voice, refusing to go outside in her kimono and nightgown. She rummaged through her drawer, putting on the first pair of shorts she could find.

The walls were crackling somewhere, the sound making her woozy. She pushed back into the dark hallways, spotting guests she'd met at the party and helping them down the steps. Turning on her heels near the smoky front desk, she went back upstairs to find others, running up just as someone was running down. They slammed headfirst into each other. Rubbing her jawline, Everleigh looked to see who it was, recognizing at once the woman's long shiny hair and pearl clips, her prominent dimples even when she wasn't smiling; it was the telephone operator from the hotel's front desk.

"Vivienne! Are you okay? I'm sorry." Everleigh noted that the young woman was no longer in uniform, instead wearing a floral dress, which seemed odd for this time of night. Then again, Everleigh had slipped on shorts.

Vivienne coughed, a plane of chestnut hair falling over her face. "I need to get out. . . . The smoke. It's too much." She pushed past Everleigh, hard and panicked, and Everleigh continued up the stairs, charging into one of the rooms on the second floor. In the bathroom, she instinctively soaked a hand towel under the faucet, wringing it out and pressing it over her face to help her breathe. For the next few minutes, maybe three, maybe ten—she was losing track of time—she went room to room, banging on the closed doors and listening for voices. On the first floor now, Roland approached, walking an elderly guest down the hallway. He hollered, "Her husband is in a wheelchair in room eleven. Will you wheel him out?"

The gentleman looked faint when she found him three doors down, and she struggled to unlock his wheelchair before rolling him swiftly through the halls, saddling her purse on the handle. Now that she was in the lobby, Everleigh found herself coughing with smoke, which was beginning to feel like thick fog, and it allowed her only to make out the general shapes of furniture and people. She felt heat gathering on her temples, like she was coming down with fever.

Everleigh sat for a moment to catch her breath on one of the lobby's chaise longues, her hands squeezing the wheelchair grips, before realizing she was disoriented. She had to keep going, she just needed to keep breathing into the towel. Flames shot out from the walls near the conservatory, and she could see the piano was completely alight, too. The kitchen burned, and in an adjacent room hot streaks of flame, spreading from a painting to a curtain to a couch. Within seconds, the back exit, the same one that Marilyn had slipped through last night, the exit that Everleigh had been heading for, was engulfed in flames, and she found herself turning around to head out the front of the hotel. Still pushing the wheelchair, with the man's head lolling, she felt the chair get stuck on something, but she couldn't see what; she simply jerked it forward, willing it to get by.

There should have been a siren by now, some sign that the fire trucks were close. She felt tears stinging her eyes, or maybe that was the smoke. There was horror, but sadness, too, like everything from the day before was slipping away from her. Roland's hotel. His face on the beach that morning, him trying to impress his father. And now. Now it was burning. The wicker settees, the seahorse mail slots, the splashy light fixtures.

There were other guests rushing to get out the front door—she could make out their silhouettes through the gray air—and she pushed the wheelchair with all of her might, wishing she were wearing shoes because the floors were melting with heat, and she found herself hopping like you did in August over hot sand. Was Roland okay? Had he made it outside?

A vase must have fallen over and shattered, but she couldn't see it and stepped on a sliver of glass, screaming from the searing pain on the pad of her foot. She crumpled over onto the couch, her camera jabbing into her stomach, and she buried her face into the cushion and bit her lip so hard she tasted the salt of blood. She thought it had probably been several minutes since she descended the stairs, but it felt like hours, and her body was leaden and heavy, her lungs tight with soot. Everleigh stared at the door, only steps away but feeling like miles.

Someone was holding her now, she wasn't sure who, and her camera was resting on her back, the strap choking her neck. She supposed it was a man carrying her, but it could have been anyone. "There's a man—in a wheelchair," she was yelling, smacking whoever it was, but then she saw that someone else was pushing the older gentleman in the wheelchair.

It was Roland steering the man now, her Rolly, with two lines of black soot under both of his eyes.

The wind off the Atlantic smacked her cheeks, and she saw the faces of dozens of onlookers, many in robes and bare feet, coughing, their faces painted with heat. Holding her was Stevie, his arms stronger than she ever thought they were. Stevie, who had been kissing the woman in the telephone booth—but who? The night seemed like a dream, and Everleigh willed herself to wake up on the beach, to feel the streaming sun on her face and the sand at her thighs, so she could roll over to Roland and drape her arm across his warm body and be reassured that this was not real life. To think that just yesterday she'd taken for granted that they were safe and healthy, living the kind of carefree summer most people in the city dream of.

"Is there anyone else inside?" It was Roland, barking at Stevie. The friends had met a year or two ago, at the bar at the Algonquin. Stevie was waitering. Soon he began showing up at the Algonquin as Roland's guest. Now he was here, saving strangers from a sea of flames.

Stevie spat, his spittle black like tar. "They're all out."

They panted, their bodies heaving with tainted air, working to replace it with the fresher salt air blowing through their hair, although something made Everleigh's chest hurt more now.

Roland yelled at the guests staring at him, waiting for direction. "Go to the ocean. It won't spread that far." He looked for Everleigh. "Where are the fire trucks?"

Everleigh, shivering and wrapping her arms around herself, tried to

speak but the smoke had rendered her throat hoarse, and her voice
came out low and strained. "They're coming," she choked.

Roland went about finding a garden hose, turning it on, and spray-
ing it at the windows, which was a sorry spectacle. The fire ignored the
water.

There were still no sirens. The hotel looked as though a piece of its
body were eaten away, a carcass rotting in plain sight. The interior
wood frame was visible on the right side of the building—window
frames exposed, wood framing actively burning. You couldn't pass
through the lobby anymore; the fire was too thick, and flames danced
up the carpeted stairs.

Roland threw down the hose, stomping on it, spitting on it in
anger, like it needed to be pummeled, until he busted a hole in the skin
and water sprayed out like a geyser. He raced off to a garden shed, running back with buckets, yelling for the wizened caretaker to help him.
They handed a bucket to Everleigh, one to Stevie, one to a random
guest, and one to Alice's fiancé, Ernest, who appeared out of nowhere,
apparently snapped to sobriety.

"We'll get sand from the beach, then throw it on the flames," Roland
said, his face wild, like a cornered animal without anywhere to run.

Everleigh couldn't stop crying as she fled to the dunes to fill her
bucket, trembling as she threw handfuls of sand inside, knowing it was
all incredibly fruitless, but she trudged back across the street to the
hotel anyway, dragging the leaden bucket with her. She threw the sand
at the fire, watching it fall into the flames. She was aware then of an arm
around her shoulders, the slender form of a woman beside her saying,
"This is awful. Just awful." It was Vivienne in her soot-stained party
dress, crying, the flames shooting skyward in the reflection of her eyes.

A motherly instinct came over Everleigh—the woman seemed like
a child then—and Everleigh hugged her. "There, there. It's going to be
okay."

The heat of the fire burned the edges of Everleigh's face, her skin feeling like it might give in and begin to melt, even though she was out of harm's way. All at once there were sirens and beams of red flashes through the trees as fire trucks raced down Gin Lane, firemen jumping out like sparks, running straight inside with axes poised on their backs. One pulled an enormous hose from a silver spindle, while another spun the silver wheel, activating the water pressure. A shot of water sprayed twenty feet in the air. A second hose felt the push of water, and its stream crossed over the other one. This time, the fire reacted, dancing down before shooting back up. But the water didn't stop.

Uniformed men who had run inside ran back out, hollering that the structure's integrity had been compromised. "It's on the verge of collapse," yelled one.

She closed her eyes, the strobing lights and sirens calling to mind a memory she wished she could stop. The damp glue-like scent of the hotel apartment's bathroom wallpaper, how humid the pink tiles felt under her stockinged feet, how the water swirled with the muddy red hue of bricks. She'd glimpsed her mother's head lolling off to the side, the life leaving her eyes. How she'd sprinted away as fast as she could to the Plaza's lobby, finding Mr. Stubbs, the concierge, who after hearing Everleigh's shrieks, stroked her forehead and gave her a glass of Ovaltine to calm her while he called an ambulance, and her father. The red lights had flashed into the lobby's windows, and she'd felt hollowed out, like she might never stand straight again, just as she felt now.

Everleigh staggered backward, falling into the rose bushes, thorns ripping at her legs and arms. She dropped the bucket at her battered feet, tasting salty goop running from her nose. She couldn't breathe or talk, but she made a wailing sound she never knew she was capable of. A high-pitched screech like a dying animal.

FIVE

❦

Several hours later, after daylight had come, after the last fireman had gone home, after Everleigh had showered at the fancy Southampton Bathing Corporation and been given a fresh change of clothes from Whitney that included a handwritten note: *I'm so relieved you're okay. Come stay here if you need to. xo Whit.* After a doctor had put a stethoscope to her chest later that afternoon and made sure she was breathing normally. After Roland had talked to the firemen about the possible cause—defective wiring, they guessed, but it could have been anything—a police detective would return and complete a thorough investigation. She awoke in a strange cottage in a strange bed next to Roland. She heard someone clear their throat in another room and, overcome with worry that it was her father outside, she slipped out of bed still dressed in Whitney's clothes from the night before.

The cottage. The sweet one with the two bikes under the awning that she'd seen from the pool. The one Roland had called an eyesore. That's where she was. It was Monday.

In a cramped sunny kitchen, she found Gordon, the caretaker. The man, with thinning lines of silvery hair combed across his forehead, seemed to be waiting for her, and he stood up, hands holding his cap at his dungarees' waist.

At least thirty years older than Everleigh and Roland, Gordon and his wife, Meg, were sitting amid several cardboard boxes and trash bags.

"Are you okay, Mrs. Whittaker?" He pointed to a tin coffee pot on the counter. "Please, help yourself."

Everleigh rubbed the smooth of her temples; she wasn't Mrs. Whittaker yet, and his mistake pushed her further out of sorts. "As okay as I can be, yes. Thank you for your help with the fire." Meg handed her a cup of weak coffee, and Everleigh stirred in two heaps of sugar. Her stomach grumbled, but she felt funny asking them for something to eat.

A creak in the floorboards announced Roland, and Meg poured him a cup, too. "Morning," Everleigh handed him the ceramic mug, the rim painted orange, and leaned against the faux brick linoleum counter. Even with his shower, Roland still had faint black rings of soot near his eyes, a crease in his cheek.

He rubbed at his hair like he was rubbing out a stain. "It hurts to breathe," he said.

The doctor had said that their lungs were clear, but the muscles around their chests would hurt for days. "He said it's nothing to worry about," she said. The cut on her foot was tender when she stepped, and even with the Band-Aids, she wished she had on a sock to cushion it. The fire had left her with an uncertain feeling, like nothing was right. Like something even more terrible might happen at any moment.

"Maybe take it easy a bit longer," Meg said, with a hard edge in her voice, sitting at the round breakfast table. It was petite, for three, with scratches on top, and the woman stood, gathering her belongings in her arms.

"Are the two of you leaving?" Everleigh said.

Meg glanced at her husband, and he placed the worn cap on his head. "Suppose you and Mr. Roland are going to need somewhere to live now. We cleaned our stuff out."

Everleigh locked eyes with Meg, who looked away, threading her fingers.

"It's not necessary, really," Everleigh spoke in the woman's direction. "We'll stay with a friend, or we can go home to the city. Right, Roland?"

Roland ignored her pleading. "It's okay, Lee. They have family."

The white-haired woman removed her pleated apron, folding it over the kitchen chair back, like she'd been waiting for confirmation to go. "We'll be with my sister. There's eggs in the fridge."

Gordon, a gentleness in his expression, nodded toward the burned shell of the hotel. "We did our best to put it out, Mr. Whittaker. I don't think we could have done more." Gordon tipped his hat. Everything smelled of charred wood to Everleigh: her skin, her hair, her shirt.

The quiet hum of the icebox was interrupted by the sound of Roland opening it, removing the carton of eggs, and placing them on the counter. The older couple's shoes scuffed against the floor as they moved to the back door, the paper bags crinkling with the weight of their things. The rest was already packed in the car, they said. The click of the latch, the rattle of the glass panes in the door, and they were gone. Everleigh watched the old man start his truck through the large picture window, he and his wife bickering about something. Gordon turned the truck off, and they heard his footsteps approaching the back door before it opened.

Her stomach swished with dread, and Everleigh fidgeted with her belt, bracing herself for whatever Gordon was returning to say, fearing it had something to do with her—with that cigarette she tossed over the side of the balcony hours before the fire. Maybe Gordon had seen the cigarette with his own eyes, maybe he believed she'd gotten them into this mess. *Had she?*

"Did you forget something, Gordon?" Everleigh said, nerves pulsing her throat.

The man pressed his thick pink lips inward, then spoke to Roland. "I know it's not really the proper time, Mr. Whittaker, but the wife is concerned we won't make our bills. To be true, the entire staff is. We were waiting on a check on Monday, today, and now, well. . . . Can we expect it?"

Roland didn't look up from his eggs, frying in butter, his voice defensive. "I just paid you."

Gordon shifted his footing. "That was a month ago, Mr. Whittaker. You said when the hotel opened, we'd get our full month's pay. I know the house here is part of . . ."

She could tell by Roland's frustration that Gordon was telling the truth, and it was wildly uncomfortable, having this man they'd just rendered homeless stand in their kitchen, asking for money. Everleigh put her hand on top of Roland's. "Roland?" she said.

"We're in a bind—" Roland started, but Everleigh cut him off, horrified by his disagreeable answer. To think Roland had expected this man to leave his home, and then didn't even pay him his salary. Fire or not, there was common decency.

"How much are you owed, Gordon?" Everleigh located her crocodile-leather shoulder bag, smoke smudged down the front, and pulled out her father's checkbook, which he'd linked to a separate trust, allowing her to cover the expenses of incidentals. The bank wouldn't allow unmarried women like Everleigh to open their own accounts, and her trust wouldn't be transferred until she was married, and even then it would be a joint account managed by Roland.

"Seventy-five dollars, Miss."

Her father required her to get permission for any spending over twenty-five dollars, but she would argue that these were extenuating circumstances. The pen made a scribbling sound as she wrote it out to cash, the ripping of the check interrupting the pop and sizzle of the eggs. She expected Roland would stop her to offer up a plan for how he would pay the man himself, but he just sat down at the table and began to eat. Everleigh wondered then how many other desperate-looking former employees would stand on their doorstep demanding back pay. She wouldn't be able to hand a check to all of them, the way she was handing one to Gordon now. She glanced wearily at Roland, then the man standing before her. "We should be clear then."

"Yes, Miss, thank you." Gordon returned his hat to his head, put his hands together as if praying, and bowed his head to them. "You're good people. I wish you well."

When he was gone, Roland stared into his plate, the yolks bleeding from the center. Everleigh stayed quiet, dropping a slice of white bread in a rusted toaster. She was waiting for him to offer an explanation, a plan.

"Remember how I told you that my father liked us to rough it—'I won't raise prissy boys,' he'd say. Well, we sometimes stayed here, too, in this tiny cottage." Roland dropped his fork on the saucer, startling her. "We squeezed into the two bedrooms. Mom and Dad in one, and me and my two brothers in the other. We had bunk beds, and me and Tommy slept head to toe on the bottom bunk."

Everleigh looked at the small bedroom off the kitchen. Now there was a wrought-iron twin bed, a dull mahogany dresser with a mirror, sheets that used to be white. She hadn't met his brothers, but she knew one worked in the office of the automotive factory while the other was a high school math teacher in Chicago. "Why didn't you stay in the big house?"

He watched her open the single cupboard and reach for a plate with rosebuds dotting the rim. "My parents didn't grow up with money, and they didn't want us to either. We had china in the cabinet, but Father kept us rowing boats and checking lobster pots and sleeping in this glorified shed. We had to earn a stay in the big house, and we'd be-have all summer, just so we could sleep a week there before Labor Day."

"Didn't you say the big house was in disrepair?" She struggled to follow where he was going with this. He looked dazed, but that was probably from the pills. She remembered that. Him opening a small glass bottle last night, swallowing two.

"It didn't matter if mice crossed into the kitchen at night or that the bedrooms were musty with dust, we felt like kings in the big house. Which is ironic. Because now this place is about losing everything." She thought he was going to cry, his face scrunching up, but he balled his fist over his face and released it with a sigh.

Every few seconds, it seemed, they heard another car drive by, slowing to gawk at the fire damage and speeding up by the time it passed the cottage. Everleigh intuited how hard it would be for Roland to bounce back from something like this. How he would become her burden to bear. She'd be forced to attend to him tirelessly back in his New York apartment, carrying over shepherd's pie, forcing him outside for walks in Central Park, and saying things like, "Cheer up, love." There was the possibility of a darker reality, too. Because what if he required more than she was able to give? She couldn't save her mother from her low moods, and she didn't think she could save Roland either.

Roland tapped his finger on the scuffed wood tabletop. "I can't just walk away from this hotel, Lee." His eyes rose up to meet hers, and he looked scared, his lean frame hunched over. "I'm not going back to New York."

Her face blanched, and she threaded her wavy hair into a ponytail just to distract herself. Even if he had sent Gordon away, she assumed they'd leave in a few days too after tying up loose ends. He couldn't possibly expect her to stay here all summer, staring out at the burned shell of a hotel, the placid extended holiday he promised haunting them both. "Of course. I don't expect you to leave it behind. . . ."

"But you said, just now to Gordon, that we would go back to the city. That he didn't need to leave this cottage."

"I was just saying we *could* go back . . . not that we must. And you built this hotel the first time while living in the city, we could do it again. I'll help you." That didn't seem very appealing either, though—returning to the city and dealing with a fine mess.

Roland's pompadour was flat since he hadn't applied gel yet, and it was strange seeing him so undone, parsed down to nothing but his tired face. "We may need to postpone the wedding, just a few months."

"But we've paid deposits." She crossed her legs, squeezing her inner thigh with her fingernails, leaving imprints of four half-moons in her skin. "Mother already printed the invitations."

"How will I stand at the altar, a perfect failure?" Roland bit at the gummy insides of his cheek. "I won't."

"Oh, Rolly. In four months' time, you won't feel anything close to that."

A newspaperman roamed the street with his camera, aiming at the hotel. Roland scooted away from the window so as not to be seen. "Can you stay with me, Lee? I admit, this cottage isn't what you're used to, but it's not terrible."

The chair she sat in wobbled under her, and Everleigh found herself sizing up the house's compact rooms. The space was worse than rustic, utterly plain and devoid of warmth, the furnishings sparse and ragged. It smelled of strangers. Yet, the simplicity was appealing. It wasn't a hotel at least, and there were marks of authenticity everywhere you looked, like those small stone homes in Provence she and her parents had driven by one summer. Out the large picture window in the kitchen, you could see ocean dunes, since the cottage sat even with the sand, and there were two bikes under the awning, a reminder that she wouldn't spend much time inside. Was it possible that they could really stay? Without a chef. Or a housekeeper. Her confidence swelled. That would be rather nice, being truly on her own.

She'd woken up scared, terrified that she'd almost died, that a hotel full of people could have perished. But perhaps she shouldn't be so frightened. Her aunt had taught her to look for silver linings. "They're the magic of life," she'd told Everleigh during a weeklong visit on Martha's Vineyard. Maybe this cottage could be Everleigh's silver lining.

"Lee, please. I need to get this hotel back up and running by fall, at least spring. I had a lot riding on it, and now everyone will know about the fire. Father will know." The glasses on the table rattled from his fist.

"Now calm down. What happened was a tragedy, not an absence of judgment. Maybe people will remark, 'What a sad thing that the hotel burned down.' But they're not going to say, 'What a bunch of dummies.' Especially not your father." She tried to feed him a bite of toast because she'd seen a woman on television do it in a bread commercial, but he turned his head away.

"Of course he will, especially if it's something about the construction that was at fault."

"That still doesn't mean you're to blame." She was harboring so much guilt that her neck grew hot, but she couldn't tell him about her late-night smoke; if she had anything to do with this, even by accident, he'd never forgive her.

Everleigh needed to eat, calm her nervous stomach, and she rose to cook herself breakfast. She'd turned on a stove only a few times during a debutante cooking class, and she'd never cracked open an egg, but it couldn't be that hard. She stared at the knobs, trying to remember how Nanny made eggs at home. The first time she'd introduced Roland to her family's longtime housekeeper, Nanny, he'd chortled: "You call her 'Nanny'? Like Eloise? The spoiled child who lives at the Plaza?" She and Nanny liked to believe that children's book writer Kay Thompson had been inspired to create Eloise and her "Nanny" after glimpsing a younger Everleigh with hers. "Well, it could be true," Everleigh had told Roland that day, "even if I was an adult when the dreadful book came out."

Roland offered her his eggs, and she squeezed some ketchup on top, determined to keep her wits about her. "You will bounce back from this, Rolly. We will bounce back from this. We'll go home for our wedding, of course, but we can stay until then."

If her parents let her. But she wasn't going to say that. She'd phoned them briefly the night before to confirm she was okay, explaining her shock and promising to call again. Her mother tried keeping her on the line, badgering her to make a decision about the place settings they'd discussed last week, which was utterly tone-deaf. Then she'd passed along a message from the decorator Everleigh was working with on the Bronxville house. "She needs to know about the color of the wall-to-wall carpeting in the living room."

Roland fell forward, his head resting on her lap, and she patted his hair, twisting her fingers in the ashen locks. "You'll help me, right, Lee?"

"Now, now," she said, trying to sound like Nanny after she rushed in when Everleigh had a bad dream. Outside, the same orange-and-white tabby cat she'd seen on her first day at the hotel peeked its head over the frame of the screen, rubbing its back against the wire mesh, purring. It was as orange as a mango.

Everleigh kissed the side of Roland's clean haven cheek. "I promise I'll be here every step of the way."

⸺H⸺

They spent the next couple of days in solemn quiet, sleeping late, taking walks on the beach, Roland writing in a notebook hunched over the kitchen table, fielding tense calls from a gentleman from United Bank about a loan, a reliable way to ruin his mood. She attempted to perk him up, making peanut butter sandwiches and telling stories from her childhood—careful to avoid the unpleasant ones, all those visits to see her mother at the hospital Upstate, sitting among manicured gardens and gowned patients. At one point, Everleigh's father called, and Roland dragged the telephone across the living room. The space was so modest it fit only a couch, the rectangular coffee table, a bookshelf, and a small television, the antennae outstretched in a V formation, tin foil wrapped around the tips.

"Yes, sir," she heard Roland remark with confidence, "we will still get the returns I promised you. It certainly looks worse than it is. . . . Yes, of course, guests will be back in by early autumn. There are no such expectations, sir. You've given me enough." Everleigh got on the phone with her mother afterward, and there was static on the line as she told her mother which wedding dress to order her—the tea-length design with a scalloped lace neckline she'd tried on last week.

Her mother squealed. "Oh, sweetheart! With the lace gloves. I'm so relieved."

Although there was little of the South left in her, Eleanor, or "Ellie" as her friends called her, had been a southern debutante who had met Everleigh's father, "Albie," at a dance when he was visiting his college roommate in Birmingham. Despite her unpredictable mental state or maybe because of it, Eleanor had always been a hopeless romantic. She and Everleigh's father had had a madcap long-distance love affair after they met, nurtured by avid letter writing. As a result, she refused to marry the nice southern boy her parents had lined up for her, and Grammy and Pappy finally agreed to letting "stubborn as a bull" Eleanor marry the New York man she loved. They told everyone they met that the biggest tragedy of the South wasn't losing the war to the Yanks, it was losing their daughter to them. As if all of New York City had swallowed her whole. Perhaps her mother's belief in true love was one of the reasons her parents had approved of Roland so easily, even if they hadn't parsed his family's background nearly as close as they had George's.

Everleigh ran her finger along a crack in the cottage's coffee table, imagining her mother's soft blond waves falling in front of her high cheekbones as she lay in bed, speaking on the telephone. How vulnerable she was to sadness, and Everleigh worried then if her mother would buckle under the weight of Everleigh's absence. The therapist had told her father that her mother's spells were getting longer, and that signaled her illness was getting worse. So with her mother still on the line, Everleigh pried into her mental state, asking details about her mother's plans, when she was seeing friends, what time she'd awoken that morning.

"Lee, sweetheart. I'm okay, really. It's essential that you stay there with Roland—he needs you. But I would like you home the week after July 4th for a fitting and to meet with the decorator. You can attend Sheila Denton's baby shower with me, too. Then we'll reevaluate your plans."

There wouldn't be an argument about her staying. Everleigh nearly threw her hands in the air; she'd never been trusted with this much independence. Her parents were actually *insisting* she stay. It was astonishing, even if their permissiveness had ulterior motives. Because she could hear their unspoken message like a trombone in her ear. In letting her remain in this unknown cottage by the sea, in letting her play all summer at the beach despite the tragedy that had unfolded, what they were really saying was, *We need you to make this engagement work, Everleigh.*

On Thursday, the sun already blinding in the early morning, there was a knock at the back door, and Roland's friend Stevie barreled in wearing a rayon Hawaiian shirt and gripping a stack of manila file folders.

He dropped them on the table, his gold chain bouncing against the thick hair on his chest. "Thankfully, I got the safe open. The dial was partially melted." He winked at Everleigh. "How is everyone?"

Roland gave him a thumbs-up. "Fantastic. Best days of my life."

"We're okay," Everleigh said. The stray cat was in her lap, purring, its fur smooth from petting. Roland didn't want the cat in the house, but she'd convinced him it was okay as long as she was holding it.

"Listen, my goddamn throat is still killing me." Stevie riffled through the papers, looking for something. "On the bright side, no one got hurt." On the table was the transfer of deed to Roland's family's land and a stack of financial ledgers.

Roland snatched the fire policy, printed on crisp white paper with a silver foil starburst in one corner, waving it in the air. "On the bright side, we have this. It's good you pushed me to get the insurance before the party."

Stevie pressed the tips of his fingers together into a bridge, his elbows on the table. "Well, there is a hiccup. A clause in the policy that I didn't give much thought to before, but it may be a problem: 'If the fire is deemed the fault of electrical systems that have failed electrical inspection, the policy is voidable and without benefit.' So if it started because of bad wiring or overloaded circuits, then we get . . ."

Roland stood abruptly, jamming his hands into his back pockets. "Goddamned nothing. You tell that police detective to put his head up his ass and look the other way."

"Have you met him?" Stevie sputtered. "He's a goddamn ball-buster."

Everleigh had been dreading the moment the investigator came to question them. She rested her spoon against her cereal bowl, alarm rising in her voice at the prospect of Roland having done something wrong. "But of course you passed your electrical inspection. The town wouldn't have let the hotel open otherwise. Isn't that true, Rolly?" It sounded right, something her father would have said.

Roland rubbed his face with his palms, slumping back into his chair. "An inspector was coming next week because we were working on some repairs. We had the party anyway," Roland nibbled his fingernail like a squirrel would an acorn, shirking Everleigh's fiery expression. "It was opening night, pet. We couldn't postpone it."

Everleigh resented that this was her life for a minute, that her fiancé had built a hotel that had burned down. She'd been trying to enjoy the last few warm days, practicing her cooking in the small kitchen and planting a small garden with old seed packets she'd found, even with Roland moping about. But it would be hard to enjoy anything if the fire turned out to be his fault. "Well, you'll talk them into looking the other way. I've seen you do it before."

"You realize I do that by adding a little grease to the wheels," he said.

She rested an elbow on the table, her palm cupping her chin. The fire had dimmed the gleam of their engagement. Now they were a couple to which bad things could happen; they'd begin their life together by climbing out of a pit.

"So, get the grease," she said, perhaps a bit too unapologetically.

"Goddamnit, Lee. Think logically here." He flashed a cutting look about the room. "Is it too early to have a drink?"

"Yes," she and Stevie said simultaneously.

Everleigh kissed the top of the cat's head once before putting up water for a second pot of coffee. She wouldn't accomplish anything by agitating Roland, but she was beginning to wonder about his finances. Their finances.

"At the very least, the adjusters are going to have questions," Stevie said. "The payout won't be immediate. First, we need the detective to finish the investigation and declare it an accident. Let's hope he doesn't think there's anything criminal here either. Then we're really not getting paid." Stevie opened one of the folders, pulling out architectural drawings, building plans with all the wiring and plumbing detailed for the lobby.

"Roland, maybe you should call home." Everleigh was always hesitant to bring up his family, but the word criminal had set her off. "Maybe your father can help us figure this out."

Roland didn't touch the mug she put in front of him. "This will give him even more of a reason to treat me like a royal pissant."

The questions she'd asked about his family were always dismissed with a chilly expression and predictable answers. His father and brothers were wrapped up in their own lives, and his father didn't care what Roland did. Roland said she'd meet them eventually, and she'd been placated by the fact that he'd given her a list of relatives to send wedding invitations to. They had a date on the calendar for her parents to meet his father at the end of August; it was supposed to happen in April, then May, but Roland said his father couldn't do it until late summer.

"Your dad might help you get it back up and running."

Roland put his hands on her shoulders, hard and rough. "This is why I love you, pet—you're always so optimistic. But there's reality, too. And the reality is, my father isn't going to help me."

It isn't the time to write off parental help, her thoughts snapped. "You could at least try, Rolly. Give him a chance."

Stevie shook his head, his grin toothy. "We all have family bullshit."

"We sure do," Roland nodded. He pushed open the back door, letting it slam behind him. It bothered her then, more than it had before, that she hadn't met his family; it was like she'd taken a photo of him, but only half of it developed. There was a very big piece missing from view.

Stevie opened one of the ledgers, holding it out for Everleigh to examine. "See for yourself, Lee. There isn't much left."

She leaned in, astounded by the amount tallied at the bottom of the graph paper: $72.58. It would pay for living expenses for a few weeks, but that was it; there was nothing for the hotel, even she knew that. "Well, Roland must have another account." His trust. His father's money. There had to be more.

Stevie shook his head and whispered, "He spent nearly everything on this place, and he took a fat investment from your father, too. But five hundred would do it, if you're willing to fetch your checkbook."

Her mind dove into a free fall, like she had fallen from the Empire State Building, a nightmare she'd had on repeat before meeting Roland. She crashed straight into the sidewalk. Roland wanted money from *her*, and he'd sent Stevie to ask for it. How pathetic, she thought, and yet, how embarrassing to be that desperate. Her father wouldn't like it if she gave Roland a large sum without telling him, especially if he'd already given him cash. It was bad enough that she'd written the caretaker a check for seventy-five dollars, and this was five times that. But even if her father was livid at the expenditure, not giving Roland the money had other repercussions, especially if he couldn't pull any from his own family's accounts. It meant that Roland's hotel would most definitely fail, which meant that her marriage could fail, too. To imagine her parents' pitiful looks if they found out the truth about his finances. She could see the headline in the Cholly Knickerbocker column: "New York Socialite's Fiancé Loses Everything on Eve of Wedding."

She poured a fresh cup of strong coffee, focusing on the chipping white paint on the windowpanes, the square of sun streaking in through the kitchen window. She was scared to give Roland this money behind her father's back, and yet how easy it would be to help—to take away at least some of his misery. Then she and Roland could make their way in this cottage by the sea, with its views of the surf, the waves pounding like a beating heart, a deep blue stretched out to the horizon in an endless plane. Sometimes wrong turns lead to the right ones. Besides, she'd already promised she would help him, and what easier way was there? He'd make it back. She'd be sure they replenished every last cent.

Pulling her red leather checkbook out of her Chanel purse, she asked Stevie, "You're certain that five hundred will be enough, to take care of things?" She caught him staring at her derriere when she leaned over to sign the check, so she moved a few steps away as he nodded at her. "Okay, Stevie. Who should I make it out to?"

The sun ducked behind a cloud, darkening Stevie's freckles. "He'd prefer cash."

SIX

⤜⤛

Five days later

Going to the beach with Whitney at the end of Ocean Road in Bridgehampton was an easy compromise—the quiet stretch of loose dimpled sand fell right between the towns of Southampton, where the hotel was, and East Hampton, where Whitney's family's Craftsman-style estate, Summerfield, sat proudly at one end of Further Lane. Neither one of them had wanted to meet at the elegant and very formal Maidstone Club, a short bicycle ride from Whitney's home, because they'd be forced to socialize with Whitney's summer friends.

They sat under a black-and-white striped umbrella, their two sling chairs side by side. It was blindingly hot for a mid-June day on the Atlantic Ocean; the summer solstice was yet a few days away. Whitney's burly tender sat in his blue truck in the parking lot, waiting for the women to call him over for whatever they needed; he'd brought down everything, including the mint-green cooler that Whitney was opening now. She unwrapped the parchment paper from one of the ham and potato salad sandwiches and handed it to Everleigh, who poured Whitney a plastic tumbler of ice water from a sealed glass carafe, a lemon slice floating at the top.

"That swimsuit is the living end, Lee—it actually gives you hips."

The sleek black-and-white strapless suit was Whitney's sister's, and she'd given it to Everleigh after the fire.

Everleigh glanced down at the three gold buttons embellishing the center of her bosom, wincing at the unattractive dimpling of her upper thighs. "In the Adirondacks, you know, some of the locals are still wearing that bulky fabric with skirts sewn into the seam."

"Sheesh. No rush to get back there." Whitney had picked Everleigh up at the cottage at eleven that morning, beeping the horn of her black Thunderbird out front, waving politely at Roland, who was still in a sour mood. This morning, after they had a spat, he threw himself back into work, directing a stream of construction workers from the lawn, even if he was still dressed in tennis whites from his morning match.

It was a scenic drive to the beach on Route 27, the only road winding east from Southampton, nothing but open meadows and wildflower fields with the occasional supper club or fruit and vegetable stand in between. As they approached the farming community of Bridgehampton, there was a Carvel and a drive-in movie theater playing *Island in the Sun*. The main drag, with its tiny row of shopfronts, had several gas stations, serving as a pitstop between towns, and a small dinette called Candy Kitchen, where men in mud-stained overalls talked crop yields on the sidewalk. A feed store stacked bales of hay and shiny tractors for sale out front, a small library sat in an old white-planked house. Truman Capote, Whitney said, was a fixture at the dark mahogany bar at Bobby Van's; he was living in a woodsy house somewhere nearby working on his latest novel.

Look at all this country, Everleigh had thought after Whitney steered onto Ocean Road, where there were only a few houses but hundreds of acres of potato fields, low green plants in symmetrical rows, paths of dark soil drawn like lines between, stretching for at least two miles with the cerulean sky open all the way to the sea.

The women gossiped the entire ride, which is what they always

did, but Everleigh found her mind wandering at times. She was thinking about her mornings at the Meadow Club. Each day she and Roland
had walked down the street to the club. On the first morning, she'd assumed they were playing mixed doubles, but as soon as they'd arrived,
Roland showed her the pro she'd be working with and a group of
women she'd be playing against. Everleigh was up for a women's
league—the skirts alone were adorable—but then her teammates
weren't particularly friendly; one of them openly pointed and gossiped
about Everleigh—"They're not even married!" one said, a little too
loudly, while another woman could be heard whispering the word "fire."
When Alice Anna arrived moments later, air-kissing her heated cheeks,
Everleigh quickly aligned herself with her old (dreaded) acquaintance,
so she didn't feel so alone. "Don't mind them." Alice had laughed, showing all her white teeth in a perfect row. "It takes them a little while to
get used to new people. I'll show you the ropes."

They played a doubles match against the women and won, Alice
congratulating Everleigh for earning their respect with her backhand.
Still, Everleigh found she was an outsider with the Palm Beach crowd
who summered here, and it left her dreading her return to the club, no
matter how pristinely the grass courts were tended. The next morning,
after Everleigh had arrived for a lesson, she went into the locker room
to stow her purse and remained on the flouncy couch for the entirety
of her session, flipping through a magazine rather than going outside
with her racquet to join the others. She could have fit in if she'd wanted
to, but she didn't want to spend a morning gossiping with women
about other women she didn't even know. When Roland asked how
her match went, she'd said, "great," and he hadn't known the wiser. She'd
done the same thing yesterday, this time bringing her camera and taking photographs of rows of lockers, positioned like soldiers at guard.
Sneaking into the locker room was a funny way to misbehave, and she
wanted to tell Whitney about it, but she also knew Whitney would

scold her for being antisocial and failing to make potentially useful contacts.

Whitney crossed her legs daintily at the knee. "You started to tell me about the latest with the hotel earlier, but we got sidetracked. Are things moving along?"

"Well, you saw all the trucks there this morning," Everleigh started. They'd pulled up at seven to park dumpsters on the back lawn, and several beefy men, guys that Stevie had hired from the Bronx because they were cheaper, had flooded the hotel like ants, carrying armfuls of debris out. "It's worrisome, though," she said, "because the fire department sent a notice that we shouldn't do any demolition until they'd fully investigated the site. Roland said he'd give them another week and then he was bringing in the bulldozers."

"I hope he doesn't make trouble for himself." Whitney abhorred people who didn't follow the rules. "They can be protective out here. Not everyone is happy to see a caravan of city people arriving."

"He says it's his right to work on his business. I'm sure he'll back down if need be." It had been upsetting, though, because he'd been short with her again, seeming annoyed whenever Everleigh brought up the hotel, and he'd told her to mind her business and he'd mind his. *Didn't her five hundred dollars earn her the ability to ask questions?* she'd grumbled. He'd fought so hard to get her to stay in Southampton with him, and now he'd become so obsessed with rebuilding the hotel that he had little time left for Everleigh. Instead of listening to music together or going for walks, he'd sit with his notebook figuring out how many new mattresses needed ordering. Dinner plans were scrapped so he and Stevie could call on an acquaintance about a possible loan until the insurance money came through. And still, he didn't come home to have lunch with her the past few days, but simply waltzed in, grabbed the sandwich she set on a plate, pecked her cheek, and headed back to the work site. It wasn't that Rolly didn't love her—she knew he did—

but she wondered if marriage always felt this lonely. She supposed it was how her own parents coexisted: her father lived his life on one plane, her mother on another, and they met up in the living room sometimes to laugh at their favorite radio program.

But instead of telling Whitney this, she said, "Remember when we used to dream about marrying brothers, so we'd be in the same family?"

Whitney smiled; she'd set her hair in rollers the night before and the curls were windswept, flying around her elastic headband. "Yes, and how we used to say we were going to get apartments next door to each other and let our kids run back and forth whenever they wanted. You would get a job taking photos for the *New York Sun*, and I'd be running the women's club."

"Mothers don't work! Only damsels." Everleigh laughed, wiping a smidge of mayonnaise off her mouth. A piping plover ran alongside the water; Everleigh thought back to how Whitney's mother often lectured them about how lucky they were that they were children in wartime rather than adults, since their generation was asked the impossible: to work *and* run a satisfying household. Both Whitney's and Everleigh's fathers were too old to join the war, but swept up in the times, Everleigh's mother had insisted on working as a stenographer for the war bureau, in what she referred to as her greatest years. Whitney's mother had volunteered in rations.

"Well, lucky for us, our houses in Bronxville are only a few blocks apart."

Everleigh took her last bite. "You better not be too busy for me when I move up in the fall."

"Too busy planning luncheons? You'll be helping. I'm not letting you off that easy." Whitney winked, twirling her emerald posts and kicking her legs out. "Isn't this just fabulous? Look at us, on the beach, having a fancy picnic in fashionable bathing suits. Take our picture."

"I don't have my camera," Everleigh said, her cheeks dimpled. "But if I did, I'd take a picture of us and name it 'Surf Sisters.'" Everleigh dug her toes into the sand, comforted by how gently the powdery grains enveloped her bare foot, sliding in between her toes and feeling like a soft blanket. "Maybe I can take portraits of you and Truman one day."

"He'll hardly sit for a *real* photographer, let alone you." Whitney squeezed her friend's shoulder, and Everleigh, a bit stung by the slight, reminded herself that her friend was right; she wasn't a real photographer. They could say things this honest only because they were so close. All those years when Everleigh's mother had gone away, leaving her only with Nanny and Daddy, she and Whitney sometimes spooned affectionately in bed. There was nothing funny about it, simply that the angst of their lives sometimes called for physical closeness.

Everleigh stared out at the sea, focusing on the point where the surf rolled and receded. She felt like she could walk the ocean's tides all day and still she wouldn't know how to find her way back to the lightness felt at her engagement party a few weeks ago. Before the hotel had burned down. Before she'd written Roland that five-hundred-dollar check. Because something else had changed, too: Stevie was a regular part of their lives now. He and Roland had been drinking most nights, carrying armfuls of booze into the cottage kitchen, staying up late and sitting on the back picnic table, like two stooges. She didn't want any part of it, and a few nights, she'd simply gone into her bedroom and closed the door.

The wind picked up, and Everleigh clasped her hair with a red satin ribbon. "Hey, Whit. When you pictured yourself as a grown-up, you know, when you were a little girl, is this how you imagined it?"

Whitney's gold huarache sandals shined with sun; her foot was so petite it reminded Everleigh of a doll's. "Sitting on the beach with my best friend? I would say so. What about you?"

Everleigh glanced at her watch's small rectangular face, thinking that just two hours ago she was fighting with Roland, that just two hours ago he'd called her a spoiled brat because she said she was growing bored with him being gone all the time. "I think it's how I thought it would be. I mean, the parts with you, yes. But then parts of it, not at all."

She *had* tried to busy herself, calling local newspapers and telling them that the Everleigh Hotel would rebuild, hoping to drum up some good press, and Everleigh *had* made a point to tell Roland, who seemed mildly amused by her reports rather than grateful. But with him out of reach, she found herself feeling malcontent—a nagging sense that she wanted something else to fill her days, a hunger for something she couldn't quite pinpoint. It wasn't that she was itching to get back to the city; she liked being here in the cottage. Oh, the freedom of it! It was more that she'd never had this kind of time, these long blocks of hours that felt like they could be stacked into something worth doing, rather than simply making the bed or wiping down the bathtub. If those sarcastic housekeepers at the hotel could see her now!

The last few nights, when she'd awoken in the dark hours of morning, she'd been unable to fall back asleep, padding from room to room, thinking up chores to keep the house organized. She wondered how Roland saw her when he left the house in the morning, what she could do to appear more interesting to him when she wasn't even interesting to herself.

Whitney handed her an aluminum tin with fruit salad. "What do you mean, 'Not at all'? How did you imagine yourself?"

Everleigh rested her chin in her hand, the cubes of pineapple tasting more tart than sweet. "I don't know. Roland said I wasn't ambitious at the party, and it got to me. Because I'm not sure I like that he sees me that way. Then I started thinking of Amelia Earhart and how she knew she wanted to fly planes, and Patricia Highsmith, and how she always wanted to write stories, and Marilyn, gosh, Marilyn, how she wanted to be an actress. And me, what do I want?"

"Did Amelia Earhart ever marry?"

Everleigh roughly crumpled her napkin, tossing it back in the cooler without care. "She did. But what does that matter?"

"You think too much, Everleigh." Whitney moved her chair so her legs were in the sun. "You know what you want. You want to get married and have a baby so we can raise our kids together. I don't plan on growing old without you."

"Well, obviously." Everleigh bit the inside of her cheek, irritating a sore spot where she'd been gnawing into the pink flesh. "But I'm afraid I'm learning firsthand that a husband is just someone else to please. I was in a panic last year about finding a fiancé after what happened with George, and I am engaged to someone wonderful. I mean, mostly. But, Whit, living out here, living with him, is harder than I thought it would be. I feel like he sees me differently, like I'm his, I don't know, toy, rather than his companion."

Whitney wrinkled her nose. "Now that's a bleak view of Roland."

"But it's true with Truman, too. He doesn't speak to you of politics or the latest headlines; he reserves those conversations for his cigar circle. It's like we're playthings."

Whitney hooted. "Playthings? Well, don't I wish?"

Everleigh dropped her head back against the chair, draping her arm over her eyes and laughing. "I sound ridiculous. I don't know what I'm saying. I don't even like politics."

"Oh, Lee. Your wedding is four months away. Don't bog yourself down with these kinds of worries. You are not someone's toy. You're someone's fiancée. There's a very big difference."

"You're right. I think I'm just getting used to this 'living with a man' thing." There was something else she wanted to run by Whitney, her stomach churning in knots over it since they'd arrived at the beach.

Perhaps now was the time. "Whit, listen. There's a photographer out here, and I'm thinking of calling her."

"Every bride gets nervous. I had cold feet the day before my wedding. What if Truman wasn't the right one? But then I searched my heart, and you know what . . . let's get you busy." Whitney pulled her planner out of her beach bag and flipped through to August. "Weren't you supposed to hold a luncheon to meet Roland's family right before Labor Day?"

This was the part of Whitney that could frustrate Everleigh endlessly. Everleigh closed the planner. "Yes, his father is flying in, but can you focus a minute? You're starting to sound like Mommy."

Whitney tucked the leather book back into her bag. "Fine. Tell me. Who is this photographer?"

So Whitney *had* heard her. Everleigh sighed. The prospect of calling any photographer, let alone one as prolific as Starling Meade, made Everleigh want to jump off the Brooklyn Bridge, and yet she felt a sort of gravitational pull. "Art Miller mentioned a woman out here, a big name, who's having a show in East Hampton."

"Oh yes, Starling something, right? Mother can't stop talking about her show, how she's the first woman this and that." Whitney rolled her eyes. "So you're going to call a total stranger? And say what? Maybe we need to have a different conversation, like whether or not Roland is enough for you. If he was, maybe you wouldn't be trying to occupy yourself?"

"I'm not trying to occupy myself. Okay, well I am, but it's not because there's anything wrong with Roland. I'm just thinking about what I'll do when I'm officially Mrs. Everleigh Whittaker. What do you do all day?"

Whitney seemed pleased by the question, like she thought Everleigh would never ask. "Well, you know I love to read. And I'm always off to a meeting here, another there. Tennis at the Maidstone. Lunch dates with friends. Tru and I try to have dinner out three nights a week with another couple." She once again opened her appointment book, turning to tomorrow's itinerary and reading specific appointments, stopping at "dinner at The Palm with the Barberries." "You just need to make connections out here. Start inviting your tennis partners to dinner. You could have a full plate within a week. I can help if you . . ."

Everleigh shook her head. It was hard finding the words for what was twisting inside her heart. If she told Whitney she didn't want that kind of appointment book—that she had little interest in keeping that particular list of engagements—her friend would be hurt. But what did Everleigh want to fill her slots with instead? She wasn't actually sure.

Two mothers splashed with their toddlers in the surf, one baby falling in and crying when water filled his nose. He choked out a cough.

Whitney leaned toward Everleigh, her voice soft. "Did you ever go to your doctor, get yourself checked? You know it takes time to prime your body for motherhood?"

"Last I heard it was a pretty straightforward process."

Whitney laughed, but Everleigh saw it, the way the corners of her mouth turned down ever so slightly. She and Truman had been trying for a year. "Anyway, you could start trying now. I wish I had before the wedding—we would have had a jump on things."

Whitney had always wanted a family from the time they were younger, playing with dolls whenever she could. Everleigh had preferred to play teacher, standing in front of a class of stuffed animals, sending the "children" home rather than following them there.

"He's trying to get me to skip the rubbers." Everleigh wouldn't relent on this issue; it was her insurance policy that if things went wrong between them before the wedding, she wouldn't be stuck with a child.

"Good." With Whitney's porcelain skin beginning to resemble a flamingo, she applied more Coppertone suntan lotion, hoping the tanning cream would turn her brown. So far, it served only to darken her freckles. "If you get pregnant in two months' time, you won't even be showing when you walk down the aisle."

With her wedding in October, Everleigh *should* be expecting by spring. Oh, how her mother would fawn over her growing belly under her patterned shift dress! Perhaps that's why her days were feeling empty here. She hadn't anticipated how much she'd miss her mother. Everleigh pressed her palm to her chest as comfort, thinking that no one had warned her how hard it was to leave home, that she'd feel the push and pull of wanting to grow up and never wanting to grow up at all. A few weeks before she'd left for the beach, her mother had mentioned she planned to turn Everleigh's bedroom into a sewing room. She'd whipped around in her room, riffling through her dresser so her mother wouldn't see the tears gathering in her eyes. All she wanted was to move out of her parents' place at the Plaza, to escape from the heartbreak that resided there, so why did it bother her that they weren't keeping her room just as it was now? That it wouldn't always be hers to return to.

Everleigh waited on her friend to continue. "So, do you think I should call her?"

Whitney tilted her face to the sun, hiding behind her sunglasses, even though she'd angled her chair so she could see Everleigh better. "Sure, get the bee out of your bonnet. Maybe ask her to lunch. Photographers thrive on patrons. Buy one of her photographs in exchange for a little inspiration. Then go home and make your fiancé a nice dinner."

Of course she'd try to make her fiancé a nice dinner. She'd dusted off a cookbook she'd found in the bottom of the pantry in the kitchen just yesterday, and she was determined to learn how to roast a chicken. But act as a patron? Her mother's closest friend, Judy, hosted a series of dinner parties with members of the orchestra at Carnegie Hall, even though she'd never played an instrument; she even rented one of the bedrooms in her house to a maestro. But Everleigh saw how she stared longingly at these artists, and Everleigh always wondered why she didn't just ask for a lesson. Why she didn't attempt to become one herself.

Whitney hadn't stopped talking. "You have to learn to find joy in the small things. When you bake a casserole, put your heart . . ."

A two-seater propeller plane flew low overhead. To the pilot, the two women must have looked like carefree summer girls getting a little color for the night's barbecue, and he was right. But even they weren't able to detect the turbulence this conversation would send up around them, how close they were sitting and yet how far away they were beginning to feel from one another. Because as excited as Everleigh was to move to the Bronxville house, as much as she wanted to be Mrs. Whittaker, as happy as she would be to have a child of her own, it didn't feel like enough, and it was lonely to think that Whitney didn't agree.

They read for a while, wordlessly trading the June issues of *Vogue* and *Cosmopolitan*, as the tide went out, leaving pools of water in the sand where children splashed about. Whitney closed her magazine, then pushed her wavy hair back with her sunglasses. "Lee."

Everleigh looked up from an advertisement for RC Cola, a woman lying on a chaise longue in a yellow bathing suit with one leg daintily kicked in the air. "Look at me—I look just like her."

Whitney laughed, then reached for her sundress and slid it over her head. "We should be going." She folded her beach towel and tucked it into her tote. "There's something else though. Something I wanted to tell you."

"Sure, what is it?" Everleigh nodded. In her head, she thought, *This better not be about Roland.* If she had to choose between Whitney and Roland, it would be the most painful decision she could imagine.

Whitney snapped shut the umbrella enclosure. "Well, Truman doesn't want to get involved with the police and neither do I, but I forgot my purse somewhere by the pool the night of the fire. Truman went back to get it. He overheard Alice and her fiancé having an argument outside before the fire started, some jealousy about her past with Roland, and there was a threat from Ernest. 'If I ever see you with Roland Whittaker again, I'll harm him in ways your pretty little head can't imagine.' Truman heard Alice crying then, too, as he rushed off."

Everleigh's cheek registered a faint twitch. "Why didn't you tell me this earlier?"

"I'm not sure it means anything." Whitney waved to the attendant. He would help carry the wooden sling chairs and umbrella to the car. "A jealous man's confrontation isn't exactly an indictment of an affair, or any wrongdoing at all. Still, I thought you should know."

"An affair!" Everleigh had considered the possibility after hearing the disdain in Alice's voice when she and Roland quarreled at the party, a bitterness that lingered between them as the others tried to redirect their bad blood. Roland wrote it off, saying Alice was resentful that he'd broken up with her cousin years back. But if Ernest was jealous of Roland, then maybe Alice and Roland had been a couple at some point, too. It wasn't a happy thought.

The attendant packed the car, and the two women drove off, each sticky with sand and salt and lotion, their hair greasy and overblown. Whitney was going on about something but stopped talking, taking her eyes off the road to look at Everleigh. "You're distracted."

Everleigh didn't even pretend she'd been listening closely. "Have you heard anything else about Alice and Roland, any kind of past between them?"

"Nothing, and I did ask around." Whitney glanced at her twice, opening and closing her mouth. "How about you join me at water aerobics this week?"

Everleigh nodded, even as her mind slipped away to Ernest's hulking stature, his anger at Roland. It seemed likely that Roland had omitted something about his relationship with Alice. Maybe to protect Everleigh. She dreaded the moment she'd be forced to confront him.

Just before sunset that night, with Roland and Stevie having drinks out with possible investors, Everleigh placed her T-strap leather heels and camera case in the front basket of her bike and slipped on flats. The ride along the ocean offered panoramic views of the inlet, thanks to the dunes that bordered the road, and as she pedaled to watch the sun go down over the lake, she peeked into the driveways of the grand homes, wondering if she'd recognize the inhabitants. Mostly, she saw house staff, a man polishing a Rolls-Royce with rags, a woman sweeping another home's grand-columned porch. She decided her favorite was a three-story shingled house that sat atop windswept dunes, the small sandy hills teeming with bright pink beach roses. Everleigh slowed, dragging her flats against the pebbly roadside, and came to a stop.

After pulling her camera out of the bike basket, she rotated the lens, scanned the landscape, and tried to capture the lush leaves, the sharp contrast of the fuchsia petals. The viewfinder was focused on the side of the manor, near the pebbly driveway, the flowers spilling over onto it. A person walked into the frame, a gentleman in colorful attire and loafers. She momentarily dropped her camera, squinting, because she knew this visitor. Stevie, with his unmistakable carrottop and Hawaiian shirt. She hunted the scene for Roland, thinking that this was the possible investor they were visiting, but there were only two people: Stevie and what looked like a preppy college boy leaning against a shiny red sedan.

Everleigh watched Stevie reach his hand into his car window, pull out a brown paper bag, and give it to the man, who stuffed a wad of cash into Stevie's hand in return. At once, the college boy opened the paper bag, and his shoulders bounced with laughter, as he pulled out a large red tomato and pressed it onto his nose.

"*Humph*," Everleigh said, even as she snapped a photo, irritated at another grown man enjoying Stevie's antics. They were yipping with laughter when Stevie turned his head at the sound of a passing car and spotted her. She was in plain view, standing on the hill with her camera, and he waved. Her mind went to Roland. If he wasn't meeting a possible investor with Stevie, where was he?

Everleigh tossed her camera in the woven basket and hopped on her bike, disappearing down a quiet lane, a road where she was sure Stevie couldn't find her. She didn't want to chance getting stuck alone with him.

SEVEN

❧

Everleigh parked the car in front of a Southampton café busy with lunch service, all the women having traded in their house pants for serious pencil skirts and colorful sundresses. She strained to see what was on their plates, noting a few women eating salmon (she hadn't attempted to cook fish yet), others munching Waldorf salads (that would be fairly easy to make) and several slices of quiche. *Quiche!* She'd try cooking that next, she thought as she headed toward Saks department store. It turned out that sautéing, roasting, and chopping were very good distractions when you were feeling blue, and the slog of keeping house could make anyone blue. Plus, with Roland beyond busy with the hotel, the cookbook she'd found was providing rather good company, giving her purpose in the otherwise empty cottage. Her latest obsession was to perfect fluffy scrambled eggs, even if this morning, yet again, they got crusted and rubbery, streaking with brown grease. Still, she'd keep trying, dog-earing other recipes she wanted to make for Roland someday in the cookbook, like those mouthwatering bacon-wrapped dates. Well, if he ever sat still long enough to enjoy a full meal with her.

American flags flapped in a row along Hampton Road when she emerged from Saks with a new dress for a party they were to attend, and she window-shopped at Keene's Books, eyeing the summer's biggest titles: William Faulkner's *The Town*, a new novel by Daphne du Maurier. Everleigh glanced at her reflection in the storefront, knowing that she was really searching for something else: an inner courage. She needed to stop pretending this shopping errand was why she'd left the house that morning when really it had been an excuse. *Don't spend another minute sweeping sand off the kitchen floor,* she heard herself say aloud on the sidewalk in front of the *Southampton Press,* the newspaper reminding her of her true intentions. Go call on Starling Meade.

With the car smelling of hot, sticky leather, Everleigh settled into the driver's seat once again, wondering what she'd do when she arrived at the art colony. Would she actually get out of her car? She glanced down at the local road map on the passenger seat to make sure she was going in the right direction, adrenaline nudging her forward, instinct bidding her to find out what exactly Starling Meade was like, if she'd even open her door. Everleigh had called the art colony again before she'd left that morning, hanging up when a man with an accent answered, too chicken to ask for the address. But she'd located it in the white pages of the phone book easily and scribbled it on an index card that was now sitting on her lap.

The roads were busy with travelers that Thursday, traffic moving slow thanks to vacationers journeying out for the weekend (next Thursday was the Fourth of July) and a dairy truck rattling in front of her on Route 27 East. After turning onto a narrow side street in Bridgehampton, her car zipped under a low train trestle, meadows of wildflowers growing to the edges. Everleigh sensed she was getting closer, and she stopped at a farm stand to check her map. Momentarily distracted by large bouquets of zinnias in mason jars, she tossed five cents in a scrubbed coffee can and selected a bunch of perfumed red and yellow flowers tied with baker's twine. She turned around to see several elm trees lining a driveway, a small hand-painted sign stuck in the ground in a patch of grass, and Everleigh nearly mistook it for a

"For Sale" sign. But when she squinted, she could read it: "Sag Artist Colony."

She'd found it.

A sparrow flew overhead, gliding over the lush meadows in the direction of the art colony, and she followed the curve of the pebble driveway, spotting several white-planked cottages built on platforms up ahead. She parked under a shade tree, carrying the flowers with her. As she got close enough to see the paint was chipping on the structures, she came face-to-face with a woman a decade older than Everleigh in bare feet, painting topless.

"Oh, I'm sorry." Everleigh averted her eyes. "I didn't mean to disturb you. I should have—"

"You've never seen a woman naked before?" The artist remained still, moving only her hand in brushstrokes.

"Oh sure, but . . ." Everleigh stood behind the artist, whose bangs made a neat line above her eyebrows. There was a small mirror connected to her canvas, and she was painting her own torso, as reflected back to her.

The artist raised an eyebrow. "It's just a body."

"Oh, I know. I have the same parts. I'm just surprised is all." It was the truth. She'd never seen someone so exposed, and it was inspiring, actually, like this woman was baring her soul to the trees in a way that Everleigh never had. "Is Starling Meade here?"

"Cabin four. But she's probably in the darkroom, that old chicken coop over there." The woman pointed to one of the little houses at the end of the row of cabins.

Everleigh sat on the rickety steps of cabin four, where a small sign above the door read "Meade." Each cabin was a tiny planked house with a small outdoor sink powered by a hand pump. She saw a gentleman next door come out to fill a glass with water, drinking it down in a large gulp.

"She usually stays in the darkroom until one," he said, rubbing bar soap and turpentine onto his hands under the water. "It's half past eleven."

He introduced himself as Jerem Soffett and said he was on a month-long grant to train under Willem de Kooning. "There's a nice path through the field there," he said in a thick Dutch accent. She thanked him, and after a restless meander through the meadow—she was nearly losing her moxie—she followed the path back to the photographer's cabin.

Starling was out of the darkroom, as Mr. Soffett had predicted, sitting at the picnic table eating noodles out of a thermos. She was tall and long-limbed with a long mane of soft white hair pulled back with a simple rubber band you'd use to fasten cellophane on a carton of blueberries. Her hair was particularly striking against her black T-shirt and matching capri pants, and she wore glasses, thick black ones like many men did, only she didn't look masculine. She looked like the kind of person you'd ask for directions, knowing she knew exactly where she was going.

"Excuse me, madame. Are you Starling Meade?"

The woman looked up, thin wrinkles spread like starbursts from her eyes, her complexion peachy and even. She wasn't too old, maybe in her late fifties.

"Yes," she said.

Everleigh handed her the flowers. "It's so nice to meet you. I'm Everleigh Farrows of New York City. But you can call me Lee." She moved to shake the artist's hand, but Starling stared at it, never lifting hers to meet Everleigh's.

"I don't believe in hand shaking—it's a phony greeting concocted by the aristocracy to make people feel unequal."

Everleigh glanced at the ground, lowering her trembling hand. "Well, it's nice to meet you."

Starling slurped a noodle from her thermos, then said, "I'm joking, darling. It's a show of peace that started back in ancient Greece. But my hand is a bit sticky." She held up the bouquet that Everleigh had placed on the table. "Aren't these lovely? They're from across the street. That's the farmer's wife growing those."

"It was hard to choose just one." Everleigh pointed to the woman's camera, the latest titanium Nikon SP, on the tabletop, the metal rusted in spots. Everleigh had seen the camera in a shop, thinking how fun it would be to spend a day trying to figure out how to use the latest technology. "That's one nice camera."

Starling smiled then, and Everleigh realized this woman wasn't wearing an ounce of makeup, and still she radiated; she herself rarely left home without thick black liner and mascara. "Why are you looking for me?"

Everleigh sucked in a breath. How much easier this meeting had been in her fantasies. "Well, this is going to sound a bit strange, but I want to be a photographer. I am a photographer, but I'm not a real photographer. I don't develop my own pictures, but I like taking them. And I met Marilyn Monroe at a party—"

At the sound of the actress's name, Starling's eyes grew round like saucers, and Everleigh continued, "And Marilyn and Arthur said that I should call you." Everleigh carried herself regally—she wasn't the type to feel uncertain—but standing here, in the shadow of a talent as towering as the elms above them, she felt like the cartoon character Mighty Mouse, who she always saw as tiny and desperate to get noticed.

Everleigh's voice dipped in volume as she reached into her tote bag, pulling out the photo she'd taken of Monroe and Miller. She'd been poring over her film from the night of the party, flipping through pictures of people dancing, along with the two photos of the famous couple. She'd stared at the celebrity couple's faces like they were part of a larger puzzle, a set of clues that were trying to tell her something—the actress's sparkly dress and tired expression, the way the writer's hand cupped the small of her back. These images felt like remnants of a different lifetime now, snapshots of a night that would live on only as a movie reel in her head.

The picture of the famous couple trembled in her hands as she dropped it on the rusted tabletop. "Like I said, I want to be a photographer, and I thought you might be able to help."

A finch landed near Starling's food, deciding whether it was brave enough to snatch a crumb of something green from her lunch bag, and Starling cooed to it, tossing him a bite. Her eyes didn't leave the photo as she offered the bird additional food bits. "Why do you think wanting to be a photographer is 'strange'?"

Everleigh tried to think of something smart, anything. "Well, there aren't many women photographers. There aren't many women anything, actually, at least among my mother's friends."

Starling waved her words away, like her line of thinking was wrong. "That only means we need to find more women photographers. You know, during the war, women did every job imaginable—I was shooting hard news for the papers—and then the men came back from Normandy and took everything from us. It was incredibly unfair. I'm not sure if your mother ever told you because the history books don't say it, but this country had an all-female baseball league, we had women trading on Wall Street, women running hospitals. And some women refused to return to domestic life after that. It ruined the ones that did. But it was offensive, really. Now that the men were back, our talents were irrelevant." Starling grinned. "I refused to quit."

"Well, I'm glad you didn't." Everleigh stood in her blush-colored belted dress, wishing she'd said something else, wishing she'd chosen something less fussy to wear. "I love cameras, and I've read a lot of books. But something is missing in my pictures."

"Because you can't learn from a book. You learn photography by doing; there's quite a bit of trial and error." Starling inquired about what kind of camera Everleigh shot with. When she told the artist about her Nikon S2, a serious camera that she knew outpaced her skill set, Everleigh was hoping to impress her. Instead, Starling slurped another noodle while settling her eyes on Everleigh's diamond engagement ring, then the rather gracious gemstone hanging from her neck. A subtle glance at the parking lot at Roland's expensive convertible. Everleigh clasped her hands behind her back, knowing that she was being judged. Because really, what was she doing here? Did she really think this photographer would take her seriously? A person like Starling, who pulled herself up by her bootstraps, taking on a woman like Everleigh, who didn't need to work at all? Starling Meade didn't need some spoiled woman from the estate section of the summer colony bugging her with questions about her craft.

"That's a pretty nice camera for a beginner," Starling said. "I think I shot on my father's old Kodak Brownie for years before I could afford my own instrument. Have you ever seen those small leather black boxes you held at your waist, looking through the viewfinder on top?" When Starling laughed, her whole face lit up, and Everleigh glimpsed the woman's younger self—how her white hair had probably once been blond, her skin smooth and satiny. "My advice to you: Put the Nikon in a drawer. Get one of those Brownie cameras and take a photography class."

Everleigh nodded pleasantly, even as anger burned inside her. She was most certainly being discounted because of her money. But she also refused to leave behind a false impression: that the poor little rich girl just got a new toy to play with. It was insulting, Everleigh supposed, for her to show up like this, asking a seasoned professional like Starling to teach her in a couple of weeks what she had spent a lifetime learning. But she was tired of the assumptions people made about her, too: that having money meant having everything. Standing before this revered photographer, Everleigh's flats resting on a patch of dirt where the grass had worn away, she pulled off her ring and popped it into her change purse. She unclasped her garnet necklace and put it in the zipper pocket of her purse.

"I don't need any of this stuff, Miss Meade, or the Brownie camera either. I want to master my 35 mm. Maybe I'm not a natural like you are, and I don't always know how to control the f-stop or how to position the frame, but I just want to learn." Everleigh couldn't believe what was coming out of her, how determined she sounded, like one of those salesmen on street corners in Midtown, handing out flyers to promote themselves. Now she understood why they followed you if you made eye contact, why they didn't stop talking until you took the flyer in hand. You had one shot with a person.

"You see, it was my fiancé's hotel that just had the big fire in Southampton, and this is the last thing I should be thinking about, but I always wonder if I have a knack at picture taking, if maybe I should at least try pursuing it, and Marilyn probably didn't even know what she was saying that night, but it stuck with me. Telling me my hobby should be a passion, and that I should talk to you. And now I'm standing here feeling very daft, but in dire need of help."

"Oh, darling, sit down." Starling patted the metal bench beside her, something you'd see in the girls' locker room. "You know, people look at Marilyn, and they write her off as a dummy. Well, I've shot her twice, and I can tell you that she knows exactly what she's doing. What she's selling. So, if Marilyn told you to come here, I'm not surprised that you're here. She's quite convincing."

Everleigh expelled her breath; she didn't realize she'd been holding it. "I've just been trying to keep it together for my fiancé, and he's trying to act as though he's fine, but he's not . . . and I cannot even make a quiche. I mean, we're eating sandwiches every day and night, but all I can think of is pictures. Of what I can photograph that day."

Starling guffawed, gulping another mouthful. It was seaweed Starling was eating; Everleigh was sure of it. "There are a lot of women out here working at their art, maybe more than you realize," she said. "You're hardly the first woman to decide she wants to be an artist."

Everleigh nodded, although she didn't know any female artists in her circles.

"You've heard of Willem de Kooning, sure, but there are women out here, like Lee Krasner and Grace Hartigan. They're living in these towns, waking up and painting something that isn't quite right but will get them to the next project. They can't stop themselves. Art isn't something you do. It's something you are. It's as certain as the sun."

Everleigh wished she could pull her knees up to her chest; instead, she sat formally, her legs crossed. "I'm not certain about my being an artist. I'm not certain about any of this, even sitting here. But I . . ."

Starling screwed the cap onto her thermos, her nails without polish. "Of course you haven't thought about it. Because women aren't switching on the coffee pot and sweeping the kitchen floor after breakfast and thinking, what can I make today? They think, 'What can I do to make someone else happy?' Look at the women artists I know. Elaine de Kooning has spent so much time promoting her husband, pouring herself into a man's work. Lee Krasner only started nurturing her own talent. But the brushstrokes in her paintings are breathtaking, and I just know she'll have her due. She lives over in Springs. Her husband died last year."

Everleigh cut in. "Her husband is Jackson Pollock."

Starling seemed surprised that Everleigh knew who he was, but she'd seen one of Pollock's paintings in *Life* magazine, shots of him throwing paint on a canvas stretched across the floor of his Hamptons barn, and noticed his wife standing behind him with a smile. All the colors adding up to something you couldn't stop looking at, even if you didn't understand it.

"So, you know the abstract expressionists?" Starling purred. "Good. I like to hear that. Not many rich girls care about that kind of thing."

Everleigh clicked her heels together triumphantly. She felt more like herself then, maybe even a shinier version.

One of the other artists at the colony walked toward her cottage, and Starling waved, making a few minutes of small talk about the quality of the light. When he was gone, Starling folded her napkin on the table and stacked her thermos on top. "Let me focus you a bit, Everleigh. What do you want exactly?"

"I want to learn about photography."

"So you want a job?"

Rapid flutters tingled Everleigh's fingertips, then her toes. She couldn't possibly. "A job? You're hiring?"

"I'm working on a project these next three weeks at a gallery in East Hampton, and I could use someone to help me with the prints— it won't pay much, but you might learn a thing or two. Which is what you want, right?"

She leaped up, then leaned down to hug Starling, her frame slight and bony in her arms. "Really?" She'd have to tell her parents. They wouldn't like it.

Starling held her wiry figure stiff, and she did nothing to return the embrace. "Really. Can you start the Monday after the Fourth?"

Everleigh clapped her hands together, breathless. "Yes, of course I can." She'd have to explain to her mother why she couldn't come home after the holiday, why she'd miss her dress fitting. But did either of those things matter when compared to the chance to work with Starling?

"Okay then, bring your lunch. We'll start at nine at Juniper Gallery, just off Main Street. I'll pay you thirty dollars for the week, but I'll up it to thirty-five if it works out."

"Thank you, Miss Meade. You won't regret this."

Starling took off her glasses to clean them with the corner of her shirt, and Everleigh could see her delicate features, how her glasses were hiding her lovely face, symmetrical and dewy, every line carrying the experience of a woman who had truly lived.

"I try not to regret anything." Starling handed Everleigh back her photograph, and Everleigh thanked her a few more times. She sallied forth to her car, wishing she had her camera. Because right now she wanted to take pictures of this whole great big world.

EIGHT

A car raced by as Everleigh pedaled out of the driveway that Friday morning on her bike. She'd been effervescent since she'd left the art colony the day before, and she'd woken this morning to see the cottage with fresh eyes. While Roland snored beside her, his blond mop damp at his temples, his skin still smelling of Ivory soap, she took in the bedroom where they'd been sleeping, deciding that it felt more like a roadside motel room than the pretty bedroom she was accustomed to; even the smaller bedroom, where she was *supposed* to be sleeping, was dull and depressing. Today, she would do something about it. She would replace the browning drapes and that awful bedspread with its swirling pattern the color of peas, something her grandmother would have chosen.

After leaning her bike up against Hildreth's, a local department store on Main Street, Everleigh opened an account in Roland Whittaker's name with chipper Mr. Hildreth himself, who walked her through his windowed store and helped her select a fresh set of dishes, two gallons of paint, three pairs of drapes, a stack of fluffy white towels, a set of new white sheets, and a simple coverlet. He said he'd have one of his clerks follow her home with her order in his van. On impulse, she'd added a framed poster of oranges for the kitchen. Then she stopped in the grocery for milk, ham slices, cheese, and crackers.

The air was soft and still when she got back to the little white house with green shutters from her shopping trip in town, the deep perfume of early rose blooms all around. Parking her bike under the green-and-white striped awning around noon, she discovered Roland lying in the backyard on a lounge chair dozing. She climbed on top of him, his shirt warm to the touch from the sun, pressing a kiss to his lips to rouse him. "Hi, pet," he said, kissing her back.

She told him about what she bought, disappointed at the smell of gin on his breath, two empty glasses on the table beside him. *Stevie.* At least his friend wasn't here now. Perhaps Everleigh could finally talk to him about Alice. And share the news of her job.

"You like playing house with me, don't you?" he said, his fingertips grazing her cheeks. In the distance, a lawnmower started, and she looked where the hotel once sparkled with sunlight. She felt out his mood another minute, then raised the subject vexing her: Ernest's violent threat on the night of the fire. "What is it with Alice that would make her fiancé hate you?"

Roland rested his palms under his head, squinting at her. "I told you, we crashed the boat, and it made her—"

"That can't be why." Everleigh cut him off, searching his face for clues. "Ernest is jealous, like you and Alice share a more intimate past."

He shrugged. "Maybe we kissed once or twice as teenagers, but I swear, Lee—I don't know where all that's coming from." She felt her chest clench in an internal sigh. There were the photographs from the night of the party, too: Roland in the background of one leaning into a tall blonde, her silhouette an inch closer than she thought acceptable. How would she bring that up now without sounding paranoid?

After the Hildreth's delivery van arrived, they put away the groceries in the skinny metal food pantry and icebox. That there wasn't a maid or housekeeper to walk in and out of the rooms they occupied gave her a sense of ownership over the space; there was no one to quiet your voice around, no one to keep you busy. By four, they had everything, even the painting of oranges, in place.

"What a transformation," she announced to Roland, who put his arm around her in the spruced-up kitchen.

"Shall I start dinner?" Everleigh opened the *Woman's Home Companion Cookbook* while Roland jimmied a lilac paint can open. He promised her he'd paint their bedroom, and he was determined to start. They could always squeeze into the twin bed in the second bedroom tonight.

"I'm happy not to have a staff underfoot, aren't you?" she said, hunting for a recipe for steaks. Perhaps she was overdoing the perfect housewife act, but she still needed to tell him about her job. "Although I would like a wash girl or a laundering service. I can't do laundry. That's where I draw the line."

With paintbrush in hand, Roland popped a blueberry into his mouth, his fingertips purple with juice, then ducked into the bedroom. "A wash girl it is," he said. "You know that's why I love you, Lee. You make your needs clear, and still, you'd do anything for me."

"Yes, but I'm done doing laundry."

"No more laundry," he repeated.

With late afternoon sun streaming through the kitchen window, casting the sagging room aglow, she heated the burner on high and dropped the steaks in a pan, the room filling with the smell of sizzling meat. The scent must have drawn out the stray cat, who began mewing at the back door.

"I'll give you a taste later, little kitty," she said. The cat, who was without a collar, sat obediently, like it understood, a pretty sit, with its tail still and eyes fixed on her. Everleigh dumped a cup of rice in a pot, turning the flames to high. Using a pair of tongs, she tried to flip the steaks, but they stuck to the pan and she had to pull hard to lift the filets. The kitchen filled with smoke. She put her hand on her hip.

"Now mango cat, what did I do wrong?" she said to the animal, turning to look for it, but it was gone.

A loud rapping at the kitchen door made her drop the tongs on the wood floor.

"Excuse me, Mrs. Whittaker?" a man said.

Roland came out of the bedroom, wiping his hands on a small washrag, his pants already stained with splotches of lilac paint. "May I help you?" Roland said.

"Well, we don't want another fire here, so you better start by turning off the burner." The man, who was in his forties, grinned, revealing a chipped front tooth.

Everleigh turned to see flames dancing up the outer sides of the frying pan, and she yelped, turning off the heat entirely, using a fork to lift the steak and set it down; it hit like a hockey puck. "Oh! I didn't add the water to the rice." She quickly turned that burner off, too.

Roland held out his hand to shake. "Roland Whittaker. I'm sorry. You are?"

"Detective Thomas Branford." The man waved the smoke away from his face. "I work for the Southampton Police Department, but I also volunteer at the fire station. Everyone agreed I'd be the best person to get to the bottom of what happened at your hotel." The detective had the alert eyes of a crow set into a pudgy face, which made him seem boy-like in his brimmed black hat, the chubby kid who grew up and was still playing with fire trucks.

They agreed to talk outside at the picnic table, and the detective set his yellow notepad and pencil down as they took a seat. She thought he must be sweating in all that blue polyester fabric. She was sweating, too, wondering if he knew about her late-night cigarette on the balcony. It wasn't that she truly thought she was responsible, but it was possible, which made her worry about emerging evidence.

"It must be a dream job working out here at the beach, where the most stressful part of a cop's job is writing tickets for women wearing short shorts." Roland was always complaining about Southampton town's strict dress code, where a man could get a summons for not wearing a collared shirt, a woman for a skirt above the knee.

"It's not as quiet as you might think," the detective said. "Certainly not the night of the fire."

Roland looked at the ruined elephantine structure. "The delay is what concerns me. I'm not sure why it took the company ten full minutes to get here, and this investigation . . . it's taken two weeks to even get started."

The detective turned his hat in his hands. "We're looking into both of those complaints, sir. Rest assured, I'm here to get your insight."

Roland gestured to his blank notepad. "At least you're here now."

The detective nodded, folding his hands atop the splintered wood. "Typically, we can tell very quickly if a fire is arson, or if it's something internal, an accident. But in this case, there are signs that it could have been either."

Everleigh felt her throat tighten. "Do you think someone purposely burned the hotel down?"

The detective flicked his pencil between his fingers. "We're still waiting on the lab to tell us if there's sign of an accelerant, and of course, it might have been caused by something defective in the construction. But the nature of the fire has us concerned—the human element side. If it was set the night of the grand opening, that feels like revenge to me. Wouldn't you agree?"

She and Roland exchanged a weary look, and he put an arm around Everleigh's shoulders.

"But I'm sure it's just a coincidence. I don't think we should jump to any conclusions about—"

She thought of Ernest's threat, how hateful his words were.

The detective, who smelled of a cigar, exhaled. "I'm not convinced, no. The investigation just started. But we need to explore all angles. Now let's start from the beginning." He was making clear that he was in charge of the conversation, not Roland, and it was up to them to cooperate. Roland fell in line immediately, answering questions about how his father had gifted him the house a few years ago, how the design took a few months, the building another nine.

Everleigh watched the detective scribble the information on his notepad, careful to look up at Roland every few seconds with an encouraging nod. He wanted names of construction workers, business partners, even guests at the party.

"You're quite thorough." Roland cleared his throat. "I didn't know small towns had resources for this kind of investigation."

"Southampton isn't just any small town." The detective smirked. "Still, there are only a few of us, and we do a little of everything. We hire college kids to help in the busy season." He had a wrinkle between his two eyebrows, deep like a valley, and it indented each time he asked a new question. "At what time did the party end, and where were the two of you between one thirty and three thirty a.m.?"

"We were in our room." Everleigh said.

Roland nodded. "We went upstairs around one-thirty, maybe. Probably had too much to drink because I fell straight into bed." He laughed in the way men did when they wanted to make plain they were drunk.

The detective looked at Everleigh. "Were you just as tired?"

She swallowed, not wanting to lie. She'd omit the bit about tossing her cigarette over the edge, but she wouldn't lie. "I couldn't sleep. So, I got up after that. I went out on the terrace." Her dimples showed, and he smiled back at her. "Stared at the ocean, thought about things I should have or shouldn't have said at the party. Our wedding."

The detective raised one bushy red eyebrow. "Did you see anyone outside? Anything that struck you as odd?" He reminded her of the school headmaster at Spence, how he only wanted to speak in facts and grew impatient when students offered opinions or arguments. *I have my suspicions about Ernest,* she wanted to tell the detective, but she knew he'd bark questions back, ones she didn't have the answers to.

"I had a headache, and there was . . . well, there was a couple fighting by the pool. Someone we know. Alice Anna Martin—her family has a house on Gin Lane—and she was with her fiancé, Ernest." He wrote the woman's name in all caps, then underlined it. She added more sheepishly, "A friend, who will remain unnamed, overheard him saying he'd hurt Roland if Alice went near him again."

"I know the Martin family." The detective nodded, unfazed. "The house is past Agawam Lake, right beyond the Beach Club. Does he have a reason to dislike you, sir?"

Roland explained about Birdie, Alice's cousin. "But this is petty gossip, Detective. From high school."

Everleigh listened as the detective made a note to investigate, waiting until he looked up. "I saw Stevie that night, too. Roland's business partner. He was in the telephone booth with a woman, and I saw them kissing." How quickly she'd ducked out of the moonlight, looking away, afraid of being caught peeping. Had he seen the glow of her cigarette?

"Oh, Stevie boy," Roland spat. She hated when he tucked tobacco under his bottom lip. A terrible habit left over from his days of playing college baseball at Michigan. "He's living over in the Springs, if you need his address."

The detective nodded, then wrote "balcony?" on his notepad. "What time would you say that you went inside?"

The question mark after balcony was alarming; what did that

mean? Was he questioning what she told him? Or was he making a note to investigate the balcony? She tried to remember if she left her cigarettes in the ashtray inside and wondered what would be left of the penthouse if anyone went up. From the street, it didn't seem like you could walk up there without risking its collapse. "I'm not sure, exactly. I had already taken off my watch."

Detective Branford stood up. "Let's take a walk over to the hotel."

After crossing the lawn and passing the pool, which, despite the cleanup, was still rippling with black water and flotsam, they hoisted themselves onto the porch, since the steps were partially destroyed. Once inside, Everleigh stepped over a few burned-out beams, saw a chair missing two of its legs, the rug no longer visible under piles of ash. One wing off the hotel lobby had partially collapsed, while the other was intact. Detective Branford's navy-blue uniform pants grew chalky around his ankles as he waded through the debris. The destruction was shocking—how fast a fire could eat everything in its path, making one forget there was ever anything there worth looking at.

The detective stood where the swinging double doors once opened into the kitchen, the walkway to the conservatory covered with shattered glass from framed artwork, the rug squishing under their feet from the water that had been sprayed on the building for hours. What the men Stevie had hired were cleaning was unclear—it looked like it hadn't been touched.

"When trying to find out how a structure caught fire, we study the patterns in the charring since they provide us with a hint as to the sequence of the fire. Think of it as a trail if you will. So if I can find the spot where the char is deepest, I can pinpoint where the fire began. We know that this fire probably originated somewhere above the conservatory." He pointed to the ceiling, parts of which were ripped away like a tear in paper, revealing the sooty charcoaled underthings. "The tricky thing is that the wind was strong that night, so it kept pushing the flames around, which is why it was difficult to control—and why this case is harder to solve. There are quite a few deep singes."

They followed the detective to the center of the conservatory, where he pointed his pencil to the ceiling. Everleigh gagged from the smell of burned wood, melted rubber, and dust. "Above this part of the conservatory, right up here, there is a guest room. See those vicious teeth eating away at the blackened ceiling?"

Branford leaned down and ran a finger along what was left of the floor, smelling it. "An accelerant will drip to spaces underneath where the fire is set, and there are often unburned trails of chemicals left over in rooms below. Sometimes they pool and leave a deep singe, which I don't see here. Still, one of my men will rip up a sample of the wood to send to lab for confirmation."

Everleigh glanced over at Roland just in time to see a shadow pass over his face.

Branford stood. "So you see, there's no evidence that the fire started in the kitchen or in the walls where there could have been bad wires. It appears that it started right here, right in this room above us."

The detective waited for a reaction, but when none came, he continued. "Was there anything different about that room? Candles that weren't in other rooms? A different lamp?"

"Of course not," Roland said. "Same view, same furniture."

The detective squinted at him. "Do you remember who was staying there? I believe it's room twenty-three."

"That I don't know." Roland scratched at a spot over his ear. "There were so many guests—the ledger didn't survive the fire."

The detective stepped over a shatter of chandelier crystals, sharp like swords. Everleigh couldn't tell if the detective liked them as people or not; his expression wasn't particularly warm. But she knew that they needed him to like them, or he wouldn't be on their side. They needed him to end his investigation. If he deemed the fire an arson, the insurance company wouldn't pay Roland anything, even if he wasn't respon-sible; they never did. Otherwise, every person would simply burn down their home and wait for a large check to build a new one.

Everleigh pointed to the detective's coat pocket, where she noticed a colored paper heart was sticking out. "You have children?"

He nodded, tucking the picture back down inside; his sharp eye-brows softened. "She's ten and is always making me these little love notes. Very different from my boy, who can't sit still long enough to write his name."

Roland flicked his hair off his forehead, asking to see a photo, and the detective pulled a black-and-white square from his wallet, two towheads on the beach in summer. "Looks like the perfect family, Detective. Everleigh and I want three children, right, pet? A gaggle of kids."

She nodded, though they'd never actually discussed how many kids they wanted. Roland never said much about having children, and she certainly didn't want three. "You are very blessed, Detective."

The detective tucked the picture back in his wallet, glancing at the yellow notepad. "Beyond this threat from Ernest, do either one of you have enemies?"

Everleigh's head became all soupy then because they didn't, did they? And yet, she knew they did. Her ex, George Sheetz—and Roland's ex, who once called his Manhattan apartment, hanging up after crying into the phone. Anyone on the staff could be disgruntled if they hadn't been paid, like Gordon, and there was the Southampton official argu-ing with Roland at the party.

"No, sir." Roland patted the detective on the back. "I fought too much with my father growing up to make another enemy."

They walked back toward the cottage and resettled at the picnic table. Everleigh went inside to the icebox, cracking cubes into water glasses, and returning outside with a pitcher of ice water. Sitting down, she pieced together what she'd missed—the detective asking about resentful employees.

The detective lowered his gnawed pencil, waiting, but Roland shook his head.

"My workers had only been there a month or so. I barely knew them."

Everleigh pressed her hand to his elbow, thinking her fiancé's approach too callow; the more information they gave the detective, the faster the investigation would go. "We do owe the hotel staff some back pay, but we plan to repay them."

Roland stared at her to stop talking, and she bore her eyes right back at him while the detective scribbled, then underlined, *debts*. Roland was crazy to think Branford wouldn't discover that detail as soon as he started speaking with employees.

The detective let the pages of his pad fall closed. "Would you mind giving me a list of staff? Someone who works the front desk might remember who was staying in room twenty-three."

"Of course." Roland turned and spat in the grass. "We'll do whatever you need, sir. But remember, I'm not a New Yorker by birth. No one in the hotel that night even knew me very well."

"But they might have been there on someone else's behalf."

Roland sat beside the detective then, straddled the bench, and pulled his wallet out and leafed inside the billfold. "You know, Detective, I know you're doing your job here, and we will do everything you need us to do. But this was an accident plain and simple." Roland removed a one-hundred-dollar bill and set it on the weathered planks of the table.

Detective Branford cleared his throat.

Roland continued. "You're a good guy, Detective. I can see that. A family man. Why not take the kids on a summer getaway, pass this paperwork right along?"

A teenager rode by on a shiny red bike, blasting a song on a transistor radio in her basket, and Everleigh tried to focus on her, rather than the detective's pockmarked cheeks. He must have suffered from acne as a child. He didn't smile at Roland or reach for the money.

Branford put on his police visor, tucking his notepad under an arm as he stood up. "I admire your generosity, Mr. Whittaker. But if this was arson, it's the worst crime we've seen in a decade out here, and I can't let that slide. Something smaller maybe, a shed burning, but this was a hotel on Gin Lane. People are upset. They're scared."

Roland chuckled. "Scared. *I'm* not even scared." He pulled out two additional one hundred-dollar bills—was this the money she'd lent him? Everleigh watched how the detective's face remained unchanged as Roland set them on the table. "I can make your job easier, Detective. You tell my insurance company, and the summer colony for that matter, that it was an unexplained accident. They write me a check. Everyone relaxes."

The detective pretended not to see the money and strode off.

Roland followed at his heels, and Everleigh joined them. "I think what Roland is trying to say is that we are all on the same side here. We all want to know what happened, but what happened probably isn't as sinister as you think."

His police car was parked in the driveway, and the detective pulled his keys out of his pocket, snorting. "You know, I've dealt with kids like you plenty when I ran that fancy precinct in Manhattan, and you can't end a fire investigation because it's inconvenient. There are steps and procedures, and we're going to run the course, whether you like it or not, Mr. Whittaker. Because if it was an accident, we wouldn't smell that chemical char so abundant in the conservatory. It's as if someone lit a curtain upstairs, and the fire followed the path of the accelerant, veering off as the winds blew it. Now I need confirmation, but if my hunch is right, someone burned down your hotel."

Roland shook his head, curling his lip and surprising them with an outburst. "That's not what happened—" He looked like he was doing everything he could not to clock the guy. He cleared his throat, returning his glare to the horizon. "I'm sorry if I offended, sir—I can see how important this investigation is to you. To the entire community. But if I—"

The detective sighed, opened his car door, and tossed his notebook onto the passenger seat. "Do me a favor: Let us do our job. And if anyone comes around and starts asking questions or saying anything unusual, please call me."

Everleigh went white. "Are we safe here? Because if there's a man—"

The detective interrupted. "I would keep an eye out for anything unusual. Don't hesitate to call me."

After adjusting the heavy silver buckle of his belt, the detective reached out his hand, waiting for her and Roland to shake his pudgy one. And Roland did, smiling jovially, as if the entire meeting had been pleasant. She felt the mud leave her chest.

They watched the police car rattle down Gin Lane, and when it was out of sight, Roland slammed his hand against the table, cracking one of the weather-beaten boards. She wondered if he'd be this angry when she finally had the courage to tell him about her job with Starling.

"What the hell was that about?" he said.

Everleigh folded her arms. "Why did you offer to pay him?"

"This investigation could take months." Roland buried his face in his hands. "Goddamn clock puncher."

"What will you do if the insurance money doesn't come through?"

He didn't look up from his palms. "I need this investigation to go away, Lee. I need it to go away or I'm sunk."

After a while, she trudged inside to salvage her steaks, worrying for Roland but also herself. She wondered if Ernest or the hotel's caretaker or that Southampton official or someone utterly unknown to them was out there watching. If someone had been watching them all along.

⁂

A night later, Roland came home from an appointment and told her to slip on a dress. He was taking her to dinner at Bowden Square. The bistro was a village favorite located in an old white-planked house in Southampton village, where tables with umbrellas dotted the patio, even at night, as a steady stream of cars coming into town cruised by. Both she and Roland ordered roasted Long Island duck and pinot noir, and for fun, she'd brought her camera, taking photos of Roland posing with the ebullient restaurateur Herb McCarthy himself, using her detachable flashbulb, since it was around nine and the dusky sky was turning dark.

When Roland got up to go to the bathroom, Herb, a colorful character Everleigh immediately enjoyed for his straight-talking personality, sat down in Roland's place, putting his elbows on the table, telling her about the first time he came out to Southampton, when he was a boy, on a fishing trip with his father. "You wouldn't believe how much this place has changed," he said, winking at her, his black mustache as thick as his glasses. "The summer colony was here, of course, but this was before the 'thirty-eight hurricane, so everything down at the beach looked different. Houses were bigger, but it was quieter too. Less people and certainly less troublemakers like your fiancé."

Everleigh chuckled, cradling her wineglass in her hand. "He's not that bad, is he?"

Herb McCarthy had to be in his forties, and still, he was charismatic, even to a young woman. "He does have a reputation," Herb said.

She took a sip of her wine, aware that she'd had enough for it to redden her teeth. "For?"

"For being an arse." The old man's eyes crinkled, and when he saw her face fall, he tapped her shoulder in jest. "I'm joking, but I have heard whispers about the hotel over the last few weeks. People don't want it going back up."

The skin on her arm prickled, and she slipped on her violet-colored dress's matching bolero jacket to warm her shoulders. "It's just a small faction with very big voices," she said, parroting what Roland had told her.

"True, but remember, everyone in the summer colony thinks their voice is more important than their neighbor's—but there are some whose sway is truly powerful. They believe they can tell the rest of us how to live, and they often get away with it. The Martins are particularly vocal."

Alice Anna's parents? "I had no idea," she said.

"Let's just say that I'm hardly surprised about the fire." The mustached man looked around at the people slicing rare steaks and sipping martinis around him, then spoke quieter. "These people like their community narrow. Why do you think some locals are building a beach club of their own down on Gin Lane? That long stretch of sand shouldn't be reserved for the rich, even if they desire it to be so."

A slowing car honked its horn, the driver waving to another patron eating outside. The restaurateur paused, giving Everleigh a moment to process what he was saying, then he tapped the table with his hand, her wine jumping in the glass. "Of course, I tell anyone who complains that I don't mind the hotel going up. It's only going to bring more business to my establishment."

"Then at least we have the truly powerful on our side," Everleigh said lightly, dabbing her clammy hands on her silken skirt before folding them in her lap. She didn't like knowing that her fiancé's idea was so controversial, and she wondered if her parents were getting whispers of it back in New York. If the dissension would be splashed in Cholly Knickerbocker's gossip column any day now.

Clearing the last of their plates, Herb winked and bid her good evening. Then he moved on to the next table, where she heard him razzing a gentleman in his sixties about the width of his old-fashioned dinner tie, his grandchildren breaking into raucous laughter.

She and Roland were finishing dessert—slices of double chocolate cake—when Everleigh finally broached the subject of Starling. After her long-winded explanation of why she went to the art colony and how the meeting unfolded, Roland begged her to cut to the point, and upon hearing the news of her job beginning in a few days, he lowered his fork, staring at her like he'd never seen her before in his life. His mouth parted, then closed, and she was ready to argue that if *he* was going to be gone all day rebuilding the hotel then *she* was taking a job. But he'd only taken another bite of cake, saying, "Okayyyyy" with a hint of sarcasm, and she'd smiled while chewing, the final bite of chocolate frosting bursting with flavor against her tongue.

Just before the check arrived, Stevie surprised them at the restaurant, pulling up a chair and joining them for an aperitif, trying to convince them both to come out to a beach party at Alice Anna's house, which turned Everleigh's mood foul. Apparently, the actress hadn't got any roles in summer stock and would be here most of the season after all. When Everleigh said she wasn't interested, they told her that Whitney might be there. Then they told her that she could take photos and try to sell them to the *Hamptonite*. She laughed, but shook her head anyway, gathering her purse and reaching for the car keys in Roland's double-breasted jacket pocket. "You go. I'll drive myself home," she said.

The last thing she wanted to do was follow him and Stevie into a party with their juvenile jokes about passing gas. Roland acted fourteen when he was with his friend, and it annoyed her to no end. The two men were beginning to feel like a team—Stevie had even tagged along with them to the beach the day before—and they only spoke highly of those with ballooning bank accounts, or women whom Stevie might want "to poke," an offensive term he said repeatedly, even though Everleigh had asked him to stop.

Off the men went to the party without her while she nervously returned to an empty cottage in the dark, bolting into the house from her car. She laughed at her overblown fear as she locked the door behind her. At first, every rustle in the bushes sent an alarm through her. At some point though, she dozed off, a novel open on her lap. Patricia Highsmith's *The Talented Mr. Ripley*.

The sound of voices was close and far away. Everleigh shot open her heavy eyes, her heart pounding. Why had she let herself fall asleep? She'd promised she'd stay awake until Roland got home, mostly out of a lingering uneasiness about the possibility of an arsonist loitering about. If someone had set fire to the hotel, they might try to set fire to this tiny cottage.

Someone rattled the back door. *Do either one of you have enemies, Mr. Whittaker?*

She peeked into the kitchen to see who was there. But it was only Roland, a cigarette dangling from his lips. "Open the door, Lee."

"You made my blood run cold." Everleigh let her breath out and unlatched the hook, realizing then how easy it would be to kick the door in.

"Sorry, pet." He smiled, his cheeks bright red, his eyes glassy and veined. He smelled of drugstore perfume, vanilla-scented, sweet and floral. Stevie stepped in behind him. She studied them as they fell into the chairs at the kitchen table, recounting some story about Stevie and a curvaceous woman that Everleigh couldn't make out. "C cup," Roland hollered like a train conductor announcing the next stop, a rain of spittle falling onto the table as he and Stevie laughed so hard they had to gulp for air.

"Goodnight, boys," she said, trudging into her bedroom and slamming the door. She wouldn't spend another minute with these two buffoons. To think Roland had been so close to another woman that her scent had rubbed onto him.

Curled into the fetal position in the twin bed, the soft air of a Long Island summer night blanketing her satin nightgown, she closed her eyes and blocked out the antics of the bombastic men, who were now clumsily cooking something on the stove.

The trill of the crickets played a rhythmic chorus through the open window. They would sound all through the night, and she loved sleeping beside the screens, listening to their dependable song, since she couldn't hear them from her bedroom in the city. Everleigh often imagined hundreds of the creatures in the grass surrounding the cottage, an army of happy singers rubbing their front wings over the ridges of their back wings, arriving at once to comfort her, to tell her just how good life could be in the darkness, even if she couldn't see them (or anything else) yet. And when she really concentrated on their song, like she was right now with her head cradled against her feather pillow, she knew that they were encouraging her to listen carefully to something else, to a voice she wasn't hearing. To a voice deep inside herself.

NINE

✢

Everleigh walked the lush lawn toward the exclusive Maidstone Club's glimmering crowded pool with her arm linked in Roland's. He lit up as he pointed to the hotel-style bar on the right side of the extensive patio, a casual snack bar to the left, and a large bright-colored awning stretched in between. Roland was a blue blood who had grown up around the finest of things, and yet he still loved the tinge of money that colored the grand architecture of the places he frequented, pointing out to Everleigh the small details that rendered a hotel or restaurant opulent. Of the Maidstone's rustic pool cabanas, nothing more than small wooden structures with picnic tables in front and private outdoor showers out back, he was equally impressed. The private changing areas were so sought after among members, he said, that families passed them down in wills like heirlooms.

Underneath the expansive shade awning at the pool were dozens of royal-blue and canary-yellow tables and chairs, the dunes and sand visible in the distance. Women in beach cover-ups and husbands in button-down shirts and shorts picked from bowls of steamed mussels and clams, children nibbling from grilled cheese sandwiches and hot dogs.

She waved to Whitney from afar, watching her friend in a shirt-

waist Oxford dress stand up. "I'm so glad the two of you could make it."
Whitney kissed Everleigh's cheek, offering Roland a terse hello. The
chatter of lunch unfolded all around them, the splashes of children
jumping into the pool. "Truman had an unexpected call with New
York, but hopefully he'll join us soon."

Pool boys delivered fluffy white towels to men and women
stretched out on loungers. At the snack bar, pimpled teenagers
dumped french fries into red-and-white paper cartons, the smell of
salt and frying potatoes as ubiquitous as chlorine. Everleigh squeezed
Roland's hand; he was dressed for a swim, wearing his straw fedora
and his bright-red bathing trunks. "Would you mind ordering, Rolly,
so us girls can catch up?"

If he cared, he didn't mention it, instead focusing on the women's
order: a container of steamers and a cheeseburger with extra pickles to
share.

Whitney's hand glided over the back of her braid, her expression
austere. "Put it on Truman's tab, Roland. Just tell them you're signing
for me."

When he turned to make his way between the colorful tables toward the cafeteria-style line, the women turned toward each other, one
cutting off the other to talk. "You first!" Whitney demanded. "I've
missed you!"

"You should see me these days." Everleigh laughed. "We've decorated the cottage, and I have a new pet, a kitty cat named Mango. I
have dinner on the table each day by seven, and I've been taking lots of
photographs. Oh! And I adore Mr. Tills at the Motophoto."

"You? In the kitchen? Am I sitting beside the next James Beard?"

"Hardly. I charred a spaghetti casserole last week, but I'm trying."

"I know a woman who gives cooking lessons to young wives out
here."

Everleigh waved her friend off—she preferred her trial-and-error approach in the kitchen—and she kept on with her sing-song voice as she shared what she'd been up to, reporting only the highlights. A visit to the Maidstone meant leaving your problems at the massive Tudor clubhouse's front door, so she didn't say that Roland had been so stressed about the fire investigation that he was charging ahead with the renovation by day and staying out later than ever at night. Or that, more than once, Everleigh and the cat nibbled dinner off brand new dishes while sitting in an empty kitchen listening to reports on the transistor radio of car racing outcomes at the Bridgehampton Race Circuit. Or that she was writing checks for all their expenses these days—her trust had become their main income—and that was most unsettling since it was beginning to feel as though her father would support them for the rest of their lives.

A child with a pink inner tube wrapped around her middle wailed at her mother.

"Enough about me. How are you?" Everleigh munched peanuts and corn chips out of a cup left on the table for guests, what Whitney jokingly referred to as "Waspy bar snacks."

Whitney smiled, placing her hand on her belly. "I don't want to say too much and jinx it, but maybe, I might be . . ."

When Everleigh squealed, her friend shushed her, glancing around to make sure nobody heard. "Lee! Will you gain your composure?" Whitney lit herself a cigarette. "Anyway, it's nothing official yet."

Everleigh looked toward the snack bar and spotted Roland talking to a Nordic-looking woman, tan and blond and athletic, standing with an air of sophistication, the sneer of royalty, like she just walked off the beach in Biarritz. It had to be the woman she'd seen in the photograph from the hotel party, her hair an identical radiant white blond. "Who is *that?*" Everleigh heard herself interrupting Whitney, who was carrying on about how tired she'd been feeling.

"Oh please, that's Opal Vandemeer. You know, the shipping Vandemeers?" She waited for Everleigh's response, and when none came, Whitney said Opal's family was from the Netherlands, but they'd been summering in East Hampton for two generations. They owned the largest house on Further Lane, a few doors down from Whitney's. "They're responsible for shipping just about all the goods the entire world over, and she flirts with just about everyone. Actually, she and Roland are quite a pair in conversation."

"What is that supposed to mean?" Everleigh had rolled damp locks of hair in foam rollers the night before, using setting lotion to achieve a cascade of pin curls around her face, and she found relief in the fact that when she met this Opal Vandemeer, she'd at least have fantastic hair.

"Well, she's gunning to be president of the Ladies Improvement Society. Her whole platform is built upon remaking the summer colonies, which is what Roland wants, too. Her idea is to offer grants to popular Manhattan chefs or hairstylists to start businesses out here. It's quite controversial, actually."

"Because the locals own the businesses on Main Street, and they'll be replaced?"

Whitney cackled. "No one in the summer colony cares about the locals." Then she shrugged. "No, they're worried that if too many businesses from the city advertise a Southampton location, every man on Madison Avenue will be punching a ticket east on the railroad. It will be overrun and ruined."

"Well, no one wants to summer with all of New York City on the beach."

"Exactly." Whitney sipped her lime-and-gin spritzer; she'd had the bartender bring two more to the table for Everleigh and Roland, who was still waiting on their food order. It was the height of lunch.

Everleigh asked if the woman was married, and Whitney spoke quietly, her eyes fixed on Opal's high-waisted bikini, aquamarine with white piping, her silken hair falling down her back. "Well, she has many admirers, but she always goes for the ones that need fixing. Last I heard, she was dating a tennis pro or a waiter here, can't remember."

Everleigh took out her camera, finding Whitney in the frame. "Say cheese." She laughed, watching her friend light up. "I'll have the first picture of you pregn—" she stopped, lowered her camera, pretending to zip her lips.

Roland walked over with a tray, Opal Vandemeer trailing behind, and Everleigh snapped a second picture of Roland and Opal, lowering her camera as he introduced the woman. The hum of ocean waves crashed in the distance.

"Now aren't you cute with that tiny little waist of yours? I was very sorry to hear about your hotel," Opal said. Her voice had a hint of a Dutch accent, and she dragged out certain sounds. "It was quite an extraordinary evening before the fire."

Everleigh looked at Roland to see if he would explain, but he was doling out their lunches at the proper place settings. She played dumb, even though she'd seen Opal in the photo leaning into her fiancé. "Were you at the party?"

"Of course, I got there late, but not too late to get some dancing in." She said it like *dahn-cing*. "Roland and I met a few weeks before, at a luncheon in town, didn't we, new friend? I'm trying to convince him to go into business with me."

"She would like to invest significantly in the rebuild." He tipped his heels back, seeming proud as punch, which made her want to punch him square in the face.

Everleigh dabbed her mouth with a napkin, trying to hide the jealousy crossing her expression. Had Roland been this big a flirt back in the city? "I think Daddy's been more than enough help, Rolly—"

"But this is different, pet." He leaned over Everleigh's shoulder, grazing his lips against her pearl earring, whispering, "Opal will be a primary investor, a business partner. Not your dad fishing me out of the gutter."

Whitney reached for a knife, and then the burger in half, catching Everleigh's eye before darting her own back to the plate. She tried to change the subject. "Lovely to see you, Opal. Will you be at the club for the fireworks on Thursday?" Roland sat at the table, placing his hand on Everleigh's; she snatched hers into her lap.

"Of course. The Fourth is my favorite night of summer," Opal said, running her pink-painted fingernails through her white-blond hair. When Opal noticed Everleigh snap a picture of the pool, she held her hand in front of the lens, causing Everleigh to see nothing but black.

"Don't let the attendants see you taking photos. They're quite secretive here. It's what keeps membership so exclusive, since everyone else is forced to stare longingly at the tall hedgerows, clamoring to get inside and see for themselves." Opal was rather serious.

Roland dipped a fry in ketchup, emitting a deep laugh and smiling up at her. "You certainly have a way of putting things, Opal."

How ridiculous that Everleigh couldn't take a single picture! It was the ultimate snobbery. But what really bothered her was that goofy grin slapped across Roland's face. He was kissing up to the Dutch woman. For a check.

Opal nodded at him with smug lips. "Let's have lunch this week and talk particulars, Roland. Bring your lovely fiancée. I'd love to get to know her."

She turned to leave, and when she was just out of earshot Everleigh called out, "I'm sitting right here, you know? You can ask me. . . ." She and Whitney exchanged an eye roll and burst out laughing, Roland instructing them to behave. They'd moved from steamers on to the burger when a newlywed couple stopped by the table to say hello to Whitney, and after polite introductions, Everleigh glared at Roland, who was humming while eating and didn't seem to notice (or care) how upset she was about him taking money from Opal.

When Whitney's attention turned back to her, Everleigh was bursting to share the news of her new job. "Guess what?" she started, then shared how she'd finally had the gumption to visit the art colony.

"We'll see how long this lasts," Roland said, snickering. To which Whitney dabbed her mouth with a paper napkin.

"Perhaps, as long as she wants it to," she said.

Everleigh slammed her burger down. "Can't you two share one meal without sparring?"

The remark caused Roland to rise from the table, striding off to refill their cocktails. Everleigh didn't protest, and with him gone, Whitney apologized for her comment, urging her friend to continue. Everleigh's excitement quickly reignited.

Whitney crinkled her nose as she listened, like Everleigh was simply the cutest thing she'd ever seen, but when it was time for her to express approval, Everleigh was met with a patronizing tone instead.

"Everyone follows these silly detours sometimes, Lee." Whitney flicked her eyelashes, then patted her stomach. "But remember, don't stray too far from the mainland."

⁂

Music spun out of the record player in the cottage's living room, a sentimental melody causing Everleigh's mind to drift, even as she rouged her cheeks in the warm light of her bedroom, forcing a smile. *This is what phoniness feels like*, she thought. It felt like she'd lived ten years in one day.

She and Roland had fought about Opal's involvement on the cottage's lawn after they returned from the Maidstone; the upset calling forth deeper emotions, making it difficult for Everleigh to hold her tongue about Opal for any longer. "Inviting her in as an investor will only invite her into our lives," she'd yelled at Roland, thinking of how intimately Roland had leaned into Opal's slinking form in her photograph. She'd put it away in her photo box, only to retrieve it and stare once more.

"It's just business, Lee. There are people I need to pay back, and Opal will give us what we need. She promises that it comes without strings."

"Us? There is no 'us' in this decision." Everleigh shut her eyes. What had he done with the money she'd already given him? She'd written him another five-hundred-dollar check just last week. "Money never comes without strings. What did you promise her? That you'll break it off with me?"

"Of course not. But she's an aspiring businesswoman, and no one will take her ideas seriously. She's willing to give me this money, as long as I call her a partner on the project." Roland sat on the lounger, burying his face in his hands, then mussing up his hair. "At the very least, I'll pay off those bozos in the Bronx that keep dropping by, and we'll clear our name in town. Then we can use the rest to finish the renovation."

As far as she knew, he'd already paid the locals with her father's money; it was why she'd felt okay letting him borrow her checkbook for lumber. It unnerved her to think he could be so callous, especially because she sensed the good will of her father would soon end.

"And then what? Opal will come to our house for roast beef on Sundays? We already have a third wheel in Stevie."

"You're too sensitive, Lee." Roland offered a tentative smile. "But no. And then the fire insurance money will come in, and we'll pay her back, and reopen, and redeem our place as the finest hoteliers on the East End of Long Island."

Hoteliers. The two of them. That would be their purpose. The role didn't even interest her.

"I'm sorry you believe that I hurt you, Lee, but you have to trust me on this. Truce?"

But you are hurting me, she'd thought. Everleigh watched him press his palms together in a cutesy prayer, squinting in the sun with a playful, pleading grin. She was tired of arguing, so she nodded in agreement, letting him off the hook, at least for now.

Roland took her face in his and kissed her hard, and she tried to remember what it felt like when they first met, the pulsing she'd felt in her solar plexus. The confidence that he was the right one. But it was ruined by the thought of Opal's advances, the flirtatious banter that had unfolded between them at the Maidstone, the money. He was being practical in taking it, she knew that, but Everleigh was too jealous to be pragmatic.

He twirled her into his arms. "Remember, if I fall down, we fall down. We need to be in this together."

JULY

TEN

❦

E'ven the blankets in the cottage were damp. A humid salt air blew in again overnight, coating everything from the pilled couch to the book covers. The fog off the ocean could rust toasters, Roland had joked, and now she could see he was right. He'd taught her to keep potato chips in the icebox to keep them from getting soggy; bread was stored in the freezer until ready for heating. Some mornings the ocean's residue was so dense that she wandered the cottage with an ammonia solution she mixed in a glass bottle, soaking it into rags and cleaning the film off baseboards and drawer handles, convinced she could smell mold, even if Roland poked fun at her compulsion. As soon as the fog burned off, she'd carry out her sheets to dry in the sun, shaking free the talcum powder she sprinkled on them before going to bed. The dampness inspired fantasies of dry fluffy towels, couch cushions that didn't perpetually feel as though someone blotted them with water, a facial moisturizer that didn't leave behind a thick grease. Living at the beach, she was learning, had its complications.

And still, Everleigh wouldn't go home tomorrow, even if her mother expected her in Manhattan by the afternoon. She'd booked them lunch reservations that Saturday. They had her wedding dress fitting, and there was a friend's baby shower to attend. Everleigh wiped the black phone with her solution, imagining the train at the Long Island rail station departing with a slow chug, right as Everleigh stood in the cottage living room drying the phone in the folds of her shirt.

How could she go home? Leaving just as she was beginning a job with Starling would be like rolling down a hill backward, her newfound freedom receding into the distance. She'd been avoiding this call for days. Filled with dread, she moved to pick up the phone to dial her mother, just as the phone rang from a caller. It was Opal, who after a couple of accent-laden pleasantries, asked if she could speak to Roland. Everleigh sighed, a bit peevish in her delivery. "He's working."

"Well, tell him that our dinner date is on for tonight at the Maidstone."

"A Friday night dinner date?" Everleigh felt the blood rising up her neck. Was there a reason she wasn't invited? At least Whitney would keep an eye on them and report details back to her.

"We're meeting with my father's friend, someone I think will benefit knowing mine and Roland's plans. Stevie needs to be there, too. I'm sorry, I could only get a table for four."

Stevie? Why would she want Stevie there? He seemed to cause trouble wherever he went. Last night, she and Roland watched the fireworks over Cooper's Beach for the Fourth of July. She'd set up their blanket on the sand, opened a bottle of claret, and poured the wine into coupe glasses she'd set inside the picnic basket; after seeing a couple sipping from them in a Budweiser ad, she'd purchased them on a whim in town. She'd seethed as Roland worked to avoid Opal, even as the woman hovered near him the entire night, the energy between them palpable. Everleigh quelled her jealousy, watching men in tan jumpsuits working to arrange fireworks on the sand, and she'd lit sparklers with the women she played tennis with at the Meadow Club. She couldn't fully relax when she saw Ernest arrive without Alice, and she'd snuck glances at his friends, rowdy horse riders who welcomed him with friendly back slaps. A glass of beer later, just before the first Roman candle went off, Everleigh went looking for Roland, eventally spying him in a dark patch of dunes beside Ernest. She walked over to them, approaching just as Roland was apologizing, promising to talk to Stevie. Of course, Everleigh wanted to know why Ernest was angry with Stevie, and once Ernest was down the beach, Roland had rolled his eyes. "He thinks Stevie's a bad influence on his cousin, William." The comment made Everleigh snicker audibly; Stevie was a bad influence on everyone. But that only irritated Roland. "Lee, that guy thinks everyone's comings and goings are his business. Well, too bad. Stevie can hang around whoever he wants."

She agreed, mostly, at least in the sense that a person *does* deserve to make decisions of their own free will, just as Everleigh was doing now as she dialed her mother's line, the phone trilling in her ear as she waited for her mother to answer. Nanny picked up, and when Everleigh told her that she wouldn't be home for her dress fitting or to accompany her mother to the baby shower, she could hear Nanny's disapproval. "You're playing with fire, Lee."

But they'd let her stay this long in the name of love. What was a few more weeks? Mango jumped into her lap, startling her, and she buried her nose into the cat's fur.

Her mother's voice bounded on the line, and Everleigh immediately launched into her plans to stay, apologizing and emphasizing how much time she'd been spending with Whitney. Her mother loved Whitney.

"Everleigh! It was my only request."

"Yes, but I don't *have* to get my measurements done this week, and the baby shower . . . they'll hardly miss me. Roland needs me here. I'm overseeing something. . . ."

Everleigh tasted the sour paste of her red lipstick, not wanting to lie. She needed to tell her mother about Starling, that she'd be starting a job at an art gallery. *An art gallery!* She needed to say that she didn't want to make any more decisions about the wedding right now, that she was still seeing red when she looked at Roland. And most of all, that she couldn't give up this freedom of living away from her parents' watchful eye. With space between them, she could see now just how much her mother's sickness had affected her. Everleigh had never done what was best for her—she didn't even live in the dormitories at Barnard during her senior year—and maybe it was okay to have needs of her own. There were fifty-nine sunsets until Labor Day—she'd counted the days on a wall calendar just that morning—and Everleigh wanted to be at the beach for every one of them.

"Just give me another week. Just one." She pleaded, vowing to herself that if things with Starling went well, she'd call her mother and explain the real reason why she didn't want to come home.

"All right, Everleigh. One week," her mother said, like her daughter had thrown a tantrum and she needed to quell it.

But even after hanging up, Everleigh continued to hear the quiet resignation of her mother's tone, what she wasn't saying more powerful than what she was. Because Everleigh wasn't sure if the call ended with her mother angry or broken or lonesome, and she'd been too chicken to ask. Too selfishly worried that the answer would stop her from doing what she wanted. Everleigh pressed a fingertip to the skin between her eyebrows and her makeup went runny, and she knew she'd have to wash her face and start over again, and yet she didn't care. Because she knew her mother wanted her home, even just for the company, and she knew she couldn't go. Not yet.

A canopy of graceful elm trees stretched over the windowed storefronts on both sides of sleepy Main Street in East Hampton. It was

Monday, and most of the tourists had left Sunday night. The bricked sidewalks were quiet except for the parking lot at the end of town near Bohack's market, where well-dressed housewives carried parcels in and out of the grocery. Whitney liked to say that Southampton is where you summered if you wanted to show off your money, while East Hampton is where you went to hide it, and the town reflected that genteel sensibility with its charming row of New England–style shopfronts. They housed everything from an impeccable candy shop to a striking French brasserie with outdoor tables modeled after the ones in Saint-Germain in Paris. The Juniper Gallery was in a small white cottage at the heart of town, dentil molding on the trim, two large-sashed windows at the front; so pretty Everleigh would have lived in it.

After missing the gallery the first time she drove past, Everleigh looped back and parked the car out front, applying a fresh coat of Chanel red lipstick. Holding a platter of cookies she baked and a brown satchel with her peanut butter sandwich and apple, Everleigh pranced up to the gallery's bright-blue Dutch door. The top was open to the soft morning air, perfumed with honeysuckle blooming in a planter, and she smiled at a stack of graphic postcards advertising the artist's photography show opening night party on August 12. It was five weeks away.

"Hello," Everleigh called out as she stepped across the threshold, her voice resounding with echo. She placed the cookies on a folding table. The gallery's walls were white and bare with nail holes where paintings from another show must have hung, the floors a dull, honey-colored wood. There were two stacks of prints on a second folding table at the center of the room, photographs tucked into sleeves of thin plastic. She lifted a picture of Audrey Hepburn wearing a men's white ribbed tank top and white shorts, and underneath found another photograph, this one of Frank Sinatra, also printed on a piece of large, thick photo paper. Sinatra was sitting on a piano, his legs dangling off the side like a child's. She played out the first few musical notes of "You Make Me Feel So Young" on her forearm, smiling; it always made her mother happy when she played that song on the piano.

"Ah, you're here. Welcome—I see that you started work already." Starling's voice had startled her.

Everleigh dropped the print, looking up at the lithe woman before her. Well, down, actually. Standing beside Starling, Everleigh felt like a giant. She was at least a head taller.

"I called out, but—"

"Sorry, I was in the back watering. You weren't here long, were you?" Starling's expression was still, a blank piece of paper, and Everleigh waited for her to smile, but she didn't. Instead, she placed a green webby house plant on the desk near a whirring steel fan.

"Barely a minute," Everleigh said. "I brought lemon sugar cookies I baked." She omitted the part that she'd nearly burned the bottoms, rescuing most of them before they crisped.

"Oh goodness. Aren't you lovely?"

Everleigh grinned. She was grateful then that she'd chosen her white Bermuda-length shorts, the red-and-white striped boatneck top and Keds on her feet—an outfit she'd labored over for hours but landed on after deciding that her original choice, a navy silk sleeveless tea-length sundress, was much too formal. Starling was just as casual in the same black capris and black pocketed T-shirt, her white hair in the same simple ponytail at the nape of her neck, her eyes the slate-blue Everleigh remembered.

Starling hummed as she moved. "We have a lot to do this week. Are you ready?"

"Yes, whatever you need." Everleigh hung her purse from the back of the black director's chair positioned behind the desk, following Starling around the quiet, cavernous space like an eager puppy. "You must be so excited for your show. Is it your first?"

"It is, but, darling—" Starling stopped, turning toward her, an apologetic look crossing the soft features of her face. "You should know that I don't like small talk, especially when I work."

"Of course." Everleigh folded her arms, cupping her elbows with her hands, her shiny brown hair, which had been set in rollers the night before, curling just below her shoulders. When she was nervous, she couldn't stop talking, but she'd will herself into silence. "I'm here to help. Tell me what you need me to do."

"It's just that the work is paramount, and we need to buckle down." Starling scrunched up her face, a wrinkle deepening at the center of her thinning eyebrows—what Everleigh's own mother called her thinking line. After Everleigh nodded, she continued, "So as you can see, here are all of the prints. A lifetime of my work really, and each one needs a home. A frame."

Starling moved with agility, pacing back and forth from one side of the gallery to the other. Leaning against one of the blank walls were rows of black frames, and Starling stopped beside them, her feet shifting into ballerina third position. The artist held up a large piece of white cardstock in one hand and a small silver knife in the other.

"You're going to use this X-Acto to cut each photograph a matte from this cardboard. Then I need you to assemble the matte and the appointed photograph into one of the frames."

The cardstock already had a small square drawn in light pencil marks, demarcating where she should slide the blade. "Sounds easy enough." Everleigh nodded, although the knife looked more like a surgical scalpel than anything to do with photography. She supposed she hadn't really thought of the actual work that would comprise her days here when she was daydreaming about her new job; she certainly didn't think she'd be mastering cutting techniques. What had she thought then? That she'd be setting up lighting for portraits, or that they'd hang a few photographs while Starling regaled her with stories from glossy magazine photo shoots?

Everleigh *had* imagined that, hadn't she? Still, she was here in the studio, working beside Starling Meade—*the* Starling Meade—so what did she care if she wasn't taking photographs as much as she was learning how to present them?

"You can do your trimming over here." Starling flicked a switch on a small light table. She pulled out a sharpened pencil tucked behind her ear, then put that on the table alongside the knife. "My sketched guidelines should be good but use this if you need to remeasure anything. And there's extra cardstock in the back if you make a mistake."

Then the woman groaned, like she'd forgotten something, placing her palms atop her crown of lustrous white hair. "Hold on! Don't start. I forgot something." Scurrying on the pads of her slight feet—Everleigh thought of her own as boats—and taking what looked like tiny leaps, Starling disappeared into the back. She *must* have been a dancer in her youth, Everleigh thought.

Now that Starling was out of sight, Everleigh clicked her heels together just once, pulsing with the same anticipation she felt before a piano recital, only she already felt the postperformance glow, too. Just standing here on these scuffed wood floors was an accomplishment, and she hadn't even framed one portrait yet.

Starling emerged, walking with an opened mason jar. "Here, I brought you a tonic. I met a Shinnecock woman out here. She's a friend, and she has an antidote for those with creative block."

"I'm not blocked—I have ideas. I'm just . . ." Everleigh swallowed the green juice, nearly spitting out the thick, sour concoction, which must have been heavy on parsley and rosemary, her face crimping with distaste.

"You have a block. Trust me. I can see it, even if you cannot." For the first time that morning, Starling smiled. Only for a beat, then the wrinkle between her brows returned, and she spun on her heels. "If it makes you feel better, I'm getting over my own kind of block. You sit in the discomfort long enough, and you'll push through. Do me a favor: keep that stuff away from the photographs."

Everleigh forced herself to take another few sips, thankful when the telephone rang and Starling became engrossed in a conversation about the art show's launch party, discussing the merits of pigs in a blanket versus herring toasts. In the back, Everleigh found a bathroom where she poured the juice down the sink, rinsing the mason jar and leaving it on a paper towel on a shelf over the toilet.

Back in the gallery's bright exhibition space, she stood at the folding table with the photographs, scanning the captivating images of famous faces. She decided to start with a close-up color print of Lucille Ball. With the redhead's hair in a bun, the comedienne lay down on her side with a green boa around her neck, her skin glowing golden to her clavicle, her expression wary even though the photograph was built around her sex appeal. In the stack of matte paper, Everleigh identified the cardstock labeled "Ball," and spent the next hour carefully cutting the lines with the tip of the X-Acto knife so it was perfectly straight. Her fingers were cramping—it wasn't easy to cut that precisely—and she'd had to stop more than once to stretch them backward. When she was done, she selected one of the frames, then assembled the matte and photograph inside with the care of a museum curator, using her fingers to press the metal edges down the back.

"I'm finished with this one. Where would you like it?" she asked Starling. The photographer had been manically arranging the prints in

an order on the table, constantly removing all of them, then reposition-
ing them, and mumbling to herself like one of those men that wandered Central Park pushing their belongings in a shopping cart. When
Starling looked up, she seemed surprised that Everleigh was there, like
her voice had come from a distant planet, and for a moment, Everleigh
felt like she'd broken some kind of spell the artist had fallen under.
Had her question breached the no-talking rule?

Starling pointed to the back wall. "Line them up there."

That she hadn't been praised or thanked left Everleigh feeling disappointed. But perhaps, she thought, it was a compliment. Starling assumed Everleigh was capable, and maybe that was the greater praise.
She returned to the folding table, wordlessly selecting another print,
this one of Nat King Cole. He was sitting at the end of a diving board
in an aquamarine pool, dressed in a bright-blue suit, his stockinged feet
and shiny black shoes peeking out of the bottom of his trousers, his
face so happy you couldn't help but smile when you looked at it.

With the X-Acto knife back in her hand, Everleigh bent over the
cardstock, puncturing it with the tip. The knife pulled at the paper,
slipping off course, slicing off a layer of her nail. She sucked on it to
ease the sting, not wanting to make a big deal of it. Glancing over at the
stacks of remaining frames, Everleigh's heart sank. There must have
been at least fifty of them.

They worked without words for another hour until the phone
rang. This time it was a reporter, Everleigh was certain of it, because
Starling's responses grew formal. She cut at a corner of the matte, her
ears tuning in.

"The images were taken for publication, yes, but that doesn't dis-
count them from being art—if anything that makes them more iconic,"
Starling said into the rotary phone. "I often ask stars I'm shooting to sit
for me for a little longer. Sometimes I have an idea after being with
them, a framing that the magazine editor may not be interested in, but

I am. I don't tell them to smile a certain way or pose them to bring out a theme a writer decided on in a news story. I let them show me who they are. I let them show me how they want to be seen."

Everleigh turned the knife over in her hands, staring down at the white paper.

Starling laughed, but in that disarming way women do when someone has just insulted them and they don't want to say anything to appear defensive. "Of course I consider myself an artist—a painting isn't the only art form worth hanging on a wall. Photographs tell a different kind of story. Pictures beg you to look deeper, to try to understand what is happening below the surface, the story behind the story. You may see one thing in someone's face, but I see another." A longer pause, then a sigh, so quiet only Everleigh would hear it. "I would say women can take photographs, yes—I've taken thousands of them."

The call ended, Starling cursing as she set the phone down. "Journalists all ask you the same thing, you know that?"

Turning around in her seat, Everleigh folded her hands in her lap. "You should ignore the questions you don't like and turn the conversation back to what you do like. It's what I do when I'm at a party. Ask me about my wedding, I'll engage for a moment, but then I'll steer the conversation to what I really want to talk about: what happened that day on *As the World Turns.*"

Starling laughed, her eyes radiating from the corners. "You shouldn't waste your time on that nonsense television show."

The chuckle urged her on. "Sometimes that nonsense television show keeps me entertained more than my own life."

Starling looked over her thick black glasses at her. "It is addictive, I tell you that. My daughter used to love it."

Now Everleigh laughed, but she reined in the volume, not wanting to overdo it. "I didn't know you had children. More than one?" It wasn't a radical question, although it did count for talking. But technically, Starling had started the conversation.

Starling scribbled something in a lined notebook. "I have a daughter."

Everleigh waited for her to say more, but the room returned to quiet except for the occasional voice on the sidewalk, cars puttering by, the whir of the fan. There were questions, obvious ones: *How old was her daughter? Where did she live? Did she take photos? Why wasn't she here for the summer?*

Everleigh pivoted in her seat, returning to her work with the matting, cutting away from the upper right corner once more. She listened to the marks Starling's pencil made, wishing she'd asked her something else, something that would have kept her talking. It was hard to work in this much silence; it made Everleigh think too much, and her mind drifted to an anxious place: thoughts of the arson. The detective had dropped by the cottage the day before to tell Roland that they were questioning a suspect in the Springs, a gentleman who worked for the hotel who had been arrested last year for burning down a friend's shed. "He's as good a possibility as any," Branford had said. Roland protested, saying that the kid was a nice local boy who helped Gordon with the grounds, trying to convince the detective to look instead for signs that a candle in one of the rooms had started a fire. "Don't you even care that someone's out to get you?" the detective snapped. Even Everleigh was shocked by Roland's arrogant retort. "I'm still standing, aren't I?"

Everleigh slid the finished matte over the photograph of Nat King Cole, then pressed both into the frame, watching Starling out of the corner of her eye. She managed to keep her head clear, her focus only on the work. She'd been standing over a photograph of a woman Everleigh didn't recognize for close to thirty minutes, and she was about to sneak to the back to take another bite of her sandwich when Starling abruptly announced, "Let's break for lunch."

Her watch read 1:30. Everleigh wanted to take a walk. She handed Starling one of the cookies on a napkin. "Do you mind if I step out?"

Starling went to the back room, returning with a leather tote slung over her shoulder. "No, of course not. I'm having lunch with a patron at The Palm, and I don't eat meat. God help me. See you back in an hour." She bit into the cookie. "As good as the baker's!" Which made Everleigh feel like singing.

She explored the village on foot, walking along Newtown Lane, passing the offices of the telephone company, until she found a lovely small park, a square of green space with lush flowers blooming at the corners. She scarfed down her sandwich, then pulled out her apple, crunching on it as cars passed by. She closed her eyes to the sun, considering what she would be doing if she were back in New York. A ghastly luncheon at Sandra Beckett's probably, sitting next to Whitney in a stuffy dress, rolling her eyes at the obnoxious comments of the newly minted debutantes. Not here. To think that she was sitting on a park bench in East Hampton on a break from her job working for a photographer. She beamed at a gentleman walking by with his dog and reached out to pet the pup.

Everleigh paraded happily back to the gallery, and once inside, she found herself in an empty room, feeling free to move about without Starling there; earlier, every creak of her chair was magnified in the quiet. Taped to the light table where Everleigh had been working was a scribbled note. "Please continue on. Go through the back when you're done, and it will lock. Answer the phone and take messages.—S"

There was a small radio in the back room—she'd seen it when she'd fetched her lunch satchel—so Everleigh brought it into the exhibition space and plugged it in. The clearest station on the dial was playing post-wartime songs from a decade before, but it was better than the quiet. Everleigh returned to cutting the matte for the Nat King Cole portrait. Then she'd get to work on the frame of a young actress, some-one named Angela Barrett, whose portrait she couldn't stop staring at every time she took a break from the cutting. She loved the desperation emanating from the doe-eyed woman's face. The actress wasn't wearing a bra, and you could see the silhouette of her breasts in her pretty yellow dress, her lips pouty, her eyes making clear she wasn't sure who she was yet. If Starling took Everleigh's photograph, she thought she'd see something similar: a woman who existed under a fashionable shell, a woman with a desire to peel off her outer skin. Is that what Starling meant about Everleigh being blocked? Standing over the portrait of the actress in the yellow dress, Everleigh thought the only thing stopping Angela Barrett from being who she wanted was the desire to be who everyone else wanted her to be: the young ingenue. She willed the ac-tress to break out of the photograph, let her perfect locks grow tan-gled, to take the Broadway role where she plays a tortured genius rather than a man's irresistible sidekick.

At four, Everleigh gathered her belongings, switched off the gallery lights, and closed the back door softly behind her. She walked around to the front sidewalk and double-checked the lock of the gallery's Dutch door. After hearing someone calling her name, she looked up into her reflection in the glass and saw a gentleman crossing the street behind her. Everleigh spun on her heels, delighted to find the young doctor from the party, Curtis Brightwell, his hand gripping his shiny black doctor's bag.

"Oh, hello there." She waved.

He grinned. "Hello. I haven't seen you since that night. How are things with the hotel?" Curtis pushed his trendy white sunglasses up into his dark hair, looking clean and freshly trimmed, like he'd just left the barber.

"We're working on the renovation—it's still a mess, I suppose." Everleigh didn't remember Curtis being this handsome, or maybe she did, but she couldn't stop looking at the doctor's dark features. She twisted one of her diamond teardrop earrings, employing her most sarcastic voice. "In the meantime, we're thinking of turning the old hotel into a campground. We figure the Boy Scouts can come learn about fire safety."

Curtis chuckled, searching her face to see if he was meant to laugh. When she gave him a wicked grin, he cocked his head. "You know that our den leader in seventh grade once told us that we shouldn't ever start a fire by capturing the sun with a magnifying glass. Some kid set his dad's woodpile on fire doing that."

"Well, my etiquette teacher once told me never to cancel a date without a valid excuse, and it only made me want to do it more. So that makes sense." It struck her that she was telling him this, a perfect stranger.

He was tanned like the smoothest of leathers, the caramel kind you saw on horse saddles. "And did you? Ever cancel a date without a valid excuse?"

"Not really. I always want to be more rebellious than I am."

"Well, that's a silly rule anyway. You can cancel a date for any reason you want." He glanced behind her, the Dutch door locked at her back. "What brings you to East Hampton?"

"She pointed up at the small engraved sign, "Juniper Gallery," painted in metallic gold. "I'm working with Starling Meade, the photographer. I can't believe it, really."

Curtis looked different from the boys she was used to meeting at mixers in the city. He wasn't like the olive-skinned Italians down by Mulberry Street, but he could never be mistaken for her brother either, even with her brown hair. "Ah, so you're a windmill girl now," he smiled.

"A windmill girl?"

His eyes were bright, shining even. "A windmill girl is a special kind of woman."

He pointed down Main Street to the village green where a tall gray cedar-shingled windmill stood; it was graceful and dignified, a charming relic of the past, with the busy rush of the present moving swiftly all around. "No matter her situation or which way the wind blows, a windmill girl stands firm to get what she wants. No one can take her down. Because she powers herself."

Everleigh emitted a high-pitched laugh, covering her mouth with her fingertips. "Is this what you tell all the girls?"

Riding past them on the street was a young couple on bikes pedaling while holding hands, a small white dog popping his head out of the woven basket attached to the woman's handlebars.

His elbow grazed hers for no reason at all, only because he'd moved a step closer, only for a moment. "Don't sell yourself short. I saved that line for you."

She fiddled with her garnet necklace, sliding the pendant in a horseshoe motion, smiling.

"It's true, though," he said. "For a woman like you to get a job, you've gotta have determination, and that's the same kind of pluck that got this local boy into medical school."

"I was wondering how you convinced them to let a country boy do surgery." Cars ambled by, one with teenagers hanging out the windows and speakers turned up so loud you couldn't help but track it as it passed; a cop car turned its lights on, pulling them over, she supposed for disrupting the peace. "What are you doing in town?" Everleigh asked.

He held up his medical bag. "House calls."

"Look," she said, leaning her face against the gallery's glass; he moved beside her and peered inside too. "I've been cutting matting and framing her photos all day. My fingers are actually sore."

Curtis tsked, like he wasn't surprised in the least. "See, I told you. A windmill girl."

"I am feeling pretty proud of myself. I nearly sliced off my finger in there. A trip to Doc Brightwell's office was nearly in the cards."

"Well, wouldn't that have been a treat?" They turned their faces toward one another, and he was looking at her like he couldn't stop.

"Dr. Brightwell, what are you doing?" A child in a pink pinafore tugged on his khaki pants, ice cream dripping down her cone onto her hand.

Everleigh and Curtis broke their gaze, pushing off from the glass.

"Hi, Beatrice," Curtis said. "My friend Everleigh here is showing me her art project." He patted the child's strawberry blond head before looking back at Everleigh, his smile full of mischief. She pressed her hands against her white shorts, returning the grin, her heart slowing its beat.

"I should be going," said Everleigh. "Meet up with you again soon."

"Maybe next time we can meet on purpose," Curtis said. "As friends, of course." He looked directly in her eyes when he spoke to her, and she waved goodbye, her breath catching in her throat. As she moved toward her car, Curtis hoisted the child's tiny frame on his broad shoulders.

"How much do you weigh?" Curtis asked the child as they strode off toward the mother. "As much as an elephant?"

Everleigh pulled on her sunglasses and turned over the engine of the car, checking her reflection in the mirror. "So sweet, aren't you, Curtis Brightwell? Even the kids in town count you as a friend."

Curtis turned to wave at her once more, and she shifted the car in reverse, embarrassed when he caught her staring.

⸙

When Everleigh pulled into the cottage's pebbly driveway, she let the convertible idle for a moment as she gathered her things. Roland was lying on the lounger strumming his guitar. He met her halfway from the driveway in the grass, handing her a bouquet of newly bloomed zinnias.

"How was it?" he asked, placing a kiss on her cheek. She hugged the flowers to her chest, grateful that he didn't bring up their fight from that morning.

"Oh Roland. She's unlike any other woman I've ever met," Everleigh gushed, the day pouring out of her in a burst as they crossed the yard, which was starting to yellow in patches, thanks to the heat and lack of sprinklers. "Her work is what's paramount in her life, nothing else, and—"

Roland lay backward in the nearby lounger, Everleigh sitting at the foot of it.

"She's probably a dyke." He strummed his guitar, a wad of tobacco under his bottom lip.

"Now, that's nasty, Rolly." She could have slapped him, his criticism of Starling feeling like a criticism of her. He could have said something innocuous like, "that's neat," and moved on.

He began laughing, egging her on with a nudge. "Come on, Everleigh. A woman artist. You've seen them at the Roc Club. They're always dykes."

Everleigh stood, carelessly tossing the flowers onto the picnic table. She would leave them to wilt. "That's nonsense. She has a daughter."

He turned his head and spit the tobacco juice at the grass. "You're not actually planning on going back tomorrow?"

"Of course I am." She kicked off her Keds, her feet sweaty, happy to sit down and feel the warm wooden picnic bench underfoot; it was her first day of actual work, and even if it wasn't exhausting, she was tired by the newness of it all. "I'm a windmill girl."

"A what?" He climbed up on the picnic table to sit next to her, holding his guitar, and began playing the repetitive chords of Elvis's

"Don't Be Cruel." He really had to learn a new song. "Lee, you already know how to take pictures. You focus and snap. Besides, there's something at the hotel that I need help with."

Roland had met with Opal. He had taken money from her. And now, *now*, he suddenly needed Everleigh's help. "Why don't you ask Opal?"

"Not that again." Roland sighed, banging out a loud haphazard riff on the guitar.

She excused herself inside to pour a glass of water, then spotted the bowl of lemons she'd picked up at the market and decided to make fresh lemonade instead. He came inside and puttered about the kitchen, where two bags of cleaned and folded laundry had been dropped that morning by the washerwoman, someone Roland knew from the former hotel.

"I'm over my head in the renovation, Lee. We have the construction moving, but I'm having trouble organizing the details. That's Stevie's job, but Stevie is wrapped up in something else."

She sliced a lemon in half, squeezing that one into the pitcher, then another. "Does his distraction have a name?"

Roland huffed outside to talk to someone working on the hotel as Mango purred at her feet. From the back, Roland looked as he always had—tall and wiry with adorable wisps of hair curling at the nape of his neck. But if she could turn him inside out like a sweater, she knew she'd no longer see impeccable stitching. There would be threads coming loose, small runs in the knit. All along he'd fooled her into thinking he was a modern man, that he wanted her to think beyond tending house, that they'd travel together and encourage each other's interests. But he didn't want that at all.

Everleigh cracked ice into two glasses, pouring herself a lemonade and storming out the back door, returning to her perch at the picnic table. Roland waved goodbye to the worker before returning to her side. She stared at the lemon slice floating at the top of her glass.

"C'mon, Lee, don't make me beg," he said.

"I've sat here for weeks, Rolly. Weeks waiting for you to come home for lunch, only to have you arrive at four, or hoping we'd go out for dinner, only to have you show up with Stevie, two cocktails in. Remember how you told me *you just needed* to take the money from Opal? Well, I *just need* to take this job. It's what I want to do."

"Well, don't forget, you don't get to tell me what you want to do." He laughed, but in that condescending way people do to make someone feel small. *Well, it worked*, Everleigh thought. *I feel as insignificant as the gnat nagging around my face.*

Across the street at the beach, someone was flying a box kite, and it soared up over the dunes, the string pulling higher and higher, like it might pop and get lost somewhere over the ocean. Everleigh imagined grabbing on, letting that kite fly her right back to the gallery.

ELEVEN

I n the sunny studio, she and Starling worked well together those first
few days, often wordlessly, with music playing on a record player
that the artist brought in. Starling played an Ella Fitzgerald album on
repeat, resetting the needle whenever it began to skip, which she said
soothed her nerves. She always had the same green concoction waiting
for Everleigh, and Everleigh always took a few sips before pouring it
down the bathroom sink.

"Even if it's a little of that stuff every day, it will help. With your
block," Starling said when she emerged from the back. Everleigh
nodded—wanting to say, *I'm not blocked.* Instead, she headed toward
her spot at the light table. She'd framed about half of the photographs
this week, growing faster at cutting over the last two days, but Starling
must have sensed her fatigue because she announced that Everleigh
had a new task today.

"I need you to use that small jar of spackle to smooth the holes in
the wall, then we'll paint over them with white. Not the entire wall,
just the spots you've spackled and sanded. We won't know until we
arrange the show where the pictures will go so we might as well fix the
walls."

"Surely I should call a handyman," Everleigh said, retucking the front of her black tank top into her pale-yellow pencil skirt; she'd paired it with her Keds, feeling stylish and cool, like she was the kind of girl who didn't care what people think.

Starling's eyes sparkled when she picked up a small metal half-moon tool with a handle. "We don't need any handyman. Watch me." Starling used the corner of the tool to angle out a chunk of the white spackle, spreading it like cream cheese into a thin layer over the wall's pinholes. "Just smooth it down. Real good, like this. Then it will dry, and we'll do a quick hand sand. Done."

"Okay, then." Everleigh smiled, admiring Starling's ability to do anything on her own. She imagined getting home that night, dragging Roland over to the walls eaten away by fire and demonstrating her new skill. How he'd grimace and tell her he was right about Starling: she was desperate to prove she didn't need a man. But it was exciting to Everleigh. It would never even dawn on her to use a saw or a hammer, let alone a spackle knife. "How do you know how to do all this stuff?"

Starling grimaced. "Years of living alone. You get tired of waiting around for people."

Everleigh removed a chunk of spackle, running the edges of the knife along the wall, satisfied when it was one smooth plane. *Years of living alone.* "Can you tell me about your daughter?" The Dutch door was open, a warm breeze blowing in and ruffling the prints remaining on the folding table. Starling placed a book on top of one stack.

"She's grown now, lives in Virginia, works as a schoolteacher." Starling returned to the row of framed portraits. She put one actor next to another, then swapped it out, indecision following her from one day to the next.

"Oh, so she's my age?" Everleigh dragged the spackle along the wall.

"More or less." Starling smiled. "She despises what I do. Most women do. What made you interested in photography?"

Why was Starling so hesitant to talk about herself? Still, it was a good question. She supposed it was Charlie Ludlow, the man who came to her parents' apartment twice a year to take formal portraits of the three of them, she and her mother posing like statues in evening dresses. The photographs always came back blemish-free, the color manipulated so their cheeks were pink and rosy, her mother's hair the golden yellow of corn. It was the way you could fool the camera that had gotten Everleigh's attention; how Charlie Ludlow didn't show how tortured her mother was inside, or how lonely it was for Everleigh to be an only child, how her smile could be forced. A photograph could tell a story, she often thought, but it could also tell a lie.

"I used to look at pictures taken of my family. It fascinated me that the portrait artist could manipulate the image and make us appear the perfect family, even if we weren't anything close. I think I saw photography as some kind of magic."

Starling folded her arms in front of her chest, her black shirt scrunched up underneath. She was listening closely, her brow furrowed. Everleigh had her interest.

"So I got my first camera for Christmas when I was fifteen—I begged my mother for it, and she made me promise that I'd take good care of it. I took a book out of the library just to learn how to load the film." A plop of spackle dropped to the floor, and she leaned over to pick it up with a rag. "Later, I told my parents I wanted to major in fine art. I dreamed about attending Cooper Union or Pratt, but they wanted me at Barnard. They insisted I major in literature. I needed a critical thinker's mind for masterful cocktail party conversations, I suppose." She paused, remembering her father's scowl when she showed him the school newspaper. "It drove them crazy that I took pictures for the paper—and they really hated how often I took pictures of them. I brought my camera into moments they felt were private, some of my mother's toughest days, but I wanted to capture what we were feeling in a photograph. It helps me to remember."

Starling was now sitting in the director's chair, crossing her legs. "And how do your parents feel about you being here?"

"Working with you?" Outside, a fire engine rushed by, the horn blaring.

"Yes." She nodded.

"My parents don't know, actually." Her voice once again wavered, enough that Everleigh realized she needed to tell them this week. It would feel a betrayal of sorts if they found out from someone else. And they expected her home on Saturday, of course. "They'll be livid with me. I should be wedding planning."

"Shit. The bride-to-be turns working girl. You're really going for it, aren't you?" Starling nodded with approval, a certain kind of pride overtaking her expression. "Well, good for you."

Everleigh smiled. She'd finished repairing one wall of the gallery, and now she was at the back, spackling while stepping around the row of framed portraits. "I guess, but I'm worried they'll tell me to quit. To come back to New York and stop 'with all that nonsense.'" She imitated her mother's dainty hand motions.

Pulling off her glasses, Starling cleaned the lenses with the front of her T-shirt. "What nonsense? Working for me?"

"Yes, well, no, living this alternate life. Staying out here with my fiancé, working with you, not moving into the house they bought us in Bronxville. It's not what I'm supposed to be doing." Out the window, Everleigh watched a little girl twirling on the sidewalk, an airplane tilting to one side, then the other.

Starling adjusted her glasses on her face. The phone rang, and she moved to answer it. "Lee, darling, you listen to me, and don't forget this: you get only one life, and you can do whatever the hell you want with it."

That Saturday morning, with Everleigh still not having called home, the phone began to trill in the living room. In her haste to answer it, she spilled an entire bowl of pancake batter on the kitchen floor, her heart sinking when she hopped over the mess to reach it, utter terror at the sound of her mother's voice. She was once again calling with a checklist of items that needed discussion, namely what song she and her father would dance to at the wedding. Everleigh quickly agreed to her mother's first choice, "Unforgettable" by Nat King Cole, hoping to wrap up the conversation quickly before she raised the topic of her promised homecoming.

"Are you okay, Lee? You don't sound right." She knew her mother's delicate hands were folded in her lap, her back straight on the living room sofa. "By the way, I've booked your ticket home for Monday."

The phone cord was tangled, and Everleigh tried to untwist it, glancing in the kitchen at the batter spreading over the floor. She tried to form the words in her head about Starling, words that would make them proud of her rather than annoyed at the "distraction" of playing with her camera. "I'm fine, Mommy. I just dropped an entire bowl of pancake batter. I need to go."

"You would tell me though, honey, if your brain felt like it was sinking in quicksand. You would say it."

I'm not like you, mother. She wanted to scream it.

"I'm not in ruins, Mommy. The pancakes are." She would get a towel to wipe up the mess, then mop the floor.

"Are you getting lost in your thoughts, like you did when that stuff happened with Elsa? Because I know the fire, a tragedy like this, can be traumatizing."

"Mommy, stop." She'd raised her voice, then immediately regretted it. Everleigh was *always* lost in her thoughts; it didn't mean she was sick. And the rabbit hole she'd fallen down the winter of Elsa was different. These days her mind wasn't consumed with anything other than the gallery. On how much fun she was having.

"Your train is at 1:05, honey. I expect you on it."

Everleigh hedged, afraid to state the obvious to her mother: That she would absolutely not be boarding the Long Island Railroad anytime soon.

After remaining silent, her mother pleaded. "Don't you dare tell me you're staying there."

Roland was whistling up the back steps. "Please understand, Mommy."

Her mother snapped. "It's your father you'll need to contend with. I didn't say it before, but he's upset about these checks you've been writing." Everleigh imagined her father's sedan pulling up out front, him rushing up the walkway and dragging her out by the ear.

"Don't worry," Everleigh said, a reserve of calm. "I'll handle him."

TWELVE

⚮

The following afternoon, just before dinner, Everleigh was clipping hydrangeas from some of the surviving bushes by the hotel when she saw the detective crossing the lawn. He'd returned to the fire scene yesterday, too, staring at what was left of the hotel from afar, arms folded across his chest.

"Evening, Everleigh. How is the fresh air treating you?" Even in the heat, Detective Branford wore his shiny dress shoes and black polyester slacks.

She pushed her woven wide-brimmed hat off her eyes so she could see him. "Quite well. I'm used to spending much of my time in thick city humidity."

He motioned to the hotel. "I asked Mr. Whittaker if he could wait to start the true demolition, but it looks like he did as he pleased." Branford's thumbs were hooked in his pockets, and even though she could tell he was irritated, he spoke to her like they were in on the same joke.

"Oh?" She clipped a branch, added it to her bunch. "Perhaps Stevie set it up?" Earlier that week, an excavator tore down the burned-out sections of the hotel, loading up several dump trucks. Since the foundation hadn't been compromised in the fire, it was nearly ready for framing, Roland had told her.

"They're close, those two?" The detective ripped at a leaf, tearing it up like a note he wanted kept secret.

"I suppose." She paused.

"How do you feel about Stevie?" the detective asked. When her mother was in and out of the hospital, her father had sent her to an analyst who asked her open-ended questions just like this, and the pressure to fill the air made her chatter.

"He's fine." She was clipping the hydrangea stems at different lengths, so the vase would seem like it was full of the bright-blue flowers.

"That's not exactly a ringing endorsement."

She laughed, standing up, wrapping the stems in a wet paper towel. "Does your wife like your best friend, Detective? I think that men pick friends that bring something out in them, something they wish they had. Roland is in awe of Stevie's bravado. Stevie is in awe of Roland's social life. So they work, giving each other a little of what the other needs, or maybe, wants."

They walked to the cottage and found Roland, still dressed from his lunchtime tennis match, on the phone. He quickly hung up.

The detective waited until she and Roland were settled into the creaking Shaker chairs, placing his elbows on the table.

"Can I get you a cup of coffee?" Everleigh offered. "A fresh lemonade?"

He shook his head, and Roland turned down the baseball game on the radio. "What have you found out?"

"Well, for one, that you cleared the hotel of evidence before I was finished investigating."

Roland's expression remained unchanged, and Everleigh saw him as the detective must have: a smug rich kid doing as he pleased. "I'm sorry. One of your guys, Lieutenant Parks, said he was done with the ash samples."

"For the day, maybe." Branford slid his chubby folded hands forward on the table. "You don't want to make an enemy out of me, Mr. Whittaker. It wouldn't be a wise decision. Wouldn't you agree?"

Roland clapped him on the back. "Of course not. It was a simple misunderstanding."

The detective took out a business card and handed it to Roland. "Don't say you don't have my number."

"Now what can I do for you, sir?" *Sir.* Roland must be anxious, she thought, because she'd never heard him be this formal. Maybe he'd talked to her father that way when he met him in his study, but his language was typically more colloquial. *Pal, buddy, good fellow.*

"You were right about the kid in the Springs, an innocent." The detective flipped through his yellow notepad. "But I have a new lead. You gave me a copy of your fire policy for the hotel."

Roland nodded, the tips of his hair bleached from the sun. "Yes, it's standard fare, I think."

The detective exhaled, and the way his lips parted halfway and paused, it appeared that he was readying himself to say something he didn't want to. "If you read the policy carefully, the last clause, in very small print, reads that if the owner of the policy is to die, then the benefits would go to a designated person. Do you remember seeing that clause?"

"Yes, maybe," he said. But Everleigh knew he hadn't. He tired of those kinds of details, preferring the big picture to the minutiae. Roland pulled a folder off the bookshelf, the shelves slanted downward thanks to the room's uneven floors. He came back to the table, policy in hand.

The detective flipped a page for him, then another. "I assumed it would be your name and Everleigh's name. Or maybe someone in your family. But it's not. . . . It's on page fourteen."

She leaned over Roland's shoulder to get a look at the typed pages, his finger running through the lines at a clip. Everleigh found the

clause a second before Roland did, pointing at it. "Alternate Beneficiary: Steven Walker."

"Stevie?" Roland laughed. "He put his own name in?"

"Well, that was my question," said Branford, pinning him with his
hooded eyes. "Did you know that?"

"Not that I can remember, but we had to replace our insurance at
the last minute, and I just signed whatever he gave me."

Branford wrote "benefit amount" on his yellow pad, then turned to
her. "Everleigh, you placed Stevie at the hotel with a woman about an
hour before the fire. Was he acting strange that night? Did he do anything that made you wonder about him?"

A knot in her throat. "You don't actually think he started the fire,
do you?" If Stevie had burned down the hotel—and failed—wouldn't
he have run off? Well, perhaps not if he was trying to cover his tracks.
Her mind went to the Patricia Highsmith novel she'd been reading.

The detective took a bite of the crumb cake Everleigh had put on a
napkin for him. "Of all the people in your inner circle, he seems to be
the one who would benefit if the hotel burned down."

Roland searched her face for any recollections from that night, but
when she shrugged, he said, "Stevie was running about with a clipboard, making sure the food was coming out, that the bar was stocked.
I couldn't tell you where Stevie was at any given moment because I
probably can't remember where I was at any given moment."

The detective stood, brushing the powdered sugar from his navy
pants. "I questioned the guy, and he said either the insurance company
misprinted it, or you added him at the last moment."

"Well, it wasn't the latter." Roland laughed. "Stevie might have invested his life savings in the hotel, but it was still paltry."

The detective sucked his teeth. "I'll question him again then."

"I can't imagine Stevie is behind this." Roland shook the detective's
hand. "But let me know what you turn up."

When he was gone and they returned to the cottage, Everleigh said quietly, "You don't think Stevie did this hoping that you were lost in the fire, do you?"

Roland slumped against the table, burying his face in his hands. His cheeks were red from rubbing. "Stevie? Of course not. They're just desperate to find someone to hang this on, and he's an easy target. You think that guy doesn't know that Stevie comes from a rat-infested tenement in the roughest part of the Irish Bronx?"

"No, of course he doesn't know that," she said. She imagined stocky Stevie sneaking around the hotel with the mystery woman, taking out a lighter and setting a curtain aflame.

"Don't be a fool, Lee. This is what detectives do—they ask a lot of questions, some pointless, some worthwhile," Roland said, folding the fire policy back into thirds and sliding it into the parchment envelope. "Look, Stevie made a big investment in this place, and if I lose money, he loses money. He only wanted it to succeed, trust me."

She nodded, but she found herself giving the investigator the benefit of the doubt. Sure, Stevie would lose money if the hotel burned down, but perhaps he was set to gain more from the insurance money. That is what the detective was wondering when he wrote down "benefit amount." Then again, as much as Everleigh disliked Stevie, it was difficult for her to imagine him purposely trying to kill hundreds of people with the scratch of a single match.

Roland fetched a Ballantine, drinking half of it at once. She grabbed it from him and guzzled some, too. It changed their whole day if he had too much too early.

She sat beside him at the kitchen table. "I don't know how you can relax, Rolly. It's like you have some alternate version of reality floating around your head."

His hand crawled up her thigh, his fingers grasping at the fabric of her skirt until they found the seam of her underwear. "Well, I have an inside tip that the detective's job is in question, that he blundered a murder investigation last year. It's why he's all over this. He needs to prove himself all over again in the department."

She yanked his hand down, holding it against her leg. So Roland hadn't been nervous when the detective arrived. It was hubris she'd seen. "You think he invented the arson? What about the evidence?"

He pulled his hands out of hers, his fingers landing on her chest, the smooth plane just above the top button of her belted dress. "It's all exaggerated, Lee," he said, struggling to undo the button. "If his investigation ends in an arrest, he'll be the hero. He keeps his job. You realize he answers to Gin Lane."

A figure cut a shape near the screen door, the dark silhouette coming into focus when Everleigh turned to look. She startled, spilling beer onto her dress. It was a curvy young woman, standing so still she could have been perched there for several seconds. Hanging from a drawstring on her wrist was a large burlap sack.

"May I help you?" Everleigh said, surprised when Roland turned, the tension in his face disappearing into a grin.

"Oh, hello, Vivienne. Come in." He gestured to the woman like she was a prize on a game show, and Everleigh wondered what the woman with the dimples was doing here. The woman she'd crashed into while running down the stairs the night of the fire.

Roland opened the screen door. "Lee, you haven't met our washerwoman, have you?"

Everleigh tried not to sound surprised as she put out her hand. "Vivienne? You poor thing, you were so upset that night. We all were. Nice to see you landed on your feet."

Vivienne wasn't shy, and she was pretty with a sweetheart-shaped face, her hair held back with pearl barrettes. She could have graced the cover of *Seventeen* magazine, even if she was twenty. "I'm helping my mom with her laundry service—something I swore I'd never do." But even as Vivienne rolled her eyes, her voice stayed perky, like a radio host's.

Roland slid an arm around Everleigh's waist, pulling her toward him. "I ran into Vivienne at the gas station a couple weeks ago, and she mentioned her mother's business. I said we needed a washerwoman, and since then she's the one who's been picking up our laundry."

Everleigh, in turn, slid her arm around Roland. "What a doll. You must have a fancy washer for the fantastic job you're doing."

Vivienne stared at the spot where Roland's hand gripped Everleigh's waist. "Indeed, we have a wringer in the barn that we crank the clothes through to extract the excess water, and it allows us to do the finest of work."

The woman kept assessing Everleigh's figure, and it was beginning to feel uncomfortable; hadn't her mother taught her that was rude? "Well, I've certainly needed the help."

Roland pulled out a cigarette, patting his pockets for his matches. "The hotel would have done it for us, of course, but the laundry was on the side of the hotel that burned."

Vivienne reached into her jeans pocket and pulled out a silver flip lighter with a filigree pattern engraved on it, then leaned over to light his cigarette, a little too close. Everleigh cleared her throat as Vivienne snapped the lighter shut, slid it back into her denim jeans, and took a step back. "I hope you don't mind me coming a day early this week, due to an appointment tomorrow."

The woman was clearly a local—perfectly articulate but studied, like she was working to avoid the slang she'd grown up listening to.

"Oh, what a dear. You're so committed." Everleigh gestured to the bedroom window. "I'll get the load together now."

Next to her bed, hospital corners neatly tucked, Everleigh crouched down in the closet, stuffing a few of her shirts and shorts into the potato sack before heading into Roland's room for his denim jeans, some dirty socks, and discarded T-shirts balled up in the bottom of the hamper. She strained to listen to Vivienne's and Roland's conversation through the window. There was a faint whisper, a giggle.

Everleigh cinched the sack closed, her temples throbbing with anticipation, and she waited, eavesdropping, expecting to hear something damning. Instead, Roland's voice returned, a question about the type of detergent she preferred, making Everleigh smile. His obsession with grooming extended even to laundry soap.

She pulled out Roland's black suit from the night of the fire, which had been stuffed into a plastic bag. His blazer, tailored for his frame but with an extralong torso, in keeping with the latest trend in men's fashion, had white ash resembling confetti pilling the fabric. She stuffed it into the laundry sack, wondering if Vivienne had a way to dryclean it, when something fell out of the pocket. A quarter, she thought, by the unmistakable sound of metal hitting wood. But when she reached down, she saw a key. It was attached to a diamond-shaped piece of aquamarine plastic with a large *E* emblazoned on it and the number twenty-three.

Everleigh turned it over in her hands with butterflies in her stomach, thinking back to their earlier conversation with the detective. Roland had denied knowing who was staying in room twenty-three of the hotel, but he had to have known if he had the key. The only plausible reason for him having it at all was if he was setting the room aside for someone, most likely his father, whose arrival he'd wrung his hands over all night. Roland must have kept it in his pocket throughout the party, anticipating the moment he could accompany his father to his room. But why had he kept the information from the fire detective when he'd inquired about the hotel's guest list? How easy it would have been to tell him that he'd set the room aside for his father. Now the information felt like a secret, and if Branford found out that Roland had this key, he'd think him a liar.

Everleigh put the room key on the highest shelf in the closet. What else could she do with it? Roland seemed more weighted than ever by his father's absence lately. One night last week, after they'd had too many cocktails together, he confided that he'd recently sent his father a letter. He'd explained what happened with the hotel, set forth a plan for how he'd rebuild it. "I just want him to be proud of me, Lee," he'd said. Still, his father hadn't called or written back.

Everleigh dragged the laundry bag outside and handed it to Vivienne, who was laughing about something else Roland had said. The woman had scars on two fingers, round pink welts, ugly and puffy. Everleigh pretended to roll her eyes at Roland. "I'm sorry if my fiancé said anything inappropriate. Sometimes pretty girls set him off."

After work that Monday evening, Everleigh stepped outside with her camera. The sun was low in the sky, turning everything the color of marigolds. That was how she was beginning to think about her time in Southampton: her golden hours. Feeling inspired after a conversation with Starling about how dusk offers the best natural light for pictures, Everleigh carried her camera outside, walking toward what was left of the hotel. If she focused on the point where the hotel's widow's walk once was, where she and Roland had spent their two nights in the penthouse, she could see a crack straight through to the front of the building. A gaping tear, and with the light hitting just right at sunset, she snapped a photo. She imagined a book sliced in half, a country divided in two, a couple with a wedge between them. *Click. Click.*

Roland hadn't come home yet—she wasn't sure where he was—so she'd devoured a quiet supper of green peppers and tomato salad with cheddar and salami chunks while petting Mango on her lap. She was dressed for a party Roland wanted to attend at the Beach Club now that their membership had finally been approved, much to her dismay.

She pointed her camera at the remnants of a window, startled by the husky sound of a man's voice.

"Cataloging the damage?"

It was Stevie in front of her, wearing his signature Hawaiian shirt, his tongue tucked into the corner of his mouth like a lollipop. She raised her camera and snapped again, feeling the rough of his elbow graze hers.

"I saw you that night. You were up on your balcony looking down at me," he said.

She was losing the light from the sun, but she snapped anyway, feigning interest in an overgrown corner of the yard. "You seemed to be having a good time."

"You seemed to like watching." He was behind her now, and he stood, hovering, which made her inch toward the stairway. She couldn't move now unless he backed up. A prickle of alarm coursed through her. She looked past his height, at the cottage, which seemed an endless distance from here, willing Roland to come outside.

He took one step closer, tipping his chin down so his lips were in line with her forehead, the heat of his liquored breath cutting through her nose. "You deserve better, Lee."

She turned her cheek away from him, longing for the cottage door to open, a car to drive by, someone to see them, when he ran a finger down the length of her bare arm, tracing a slick path with his oily touch. She hoped he couldn't feel her trembling.

In an awkward attempt to get away, she leaned backward from her neck, focusing her camera on his face, using it as a barrier between his body and hers, disgusted at the way his pink bottom lip stuck out over the top one. Where was Roland?

Using all her body weight, she pushed past Stevie's doughy center, her pulse pounding in her chest. There was sweat on his ruddy forehead, his lips slimy like a slug.

"I'm quite happy with my choices, thank you," she said, echoing the formal tone of a headmistress. She could feel his presence lurking behind her as she crossed the lawn, and she jumped when his voice appeared close again, calling to her. She considered the detective's suggestion that Stevie might have had something to do with the fire. Perhaps he could hurt someone.

After several more paces, in which she feared Roland wasn't in the cottage at all, that Stevie had come knowing he was out, Roland finally emerged. He called to them, and seeing him made Everleigh feel safer, like she could challenge Stevie and not worry about the consequences. She put her hand on her hip.

"Do you have something to hide, Stevie? Because your name was listed as a beneficiary on the insurance papers."

Stevie's blue eyes lolled up to his feet, a half smile taking over his freckled face, the ping-pong laugh again. He slurred, just enough to mark him drunk. "If I'm hiding something, then Roland is, too. Think about that, Miss Everleigh Farrows."

She slapped him across the cheek.

"Hey, hey," Roland called out, running across the lawn. He grabbed for her hand, his straw fedora falling off his head into the grass. Stevie strode off, smirking. "What was that about?"

Everleigh didn't look up from Roland's warm chest, not until she heard Stevie's car start. "He threatened me, Rolly," she sputtered out of his arms.

He held her chin between his thumb and forefinger. "Did he hurt you?"

"Not exactly. But he—" she hiccupped. Why was Roland only concerned that she wasn't physically hurt? Could Stevie do or say what he wished as long as he didn't lay a hand on her?

"Well, what happened exactly?"

"He touched my arm, but in this creepy way."

"Your arm?" He waited for her to continue, but what *had* Stevie really done? He'd cornered her, made clear he liked her. He didn't force himself upon her. Perhaps if things hadn't happened with George Sheetz, if she weren't so sensitive . . .

"I just don't like how he talks to me, Rolly." But even as she said it, she knew that to a man, those were empty words. Men could talk to women however they wanted.

"I'm sorry, pet. I'll talk to him."

At least he'd keep an eye on Stevie now. Roland trusted him so thoroughly, but maybe he shouldn't. Maybe Rolly needed to open his eyes.

THIRTEEN

The locker room at the Southampton Bathing Corporation smelled like ammonia and chlorine, thanks to an aging woman wiping down the metal cabinets with a washcloth, and Everleigh was immediately brought back to the gleam of the floors in the Plaza's lobby. Once, when they were teenagers, she and Whitney played a cruel prank on one of the front desk attendants; they wrote her several love letters and signed them from one of the elevator operators, manufacturing an entire affair between the two, which had actually culminated in a month of serious dating. They never did find out if the couple realized she and Whitney had authored the letters.

Whitney seemed to be avoiding her these days. She may have canceled plans the last few times in innocence, but last week's call was particularly upsetting, since it hadn't even come from Whitney. Her housekeeper rang Everleigh to say her friend was returning to the city and would be in touch next week. She'd heard through Roland—*Roland* of all people!—that Whitney had returned to the beach a few days ahead of schedule, that he'd seen her when he'd met up with Opal again at the Maidstone, but still no phone call.

"You met up with Opal? Again?" Everleigh had seethed. Roland's temper flared. He argued that he'd invited Everleigh both times, and she'd declined. "Meaning," he'd said, "it wasn't a private rendezvous."

The pool attendant arranged her and Roland's towels on loungers at the rectangular pool, the cool water beckoning. She'd come to the Beach Club every day after work this week to swim, and now, on Sunday, she'd had to sign an agreement that promised she'd never release photos of the clubhouse or talk in detail to reporters about it.

"Why are the social clubs here all shrouded in secrecy?" she'd asked Roland as he greased her back with lotion.

"Because members don't want anyone to know they pay through the roof for what is ultimately a community pool."

And still, it was an entirely beautiful place to summer, she thought now, her lounger facing the swimming pool. From here, she could see Lake Agawam and hear the crashing waves of the Atlantic, making her feel even more exuberant after finishing her second week of work. Cattails rose up through the dunes in front of the Spanish-style clubhouse, an elegant almond-colored stucco with arched doorways and rows of red clay tiles on the roof.

Around the pool, women were clustered under umbrellas, the men in their own groups smoking cigars, which injected a sour cinnamon smell into the chlorine haze. She saw several familiar faces from the city, and she began narrating their stories to Roland.

He loved hearing about people whose families had nearly disavowed them, of which there were quite a few, since many rich kids tended to behave badly until given an ultimatum by their well-heeled parents. Bouncing on the diving board was a blond gentleman known for his magnetism who was kicked out of Harvard only to have his father pay the administration "a significant sum" for his readmission; he was now a vice president at one of the big banks. Roland grinned and sauntered off in his plaid swim trunks to meet the scoundrel.

Everleigh picked up her novel, determined to finish it that day by the pool, when a shadow passed over her. There was Alice Anna, with her sickening stick-thin legs, coral-colored sandals matching her bathing costume. "We need a fourth for canasta. Will you join?"

"Oh, I . . ." She tried to formulate an excuse, one that didn't sound rude, but Alice was already pointing to a table of women Everleigh knew from tennis. They waved, and now there was no denying them. Everleigh reluctantly rose, wrapping herself in a terry robe.

The women had a gin and tonic waiting for her, each of them greeting her pleasantly, the one with tight curls, Betty, dealing her fifteen cards. Their table was near the diving board, and every time someone did a cannonball, Everleigh felt the splash. As they played through the cards, there was small talk of the pettiest kind: someone's husband was staying in the city too much, famous names that the club's admitting board had rejected that summer.

"I suppose we're lucky we made the cut then," Everleigh quipped, watching Alice discard the queen of hearts.

Betty snorted. "The jury is still out."

Alice kicked the woman's ankle under the table.

Everleigh smiled, picking up the queen of hearts, putting a pair down; she was winning now. "Is there something I don't know?"

Betty launched into a long, boring story about how her father was on the board with Alice's father, how much thought was put into who your associates were, who your sponsor was. She said nothing of consequence; it was her own voice she liked to hear.

Alice batted her eyes and asked Everleigh about the fire investigation, remarking how slowly the restoration was coming along.

Betty shifted in her seat. "It was a terrible, terrible fire."

"Well, it seems like Alice's parents are putting up some unnecessary roadblocks to rebuilding it." It was Everleigh's turn again; the game moved fast and seemed to be moving even faster now. "Aren't they, Alice?"

The woman twisted up her long hair and knotted it at the nape of her neck. "It's not just my parents. Truth is no one wants that tacky thing back up. I'm sorry because I know Roland must be suffering with all that financial loss. You realize that he still hasn't even paid the second half of his dues here. The Board may cancel your membership."

Ernest whistled in the pool, and he reached over to tickle a woman in a flashy high-waisted red bikini with white piping. The woman laughed, pushing him away. "Behave, Ernest," Alice hollered to him. Her fiancé yelled back, "Come swim with me, love." She ignored him, and Everleigh was grateful for the break in conversation. She'd had a moment to gather herself, even if her cheeks were still aflame.

"I suppose I better take a trip to accounts payable," Everleigh joked.

"I'm sorry, Lee," Alice sighed, waiting for Betty's next move: a four of spades. "I'm being awful. But this is what Rolly does. He makes a mess of things and gets the women in his life to clean it up. I'm worried about you is all."

"Worried about me? Well, don't be." Everleigh threw down her last pair, standing abruptly. "I'm out, and I'm pretty sure I won." She gulped down the last of her cocktail, wishing it would make her disappear. The gin stung her throat. "Thanks for the game, girls."

Back on the striped pool lounger, Everleigh buried her face in her novel while watching Roland over the tops of the pages. She'd always assumed he was at the center of the men he was talking with, but now she realized Roland was on the periphery, trying to edge his way into the conversation, laughing at someone else's jokes. He was trying too hard.

Starling had given her the morning off since she had an appointment, but Everleigh got up early anyway and prepared two bowls of milk toast. She sprinkled some sugar and cinnamon on the bread but decided to wait for Roland to pour the milk and butter mixture over the top so it wouldn't get soggy. The terrible day before had chased her in her dreams, and she'd woken feeling as though she hadn't slept at all, a light tremble in her hands as she prepared breakfast. She dressed in a pretty floral crepe sundress to pick herself up.

"I want—I want—I want—was all that she could think about—but just what this real want was she did not know." She'd read that line in her Carson McCullers book the day before at the pool, and she turned back to it now. What did she want? She was tired of tiptoeing around Roland with her choices when he was making awful ones himself. And she really wanted to talk to Whitney—maybe that's what she wanted most—but when she tried her, her housekeeper said she was at the Maidstone Club with friends. *Friends!* She seemed not to count Everleigh one of them lately.

Roland woke up after nine, missing his tennis match and emerging outside to join Everleigh for breakfast, Mango sleeping at her bare feet.

"How are you feeling?" She could see a crease in his cheek from the pillow. While Everleigh had come home after dining at the pool, Roland had stayed, stumbling home sometime after midnight. He'd gone on to a party at the Maidstone with Opal and Stevie. He'd seen Whitney.

He rubbed at the part of his hair with his palm. "She asked after you."

"Who?" she snapped. "Opal or Whitney?" In an instant, she was upset with Whitney. She should have called and reported that she saw Roland and Opal together. If Roland was cheating on her with that woman, someone needed to walk Everleigh through what to do next. How would she confront him and demand he end it with his mistress—without losing him? Or how would Everleigh move forward and find a path for herself if they actually split up?

There was a bowl waiting for Roland on the picnic table, and she broke the milk toast into pieces with her fork, pushing it toward him, uncertain and not really caring if it had spoiled in the sun. A trio of magpies chirped above them on a wire; they were surely talking about her, wondering what she would say to him.

Everleigh placed the book spine-up on the picnic table. "Rolly, why did Alice say our membership at the Bathing Corp is in question? I felt a fool sitting there."

His T-shirt was rumpled and sour smelling; he should have taken a shower before he'd come out. "So what? I owe another payment. Doesn't everybody? She's just messing with us."

"You don't deny it then?" When he didn't answer, she picked Mango up from the grass, stroking the cat; the smooth of her fur calmed her, and she needed to remain calm. "Okay, but why is she messing with us? You keep saying it's because of this accident back in Michigan."

Roland scarfed down the bread, lifting the bowl to his mouth to drink the cinnamon-flavored milk. He placed it softly on the table. "It's not just the accident, pet. It's my breakup with her cousin. Alice blames me for her unhappiness. She thinks I should have married her, provided for her in some way. Can't you see? She's just angry I'm marrying you."

The phone rang from inside the living room, and she ignored it. "But why would they expect you to provide for her? Were you engaged?" she asked. When he didn't give a clear answer and the ringing didn't stop, she excused herself for a moment, dashing in to pick up the telephone on the small table by the picture window. She hoped for Whitney's voice.

"This is Saks Fifth Avenue Southampton, the accounts department," said a soft-spoken elderly woman who might have been Everleigh's grandmother. There was a problem with Everleigh's check. She'd submitted payment for items on her account the day before, but the check was returned for insufficient funds.

Everleigh twirled the tight coil cord around her finger. "But that's impossible, madam—it's my checking account. Well, a joint account."

The woman's voice was kind. "I'm just telling you it was returned, dear."

Everleigh ran her hand down the pleats of her dress. "Well, there must be a misunderstanding—that's our family's account."

Everleigh struggled to remember what the balance was in her checkbook, although she never recorded her expenses in the small ledger. There wasn't any reason to think anything would bounce; the account had to have at least several thousand.

The woman's voice was tentative. "Miss Farrows, you're one of our valued customers, and I agree that there's some kind of miscommunication. Let me read the numbers from the check. Will you tell me if it's your current account?"

Everleigh fetched her checkbook from her purse near the backdoor hooks, and the woman read back the numbers. They were, in fact, the numbers associated with her trust.

After hanging up, Everleigh immediately dialed the switchboard operator, asking her to connect a long-distance call to Manhattan Central Bank. She heard the click and pop of other lines being pushed into jacks in the background, the voices of the other operators connecting calls.

A minute or so later, a gentleman she knew at the bank picked up, and Everleigh told him about her predicament with Saks. The teller put her on hold, and when he returned, his friendly tone had been replaced by remorse.

"Miss Farrows, your account was closed on Friday. We had to return another check, one for a department store, Hildreth's, in Southampton. I'm sorry."

Outside, Roland lay on a lounger, relaxed and unaware of the panic rising in her throat. "What do you mean? Closed?"

"We got a call last week. The note says to take your name off the account. I'm sorry."

"It's okay. Thank you." She forced confidence into her voice, setting down the phone.

No one had access to that account except her—and her parents. Which meant . . . it meant that her parents had taken away her bank account. Her head felt woozy, like she was on a carousel moving too quickly, and she fell into the tufted chair where she'd sat earlier. Her father was clearly making a statement. Perhaps they'd learned about her job with Starling. Maybe they were angry at her for giving Roland too much money, or maybe they were tiring of her reluctance to return home. She hadn't called them in over a week.

"Lee, can you mix me a Bloody?" Roland called through the kitchen window, and she could see him on the lounger, the sun wrapping him in a blanket of bright light. Why did the house feel so cold? Her body was shivering, goosebumps prickling her arms.

Her parents had threatened to take away her trust only once before. She was in college and a handsome history student she'd fallen for had broken up with her and then she'd failed her French midterm. She came home to her parents' apartment and crawled into bed. Her mother went along with her refusal to get up, seeming to like serving her only daughter tea and rubbing her forehead, the way her daughter often cared for her. But the following week, her father marched into Everleigh's room, sat on the edge of her canopy bed, and scolded her. "You will not be like your mother, or I will take away your trust, which means I'll take away your whole goddamned future." Everleigh had immediately returned to her classes.

She pounded the grass with her feet when she got outside, carrying a large piece of a too-dry strawberry loaf she'd baked, slamming her bottom down on Roland's lounge chair. She bit nearly half off, stuffing her mouth.

"What happened to my Bloody?" Roland said, sitting up expectantly. He noticed her tear-stained face. "Lee, are you okay?"

She wedged another chunk of cake into her mouth and stared down at her painted red toenails. "My parents. They closed my account. That was Saks, but I called Manhattan Central Bank, and my trust—it's gone."

Roland pushed his sunglasses on top of his head, sitting up. "They couldn't have. Your father, he wouldn't do that to us. The money from Opal, there's only so much. We need your trust for incidentals, for gas for chrissakes."

"Roland! It's gone. I don't even know if they'll speak to me." Everleigh wanted to bury her nose in the honeysuckle growing in a tangle up the cottage gutter, smash her face into the flowers, smell nothing but the sweetness of its blooms. Or maybe she'd just tear it all down. Anything to not have to look at Roland right now, his face blanching, the speed with which he was biting at his fingertips.

"He's angry that you gave me that money. I told him I'd repay him, and I didn't."

"But Roland! You had it in the bank."

He spat a fingernail into the grass. "Had it. I had it in the bank."

Her stomach turned upside down. Everleigh thought of her last call with her mother, how she'd planned to tell her about Starling but lost her nerve. "No, it's my job at the gallery. They must have found out."

"Then you need to quit. Call your father immediately and apologize."

She would do no such thing. Not now. Not after how far she'd come.

Roland bounded toward the hotel, picking up a rock and ramming it at one of the hotel's windows. He found another and lobbed it even harder. A window shattered. He picked up another. And then another.

Her head felt like a bowling ball in her hands, tiny spasms knotting her neck. It was one thing to walk away from your inheritance. It was quite another to have it taken away. Because in the end, her parents were taking away something far greater than money. They were taking away her freedom to do as she pleased, and they wanted her to know that.

FOURTEEN

⁂

Everleigh called into work that Tuesday, spending the morning moping about the cottage in her nightgown, eating from a pint of ice cream and picking at blueberries she'd bought to make a pie. She couldn't focus enough to read or summon the energy to turn on the stove. A wave of anger would take hold of her, and she'd see her father's pinched face sneering. Minutes later, she'd fall into a heap on her mattress, envisioning water pooling in her mother's eyes. Still, there were moments of clarity. She began forming an argument in her head about why it was good that her parents had revoked her trust: for one, she wouldn't have to return to the city at all this summer.

With Roland working at the hotel, Everleigh picked up the phone. She would have to face her parents at some point. After she exchanged pleasantries with Nanny, neither of them acknowledging the elephant in the room, her father blustered onto the line. "You may think that what we're doing is harsh, but your mother and I are both in agreement. Do not give Roland another dime of our money. I've given him plenty, and I expect you both to pay me back for what you stole."

"So that's it. I'm a thief, and you're setting me loose, your criminal daughter." She put her hand on her hip, wiped her wet eyes. "I was only lending it to him, Daddy."

"And I had to hear about this radical you're spending time with from Alice's parents the other night. The embarrassment, Lee."

"And what if I quit that job and come home?"

There was a long pause, and she could hear voices in the background, perhaps a television laugh track. "*Are* you coming home?" he asked.

Everleigh considered this. She hadn't called home with bargaining in mind, and it had occurred to her last night that she could end this and do just as her parents wanted. Get on the Long Island Railroad and return to Pennsylvania Station, hop in a cab, and, after chatting with her favorite doorman, ride the elevator up to the fourth floor where they lived. But the thought turned the floor underneath her feet to quicksand. Everleigh was tired of her parents dictating her every decision. She'd asserted herself to them for the first time in her life, and their response was to cancel her trust. Was this to remind her that she didn't have any say in her life at all? It was maddening.

Everleigh glanced out the cottage window, thinking about her mother. She wasn't getting on the phone, and that could only mean one thing: she was too upset to talk.

"Roland needs to look outside our family for help," her father said. "And Everleigh, I swear it, you need to stop gallivanting in Southampton as though your reputation—our reputation—isn't on the line here. Because it is. Now, are you coming home?"

Her reputation? She hated that her parents were always reminding her of how other people saw her. If her parents finally stopped caring what others thought, would they still disapprove of her decision to work for Starling?

"Of course I'm not coming home," she said, hanging up.

Everleigh pressed the back of her wrist to her mouth, a laugh slipping out, her cheeks dimpling. Her hopelessness vanished at once. She wouldn't put up with her father's demands any longer. She wouldn't let his money control her. It was three in the afternoon and she was in her pajamas, but she would shower and slip on a dress and take her camera outside to take pictures of that dead patch of grass, focusing on the lush lawn beside it, the square that looked so alive.

And then, just because life felt sweet again, she would bake that blueberry pie and savor every last bite.

Three nights later, the party at the Bathing Corp spilled out onto the beach, the sand colder than Everleigh expected on her bare feet. Roland led her to a beach blanket he'd set up near Stevie, who was tending a bonfire, a large pile of firewood set up in a crosshatch tower in the sand and illuminating the darkened beach. While Roland tried to uncork a bottle of claret, Everleigh settled onto the striped woolen camp blanket, the fire warming her rising goosebumps. She'd avoided Stevie since that day he'd cornered her at the hotel, and she watched him poke at the flames with a thick piece of driftwood. How determined he seemed to grow it, his jughead focused on the flames shooting upward.

"To you and me making it on our own," Roland said to her, raising the glass he'd borrowed from the bartender at the club. She'd spent the night before convincing her fiancé that her parents were calling their bluff. Of course, they'd reinstate her trust after they realized their only child wouldn't cow to their every demand. Think about it, she'd told him. *They're not taking away the house they bought us in Bronxville. They're still paying for the wedding. They want us together,* she'd said, fully aware she sounded bratty. *But we'll make clear it's on our terms.*

What she really meant was: *her* terms.

Everleigh tucked the crinoline of her A-line skirt under her folded legs, toasting him back. "We will answer to no one." She giggled, sipping the wine, loving how deep and rich it tasted.

Word must have gotten out about the impromptu gathering because it seemed to be doubling in size, with people walking down the beach from public entrances to join in the revelry, although the Bathing Corp members were still in slacks and cocktail dresses. She'd barely registered Roland's announcement that he wanted to talk to Stevie when Whitney sat beside her, her petite friend falling against her with a *thunk*.

"Oh Lee, I've missed you. I'm sorry for canceling twice." Whitney tried to hug her, the smell of her gardenia perfume overtaking the burn of the fire, but Everleigh turned away sharply. Whitney had seen Roland and Opal together at the Maidstone and hadn't called Everleigh to warn her. Not because she was trying to protect her, but because it was easiest.

"You're back from the city, I see." Everleigh needed a cigarette, to exhale her stress.

Whitney launched into a long-winded explanation about a last-minute luncheon she needed to organize to support the New York Public Library's Children's Room. She'd been back and forth a few times, but she hadn't had a chance to get together because she needed to check on all the planters that the Ladies Village Improvement Society had placed in the villages, then some nonsense about a proposed renovation of the pool house at the Maidstone.

Opal ambled into the glow of firelight. Walking barefoot and holding a pair of sandals, a mane of blond hair trailing down her back, she approached Stevie. A dreamy look overtook his face, and they began laughing about something when he threw another log into the blazing fire. She looked to see if Roland noticed her, but he was deep in conversation with men from the club.

Whitney chattered on, and Everleigh felt like she couldn't swallow her wine, she was so bitter at how clueless her friend was. Everleigh cut her off. "Did you know about Roland spending time with Opal?"

Whitney cleared her throat, buttoning her cream-colored cardigan, a navy ring around the neckline and wrists, a string of dainty pearls hanging at her chest. "What do you mean?"

Everleigh poked her hard in the shoulder. "You think I don't know that you fiddle with your clothes when you're lying?" It was a joke between them. Everleigh pressed her lips inward after fibbing, while Whitney often pushed her hands into her skirt pockets. "How could you not tell me he was with her at the Maidstone? You had to have seen him."

Whitney looked about, concerned that someone was going to hear Everleigh's rising voice. "I only saw him once, Lee, I swear. But there were whispers."

"And you didn't say something? You didn't tell Opal to leave my fiancé alone?" Of all the causes her friend had taken up over the years, she couldn't have made Everleigh one of them? She couldn't have shown an ounce of passion in sticking up for her friend?

Whitney waved to a woman in a zip sweatshirt warming her hands by the fire, where two men were opening a box of pizza and handing her a slice. "Are you that insecure about your fiancé that you need me to tell him to behave?"

A flash of resentment struck like lightning, breaking open old wounds, and Everleigh felt hateful, like she wanted to hurt her friend right back. "Are you so scared of losing your place in the pecking order that you can't tell someone to stop sniffing around my life?"

This had always been a sticking point between them. In their school days, if someone was unkind to Whitney, Everleigh was the first to shut them up. But when the most popular girl in school made a snide comment about Everleigh's skirt as she was about to give a speech in tenth grade, Whitney never demanded an apology, and when that same girl left nasty notes in Everleigh's locker for no reason at all, Whitney didn't say a word then either. Whitney refused to step into the fray, always afraid of becoming a target herself.

Stevie kept gathering kindling, tossing it in, poking the embers. The glow of the bonfire turned half of Whitney's face golden as her voice turned apologetic. "You would have hated me if I told you, Lee. I was hoping Roland would make the right choice."

Everleigh imagined herself in a boxing ring, Rocky Marciano about to throw a punch, as though all her upset, much of it having nothing to do with Whitney, was her friend's fault. "No, you were waiting for him to fall on his face, so you'd get your way, and I'd marry someone else, someone you approve of."

Whitney sighed, twisting the pearls with her fingers. "See, I knew you would do this. Make this about us."

"But it *is* about us. You haven't even called to ask about my job with the photographer. My first real job, but do you care? No, because it doesn't involve your precious little social club."

Whitney rolled her eyes. "Well, I'm sorry if I'm too busy making a life, rather than trying to escape one."

Truman ducked down in front of Whitney then, saying hello to Everleigh while humming a showtune without any awareness of the tension between his wife and her best friend. "Let's get out of here, love. This isn't our crowd," he said.

It didn't take Whitney more than a second to jump to her feet, and she didn't even turn back to say goodbye as the couple linked elbows and disappeared into the darkness of an unlit beach.

Everleigh turned around and walked toward the fire, her mood sinking into sadness at Whitney's sudden departure. The hateful things Whitney had said! And Everleigh had needled right back. Why were they both so quick to be angry at one another this summer?

Someone turned up a transistor radio, a song with sappy lyrics about breaking up with someone you love, which only made Everleigh feel more glum. It felt like Whitney was a different person this summer, wrapped up in everyone else's life but Everleigh's. It was embarrassing to admit, but out east, without her usual routines and friends on hand, Everleigh wanted more attention from her best friend, not less. She was already defying her parents in taking the job with Starling. It would have been reassuring to have her friend's stamp of approval, let alone a little extra support.

From her position near the fire, she made out the form of Alice Anna, one hand on a slender hip, facing the statuesque Opal. Everleigh drew closer in the darkened perimeter, breezing by as if she didn't care what they were saying, even though she wanted to know why they were arguing. It was easy to hear Opal's priggish tone. "I absolutely will not say that, and I will not indulge your threats, Alice. You're acting as some toffee-nosed princess."

Alice stepped closer to Opal. "Then I will come forward. I will tell."

Tell what? What kind of secret did the two women share? Everleigh strained to hear Opal's retort, but when the woman saw her, they both fell silent, waiting for Everleigh to pass. By then Everleigh was back by Roland and Stevie, both roasting marshmallows by the bonfire. "You want a s'more, Lee?" Stevie grinned, kicking a log closer to the others, setting it aflame.

"Sure," she said, reaching for the dessert.

She wondered what Alice knew about Opal, what information she harbored that was so damning that Opal wouldn't want others to know. If Everleigh wasn't already suspicious of Alice's fiancé because of his threat to Roland the night of the fire, she might have written it off as something benign, one woman's jealousy over something trite. But Alice's words "I will tell" sailed off her tongue like a storm, like Alice knew the very idea of this information emerging would frighten Opal into whatever submission she was requesting. Even more intriguing was that Alice was asking Opal to do her a favor of some kind, to say something to someone that Opal deemed untrue. What if Alice was asking Opal to tell a white lie to the detective? Something small, one solid detail suggesting her whereabouts, that would give Alice a solid alibi. Everleigh already knew Alice and her parents believed Roland's hotel was sullying Gin Lane, and the business with her cousin made Alice despise him. This all added up to one terrifying possibility: Alice and Ernest had to be serious suspects in the arson.

Everleigh needed to go home; she'd crawl under the covers and snuggle with Mango until she fell asleep. She said a quick round of goodbyes, unable to locate Opal or Alice anymore, insisting she'd be okay to walk home alone. Roland didn't put up a fight, even though it was pitch-black, the only lights twinkling off the houses just behind the dunes.

After grabbing her heels, she walked toward the beach path and came face-to-face with Detective Branford, who was standing with his arms crossed against his barrel chest, a cigarette dangling from his mouth, his portly middle stretching the fabric of his uniform. "They have a permit for that fire?" he said.

Everleigh shrugged, playing dumb; she doubted Roland even knew you needed one. "Maybe?"

Branford laughed, his doughy face round in the moonlight. "Stevie seems to know what he's doing."

"Maybe too much," she said, hoping he would catch her point.

The detective shrugged. "I don't have anything solid on him yet. Do you want a ride?"

The summer cottage was at least fifteen minutes by foot and she was wearing heels. "That would be lovely."

The police car smelled of cigarettes and cracking leather as the headlights shone along the road, snaking through the dune grass and tall hedges. "I was going to drop in on Monday, but I might as well tell you now. We found a flammable residue at the hotel."

"There was gasoline?" It was the only thing she could think of that would catch fire.

He popped open the car's stainless steel ashtray, stubbed his cigarette inside. "Not quite. We found something else—a chemical called acetone, lots of it." Outside, a group of men in their twenties passed them going in the direction of the Bathing Corp, no doubt on their way to the bonfire.

Fear tickled her throat. "So it was definitely the work of an arsonist."

The detective gripped the steering wheel, his hands at eleven and one o'clock. "In my work, I think a lot about context—most of the evidence I'm looking for gets destroyed as soon as the firemen aim the hose and wash away the evidence. If we find residue in a garage, where people might keep a canister of gasoline, then we'd wager a guess that the fire was an accident. If we find it in a bedroom, though, somewhere you don't typically see an accelerant, then we get curious."

Everleigh's mind rewound to the night at the hotel when she'd run through the hallways, the walls hot to the touch, trying to help guests escape down the stairs in the thick black smoke. "Is that where you found it? In a bedroom?"

"It was in room twenty-three, as I suspected. Acetone droplets, in whatever was left of the rugs. We found some along the baseboards, too, maybe fragments from the bedding or curtains. We even found residue in the floorboards directly underneath."

The key to room twenty-three had been in Roland's suit pocket the day she was gathering the laundry, and she'd tucked it on the shelf in his closet. It was still there. All Everleigh had to do was run her hand along the top of the wooden board, her fingers gathering dust as she felt for it. If the fire truly started there, she needed to tell the detective about Roland having the key before they could be accused of concealing evidence. They never did find the ledger with guest names listed.

"My fiancé reserved that room for his father's stay," she said. Although she'd never confirmed her thinking about why he had the key in his pocket, something she was regretting now.

The detective parked the car in the driveway. He lifted a mug of what appeared to be cold coffee to his mouth; discarded ceramic mugs littered the floor of the passenger side. "I figured that out. But it's strange that the room where the fire started is the only room in the hotel that sat empty that night."

The cottage was dark other than the light over the kitchen door. Mango was sleeping on the doormat, waiting for her. "If you're trying to say that Roland tried to burn down his prized show horse, you'd be wrong." Everleigh splayed her fingers out on her chest. "He loved that hotel."

"Well, someone knew that room was empty and that same someone took something with acetone, like varnish or paint thinner, and poured it all over. That stuff ignites with the speed of a warhead."

It scared her the night of the party, how her clothes had nearly caught fire as she pushed through the burning lobby. But what had Roland wanted of room twenty-three before guests began arriving? She pictured Roland approaching the front desk earlier that morning and taking the room key, sliding it into his silken trouser pocket. Inside the room, beside the taut white bedspread with small pearl beads sewn along the seams, he'd pull an envelope from his dinner jacket breast pocket and set it on the nightstand. It contained a handwritten letter she'd seen him compose on Everleigh Hotel stationery—an apology letter, he'd said—waiting for his father's arrival.

I'm sorry for . . .

What was he sorry for, though? A private matter, he'd said. She wondered then if room twenty-three had remained empty for the duration of the party. Or, after she'd turned off the light in the hotel penthouse, once she'd finally drifted off to sleep, had Roland crept downstairs and entered the room? Had he lain down at the center of the unwrinkled bed, pressing his fists over his eyes in the dark, upset his father hadn't come? Had he torn up the letter, leaving the confetti at the center of the bed, and in a rage, grabbed the first flammable thing he could find in the maintenance room down the hall?

Branford pushed open his car door, walked to the passenger side, and opened hers. "You can tell Roland that anybody can walk into a hardware store and buy paint thinner. Which means the arsonist could be anyone, anyone at that bonfire. Anyone at all."

These former city cops, Roland had complained of the detective's languishing investigation. *They come out here, think it's going to be cake, and then something out of the ordinary comes up, and they look for clues where there are none. He needs to stop trying to be the hero.*

She hated walking toward a dark house. "I feel uneasy," Everleigh said. "Do you think we know the person that did this? I think of Stevie with the bonfire on the beach just now. He had lighter fluid."

Branford walked her to the kitchen door, leaning down to run his stubby fingers along Mango's head. "Remember, it's common for arsonists to stay close to the people they intend to harm, even if they don't know them well. They use fire for revenge or to cover up evidence of some other crime. Most are depressed or lonely. Or they might be proud of the fire and secretly want attention for starting it. Maybe the guy wears a shirt with a burn in it, or he works for the gas company."

Once, when she and Roland were in the city at a bar called Don's, Stevie had used a match to light a shot of gin on fire. He laughed as the flames shot up from the metal bar top. So had she and Roland, clapping after their initial surprise, as though it were some kind of magic trick. It hadn't been scary—the flaming volcano was the most popular cocktail at the Midtown Tiki Hut—but maybe it was evidence, a shred of proof that Stevie liked playing with fire. The bartender had hollered for Stevie to put it out, and Stevie had poured his beer over the flames.

"Fun factoid." Stevie had grinned, his two bottom teeth overlapping the top ones. "Lager always puts out flaming cocktails."

"There's one more thing." Branford pulled a small velvet pouch out of his trouser pocket, opening the cinch and letting a heart charm drop into his calloused palm. "My guys found this in room twenty-three, in a crack in some surviving floorboards."

It was a locket, missing from its chain, clearly belonging to a woman, a melted setting where a single-carat gemstone must have been. You could make out an engraving, a scripted *A* on the face, although it was tarnished. "Shouldn't it have burned in the fire?"

Branford put his hands on his hips. "Not necessarily. Gold doesn't melt until the fire hits nineteen hundred degrees; ours probably burned around twelve hundred."

"The engraving. It's an *A*." *For Alice?* Although, nearly every woman in the summer colony had a locket with their initial on it.

He nodded. "I will question Alice, of course, but she's hardly the only one with that initial. What we do know is that a woman was inside room twenty-three before the fire was started, and this is too fancy to be the help's."

Everleigh said goodnight to the detective, then opened the cottage door, flicking on the kitchen light. Her cheeks were flaming. Had Roland invited a woman into room twenty-three with him? She didn't think it was Alice because Roland was truly shocked to see her at the party. So if Alice had been in the room, Roland wasn't with her. What had she gone in looking for? Or had she followed someone else inside?

She pulled the photos from the night of the party out of a box, studying the women's necks, looking for someone wearing the locket, particularly Alice. But Everleigh remembered how she'd avoided taking the woman's picture that night, even at a distance. Feeling frustrated with herself, she repacked the pictures.

Everleigh crawled into bed in her cocktail dress, her mind laboring to remember if she'd ever seen Alice wearing a monogrammed locket, but she came up blank. Even if the evidence on Alice was only circumstantial to the detective, it was damning to Everleigh. She knew Alice Anna was involved in this fire somehow, whether she lit the match or not.

FIFTEEN

It was raining when Everleigh woke that Monday for work at the gallery, an increasingly strong pitter-patter on the roof. After unlocking the Juniper Gallery's Dutch door at eight that morning—Starling had said she'd be late—Everleigh walked into the quiet of an unlit studio, sighed, and leaned against the front desk. She watched the cars puttering by, the rhythmic swing of the windshield wipers sometimes in sync, making their way down the charming street. The morning had a tense quality to it, like if she didn't do something to keep herself busy she might pick up the phone and tell her mother she was coming home. Instead, she scribbled on the back of one of the postcards advertising Starling's show, "Dear Mommy, I miss you terribly, but you would love to see me as I am. Happy. Love, Everleigh."

She would mail it at her lunch hour, and as she glanced out at the post office across the street she saw Stevie's cherry-red Buick Skylark pull into view. It idled in front of Weigel's Fish Market. He ran out of the car into the fish store, trying to avoid the torrents of rain.

Everleigh turned toward the sea of frames now flooding the gallery floor. She had to finish several more "packages," as Starling had taken to calling the finished products, but she was distracted by the sight of Stevie. The fish store wasn't even open for customers.

Out of the corner of her eye, she saw him again, a blur of red hair, his signature colorful Hawaiian shirt. He popped his trunk, and one by one he lowered wooden crates into the back. It must be fish packed on ice, she thought, but it was hard to see through the whipping rain. A woman with white-blond hair parted down the middle rushed out of the market and around to the passenger side, hopped into the front seat with the energy of a bunny, and slammed the door. Opal. It had to be her. Who else had hair that glowed like sunflowers when sun hit it?

Dropping the needle on Ella Fitzgerald and Louis Armstrong's "Cheek to Cheek," she went to work almost obsessively in the space, her every sound echoing back at her. Every day she'd watched Starling labor over the order of the photographs, which she said would frame how people experienced the show. Everleigh grabbed a notebook and scribbled down the order that Starling had the artworks positioned, so she could return the frames to their rightful places if need be. But for now, she tried to envision what would draw in patrons. They were framing over fifty images, but only twenty-five pictures would make the show. Everleigh had a hunch they should use Marilyn Monroe's image to lure people inside; everyone was buzzing about the actress's appearances in town. To see her up close, to be able to stare at her face, would allow guests to get to know her more intimately. Perhaps, it would even lure the actress to the show.

Everleigh imagined constructing a temporary wall up front where the Marilyn photo could hang. Then people could walk around the gallery either way. So they needed two photographs with emotional punch to beckon viewers deeper into the show, past Marilyn's famous face. Everleigh hunted for the portrait of the young singer and actress Debbie Reynolds; she looked so confident and yet so desperate to be liked with her perfect brown curls. Everleigh placed her image on the left side of the initial portrait, then tried out Paul Newman on the other side. It was shot on a film set, and he was shirtless and tanned, lying on the sand next to his costar Jean Simmons, both of them on a striped black-and-white beach blanket, looking like they wanted to inhale each other.

After an hour, Everleigh had most of the show laid out, and she stood back to consider her work, already hungry for the tuna salad sandwich she'd packed for lunch. She checked her watch—10:12. Too early to eat.

"What is this?" Starling had come in through the back door, zipping off a utilitarian rain jacket soaked at the seams.

"I meant to finish the frames, but you weren't here, and I've been watching you arrange the show for weeks, so I decided to give it a try." Everleigh rushed to the desk to pick up her notepad, unable to tell from Starling's furrowed brow if she was angry or not. "But I wrote down the order that you had them in before. Just in case."

Starling set her hands on her hips. She had the slender arms of someone much younger than her, and she pursed her lips, taking in the order of the prints. She nodded her head at the first few photographs, her silvery hair shining under the gallery's bright lighting. Everleigh wondered what she was thinking. She nudged her purse out of Starling's way since she'd been so wrapped up in the work that she'd forgotten she'd left it in the middle of the floor.

Starling crossed her arms. She pivoted from the first three photographs to the next three, and back again.

"Yes," she said, drumming her fingers against her elbow. "The emotion to start. Debbie, then the playful Paul Newman. I appreciate the transition to Frank Sinatra and his mobster expression, which warns that things aren't what they seem." Her eyes moved to the next several shots. Everleigh had placed a photo of Pablo Picasso, whose mind seemed to be brimming with ideas, and then Gloria Vanderbilt, who sat upright in a formal chair wearing a brocade skirt suit, her legs crossed at the knee. The next two were of Nat King Cole and Brigitte Bardot. She loved the contrast of Nat King Cole's look of delight, the way his eyes flicked with joy, beside Brigitte Bardot's pouty expression, how she relied on her lips to tell her story.

Everleigh looked from Starling to the photographs, then back again.

"That is not quite right." Starling touched the frame housing Brigitte Bardot, then took a step back. "Nat is okay here. You were spot-on, and I get the contrast. But we may want to consider swapping them."

Everleigh nodded.

"Brigitte is sex appeal. Nat King Cole brings humanity. We need a bridge. But this is wonderful, Everleigh." She made her way through the last few, nodding at Marilyn again, now that she was back to the beginning. "I agree, we need to begin or end with her. This is the beginning of something though." A horn honked outside, a screech of tires as a car missed another, and they both looked up. Everleigh could have crashed, too, at this moment, but she didn't.

"I'm happy you like it," she said.

"A very thoughtful curation," Starling said. "I think you might have unblocked me!"

"Thank you," Everleigh said, turning on her heels triumphantly. She returned to the light table with her X-Acto knife, readying a matte for cutting. She'd get to the questions she had for Starling about the f-stop later. For now she would relish the feeling of being on the good side of someone else's genius.

Starling spent the rest of the morning thumbing through the portraits looking for the best foil to Nat King Cole. Each time she'd interrupt Everleigh, no matter what she was doing, and ask her for an opinion. They'd discuss why the selection worked, then why it didn't, and Everleigh heard herself using words she didn't know could be a part of her everyday vocabulary, calling one pairing "provocative," and another "fraught."

The rain had stopped by the time they finished with lunch, which they ate at their desks, and the sun came blasting out, turning the slick village streets—and the inside of the gallery—reflective and bright. Truly, it was entirely too steamy to be inside. She took a break from cutting to cover the prints with plastic so she could lightly sand the spackle on the walls. Then she'd paint the walls white.

"It feels good to do things yourself, doesn't it?" Starling chuckled, watching Everleigh take a piece of sandpaper out of a small box recently bought at the hardware store.

Everleigh grinned and began sanding the rough patch. "It most certainly does."

Out the window she saw Ernest crossing the street near the fish market. His tan riding pants and tall leather boots were much too hot for the humidity.

Everleigh moved to the side of the room where the fan oscillated, hoping he didn't see her, the moving air cooling the sweat gathering on her silk dress. They'd opened the top panel of the gallery's Dutch door an hour before, hoping to let in a breeze that never came.

Her eyes pressed closed. Everleigh didn't want to hear the *ding* of the door opening, the bell announcing that she'd have to make conversation with a man whose fiancé was trying to stop Roland's hotel.

The door *dinged*. She opened her eyes, waiting a beat before smiling so she would seem surprised.

"Ernest!"

He came straight toward her, like a bullet, kissing both her cheeks, his ruddy complexion and charm exceedingly British. "Everleigh, lovely to see you. Alice told me you were working here."

"Apparently she told everyone."

Ernest grinned. "I'm surprised you're not at the Maidstone, lunching with Roland."

"Oh?" She couldn't hide her surprise. Roland told Everleigh that he was going to be at the hotel the entire day. "He was at the Maidstone?"

"With the lovely Opal Vandemeer," Ernest said, and as a way to reassure her, "and many others, of course." Everleigh steeled herself. Not only had he lied about his whereabouts, but he was with Opal?

"Were you riding this morning?" Everleigh asked, a safe question since she already knew the answer. Ernest spent most of his days in the barn, that's what Alice said, but they lived nearby, so it wasn't unusual for him to be in town. Still, she didn't like that he was here. He backed off from the kiss, taking in the photographs propped up against the walls, and she was grateful that Starling was in the back.

He nodded, running his wide fingers through his big head of mussed hair. "A few girls had lessons. It's bloody awful out there. The heat could kill a horse."

Kill. That he even used the word sent a tingle up the back of her neck. She imagined him at the hotel that night, the click of his lighter, a blaze shooting up. Had he been trying to kill Roland? "I hardly think that. Where is Alice off to?"

She hoped asking after her friend would send him a message: Why are you here?

"Alice is back in the city for a couple of days, but I have some riders with competitions coming up."

"Ah, a lone bachelor." It was a silly joke since they both knew he had a housekeeper picking up after him. Starling made a noise in the back, dropping a cardboard box, but it was enough of a hiccup to put her at ease, reclaim her need to return to work. "Well, I best be getting back to—"

"Yes, of course," he said. "But Everleigh, there is something I need to tell you. Something important."

He leaned against the table, edging nearer to her; broad-chested and strong, he had the body of a lifelong equestrian.

Starling emerged. "Lee, is this a friend of yours?"

Ernest politely reached to shake Starling's hand, saying he was a fan of her work and that they had friends in common. He knew patrons who had been supporting Starling, who lived in London where his family was, and Starling believed she'd once met Ernest's mother at an afternoon tea. For a few minutes, they stood over a picture of someone Everleigh didn't recognize, a lithe young woman with two large front teeth. A duchess, apparently. They said their goodbyes, but before leaving, Ernest asked Everleigh to walk him outside for a moment.

Ernest, who was much taller than her, bent forward slightly so he could talk quietly.

"Everleigh, you should know that the police investigator, I'm forgetting his name, but the short one, a bit portly in the middle . . . he's been asking questions about you. Has he come to see you yet?"

"Yes, about the hotel, of course." She pressed her lips together. "But questions about me?" Clearly, he had interviewed Alice, too, and it had spooked Ernest. Perhaps, the two of them were hiding something, and this was his way of poking around for information. She thought of the fight she'd overheard between Opal and Alice at the bonfire; her instincts told her it had something to do with the investigation. But what?

"Well, you know he's looking into the hotel fire, but he appears to be investigating you. For the arson. He's asked Alice and me all sorts of questions, and—"

The sidewalk no longer seemed flat. It appeared wavy, like it was undulating underneath her. The cars, the buildings, the American flags hanging from the shopfronts moved up and down, too. "Me? He thinks I started the fire?"

Ernest looked behind her, and Everleigh turned to find Starling passing by the window, with sandpaper in hand.

"I don't know, Everleigh," he said, pressing his hands on her shoulders, only for a moment. "But I wanted to give you warning. He made it sound as though he was going to question Roland, too. Has he talked to you about additional suspects? I can't imagine you're the best he has, and yet, you were the only one he seemed interested in."

Ernest had taken off his horse-riding jacket and draped it over one arm, and his white shirt was unbuttoned and open, a patch of chest hair curling out of the neckline. She didn't trust Ernest. He had been at the fire that night, lingering, and he'd made the threat about Roland. Yes, he was being a good citizen in warning her, but he also seemed like he was trying to scare her. There wasn't any chance she was the only suspect in the fire, even she knew that.

Still, she was unable to form words straightaway, panicked at the prospect that he was telling the truth. "Thank you," she said, finally. "Thank you for telling me." After the bonfire, when the detective dropped her home, she'd asked Branford if the police would arrest someone like Alice's parents if they were responsible, even peripherally, since they were so powerful. Everleigh had wondered if the crime would be pinned to someone else. Was that someone *her*? Was Alice Anna leading the detective straight to Everleigh?

Ernest cupped his palm over her cheek. "Be careful, Everleigh. Truly. You don't want to tangle in the system."

"I'll be okay." She took a step away, not liking the clamminess of his touch. He seemed sincere, but she doubted his intentions were true. She would ask him about the locket. She would press him right back for information. "Ernest, wait, does Alice own a—"

That's when she saw it: a flaw in the waistline of his shirt. At the very bottom, where the seam was normally tucked in, the shirt had pulled loose. There was a circle no larger in diameter than a cigarette tip, the fibers singed yellow like a halo around the sun. Once she spied the burn mark, she couldn't stop looking at it. There it was, a singe, calling out to her like a radio advertisement.

"Does she own a what?" He kissed her cheeks to say goodbye.

There were two reasons why Ernest may have come today. First, in an attempt to understand how much the detective knew about the arson, he'd try to shock Everleigh into revealing information he'd given her. Or, he was truly delivering a warning. But she kept coming back to the burn mark. The detective said to keep her eye out for clues that someone set fires—he'd even mentioned that an arsonist may wear clothes with a singe—and now Everleigh couldn't take her eyes off the one on Ernest's shirt. "Oh, nothing. Forget it."

As she stepped into the gallery, Everleigh fell backward into the rolling chair by the light table. She was still dizzy, but she felt better now that Starling was in the same room with her. She was grateful she hadn't asked about the engraved locket, thinking it would have revealed too much.

"Is everything okay?" Starling asked.

Everleigh kept her eye on Ernest across the street as he got into his car. "Someone led the detective to believe I started the fire." She thought of the burn mark on his shirt. "But it just may have been him."

SIXTEEN

❦

When they broke for lunch the following day, after spending the morning tweaking the order of the prints in the show once more, Everleigh pulled a brown bag out from under her desk. She pranced into the back room, singing out to Starling that she had a surprise for her. "I think I can lay claim to the best luncheon recipe ever," Everleigh called out. "The farmer near the cottage taught me this."

Starling poked her head around the doorway and found Everleigh slicing plump beefsteak tomatoes on a table, placing them on fresh-baked bread she'd picked up at the bakery. "Here," Everleigh said, handing her boss a butter knife. "Smother it with mayo, and I'll sprinkle on the salt and pepper, but don't slice them in half." Starling helped her plate the sandwiches, and together they carried them out back, beyond the trash cans, to a patch of sunny grass behind the parking lot.

"This is my version of the green juice." Everleigh smiled, picking up her sandwich with two hands. "You will never taste anything better."

Red juice squirted out the sides as she bit into the tomato sandwich, and her eyes crinkled as she watched Starling do the same. It was truly her new favorite thing to eat; the salty coat of the mayo meeting the sweetness of the fruit, the crunch of the bread against the juicy ripe tomato slices.

"Wow." Starling's eyes widened. "I mean, wow. Everleigh!"

"I told you! It's summer in a sandwich." Everleigh grinned joyfully, tucking the slippery contents back into her bread. "You don't need to know how to cook a single other thing."

"We need to photograph this," Starling said, closing her eyes. "These tomatoes. I need to remember."

They broke into laughter, like old girlfriends, and she wondered if Whitney had ever experienced the pleasure of a simple tomato sandwich. She wished she could drop one at her house, sharing the satisfaction she was feeling with her newest friend with her oldest one.

Truly, Everleigh wished Whitney would come to the gallery and talk to her. Because she really needed to talk. So much was changing in her life, and it felt strange that Whitney didn't know. She popped the last bite of her lunch into her mouth, Starling making plain it was time to return to work. *Her work, her job, her life.* Everleigh grinned once more.

That night, though, her mood plummeted as soon as she stepped into the cottage. Roland sat her down to say that he had called her father to apologize and try to get her trust back, but his call had the opposite effect. Her father wanted details of Everleigh's job—and her mental state. "Which apparently is the real reason he canceled your trust. Because he's worried you're going cuckoo."

"Roland, stop," she'd said.

"You need to quit," he told her.

Everleigh felt silly that she hadn't seen this coming, how Roland would turn on her; she'd been so resentful of his focus on the hotel, the affair she was convinced he was having with Opal, and his nights out with Stevie that she was blind to the fact that he was developing his own resentments, too. He was nothing but a spoiled child. He'd lured her out here, convinced her parents to let her stay, and now that things weren't going his way, he'd tattled on her.

"Oh, Rolly. I'm having a summer fling," she'd tried to make light of it, the Yankees game on the radio. "It's my last chance to do a little something before we settle down and have our own family. Can't this be my little dalliance?"

Roland turned up the radio.

The cottage felt smaller then, her anger melting into a puddle of tears, and Roland listened impatiently as she launched into anxieties having nothing to do with her work at the gallery: how she was being investigated for arson, and how she hated that Roland was always with Opal.

"No one actually thinks you burned down the hotel," he snapped. "There is no arson. I told you this already."

"But they found an accelerant!"

Roland shook his head like it was funny. "What is so damning about that? We had varnish in every supply closet. You realize that if it's arson, I may not ever see a dime of the insurance money. You know that, right?"

"And what about the locket? How do I know you weren't with someone that night? With Opal?"

"Oh, pet. You're connecting all the wrong dots. I'm not interested in Opal. Something terrible has happened to us, but it doesn't mean that a lot of other terrible things are happening, too. That locket could belong to anyone."

He'd kissed her across the kitchen table, softening his tone. "Listen, I know I've been enjoying my cocktails and my nights out, but your work is becoming a problem, too. It's driving us apart."

That night, they shared a bed. Everleigh spent the wee hours tossing and turning, weighing whether she should quit the following morning. She woke up frustrated and uncertain, hoping to talk to Roland once more, but found herself in an empty bed. An empty cottage. She made coffee and fetched the newspaper from the driveway, letting the morning sun warm her. As she dipped her milk toast at the kitchen table and blindly flipped through the newspaper, she wondered what she'd say to Starling if she left her job at Roland's request. Suddenly she stumbled on a large photograph of Roland in the Cholly Knickerbocker column on page three.

"With plans to rebuild the troubled Southampton lodging by the spring, Roland Whittaker, one of the heirs to the automobile fortune, says, 'this hotel will be even more stunning than the first', and will also offer stays at a sister hotel, The Opal Beach Hotel, in East Hampton."

The Opal Beach Hotel? Everleigh threw the newspaper across the room like she'd discovered a cockroach in the folds. Clearly, Roland didn't have plans to tell her that he was partnering with Opal Vandemeer on a second hotel. How cozy would that bring the two of them now?

She dumped her breakfast in the trash, seething. To think she'd even considered quitting her job last night. Whether or not Everleigh went to the gallery was her choice to make; she wouldn't let Roland try to stop her again. Her job wasn't a problem between them. It was only that Roland worried the gallery would snatch her away from him, like one of those UFOs you saw on television coming down to earth and forcing someone to another dimension. Well, too bad. He would have to deal with his insecurities. She was certainly working on hers.

Everleigh was right on time for work, and she and Starling were busy straightaway, working on the show at opposite ends of the gallery. Everleigh was perfectly content when Starling gave her the mindless task of shining the glass of the portraits they'd selected for the viewing. She would have done anything to stay with her. She would have worked weekends if Starling had asked. The gallery had come to feel like a conch shell in a turbulent ocean, and she wanted to disappear inside its walls entirely.

About an hour later, after Starling puttered about lost in thought, she yelled, "Everleigh, look, I got it." The artist had let her hair loose around her narrow shoulders, and even with her severe black glasses, she looked more feminine than usual in her black pencil skirt, a black tank tucked in, a sheer red scarf tied about her neck. She held up a portrait of Lucille Ball.

"This is who should be next to Nat King Cole. Think about it: her funny face, those lips sucked in like a fish—she really offsets him, even if he's happy, too." Her slate-blue eyes sparkled. "What do you think?"

Everleigh dropped the cleaning supplies and went to stand beside her. "Yes, it's almost like she's shaking her head in the picture, like she's making clear she doesn't agree with how Negroes are treated, which gives weight to the marches. Then Nat is playing to the camera, daring you not to take him seriously. Oh, it's perfect."

Starling exhaled, grinning. "Yes, yes." She went into the back and returned with two plastic tumblers of orange juice. "Let's celebrate with a Mimosa."

They toasted, "The Show!" which was opening in two weeks, and admired their work, when the phone rang out like an alarm. Starling rushed over to the desk to answer it, and Everleigh felt a rush staring at the order of the prints. They were nearly finished.

"You know, Sheldon, I cannot take your picture," Starling said. "But I know another wonderful photographer."

A voice on the other end of the phone sounded squiggly and deep, but Everleigh couldn't make out what he was saying. A large garbage truck stopped outside, and with the Dutch door open, the idling noise of the engine kept her from hearing Starling talk. When the rumble of the garbage truck quieted, Everleigh heard her name.

"Yes, exactly, Everleigh Farrows. Friday at eight a.m. Of course, yes, the new raceway. Do you want action shots as well?"

Everleigh shot her gaze at Starling, who scribbled numbered points on the legal pad she kept next to the phone. She looked up at Everleigh, and her eyes crinkled, beckoning her over with her hand. Beside her, she could see that Starling had written "Bridgehampton raceway" and "action + sweet + danger." She'd underlined it three times.

"*Mmmhmm.* Yes, Sheldon. I'll have her file the film with you the following day. Okay, thank you." Starling hung up the phone, a mischievous smile creeping into her cheeks. "You've got your first job."

Everleigh's chest flushed. "Taking pictures?"

Starling was quite pleased with herself, like she'd gotten her a hot date. "That was the photo editor at the *East Hampton Star.* They need someone to take a picture of some race car driver, and I suggested you." She tapped Everleigh's arm with her pencil.

"But Starling, I—"

"I simply told Sheldon you were my talented assistant, someone studying under me, which is the truth, and now you've got your first assignment. Paid, I might add."

The last time Everleigh shot a picture on assignment was for the campus newspaper. This was bigger. "But I can't do what you do."

"Oh, darling. They don't want anything like what I do here," Starling gulped back her Mimosa. "Newspapers keep it simple. Besides I can't afford to offend old Sheldon at the *Star* since we need a good review in his arts pages. He was happy to try you out."

Everleigh's initial shock turned to panic. Not only did her photograph need to succeed to make it into the paper, but it needed to be good so she didn't make a fool of Starling for recommending her. "Okay, so what kind of picture do they want?"

Starling sat in her desk chair, crossing her legs at the knee. "For one, you have to get that deer-in-the-headlights look off your face. Every photographer starts somewhere. And if your pictures stink, then you'll try again."

Everleigh ripped out the page with Starling's notes. "But I have questions that I've been meaning to ask you. Like the f-stop. How do I—"

"The f-stop is your friend. Let in more light if it's dark. Less light if it's bright."

Starling went gliding into the back room, returning with her camera equipment slung over one shoulder. She placed it down on the desk. "Let's go over it. You ready?"

Everleigh had had an awful night with Roland, and now she was standing in the gallery having an unforgettable afternoon with Starling. She could have cried.

Starling unpacked her camera. "So a wide aperture is going to isolate the person from the background. I suspect that's what you'll want if he's driving in the car. You want him in focus but the background to blur." She unzipped a large black bag with soft foam pockets, and she pulled out a few telephoto lenses, demonstrating how to get what you wanted from each one. "These will help with clarity, too."

"How do you get them to look at you through the lens like that?" She fiddled with one of Starling's lenses. Most people grew stiff when you raised a camera. She'd need to put the race car driver at ease. "I mean, the f-stop, aperture, these are technicalities, right? But how do you get them to give you something?"

Starling seemed to be considering this. "Some of this is second nature to me. Let me think."

"It's like you get them to forget about the camera."

Starling tapped her unpainted fingernails against the desk. "Well, I do have coffee with them first. Or tea. Or a cocktail. Whatever they like. But I sit with whoever I'm shooting for as long as I can get them, and we talk. Some photographers like to show up on assignment and see a person only as the camera sees them, but every subject is quite needy, actually."

Everleigh pointed to the portraits, the raw emotion emerging from each face. "But you're able to capture their essence."

She adjusted her glasses. "I'm just curious is all. I want to know people. Strangers interest me, and when I take their photograph, I make them laugh, and they make me laugh, or they tell me a sad story, and I listen, or I tell them a sad story, and they listen, and I snap the entire time, and by the time we're done, something has been revealed. Be it anger or love, sadness or beauty. Something always emerges in the prints. Sometimes I know which picture is the one before I even develop it; sometimes there are surprises."

Everleigh feigned taking a photograph of Starling; there wasn't any film in the camera. "You just have to wait for it."

"That's right. You just have to wait for it."

Everleigh put down the camera. The words hung in the air for a bit, Everleigh trying to figure out what that meant for her photo shoot with the race car driver. How patient would he be if she took all morning? There was a possibility he'd only give her an hour, that she'd have to rush through her photographs and hope for something interesting.

Starling took her camera from Everleigh's hands, lowering the lens to waist height, the shutter clicking a few times. "But shooting from the hip helps, too."

Everleigh fidgeted, then she broke into a nervous smile. "What are you doing?"

Starling clicked the shutter once more. "Shooting from the hip. It's a little trade secret. When the subject thinks the portrait session is over, when they least expect it, lower your camera to your hip. Chat with them, make them think you're no longer taking their picture, but point the camera up so it's angled at their face and click. Some of my best shots come from shooting at the hip. Sometimes the subject isn't even in the frame, but sometimes"—Starling pointed to the framed candid of Angela Barrett, the young actress whose picture Everleigh had stared at on her first day—"sometimes you get lucky."

Everleigh gaped at the photo with newfound appreciation.

"You don't need the other lenses, but you'll want this one. Practice on it for the next few days. But don't goddamn break it. It cost me three hundred bucks."

Everleigh cradled it like a newborn. "I'll guard it with my life."

Starling began packing the equipment into her black bag. "Okay, now let's get back to work. I need your head back in my show."

Starling spent the rest of the afternoon typing out her artist's statement on a typewriter; her biography would appear on one side, a synopsis of her work on the other. It wasn't going well.

"No one ever said I was a writer," she huffed, lolling her head backward, straining her neck almost as a form of self-punishment. There was the crumple of paper, then another, and when Everleigh turned around, she saw Starling aiming them into the trash, missing both times. She stood, pressing the seam of her skirt straight. "I need a break. Will you be sure to paint the walls today?"

Everleigh agreed, watching Starling rush off down the sidewalk toward her car. She appreciated the quiet of the gallery after that; she didn't switch on the turntable, instead letting the silence tease out her thoughts. As she painted the walls, she considered how using her hands was particularly satisfying. She thought of all the things she'd never attempted doing, like twisting a wrench on a sink pipe when it leaked or using a saw to cut a piece of wood or pumping air into a bike tire. She was accustomed to asking men to do such things, but her hands were capable, too.

In the bathroom sink when she was finished, she washed with turpentine. She picked at the paint specks on her fingers, wondering about the words Starling had left half-finished in the typewriter. It seemed difficult to summarize your life. She considered how she'd write her own personal summary: *Everleigh Farrows grew up on the Upper East Side of Manhattan, the daughter of Ellie and Albie Farrows.*

What else could she say? *She attended the Spence School before graduating with a degree in English from Barnard. She's carried much of her mother's emotional baggage her entire life, and she fights often with her father about what she should be doing now that she's graduated. She died of boredom. She was twenty-four.*

A sigh came out louder than she expected. She dried her hands on the cloth towel hanging from the rack in the bathroom. Her life was better than that, she knew, yet she labored to think about what she would want someone to write about her. She stared out the small square window in the bathroom, the speckled glass overlooking a dumpster.

Everleigh Farrows of Manhattan spent her youth roaming the Metropolitan Museum of Art and begging friends to let her take photographs of them. She was particularly proud of a series she took of her friend Whitney Barrington, who posed in her prom dress in the lobby of the Waldorf Astoria, one photograph of which won an honorable mention—under a pseudonym—at the New York Public Library's Photography of Tomorrow contest. When she was twenty-four, Miss Farrows began working with famed photographer Starling Meade, who taught her the art of taking pictures, and now she—

Through the bathroom window, she heard a man walk behind the dumpster outside, startling her. She emerged from the bathroom into the afternoon sunlight of the gallery. *And now she* . . . what? And now she married her fiancé and lived happily ever after? She was beginning to have her doubts.

It was a few minutes after six, so Everleigh picked up her purse from Starling's desk, leaning over to see what the woman had written so far. *Starling Meade isn't sure if her show will be a flop, but she hopes for the best* . . . . The rest of the page was blank.

Beside the typewriter, there were faded newspaper clippings, stories the *New York Times* had done about Starling's rising stardom, another from the Talk of the Town column in the *New Yorker*, where one of the editors recounted an amusing lunch with her. There was a very old glossy magazine on the desk, too—*Photography World Today*—open to a short profile, a picture of Starling when she was younger, as blond as Opal, with the inviting kind of face that photographers wanted to take pictures of. It was ironic, Everleigh thought, that she'd become one herself.

Starling Meade, 43, learned photography from her father when photography meant standing under a black curtain and squeezing a trigger.

"Even before he let me hold a camera, I'd cut a hole in paper squares and pretend to take photographs of squirrels in my back-yard." Mrs. Meade laughs, sitting in the living room of her Virginia home, with her eight-year-old daughter, Sally, playing at her feet; the child's nickname is Squirrel.

Mrs. Meade got her break when her husband was called to fight in World War II, and her widowed father, who agreed to care for her daughter, encouraged Mrs. Meade to earn money by shooting for the Richmond Times-Dispatch. *Her images, known for their human quality, were picked up by the Associated Press, and by the time her husband returned from France, paralyzed from the waist down, she was shooting for* Vogue *and* Life *magazine. She's made her mark capturing the vulnerabilities of the rich and famous, and for seeing within them something they're often unable to see themselves.*

Everleigh dropped the magazine. A paralyzed husband. A young child left behind so her mother could shoot photographs of the rich and famous? Beyond the glossy photographs and tidbits she'd picked up about the photographer spanning the last ten years, Everleigh hadn't really considered Starling's personal life—where she had come from, how that impacted how she shot and what she saw when she looked through the lens of the camera. At that moment, she considered, for perhaps the first time, what it meant for a woman to be an artist. Not a woman who held any old job, but a woman whose desire was to create something original in a room of one's own. A woman who had something to impart to the world, who felt like making something was as imperative as breathing. Was it possible to be a loving mother and an artistic photographer? Or did you have to choose?

Because Starling had most certainly made her choice, and Everleigh wanted to know: Had it ripped her heart in two? Her mind in two?

The thinking brain was mysterious because it could slip into a deep study of one topic and another and another. But juggling emotional intelligence with creative wit was more difficult. Even Everleigh knew that when she lived in her creative imagination, say, coming up with plans for photo compositions, there was less of her for everyone else. Her mind became a locked room to which only she had the key, making her distant from everyone around her as she made adjustments to her photographic visions. In fact, she could grow so immersed in her ideas that household tasks—and, yes, people she loved—could feel secondary to getting her ideas on film. It was partly why she adored photography: it took her out of her everyday life. Less meaningful commitments receded to whispers, and appointments became things to be canceled.

Creation could feel like an obsession. And if you were a mother, a wife, your family must always be tugging you out of your head. Perhaps it's why Starling had left her family altogether. There wasn't enough space in her brain to put her ideas on paper, print them, *and* be fully there for her husband. In order to be the artist she wanted to be, she had to leave.

Maybe this was what her fight with Roland was really about. What he was saying to Everleigh was: If you choose the creative life, then you're not choosing me. You don't have room for me. Did that mean that someday, at some point, if Everleigh pursued her love of photography, she would also suffer heartbreak, and that she, too, would need to make the same impossible choice?

SEVENTEEN

※

The Bridgehampton Race Circuit wasn't a predictable circular track where cars orbited around a visible grassy middle, even if it did have a couple of shiny grandstands, a shingled announcer's podium and three parking lots for spectators. Instead, the raceway snaked through recently graded sand dunes and bulldozed forest, the spit of land elevated just enough to offer views of the majestic Peconic Bay stretching to Shelter Island and beyond. Thanks to its hilly topography, "the Bridge," as the track was nicknamed, would become famous for two hairpin curves that one world-class auto racer called the most difficult in car racing. Everleigh was surprised to learn that the races were a must-see event every summer in the Hamptons that started with drivers racing through the streets of the small villages before spinning off into the roads lining the potato fields on Ocean Road for the finish. A few years before, when one of the speedsters flipped and killed a spectator, the town insisted on a formal raceway, which is where Everleigh was now.

She parked in the pebbly lot and walked over a pedestrian bridge to an area labeled "the paddock," where several race cars were parked. A checkered flag rippled in the light breeze.

The final days of July had brought the emergence of cicadas after seventeen years underground, their singing so loud it was hard to sleep, the nights so warm now she went to bed in her underwear, her thighs sticking together with sweat. Everleigh had taken a cool shower that morning to wash off the heat, but already, the humidity was overbearing in her pleated skirt and T-strap sandals. Certainly not ideal weather for a photo shoot, especially one on hot, tarry pavement. Was it possible for film to melt?

With her camera hanging from her neck, Starling's telephoto lens in position, she carried a brown paper parcel holding a thermos of Sanka, two mugs, a second thermos with cream, and a small Mason jar of sugar. Butterflies fluttered in her stomach.

There was a man by a shiny yellow two-seater, she could see him now as she walked the row of parked cars, the number ninety-nine painted on his hood. He had a tan linen cap pulled low on his forehead, and he was tinkering with the engine. Starling hadn't given her the name of the gentleman she was supposed to photograph, and it was awkward now, showing up without knowing who to ask for. With her footsteps edging closer to a shuttered first-aid station and pit stop, the man walked around the side of the car. She noted his gray Converse All Stars high-tops.

"Curtis?" she managed, a ripple of surprise traveling through her.

His face shined with curiosity, his dark brown eyes studying the sight of her. "What are you doing here? I never told you that I raced. . . ." Curtis drew nearer, his focus settling on her camera. She took a step backward.

Everleigh shielded her eyes from the sun, trying to figure out why he was greeting her at the racetrack at eight in the morning—didn't he have patients? Then she remembered Starling, the photo shoot, that this was her first job.

Rising up on tiptoe, Everleigh tried to peek over his broad shoulders, where his tan racing jumpsuit zipped up the middle, a white patch labeling him "Curt," but she found only a stretch of scrub grass, a starting line and roadway that snaked off toward a glimmering blue bay, no other person in sight. "It's just . . . I'm supposed to be taking pictures of a race car driver, and I don't see him."

Curtis pulled off his cap, his eyes crinkling with a smile. "You're the photographer?"

He certainly looked the part of race car enthusiast, a black racing stripe running the length of his sleeves, but he couldn't be the auto racer she was seeking. "Yes, we were supposed to meet here, a shoot for the *East Hampton Star.*"

Curtis threw back his head to the sky and laughed with a white-toothed grin. "Do I seem like someone too afraid to race cars?"

His amusement was palpable, and yet she didn't laugh. She still hadn't adjusted to the idea that she was here to take pictures of him. "Maybe. You care for the sick and wounded; why would you risk maiming yourself?" Curtis Brightwell—*he* was the race car driver she was sent to photograph?

"I'd like to say this was my idea." His cheeks were rosy with heat. "But the *East Hampton Star* told me to be here at eight this morning for a photo shoot."

Her brain labored to catch up to what she was seeing: the handsome gentleman, the doctor, was here; he was her first subject. It was more entertaining than a twist in the soaps. Tongue-tied and unable to formulate a coherent thought, Everleigh held up the brown bag. "Well, I brought coffee." She looked at his car, the glimmer of the polished hubcaps, setting the coffee down on a nearby picnic table.

On a cloth napkin, she arranged the cups, creamer, and sugar, and poured the coffee. She handed it to him, his face crumpling into laughter.

"What is it?" she said, stirring her own coffee with the silver spoon she'd brought.

"It's just . . . can I fetch you an ice water instead?"

Her laughter loosened the anxiety that had been building inside her. "It does feel like we're standing on the surface of the sun, doesn't it?"

He placed the steaming cup on the table. "There's hardly any tree cover here. It can be brutal."

"Water it is then," she said.

"Water it is. I'll get my canteen. But let's use these dainty teacups you brought. The set-up is so decadent. Like high tea at the Plaza." She winced as he brushed past her, his arm touching her briefly, sending her heart to her throat.

She cursed herself for not bringing paper cups. "Don't say that, or I'll pack up."

"Why? It's so darn pretty." Curtis walked over to the race car, his build taller than what she imagined a race car driver should be.

"I'm not trying to be pretty." She dumped the coffee out of the thermos into the dirt. "I was simply trying to break the ice."

He grinned, next to her again. "And we certainly could use some ice."

One, two, three. Deep breath. She'd started the morning nervous about taking these photographs; now she was nervous about spending the morning with this man. She would find him in the viewfinder of her camera and follow the height of his cheekbones, the symmetry of his features, his sturdy silhouette. It felt much too intimate to do with a man she knew—a stranger would have been better—and she cursed the newspaper's photo editor for not assigning her a woman to photograph.

"To you taking my picture," he said, after pouring them ice water. His hair was the color of a raven's wing.

"To you, for making it easy on me."

"What makes you think I'll be easy on you?" His smile was full of mischief.

She refused to let down her guard today, determined to present the way she thought Starling would: focused on the shot, not the subject. Everleigh dabbed her neck with her handkerchief. "Because you want a good picture in the paper, don't you?"

It was her favorite hankie, purchased at the art museum one Sunday when she visited with her mother. What her mother would think of her sitting alone with this man right now! Last night, she'd called home, unable to go another day without talking to her, but Nanny had answered, saying that Mommy was asleep. Still, she'd stayed on the phone with Nanny for a half hour, catching her up on the gallery, what Starling was like, how she and Whitney hadn't spoken since their fight at the bonfire. *Call Whitney*, she'd said. *You are misunderstanding each other—it happens with friends.* Then she'd delivered the reassurance she needed about her mother, that Mommy had been lunching with friends. She was angry with Everleigh, of course, but she and her father were packing for a long weekend in the Adirondacks that Friday. They both knew what that meant: Mommy was healthy.

While sitting at the picnic table, Everleigh took a couple of candid shots of Curtis to warm up. He didn't shirk from her or go stiff; he seemed to jump into the frame, relaxed and carefree. She focused the lens on his face, knowing that when the film was developed, the trees would be a blur of green behind him. "I'm just checking the light exposure," she said, which wasn't entirely true. She kept staring at the chisel of his cheekbones in the viewfinder, how when he grinned, his smile was bold and confident but also mysterious, like his lips alone were trying to tell her a secret.

There was nothing but the sound of birds around them, the Peconic Bay so still in the distance, it looked like glass. He motioned toward the road where some of the sand had blown onto the track. "Can I take you for a ride in a really fast car?"

"Is it *your* really fast car?" She wished he would stop flirting, because it was too hard not to flirt back, and she didn't want to get side-tracked. She lowered the camera.

His lip curled up. "It is."

"But first, you must tell me why the *Star* is running a story about you."

Apparently, a reporter was writing a feature on the upcoming grand opening of the track, and Curtis had been instrumental in developing the three-mile loop. Some people also believed, although he said this part quietly and quickly, like he didn't want her to hear at all, that he was favored to win the Bridgehampton Sports Car Races in August.

She imagined a photograph of him then: Curtis in the front seat of his yellow sports car, his stethoscope around his neck, one hand on the three-spoke steering column, the other on the beechwood knob of the gearshift. "Did you ever race in the streets like the other drivers?"

"Twice, but I didn't qualify in the local race a few years back, and maybe luckily so, with that awful crash. I lost a friend that day." He leaned up against the passenger window. "I'm dedicating my race to him, Mr. Jimmy Matthews—he brought me into the raceway when I was a teenager, much to my mother's dismay."

"Your old friend will be watching you," she said. "He's probably watching right now."

Everleigh steered her mind back to the shoot. Should she use the open window of the passenger seat to frame him, or should she sit beside him? She'd try both. "Do you have a stethoscope with you?" she asked, and he nodded. She followed him over to the car that she'd seen him driving in town, a gray traditional four-door sedan. He popped open his medical bag, the sun catching the silver of the stethoscope as he looped it around his neck.

"Perfect," she said. "Well, just, let me . . ." She centered the stethoscope on his chest, trying to ignore that her pulse was thumping while grazing the smooth front of his racing overalls with her fingers. She turned down her glance, blushing, noting the book on his passenger seat, a frayed copy of *Peyton Place*. It was a curious choice for a man: did men really want to learn about the inner workings of women in small-town New England?

"Do you like it?" she said. It had been one of her favorite books of last year. "*Peyton Place?*"

He recited one of the book's famous quotes. "'There can be neither beauty, nor trust, nor security between a man and a woman if there is not truth.'" Then he said, "Mom has me reading it to her. But, yes, it's quite good. Do you know the movie is coming out in December?"

"Lana Turner will star. I heard that," she said. He'd actually repeated her favorite line in the novel. The infamous sentence that was inspiring women across the country to question their marriages altogether. She'd seen it with her own parents: an emotional divide that kept them from truly knowing one another's inner emotions. But it was funny that Curtis was reading it to his mother; was she not learned? Besides, it would have embarrassed Everleigh to recite some of those sentences aloud to her parents. "Do me a favor? Can you go sit in your car?"

"Sure, but . . ." Curtis put his back against the car, folding his arms against his chest. "My mother likes to say there are no such thing as coincidences, that the universe lobs signs at you, to guide you, like the stars. But I'm a man of science, and to me, that's always sounded like the talk of mystics. But right now, I have to wonder if she's right."

"You mean, you think I was destined to stand here and take your picture?" She laughed, even if she blushed while pretending to fiddle with her camera. "That's my one life purpose?"

"Well, when you put it like that, I sound quite arrogant." He grinned. An energy radiated from him, small particles bouncing off his edges, igniting the side of her body standing inches from his. His hands pushed into his pockets. "I only meant that it's a rather nice coincidence meeting up with you like this."

"Yes, it is. But you know, I'm not sure I believe in fate. I mean, one could argue that we live in a small town, and we're always meeting up with strangers on repeat."

"Well, true, but I'd much rather find you in my path than old Archie Jones, who I've met in the aisle of the hardware store twice this week."

She laughed quickly while she lifted her camera to her eye, relieved to get back to work. "Can you get in the car now?"

He ran his palm over his shiny slick of hair, parted at the center and falling forward ever so slightly. "Don't make me put on my lab coat. This is my chance to be the cool cat."

"Because you aren't always the cool cat?" Everleigh smiled, removing the flashbulb on her camera; it was too bright to require it. Then she asked Curtis to position the car on the raceway, drive by her slowly, and turn toward her as he passed. They tried a few times. But she couldn't get the right angle in her frame, and she feared he wouldn't look the way she intended: an air of authority providing a counterpoint to the singular focus of a race car driver.

"How about that ride?" she said, positioning her camera at her hip, her finger on the trigger as she settled into the black leather bucket seat.

Curtis positioned a pair of driving goggles over his eyes. "Ready?" he said, his foot revving the engine.

He tossed her a pair of goggles to put on, too, but she held them in her lap. She needed to see him clearly, and a half second after she nodded, he hit the gas, the car gaining speed in a way she'd never felt any car move. Propelling down the pavement like an airplane, she watched as the speedometer climbed upward of forty, then fifty, the sand dunes becoming a flash of color. The road ducked into the trees, and she glanced at him, thinking it interesting that even at this speed, he was at ease with himself. He knew exactly where he was going. With her eye in the viewfinder, she began to snap, trying to capture his adrenaline in the tension of his shoulders, how he gripped the steering wheel, his face turning up with glee, even if his goggles covered him like a mask.

She clicked away, having to reload her film while she slid about in the seat, gripping the leather with her fingernails, until they were going so fast that her cheeks felt like they were pinned to her face. Ninety, one hundred. She rested her camera in her lap, afraid it might fly out the window. The track twisted sharply around a bend. "The hairpin," he yelled to her, and she wondered if they'd make it around. But then they were shooting along a linear part of the track, following a gradual s-curve and jumping an incline, getting at least six inches of daylight under all four wheels.

Everleigh glanced at Curtis, and he hollered over the roar of the wind. "You okay?"

She nodded, unable to say that she loved driving fast in cars, she always had—it was a fast car that had brought her out to Southampton only weeks before—and this felt like they were flying. One hundred ten. One hundred twenty. *Faster*, she thought. If they went fast enough, the outside world would blur, and she could forget about Roland and the Opal Beach Hotel and the fire and her parents and her lost inheritance. In the car, with the windows down, and her dark hair flying about her temples and into her mouth and tickling the pearls in her ears, all she could think about was right now. How she was free. How none of that awful stuff mattered as the air rushed her face, the sun blinding her eyes, her insides beating with one thousand drums, as she rocketed around a racetrack with a local doctor. On assignment!

Curtis swerved to avoid a surprised squirrel, and she thought of James Dean, that awful car wreck he'd been in two summers before, and how lucky some people were, and how unlucky others were, and how she needed to stop forcing herself to feel eternally grateful for a life that, perhaps, she didn't want. So what if she was lucky on paper? A privileged upbringing, a fancy private school education, an impressive address. What did any of that mean if she wasn't happy? This was making her happy. This moment in this car with this man with this camera around her neck—this was filling her up inside.

Curtis turned off the track onto a dirt road, slowing the car until the dense tree cover opened up to the sky, a crescent of sand stretching along the Peconic Bay, a row of plastic loungers positioned on the beach. Everleigh picked up her camera once more, finding Curtis's profile in her frame, and he looked at her, knowing she would snap, even if he was still catching his breath. A million questions popped into her head. and she suddenly wanted to know everything about him. Silly things like why he painted his car bright yellow, and probing things, too, like where he learned to look at a woman the way he was looking at her now.

"How did you get into racing?" she wondered aloud. *Click, click.*

Curtis put the car in park. "I worked the races as a teenager, and I made friends with this really nice guy, Jimmy, the one I was telling you about. He came out from the city to race his Porsche in summer. I took care of his cars, and he took an interest in me. He became my benefactor, paying for me to go to college, then medical school. My whole life started with the racing club."

"Did he give you this car, too?" She had wondered how he'd afforded it; doctors were known to make a comfortable salary, but they didn't have the deep pockets of an attorney.

Curtis patted the leather dash. "Nope, I found this baby at a garage in Garden City, rebuilt its engine myself." He turned to face her. "My parents really hate that I do this. Actually, my mom. She's afraid she's going to get a terrible call about me someday."

"Have you ever taken your mother for a ride?" Everleigh had to have at least one usable photo, even though once they were speeding, it was doubtful her camera had been able to keep up.

"Mom? No way." He killed the engine. Someone was fishing in the harbor, a father and son in a small powerboat.

"Well, that's the problem then. She doesn't know what a good driver you are."

He touched her hand, just once. "You were never ill at ease, that whole time?"

She closed her eyes. "It was like speeding through the scenes of a movie. Too fast to process." She looked at him, grinning. "I want to do it again."

He opened the car door. "Let's walk first."

"Good, yes. I may get something better of you." Everleigh reloaded her camera, then pulled down the visor to see if there was a mirror, checking her reflection, and when she saw herself, she found proof that she liked him. Her skin was dewy, her eyes gleaming and full of possibility. They walked the beach for close to an hour in the warm sun, their bodies heating up all over again, chatting about racing and their jobs, music and the drive-in movie theater, the easy conversation of two people who didn't want the exchange to end.

"How are you liking Southampton these days? Dramatic life-changing fires aside." He handed her what he said was a tiny whelk shell, ringed with small knobs.

She took a picture of it in his open hands. "Southampton is growing on me, actually." She wanted to say, *You're growing on me.*

"I told you," Curtis said. "Small towns are pretty nice."

They walked back to the car, and he opened the passenger door. She'd stopped taking photos but now she raised her camera once more, liking how chivalrous and kind he was, opening her door. He tucked a lock of her hair behind her ear, and she couldn't stop the tingling from starting up, a sparking that put her on edge. She felt him lean toward her, and she tilted her chin up, ready for him, her feet floating off the ground, but when his eyes locked on hers, she realized what was happening. Overcome with panic, she ducked into the passenger seat.

When he started up the car, she threaded her fingers together in her lap, staring ahead at the sea. She said, "I'm sorry, I just . . ."

Curtis turned over the ignition, the engine revving. "Like I said earlier, someone wants us together. As friends." He smiled, then hit the gas with a force she didn't anticipate, and they shot off, the car once again getting air. She wouldn't have been surprised if they flew all the way back to the parking lot.

⌐⫫⌐

That Monday, Everleigh and Starling left the gallery an hour early to go to the art colony in Sag Harbor where Starling lived. Starling held open the door to the darkroom, a converted utility closet that barely had enough room for two, and closed the door to darkness, a red light clicking on. They opened the small canisters of film and went on to develop the pictures of Curtis, the artist giving her tips on how to evenly develop the film into negatives, a "wet process" that Starling said was critical to printing a fine-art level picture later. They wound the film around a steel reel, tight and even, to guarantee uniform exposure.

"Let's be careful now—this may be the most important step," Starling told her, her hands just visible in the ambient light. Starling turned the reel into a tray of Kodak D-76 chemical solution, a powder mix she'd combined with water, controlling for temperature and dilution. After, she poured in a measured amount of fixer, a chemical used to stabilize the image. Last came a "wetting agent" to reduce water spots or streaks from forming as they hung the negative plastic strips to dry on a clothesline with clothespins.

"I feel like I'm in chemistry class," Everleigh said.

Starling smiled, her skin taking on a reddish tinge from the muted crimson lightbulb overhead. "It's just as much science as art."

Everleigh's physical body wasn't in any of the photographs she'd taken, but she was certainly in every shot. Her gaze, how the lens always landed on the barrel of his chest, the soft part of his hair, the cinnamon color of his skin, the square of his jawline, that luminescent way his personality shone through his eyes. Even Starling had seen it. *You like looking at him, don't you?* the artist had said. And she did. Sometimes she stared into the solution, her eyes tracking the blank photo printing paper, waiting a few seconds for his silhouette to emerge as it developed, then his features. She left that day with a stack of photographs, negatives, too, to drop off with the photo editor at the *East Hampton Star.*

But Everleigh kept one picture for herself, a photo she'd taken of him grinning in the driver's seat, his eyes searching for hers on the other side of the lens. That night, with Roland snoring in the next room—the excitement of them sleeping together having worn off—she tucked it into a book on her bedside table.

AUGUST

EIGHTEEN

⌘

With her floral apron tied at her waist, Everleigh tipped extra salt into the creamy chipped beef, tasting it once more. *Perfection,* she thought, admiring how similar her dish looked to the photo in *Ladies' Home Journal.* The guiltier she felt about the business with Curtis Brightwell, the fussier her meals were becoming. Tonight featured the beef as well as a tomato salad *and* roasted rosemary potatoes. All this cooking wasn't romantic as much as it was purgatory. She'd brought home armfuls of groceries yesterday, tying on an apron and working at the stove, so when Roland stepped inside, she was right where he expected her.

As the beef tips warmed, the sun shining like three o'clock even after seven on a Saturday night, the smell brought her back to Whitney's house, where they often ate creamy beef potpies, Whitney's favorite. She'd nearly called her a few minutes ago, a bout of loneliness overtaking her, but Everleigh didn't know how to start a conversation with Whitney without all her other emotions resurfacing. She'd felt so abandoned by her friend at the bonfire.

Through the living room window, she spotted Roland crossing the lawn toward the cottage in a suit. When he entered the cottage, she handed him a plate of steaming meat, her nerves keeping her moving, putting napkins out, pouring claret into two coupe glasses. All her anger at him working with Opal overshadowed by the fact that she was feeling equally dishonest. "It's been nice having dinner together, hasn't it?"

The phone rang, a trilling that put her on edge, and Roland waited for Everleigh to rise, but she only smiled at him; there wasn't a rule that said women had to be the ones to get up from the table. "Can you get that, Rolly?"

He huffed, his dress shoes rattling the living room. "Hello," he said and explained that he was in the middle of dinner. "The delivery is for Friday after lunch. Not tonight . . . No. Friday." She peeked in on him, watching his foot tap impatiently, and his voice became low and angry, just for a second. "No, you cannot come now. I already told you . . ." The floorboard creaked underneath her as she whipped back to the stove, Roland's voice returning to its chipper tone. "I must return to dinner. Yes, Friday afternoon it is. Thank you."

He had no sooner returned to the kitchen table, Everleigh's blood pounding like it did when racing the hairpin curve, than there was a rapping at the back door. "What is it now?" Roland said, cranky at another interruption.

Stevie stood on the other side of the screen, his red hair freshly cut in a flattop boogie, looking like a neatly trimmed hedge on top, the back feathered and tucked into the center. He was grinning like he just won a poker game. "Hey, Rolly. I hope you don't mind, but I brought . . ."

Opal appeared in the doorway, her knee-length ruffled dress tied at the waist with a violet sash, a blond braid rounding her head like a crown. "Hi, Everleigh," she said, prancing in like they were old friends.

It was one thing to have an affair. It was another to parade it in front of your fiancée's face.

Everleigh calmly turned to Roland, everyone suddenly registering the tension coming from her. "You need to ask her to leave."

Opal kicked off her two-tone Chanel slingbacks by the door, then sat down at the kitchen table. "Oh Everleigh. I'll go if you want, but—"

"There's nothing between us," Roland said, taking two more fast bites. Everleigh's cheeks burned. Couldn't they have this conversation in private?

The scent of Stevie's aftershave overpowered the room while Everleigh considered blasting out of the house for the beach. Opal looked about, grimacing. "You've been living *here*? Has Whitney seen this place? My parents would flip if I stayed in something like this."

Everleigh laughed, a little too loudly. "They're not thrilled."

"Lee does as she wishes, no matter what the cost is to everyone else." Roland didn't mean it as a compliment—she could tell by his snarky tone.

"Oh, Rolly, don't be such a baby. Us girls always do as we wish." Opal winked.

Everleigh pushed her plate away.

"Are you still coming to Sharon Southard's party tonight?" Stevie had traded his Hawaiian shirt for the smooth cotton of a golf shirt, a linen blazer, his shoes trendy slide-ons made of canvas. On the middle finger of his right hand was a cocktail ring with a flat onyx rectangle at the top. His new look cost money that Lee certainly didn't think Stevie had.

"What's happening again?" Roland pushed up on the balls of his feet, rocking in his chair. If Roland left her here alone yet again—because Everleigh wasn't going with them—she would call Whitney and pack up her things and she'd be gone.

"It's some Boston chick's twenty-fifth with a band and a full bar and guys in tuxes serving food."

"You mean, it's catered. The word is 'catered', Stevie." Everleigh rolled her eyes.

Opal burst out laughing, raising her hand to her mouth. "Actually, she's from Palm Beach, and her parents have organized a lawn party. It's quite formal. That's why I'm so dressed up."

"Whatever." Stevie shrugged.

Roland went to hand Everleigh his cleared plate, and she turned away without taking it, then stood with her back to them at the sink. Roland offered them brownie sundaes.

She raged while soaping her plate, listening as Stevie and Opal said yes, in fact, they'd love one. Opal offered to help serve, and the men went outside to the picnic table. Everleigh fished out the tub of vanilla she'd picked up at the local dairy, while Opal stood beside her, watching her struggle to scoop it.

"Rolly tells me that the terms of our agreement are unacceptable to you, that you're uncomfortable." Opal's mild Dutch accent shined through, with "that" sounding like "dat."

Everleigh placed a brownie square beside each scoop.

Opal's voice was placid. "I want you to know that my intentions are pure, not some desperate attempt at romance. I will benefit as much as he will from this hotel." Everleigh could tell that Opal was a woman who always got what she wanted, whose parents probably called her a "good girl," even when she was throwing a tantrum. She moved through the world seeming sincere, a person you would vote for on Election Day even if you didn't know their politics.

Everleigh yanked open the silverware drawer. "Then why are you here?"

"I want to make peace." Opal smiled. "Whitney said that you're upset, and I want you to know that I'm with someone, yes. But it's not your Rolly. It's Steven."

Everleigh's mouth fell open. "Stevie?" She returned the ice cream to the freezer, retrieved the whipped cream, and put a mountain on each sundae. Of course this was a lie, concocted so Everleigh would go along with Opal and Roland's obvious charade.

Opal sighed. "He's untamed, I know, a wild horse bucking, but Stevie actually listens to my opinion. He takes me more seriously than the men in our circles, and he wants to help me with my business."

It was preposterous. "And your parents like him?"

Opal waved her off, but with the daintiness of a princess. "I'm simply making the most of a fling, Lee. I'm not marrying him."

Everleigh and Opal carried the sundaes outside, and as she put one in front of Roland, his eyes lighting up at the confection, her thoughts turned wicked. Because if Opal wasn't the one distracting Roland, if Roland really wasn't stealing off to meet her, then who was he meeting? Everleigh ran through the faces of women she'd seen pass by the gallery, women who'd been at the hotel party, women Roland greeted in town or on the beach. But he was friendly to everyone.

Her mind wandered to the gallery. Starling had asked Everleigh to stay working through Labor Day when the show officially ended, and she'd agreed. She wouldn't leave that job, no matter what happened with Roland, even if she'd just promised herself she'd ditch him if he went out. Her professional debut was in sight, too. The editor at the *East Hampton Star* had had her negatives for over a week now; the paper was set to run the story on Curtis in a few days.

With the sundaes finished, Roland announced he was leaving for the party, inviting Everleigh along. But there wasn't any part of her that wanted to go, especially not as a foursome. She said she was tired, and Roland moved to kiss her goodbye. That's when she turned away her cheek. When they all left their empty ice cream bowls for her to clean, she flashed a dirty look at the closing door. She'd leave them in the sink.

She continued to fight the urge to call Whitney.

H

When Roland left for his match at the Meadow Club the following morning, Everleigh raced into the car for her morning's secret activity: taking pictures for *Hampton Summer Life* magazine's Best of Summer Photography Contest. Starling had told her about it by clipping the advertisement out of the lifestyle pages and leaving it on the light table with a directive: "Enter!" The winner won twenty-five dollars and their photo would be on the cover of the glossy magazine.

Even though the beaches near Gin Lane were beautiful, Everleigh thought everyone would try to capture the ocean's brilliance. Instead, she was set on taking photos of the windmill in East Hampton, and she headed there now, hoping to photograph the gallant gray arms against a clear blue sky. Everleigh parked under one of the elms on Main Street and walked to the village green with her camera around her neck, finding the windmill in her frame and snapping. She was overcome by its stature, but the more pictures she attempted, the more disappointed she became.

Crouching in the grass a moment, Everleigh wished her camera allowed her to see pictures straightaway, that she didn't have to wait to develop them. As elegant as the windmill was on sight, it looked either too small in the frame or so large that you didn't know what you were looking at. Some of Starling's portraits were taken with a stunning backdrop, but they worked because there was always a person animating the foreground. It occurred to her then: she needed to find people living the carefree summer life that everyone waited for each year and capture the feeling. No, the sensation.

She made quite the spectacle, walking down East Hampton village sidewalks in her button-front, A-line pink skirt and sleeveless Peter Pan–collared blouse, snapping photographs. An American flag flapping off the bookshop (*click*), two teenage girls leaning against their road bikes with matching white sunglasses blowing her a kiss (*click*). Bubbles. Everleigh needed children's bubbles, and she bought a bottle of bubble solution at White's Pharmacy, using the wand to send them into the sky while taking photos of two children in sailor suits trying to pop them as she grinned into the viewfinder. Everleigh followed the kids along the sidewalk, snapping, and pausing in front of a jewelry shop to reload her film when a familiar silhouette took shape at the door.

It was Alice who stepped outside, her mother at her side. On instinct, Everleigh snapped a picture of the nearly identical women, noting the droll smile overtaking Alice's pretty features and the smug one on her mother's aging ones. The latter swatted at the bubbles like flies.

"Shouldn't you be at the Bathing Corp?" Alice said, her voice full of sarcasm, like she'd caught Everleigh doing something illegal. Her mother announced she'd meet Alice at the car.

"I'm on assignment," Everleigh fibbed, the children begging for a turn with the bubble wand. She handed it to the girl, maybe eight, who ran about with it. "Shouldn't *you* be at the Bathing Corp?"

Alice held up a small, shiny black bag, satin ribbons as handles. "I had something to pick up."

Everleigh lowered her camera, trying to stay cool, her hand reaching for the garnet necklace clasped around her neck. The locket found in room twenty-three had been one of a kind, a 14-karat gold heart with a missing gemstone in the setting, an *A* engraved on the front. Perhaps Alice was ordering a replacement. "I've been looking for a new watch for Roland and a jeweler who would engrave it, but so many shops have these terribly boring watch faces. Would you recommend this one?"

Among younger women, there was a shared distaste of housewives from the previous generation who, without access to fine fabrics and precious metals during wartime, wore jewelry made of Bakelite and plastic. Alice nodded. "I *only* buy my jewelry from Arthur. His prices are better than those in the city, and he does a fine job with engravings."

In the window, there were velvet stands shaped like necks with glittery strands hanging from them. On a shelf in a window display were rows of golden locket charms of various sizes. "May I see what you have? I'm curious about the quality."

The children handed Everleigh the bubbles, waving goodbye and rejoining their parents at a café table at the French brasserie.

Alice demurred, hunting the street for her mother's approaching car. "Go inside and ask him to see his work. Like I said, his name is Arthur."

"But I'd love to see what you ordered. I envy your impeccable taste. I'm looking for a necklace. Maybe a locket to house a photo of Roland and me."

Alice stood on tiptoe. "Where is Mother? We're going to be late for Marsha's."

The bag in her hand was small enough to hold a locket, but Everleigh supposed it could also hold a ring or a bracelet. "It will only take a moment."

Alice snatched the bag closer, noticing Everleigh trying to peer inside. "I'm hardly going to take my jewelry out on the sidewalk, Lee."

"We're hardly in rough New York," Everleigh raised her camera, just so she could focus on what was around Alice's neck now: a simple gold chain with a row of emeralds forming a pendant. *So she did favor gold.* "Please, just a quick peek at the necklace."

Alice sighed with irritation, holding tight the ribbon handles of the glossy shopping bag. "It's a bracelet, Lee, and the engraving is small. You would be better going inside. . . ."

Alice's mother swooped up in her Cadillac and beeped its horn, causing Alice to shove her fingers in her ears. "Mommy, stop! Lee, see you at Whitney's luncheon."

What luncheon? Everleigh hadn't been invited. She ignored the slight for a moment, waving goodbye.

The bell on the door dinged when Everleigh stepped inside the jewelry shop, a man in a linen vest leaving his cluttered worktable to stand behind the counter. Everleigh gave a charming smile and explained that her friend Alice Martin had just shown her the stunning piece he'd made her, and she absolutely loved it; could he make her one, too?

"Of course," he said, asking if she wanted to mimic the style of the bracelet entirely. *So it was a bracelet, not a necklace,* she thought.

"I'm not sure." Everleigh wrinkled her nose, pretending to be a picky customer. "I adore your design, but she showed me quickly. Could you show me something similar so I can be certain?" She pretended to be interested in ruby rings in a glass case, but out of the corner of her eye, she watched him fetch a file from a metal cabinet, sliding the drawer shut. He opened a folder on the counter and pulled out what looked like an architectural drawing of a simple bracelet, a small locket sliding along the gold bangle, an engraved letter *A* in the center of the heart, an outline of tiny diamonds around the rim. It wasn't identical to the locket found in room twenty-three—that hung on a necklace—but it was a sensible replacement. Perhaps that was why Alice had hidden it from view; she'd lost it at the hotel and feared someone knew and might connect her to the fire. Then again, if she was hiding her connection to a locket, she wouldn't be running out for a replacement.

"It truly is just what I'm looking for." She smiled. "May I borrow one of these sketches to show my fiancé?" He handed her one of the designs in Alice's file, and after thanking the jeweler for his help and promising to be in touch, she stepped outside onto the quiet sidewalks, her head reeling. If there was a time to go to the detective, it was now. Everleigh needed to show him the bracelet design, the locket, how close its engraving was to the one on the locket that was being held as evidence.

Her foot weighed like lead on the accelerator as she peeled out onto Main Street, heading straight to the Southampton Police Department, towns and farms racing by her windows. She kept glancing at the drawing on the passenger seat. This could be a coincidence, of course, but if the locket was Alice's, if this jeweler had embossed it for her, the detective would be able to demand records as proof. Maybe Alice had been in room twenty-three uninvited and somehow lost her necklace in the process of spreading acetone over the bed. Or maybe Roland had invited her up to the room during the party. They spent time there, possibly undressing—Everleigh bit her cheek then, tasting blood—with Alice forgetting to put on her necklace before re-dressing and returning to the party.

Twenty minutes later, she pulled into the police station. She found Detective Branford, who led her outside to a patch of grass with a faded wooden bench. He acted as though he was expecting her, even though it was a Sunday. He'd been working more weekends than he'd like, he said. "I was certain that this investigation would be a cut-and-dry case. Interview a handful of people; confirm that it was an accident. But it turns out, you and Roland have woven a twisted web out here." He sat on the bench, and she followed, feeling confused. She'd come to tell him something, but it seemed he was trying to tell her something first.

A *twisted web*, now that was a bit dramatic. Their lives weren't that interesting as far as she could tell. She, for one, didn't fraternize with anyone but Starling. "I hardly think we're naughty children that need minding."

Holding a chewed-up pencil, the detective opened his notepad to a blank page, the edges tattered. "Can I ask you a few questions?"

Everleigh fiddled with the pearls on her wrist. "Yes, of course, but first, I'm here because I need to tell you about Alice."

This seemed to amuse him, and he sipped his coffee, chuckling. "That's funny because she has a lot to say about you, too."

Cars whooshed by, some speeding, and Everleigh thought it must be frustrating to be a police officer, to watch people break the law all the time and not always be able to stop them.

"Oh? Like what?" said Everleigh, surprised. They'd met in grade school, attended finishing school together, and sometimes crossed paths at the Rainbow Room. They'd never been close.

"Well, she isn't particularly fond of you."

Everleigh was growing uncomfortable, even if the previous meetings with the detective had been benign. A sting burned her cheeks. "Like I said, we've never been close. Did you question Ernest? He made a threat that night. And today. Today, I saw Alice . . ."

The detective dropped his pencil. "Tell me about Elsa Loring."

Everleigh felt the blood drain from her face. What had made Alice talk about Elsa? She cleared her throat, tucking her hands under her skirt to keep them from trembling. "Elsa was one of my high school friends, and she went missing senior year." She smacked at an ant crawling up her leg. How many were at her feet, poised to sneak up and surprise her?

The detective seemed to be gauging her reaction. "It seems relevant, these details."

So Ernest *was* telling the truth: the detective considered Everleigh a suspect in the arson. But why had Ernest told her? Alice had clearly let slip these details about their former classmate, so wasn't Ernest crossing Alice in some way by letting Everleigh know?

"It was awful," Everleigh managed. The police had questioned her for hours, more than once, and she'd been cleared of any wrongdoing, but it didn't keep the rumor mill from churning. She'd fallen into despair, refusing to leave her room for weeks.

"Alice said Elsa was enamored of you. She copied your clothing, mimicked how you spoke. You hated it and had a huge fight in the hallway at school, and the next day, Elsa disappeared."

It was true. Her parents' car was discovered hidden under an underpass along the East River, a burned-out shell with human remains inside. It was awful, because Everleigh had felt guilty, like their fight had caused Elsa to do something stupid, and it took months of therapy for her to see that it wasn't her fault. During one particularly grueling session with police, they'd forced her to listen to a play-by-play of the alleged murder while gauging Everleigh's reaction, her father instructing her when to speak and when not to. Later, when detectives confirmed that Elsa had shot herself—and it was clear that Everleigh was at a friend's house the entire night—they finally left her alone. Still, witnesses had heard the gunshot before anyone saw the flames, so it remained a mystery who set the car on fire.

She swiped at her eyes, even as her temper flared. "I would never be a part of something that horrible."

"But you can see why I need to ask." The detective's tone softened. "The hotel would not be the first fire you were questioned about."

Two fires, and Everleigh on the periphery of both. It was odd, even she could see that, but it was hardly incriminating. "I had nothing to do with Elsa's disappearance, and I didn't start the fire at the hotel. Okay?"

Branford flipped through the pages in his notepad. "There's more, though."

Alice. She wanted the detective to suspect Everleigh, and why? To send him sniffing down someone else's path. It was yet another reason to believe she was guilty.

The detective found the page in his pad he'd been thumbing for and read it aloud. "She also said, and I quote, 'Roland built his entire fortune around the hotel, but she told him she hated it—'" He licked his pointer finger, then turned back a page. "And then: 'She complained of other girls. She is very jealous.'"

These were private matters—how did Alice even know these things? Had Roland spilled his sorrows to her one late night at a party? "Some of that is true, but detective, relationships take fine-tuning."

A patrol car parked in front of the station, and the detective nodded at the emerging officer. "Were you angry at Roland on the night of the fire? Sometimes fire starters don't intend to do so much damage. Sometimes the fire slips away from them."

"Of course not," she snapped. "But Alice, she was at the jewelry store today. She . . ."

Branford smacked the pad against his thighs. "Did you hire someone to start the fire for you?"

"No, I didn't. Why would I do that?" She was nearly crying, and it occurred to her then. She needed a lawyer.

"That's easy," the detective said, swagger in his voice. "For making you live out here for the summer."

She would stand up, she would walk to her car, she would tell him he had no right asking her these things.

Miss Farrows?

Everleigh sighed. She replayed the night of the fire one more time. Her cigarette on the balcony. Locking eyes with Stevie kissing a stranger. The voices of Alice and Ernest fighting by the pool. Tossing her cigarette to the ground without stubbing it. The detective had her confused. Had she purposely thrown that cigarette into the bushes hoping that the hotel would alight? Was she trying to sabotage Roland's dreams? Once the hotel was burning, she couldn't stop crying, watching the flames, hauling sand from the beach. Was it because she knew deep down that she'd started the fire? That in tossing the cigarette into the bushes, she'd taken it all away from him?

She had felt a burden lift when it burned, yes, but only because it was seemingly an act of God. It gave her a sense of freedom. She would never have to live in that hotel, or any hotel, again. All those terrible memories of her childhood slipping into the plumes of smoke: Her father sitting at the polished dining room table without ever calling out to her. Her mother in a darkened bedroom rarely getting out of bed. Nanny applying Band-Aids and running baths, taking her to birthday parties, and attending teacher conferences. The whispers of parents at school drop-off—*electroshock therapy, home from the hospital, mentally unstable.* Everleigh couldn't explain why watching the flames that night had released her from some of that baggage, but it had.

How far off this detective's investigation was! He didn't ask one question about Alice or Stevie, who could be placed at the source of the fire, who had motives. His best theory was that Everleigh had set it ablaze to punish her fiancé.

"Detective, let's think logically. Why would I swindle myself out of thousands of dollars? You realize that the fire rendered my fiancé penniless."

Branford stood, his tongue sucking at his two gapped front teeth. "You might if you planned to cancel your wedding. If you discovered your fiancé was having an affair. If you wanted to get even."

"And what do you know of Roland's extracurriculars?" It was hard to swallow. *How many other people knew that Roland was off with someone else?*

"I'm just saying *if* he was," Branford said, his cheeks flushing. She'd made him uncomfortable. Well, good.

She crossed her arms. "It's Alice that you need to question. I ran into her today picking up a custom order at a jewelry store in East

Hampton." Everleigh unfolded the sketch she'd taken from the store, waiting for him to notice that the engraved *A* was identical to the locket's.

"What is the jeweler's name?" The detective's voice was steady, and Everleigh offered his name and address. He jotted it down on his notepad. "Even if it is Alice's locket in the room, even if she was involved, I can tell you she didn't light the match. Her chauffeur was driving her back to the city by eleven that night; she had an early-morning meeting the following day and I have witnesses vouching for her presence."

Everleigh chewed on her cheek, tasting the salt of a wound; the fire had to lead back to Alice. "But I heard her voice, at the pool, after one a.m. I saw her. And her parents, they hate the hotel—Alice has admitted as much. They want it gone."

"You saw *a woman*, you heard a woman's voice. It doesn't mean it was Alice. It was late, you'd been drinking, and you were at least three stories up."

"But it was definitely Ernest on the lounger—I heard his accent. A friend saw them both, too." On the night of the party, Alice had certainly annoyed her, acting like she knew Roland, that there was a secret in their past, something he wasn't willing to share with Everleigh. And Whitney's husband saw them both.

"A friend that you said isn't willing to be questioned. Correct?" His tone was accusatory, making clear he had every reason to believe she made the whole thing up.

She nodded; Whitney had sworn her to secrecy at the beach. "But, Detective, you're trusting Alice's chauffeur, someone she pays for a living." It was so obvious that Alice was falsifying her alibi to avoid suspicion, which made her only more suspicious; why was the detective so willing to overlook that possibility?

"Miss Farrows, there's no need to be hysterical. Ernest was there, yes, but passed out on the lounger. And Alice's parents whispered that

Roland needed to rethink the size of his fancy hotel; that doesn't make them hateful."

"How can you be so certain?"

Everleigh's mother was often called hysterical because her mood swings rendered her illogical, unreliable. When she was upset, she could do unthinkable things, like what she'd done in the bathtub all those years ago. Had Everleigh been overcome with a similar insanity? Had she been *hysterical* the night of the party? Had she lit a match in room twenty-three, and somehow didn't remember?

"It isn't me you should be after," she said, leaving behind the design of Alice's new locket on the bench. Everleigh rushed off to her car, thinking how easy it would be for Alice and Ernest to get away with everything.

NINETEEN

The next day went by much like the ones before. Everleigh reported to the Juniper Gallery each day by ten, so she and Starling could finish hanging the artwork in the space. In the afternoons, she'd return home to an empty cottage with Roland still at the hotel, overseeing the installation of electrical wiring, the fresh plastering of walls. Already, you could walk through the hotel's rebuilt lobby, even if it was still unpainted with a plywood floor. Then she'd prepare them dinner, and they'd eat at the picnic table outside, Everleigh attempting to talk about the gallery and Roland feigning interest. Neither one said what they really wanted to say: that things weren't right between them.

She didn't bother telling Roland about the business with Alice's locket or her conversation with the detective. These days he refused to discuss the investigation at all.

"It's their job to figure this out, not ours," he'd scolded her last week. "Our job is to move on with our lives."

Some nights, Stevie picked Roland up, Opal sitting pretty in the passenger seat, and off they went to Bobby Van's or a beach bonfire or a lawn party. There always seemed to be a party she was missing out on in these quiet towns.

It was Tuesday, and Starling's photography show was set to open in the gallery in six days, the twelfth of August. Each picture hanging on the walls needed an information card, and Everleigh was typing them up: the title, the year it was taken, and the location, which was sometimes a movie set, sometimes a city, or obscure town. She had just finished the one for Paul Newman and Jean Simmons: " 'Star-Crossed,' 1957, on the set of *Until We Sail*; Hollywood, California."

A jittery excitement overcame Everleigh when the familiar smack of the newspaper hit against the front door. The story about Curtis was in today's paper, which meant her photos were, too. She fetched it, scanning the front page.

Starling paced the gallery, seemingly agitated, while at the desk Everleigh paged through news to the features section. Opening to half a page of Curtis's handsome silhouette, she saw a large headline, "Local Doc's Fast Track to Winning." Everleigh's lens, Everleigh's eye, her hand-crafted negative, her prints. She brimmed with satisfaction.

"He selected my safest composition," she told Starling, who came to stand next to her, making Everleigh self-conscious and more critical of her photo than she would have been alone. "I took so many others while he was racing. You saw them, where you could see the speed in his face." Everleigh wrinkled her nose. "This one is so static. A portrait." It was one of the first shots she'd taken of him sitting in his car, leaning in through the window, but you could see the track snaking into the distance behind him, Curtis's face grinning like he'd already won the upcoming race.

"Don't expect a newspaper editor to appreciate art. Just the facts, ma'am." Starling ran her hand along the racing stripes of the car, the sleek contours of the coupe. "That's quite a driver."

Everleigh smiled. She thought Starling was going to comment on the car, not Curtis. "I told you, right, that I know him?"

"It's wild." Starling went back to the corner of the gallery where she was working to re-center the photograph of Nat King Cole. "The photo you took is exactly right. You gave them what they wanted: a clear portrait of the young doctor. Good job, Lee." It was the kind of praise you wanted from your mother. A spotlight shining on you and only you.

"Photograph by Everleigh Farrows." Her first photo credit. She'd done something spectacular. She'd made a mark. It certainly wasn't enough to earn herself the title of artist. But she was learning how to be one. Later, after work, she'd buy extra copies, cut out the article and circle her name in the photo credit, drop it in an envelope, and address it to her mother. *Look at what I did*, she'd write on a piece of stationery.

Starling turned down Ella Fitzgerald's album, tapping her fingers against her folded arms, her bony elbows. "Something's not right, Lee."

Everleigh folded up the paper. "What is it?"

Starling took one of the photographs off the wall, then another. "The portraits. They shouldn't all be the same size. Or maybe it's that they're too small? What if I blew up eight of the best ones? Twenty-five-by-twenty-five-inch square. No, thirty-by-thirty. Big faces jumping off the wall. Yes, that's what I need to do. We need to redo this. We'll need larger negatives."

Everleigh swallowed. All the cutting, the framing, the time she spent arranging the order of the prints. It was unclear there was even enough space on the wall to hang that many oversized prints. And the frames. Where would they find frames that big within a week?

"But this looks so incredible. I'm not even sure we have the time . . ."

"We'll make the time." Starling continued to pull the frames off the wall, and said she was certain about who should be included: Marilyn, Paul Newman, Lucille Ball, Nat King Cole. Only the biggest names. Starling was light on her feet, shifting from side to side, like a boxer readying for a fight. "This will punch them. This will make them pay attention."

Everleigh wasn't sure how you'd make prints that big. Where would they find a big enough tray for developing solution? "But Starling, who will pay such close attention?"

Starling went still, a lock of hair pushed the wrong way across her forehead. "Everyone."

"Well, okay, but . . ." It was Everleigh's instinct to accept the status quo, and here was Starling, her instinct to push. To be bold. Not to shirk from what's difficult, not if it got you what you wanted. It was a lesson Everleigh needed to learn.

Starling rested her smooth flattened palms on Everleigh's cheeks. "The show has to be right, Lee. It may be my only gallery showing ever. We need headlines, like your race car driver. He didn't get in the paper by going to his medical office and seeing sick kids. He got in the paper by surprising us. We need to surprise this little seaside town. These photos will be so big, so sexy, they'll get people off the beach."

The photographer moved frantically about the studio, knocking into things. Like if she didn't figure this out now she never would.

"Okay, okay." Everleigh took out her notepad, following Starling. "What do we need to do?"

Starling listed tasks, her eyes slits of focus. "We need a new darkroom, a tremendous one. Maybe we set up in an old barn. Write this down: Get enormous bins to pour the printing solution, maybe baby pools could hold them. Forget buying frames that big. Do you know a local woodworker? We need someone to build them, and fast. It may be expensive, but I have some money from my fellowship. I know where to get a large roll of photo paper. Let's forget the matte in the frames—we won't have time to cut, so we'll insert the photos only in glass."

Starling stared out the window at the sunny sidewalks of East Hampton, women in sundresses, men in pressed shorts ambling by in Top-Sider boat shoes. A green Mercedes convertible drove slowly through town, two little dogs scampering back and forth in the back seat. All the people on the sidewalk started pointing at the driver, who had a perfectly coiffed head of blond hair. There was Marilyn Monroe in full makeup and red lipstick, her car moving lazily along. It was uncommon to spy the actress about town, so much so that the Shouts and Shushes column had begun reporting rare sightings in the paper. Everleigh hoped to run into her again at some point; she wanted to thank her.

Starling didn't register the actress as she passed, lost in thoughts of the show, and when the car was gone, Everleigh's eye caught Stevie across the street. He was at the fish market, yet again, loading the same crates into his trunk as last time. The passenger seat was empty.

"What exactly is he up to?" Everleigh didn't mean to say it aloud, but she had, causing Starling to come stand next to her, tapping lightly on the glass in his direction.

"You use him, too?" Starling said. "I didn't know you smoked."

Even though she'd had a cigarette on the night of the fire, Everleigh rarely smoked, only when she and Whitney were teenagers and they'd snuck out to dark and smoky jazz clubs in the East Village. "I've never been into cigarettes."

"Not tobacco, dear, grass. I could use some right now actually. I'm on edge." Starling removed her glasses, cleaning them on her black shirt.

She glanced back out the window at Stevie with his flattop hair. She was right in not trusting him. He was selling grass to all the rich people in town. Opal probably introduced him to half his clients. It made sense now why he seemed to know so many people here, why he showed up on Gin Lane handing someone a bag of tomatoes: there was something else in that bag, too. Apparently Whitney was right when she said Opal was drawn to lost puppies. But it also pained Everleigh to think that her fiancé chose someone so wayward (and impressionable) to be his best friend. Because what did that say about Everleigh? Had Roland met her on the steps of Madame's townhouse a year ago and thought *This wobbly woman needs someone to fix her, too?* Everleigh's stomach lurched.

Starling clapped her on the back. "We need to move fast. Will you get everything on that list? I'll scout the barn." Starling tossed her canvas tote over her shoulder. "Can I count on you, Lee?"

Everleigh nodded, grabbing her purse, pulling out her keys. "Of course."

She'd head to the five-and-dime for the baby pools, then the hardware store for the wood for the woodworker to build the frames, and the lunch counter at the pharmacy for tuna sandwiches, and, if possible, a list of woodworkers. Starling said they were to meet at the Sag Harbor artist colony in two hours' time. Everleigh slid into the driver's seat and turned over the engine when the passenger door opened. Someone was getting inside. Instinctively, she grabbed for her purse, but then she registered the person sinking into the seat next to her. It was Roland.

"This is a happy surprise," she said, confused at the sight of him, his hair slicked back, small golden curls at his neck. He hadn't come to the gallery once since she began working there weeks before.

"Everyone's calling me about my fiancée's photograph in the paper. Why didn't you tell me you spent the afternoon fraternizing with that guy?"

Her chest rose in a deep breath. "It was an assignment, and I wanted to surprise you."

"Surprise me, or hide it from me?"

She slammed her hands on the steering wheel. "You haven't cared about one thing I've been doing since we got here. Why would I tell you anything?" Lately, she'd stopped picking up the clothes he left on the floor of his bedroom, tending only to her things in her bedroom next door.

"I need my car back," Roland said.

She could walk to the five-and-dime from here and the hardware store, too, but she needed a car to get to the art colony. She never needed a car as much as she did now. "Well, you can't take it, Roland. I'm in the middle of my workday."

Roland's navy dinner jacket was new. She wondered when he bought it, stung that they had drifted so far apart that he went shopping without her ever knowing it. She wished they could open up to each other, talk through whatever was happening. Instead, each morning, with a swirl of anxiety in her stomach, she made the choice to keep up this charade between them, like everything was fine.

His showing up like this was not fine.

He took the keys out of the ignition, closing them in his palm. "I have appointments—and I'm tired of hitching rides. I should have taken my car back weeks ago." She suspected that Roland was running out of money again. The several thousand from Opal would only get him so far. Then there would be another promise to her, another loan with strings attached.

Everleigh pressed her forehead against the red leather steering wheel. Starling needed her. "Can we figure this out at home tonight? The show is changing, and Starling needs me to meet with her."

"I don't care about that woman. I need my car. *My* car. You hear me?"

Roland got out of the automobile and walked around the front. He ripped open the driver's side door, holding his hand out to the sidewalk like an arrow.

"So you're going to leave me stranded here. On the side of the road?" she said, emerging into the sunshine. She realized then that she didn't care anymore if she made him happy or not. She wasn't some lovesick teenager. It was naïve of her to think she could live with the freedoms that Starling did, and yet she wasn't as scared by the idea of things not working out between her and Roland either.

Roland flopped into the driver's seat, starting the car again. "I brought you out here to sun at the pool and sip Bellinis on the beach. Whatever *this* is, whatever you're doing every day, it's not what I signed up for."

It was only a matter of time before Roland grew angry, and she'd expected this kind of backlash. Not only because she pulled away from him when he'd invited her into his bed the other night, but also because she was pulling away from him mentally.

Roland waited for her to look at him, and when she did, he shook his finger at her. "This is not the woman, *you* are not the woman, I fell in love with."

Her fists slammed into her thighs. "Well, maybe you don't know me. Maybe you should have asked me if I wanted to sip Bellinis by the pool. Because I don't even like goddamned Bellinis, Roland."

He revved the engine. "You said you were ready to be married. You said you wanted to be my wife. You won't even go to lunch at the Bathing Corp, the club I spent a mint to get us into. Do you know how many excuses I've made for you?"

The thought disgusted her. "Try telling the truth. It's hardly a secret that I'm working here."

"Well, I never asked for this. A woman so mixed up inside she can't find her way home to me."

He sped off without a goodbye, the tailpipe blowing black exhaust in her face, leaving her feeling angry and let down. She stilled the tapping of her foot. *Starling needed her.* There was no time for this petty drama. Which meant that Everleigh needed a car. Right now.

A woman mixed up inside. Isn't that what everyone was until they found their way? After unlocking the gallery door, she settled herself down beside the phone, dialing the hardware store, which, after taking her lumber order, offered the name of a woodworker. She placed the wood order, then called the five-and-dime for the baby pools. She would pick them up within the hour.

Then, with a heavy heart, she dialed Whitney. After the first ring, she nearly hung up. *You have no other choice*, Everleigh thought. The gallery was silent, so quiet she could hear the beat of her heart. A housekeeper picked up, and Everleigh tapped a pencil on the desktop while waiting for her friend to get on the line. Across the street, she saw the detective standing in front of the fish market, questioning a squat gentleman. Was he onto Stevie's illegal dealings?

"Hello." Whitney never greeted her this formally. It sounded as though her hands were folded in her lap, her legs crossed at the ankle.

"Hi, Whit. I'm sorry to bother you, but I'm in trouble." There was a rattling in Everleigh's throat, an earthquake rumbling her heart. "Will you come to the gallery in East Hampton?"

Birds chirped in the background, and she pictured Whitney taking the call in her sunroom on one of the wicker chairs by the window overlooking the rose garden. "You haven't spoken to me in weeks, and now you suddenly need me."

There were years of friendship in their past, and Everleigh knew that no matter how mad she was at Whitney, or Whitney at her, she'd be the first to come to her aid if she needed her. "Yes, I do. I need you."

There was rustling on the phone, her friend moving about. "Okay. What's the address?"

Everleigh rushed to the hardware store, asking the gentlemen to help her carry the wood to the gallery. She fetched the baby pools herself, leaving them on the sidewalk while picking up the sandwiches, and returned to the gallery to wait on the curb. An hour and a half had passed since Starling left; she had thirty minutes to get to the art colony. Minutes later, Whitney's dusty pink Chrysler La Comtesse with the gray plexiglass top pulled up next to her. Her friend parked and got out.

"Thanks for coming." Everleigh rose to her feet. Whitney's chilly expression made her forget everything she planned to say. "Roland took the car, and now Starling wants to reprint all of the photographs, but I had to run to the hardware store. Anyway, I hope I didn't pull you away from anything important. I swear it was an emergency."

Whitney's hair was tied in a loose twist. She wore a pleated navy dress with yellow lemons printed on it. "It's nothing," she said. Whitney popped the trunk of her car, letting Everleigh place the baby pools in alongside the skinny-cut pieces of lumber. "Is this really how you spend your days now?"

Everleigh stopped arranging the items in the trunk. "I know, you don't approve, but I hope you come to the opening." She'd made sure that Starling sent Whitney an invitation to the show and fete that Monday night.

Whitney slammed the trunk closed, her heels tapping their way to the driver's seat. She opened the door hard and propelled herself inside, shutting the door like she hated it. Everleigh closed her eyes. She had to be at Starling's in less than thirty minutes. And now, this was the moment Whitney wanted to talk, the very moment that Everleigh couldn't.

The white leather of the passenger seat was hot when Everleigh sat down. "What's wrong? I mean, I know what's wrong, and I'm sorry. I was just so angry at you at the bonfire."

In her cat's eyes sunglasses, Whitney pulled into traffic. "What's wrong? Other than that my friend has been so utterly immersed in herself that she doesn't even ask me how I am."

"But I did ask—when you arrived. . . . I should have called sooner."

"Yes, you should have." Whitney pulled the car to a stop on a back road. She turned in the seat to face Everleigh. "Do you realize what I've been going through out here? Do you even know that Sandy Donaldson put a slip of paper in my hand with a doctor's name to call to help me have a baby? The humiliation I feel when I see these women with their kids in tow, the pitiful looks they give me, the whispers."

Everleigh's face fell. "I'm sorry. I didn't know how bad it was."

"Of course you don't. Because you have your fiancé. And your gallery." Her friend's face scrunched up in a ball. She was wearing pearls, looking utterly pulled together, but really on the brink of falling apart. "Remember when I was pregnant a couple of weeks ago? Well, the bleeding started, and it won't stop, and the baby's gone. That's why I'm wearing this awful dark color."

A soft trembling that started in Whitney's lip spread to her fingers, and Everleigh grabbed her hands, squeezing them hard, wet drops falling from her eyes and plopping onto her lap. It was as though the dam that had built up over the last few weeks broke, and Everleigh was suddenly angry with herself. *How could she have let this happen?*

"I don't know what that feels like, but it must be awful." Everleigh hugged her friend, not wanting to let go. If she could take back the last few weeks, she would. She'd put her lifelong relationship with Whitney in jeopardy over Roland. And for what? Because she didn't want Whitney to be right about him, that he was needy and a flirt?

Whitney pulled back from the embrace, dabbing her face with her handkerchief, clearing her throat.

Everleigh stared out the windshield at the car parked in front of them. "If it makes you feel any better, things haven't been easy for me either. Roland has been coming home smelling of the same woman's perfume, if he comes home at all."

"Oh, Lee, I'm sorry." She let her face fall forward into her hands, then peeked up, her lips betraying a slight smile. "We're a pair, aren't we? To think that at the beginning of the summer we had everything figured out."

"I'm so sorry, Whitney."

Her friend nodded. "Me, too. How did we actually make it four weeks without talking?"

"I know. There are so many things I have to tell you."

Both women used the backs of their wrists to wipe the corners of their eyes. "We better get you to the art colony," Whitney said. They drove by the handsome, columned Maidstone Arms Inn, which was across from a small graveyard near two interlinked reed-ringed ponds, before turning off in the direction of Sag Harbor.

"Truman says that we need to see yet another special doctor in the city, so I have an appointment again, but most of these men say it's something I'm doing wrong. I'm not keeping my legs in the air, or my vagina is sideways—yes, sideways!—or my ovaries are too small. Like everything is my fault. And I leave each appointment ready to down an entire chocolate cake."

"I can bake you one next time. I make an addictive frosting." That made her friend laugh, even if Everleigh grew serious. "It could be Truman, though. I read an article about how women blame themselves for infertility, but it can be the man's fault. Maybe it always is."

"I could never tell Truman that his boys are weak; he thinks of them as soldiers invading for battle."

It was true; the male ego could rise and fall if attacked. She'd seen it with Rolly. "But heartbreak should fall on both sides, Whit." Everleigh pressed her bare feet up on the dash, making herself at home, like she always did when they were together. "It's only fair to share that burden."

Still, Everleigh knew Whitney would never talk to her husband; having a baby was in the women's department as squarely as the makeup counter.

Whitney asked after her, if only to change the subject, and Everleigh explained about the photograph in that day's paper, how the shoot with Curtis had unfolded into a near kiss, how she and Starling were experimenting with larger prints this afternoon. Whitney listened carefully, not showing support or disdain, a juror hearing a case.

They passed under the train trestle on Butter Lane, lumbering past the Bridgehampton Long Island Railroad station before the road opened up to meadows. The artist colony was just up ahead. "Are you sure you're not just overcorrecting, Lee?"

Everleigh noted how the sun hit the tips of the wildflowers in the field, how if she could get high enough with her camera, she would capture a carpet of pinks and purples. "What does that mean? Overcorrecting?"

Whitney glanced over at her. "It means I understand that you're having second thoughts about Roland. But just because he's feeling wrong for you doesn't mean you have to flee to some opposing existence. You can still be the Lee I've known and loved since we were schoolgirls; you don't have to be so dramatically—"

Everleigh took out her lipstick, applying it, anything to make it seem like she didn't feel judged. "What? Different?"

Whitney's shoulders relaxed. "Yes, exactly."

She couldn't help but grin. "Oh, Whit, but I want to be different, and that's okay. I'm not going to love you any less."

Whitney opened her mouth, then closed it, as if she changed her mind about something. "But I thought we wanted the same things. I thought you were excited to move around the corner from me. Raise our kids together, remember?"

"I'm not disappearing. We will still sneak into dive bars for cocktails on Friday nights. You're my best friend, Whit. No matter what direction our lives take, my heart will always lead back to you."

Whitney wiped at the corners of her eyes again, forcing a smile. "I know. It's just been a hard few months, with all this uncertainty, and I'm not used to being this uncertain about you, too."

Once they pulled into the artist colony, they parked in the pebbly lot, Everleigh turning to her before she opened the door. "We can't keep spending so much time apart, okay? We need to make time, no matter what our lives or our husbands require of us."

Whitney laughed and sing-songed, "Cute boys make you blush. A funny boy, you'll fall in love. But girls will never leave you." It was a saying they'd made up in middle school, back when they wrote each other notes on lined paper, every *i* dotted with a heart.

"Girls will never leave you," Everleigh repeated. They hugged once more, and while unloading the contents from the trunk, she begged Whitney to come and meet the artist. Her friend kissed her on the cheek.

"I'll meet Starling at the show," Whitney said. "I have a meeting, and I . . ."

Everleigh nodded, knowing it was an excuse, and Whitney looked off toward the cabins, where Starling had emerged, waving. "Lee, can you promise you'll try to come to my luncheon for the Ladies Village Improvement Society on Friday? Twelve thirty p.m., my backyard."

"Promise," Everleigh said, the stuff in her arms cumbersome and making her unsteady.

Whitney blew her a kiss. "Let's never do this to each other again."

After rushing off to a Sagaponack barn, she and Starling spent the next several hours converting it into a large-scale darkroom. By eight, they were exhausted, and they decided to stop working for the night, both of them ready to fall into their respective beds. Starling let her off at the darkened cottage, Roland's car nowhere in sight.

"Great work today," Starling said. "Tomorrow, we'll start printing."

"Good night," Everleigh said.

She longed to put on her pajamas and make a cup of Earl Grey. She'd snuggle with Mango and read a book. Inside the cottage, she was met with a sink full of dishes and the smell of rotten milk. Mango didn't meet her at the door. She normally rubbed her nose against Everleigh's ankle, purring. She'd follow her about as she changed in her bedroom, sitting beside her as she cooked.

"Mango," she called to the quiet house.

Everleigh shrugged, padding into her bedroom to change. The cat was a stray and could survive outside if she needed to. After kicking off her flats, she startled when she heard a wheezing. On the bed was the cat, her chest sucking into her ribs, like she was struggling to breathe. Everleigh dove into her bed, trying in vain to comfort the animal. Mango's pupils were dilated. Everleigh pressed her lips inward, feeling like she couldn't breathe herself. She needed to call someone to help, but who? Starling was driving home, and Whitney said she was playing canasta at the Maidstone. It was after office hours for a veterinarian, and Everleigh hadn't even seen one advertised around town.

She spotted her photograph of Curtis in the newspaper. *He was local.* He would know where to take the cat for help. Frantic, she called the switchboard operator, hoping they would know his home number; Everleigh didn't have a telephone directory and Curtis had never shared his town code or five-digit number. "Do you have a connection for a Curtis Brightwell? His family is in Bridgehampton, I think." Soon enough, after a few *clicks* and *pops*, the lines were connected, and Everleigh heard the phone ringing. Curtis answered straightaway and she relaxed just hearing him. She explained about the cat, that she didn't have a car.

"I'll be right there," he said. In the meantime, Everleigh lay on the bed, soothing Mango, singing her songs the way she used to sing herself to sleep as a girl. While she wasn't sure if she ever felt true love for a man, she felt it for this cat, especially on those days when Roland had disappeared and she and Whitney weren't speaking.

When Curtis arrived, which seemed like hours later, he placed two fingers on Mango's furry chest. "Her pulse is too fast."

He was dressed in shirt and tie, as though he'd come straight from his office, even though it was nearly nine at night. They drove in the dark to his friend's house in Amagansett who had an animal hospital in a converted garage out back. The vet, a balding gentleman at least twice their age, examined Mango on a small metal table.

"Has she been throwing up today?" he asked, pulling his head mirror over his eye to examine the cat's eyes, ears, and throat.

"I don't know." Everleigh said that she hadn't been home. The smell of sour milk in the kitchen. Maybe that was the cat's sickness left behind on the floor.

The vet took out a damp cloth and softly wiped the cat's flicking eyes, even though Mango struggled in his grip. Then he forced open her mouth with some metal device, using a dropper to insert a water solution. "Her heart sounds fine, and so do her internal organs. I think she probably ate something funny, threw up a couple of times. It was hot, and she got dehydrated. That's why she's heaving. She scared herself is all."

Everleigh buried her face in the cat's fur. "You scared me, too."

The vet asked to keep Mango overnight just to be sure, and they left feeling a thousand tons lighter than when they'd arrived.

Everleigh exhaled. "Gosh. What a day. If you only knew."

Curtis pulled the car onto the main road. "How about a walk on the beach before I drop you home?" She nodded, wishing she had a sweater; the night was warm, but the wind kept blowing against her bare arms, giving her chills.

They walked Flying Point Beach in the dark, the only light coming from a solitary boat on the water, zipping by in the light of the crescent moon. The ocean was rarely this calm.

"Thank you for your photograph," he said. "My parents are treating me like I'm in the movies. Every time they see me, they pretend to roll out a red carpet."

She laughed. "You're welcome. You were an easy subject. I could print you more if you'd like. Some of the racing shots."

"Sure," he said.

In the distance, a bonfire made a fiery dot on the horizon. She thought of the picture she'd hidden in the novel on her bedside table. In it, he looked a little like he did now: approachable, sensitive, in tune with the woman beside him. Talking to him made her feel like she was talking to someone she'd known for a lifetime.

Curtis plopped down in the sand on his knees, a fun-loving expression on his face. He was cast in blue from the moonlight, and he reached his hands up toward her. She couldn't stop giggling as she put her soft palms in his, which made her think of that day at the racetrack. How he'd look back at her in the viewfinder with his deep amber eyes, how the camera had been a barrier between them the last time they were together. But now, the camera wasn't here. It freed up the space between them. He pulled her down, but she wouldn't let herself fall on top of him, even if she was smiling out of sheer awkwardness.

They sat with their hips touching, their legs outstretched, facing the foamy surf. She refused to like him. They were friends. That's all.

"I've been trying to run into you," he said. She wondered for the one hundredth time that week what it would be like to kiss him.

"Isn't that the way? When you're looking for somebody, you never seem to find them."

The sand sank under them, seeming to pull them closer, or was he edging nearer? "Or maybe they're right there, and you haven't noticed before."

"Maybe." She felt his hand press on her thigh—she was still wearing shorts. *His hands.* The ones that gripped the steering wheel of his race car with might. The ones that turned the wheel, that maneuvered the gearshift, knowing exactly where his fingers had to be to get the car to do as he wished. To get a powerful boost.

She absolutely would not kiss him. Even if she felt her breath catch, even if it's all she wanted to do. She picked at shells in the sand, turning over a scallop shell, keeping her gaze on the ground. It was too dangerous to look up. Seconds dragged on like hours. Curtis tipped his head down, cocking it to get her attention, and when it didn't work, he cast his finger out to gently move her chin in his direction. Everleigh peered up at him.

Do not kiss him. You are forbidden, she told herself.

But then that is exactly what she did, his lips soft and full and powerful, just like the car, and they lay back in the sand, kissing like two people who might never see each other again. She imagined him racing around the track, faster, then faster still. Her tongue couldn't get deep enough inside him, and she'd arched her back, wanting him to explore her body with his lips, imagining that he was. She felt him move to unbutton her shorts, and she sat up, stunned at how inappropriate this was, Curtis pulling back his hand and apologizing.

Even in the dark, she knew his cheeks were on fire. "Should I smile because you're my friend, or cry because that's all we'll ever be?" Then he did smile, one that could open a thousand doors. "I actually read that on a card in the pharmacy today."

She leaned back into his arms, huffing in frustration. "Why couldn't we have met a year ago?"

"If you had only visited your friends more last summer."

They talked for the next hour, Everleigh telling him about her family. About Whitney. He spoke about growing up as a local, what it was like to be back as a doctor. How sometimes people still treated him like a farmer's son. How the summer colony didn't trust him at first with their health. A truck drove down the beach, the headlights causing them to shield their faces. Fishermen, their poles standing upright in the back of the truck, the crackle of a radio coming from inside.

"Can I ask you something personal?" Curtis said when the vehicle was gone.

She nodded. They had started to walk back to the parking lot.

"What is it about Roland? That made you say yes?" Curtis brushed off his feet with one hand, steadying himself against the car. "You're so wonderful. And he. Well, he has a reputation. He's doing things out here that you probably wouldn't approve of."

She sighed. *Roland.* She didn't want to know what corners he was cutting to finish the hotel anymore. Tensions were already high between them, but walking away from him now would mean walking away from her entire life. "You may not see it, but he's charismatic and fun and he fits into my world back in New York. We may not make sense out here, but we make sense there."

She wasn't sure anymore if this was true, that they'd fit together so perfectly when they moved into the house in Bronxville come fall. She was certainly giving him a taste of his own medicine right now.

"But we make sense out here—you and me," Curtis said, holding her hand.

Everleigh nodded, offering no explanation, no defense of Roland, and Curtis took a step toward her. He tucked a lock of hair behind her ear, like even her tresses were so special that he had to handle them with the utmost care.

"I'm in trouble with you," he said, kissing her lips softly. He pulled back. "Big, big trouble." They kissed again, and Everleigh didn't pull away. This right here was the best kind of trouble.

TWENTY

❧

Starling washed the chemical solution over a square of developing paper in the baby pool they'd blown up with a bike pump. With a battery-powered camping lantern they'd hung precariously from a barn rafter, Everleigh stood beside the photographer in the red-hued light waiting for the face to emerge from the blank page. There wasn't a sliver of sun coming into the barn since they'd covered every crack with black duct tape, and the darkness, necessary for the photographs to expose properly, was thick as night. The enlarger, specialized and made of steel, had been the most challenging part to set up. The instrument, which required the help of a few men and a truck to transport from Starling's narrow dark room, allowed them to expose the images on photographic paper and manipulate the size, but to do so meant that they had to position it high up to get the image large enough. Starling had borrowed a tractor with an excavator shovel, suspending the enlarger with chain links from the machine and raising the shovel as high as it would go, so it dangled above the photo paper. She sat in the driver's seat, raising and lowering the enlarger until the image projected was the size and clarity she wanted.

Everleigh thought the entire contraption was bananas, but it had worked after a few grainy first attempts. Starling applauded herself when they'd superimposed a crisp black-and-white image on an enormous piece of photo paper.

"What a drama!" Everleigh laughed, caught up in the artist's joy.

"We women can figure things out for ourselves, you see." Starling climbed down off the tractor. "Having a crazy idea and then figuring out how to make it happen . . . That is the creative process, Everleigh, and you should know that that's art as much as taking the original photograph is. It's you who has to dig into your vision. It's you who has to put in the work."

"A little every day," Everleigh said.

Starling looked over her glasses. "No, a lot every day."

The barn smelled dank and musty, like no one had opened these doors in a decade, maybe more. The rustic wood walls chipped and peeled, and in one corner was a stack of rusted tools—two hoes, a shovel, a plow with a crack down the center. They'd cleared away dusty boxes with books covered in mildew, tablecloths and sheets speckled with mold, curios like ceramic statues of children praying, their shine dulled, the corners chipped.

They waited several minutes before the edges of the photograph came into focus.

"Now look at that," Starling said, watching Marilyn emerge in the developing solution. "Her eyes are as big as walnuts."

Everleigh had hung a double strand of thick rope like a clothesline overhead. When Starling lifted the picture from the developing solution, it had to go into the stop bath, and, after that, a fixer, which they'd also put in large baby pools. The chemicals were noxious and dizzying. "You were right. You can't look away from her."

Starling let the solution drain off the image. "Imagine this on the wall in the gallery, famous faces suddenly feeling like friends. Like someone you could talk to."

Everleigh hadn't considered that before. Maybe Starling liked pictures that invited people into others' inner lives because hers was so pained. "Do you want people to feel like they know them?"

Starling studied the contours of the paper, the print for splotches. "I suppose, but I also find faces fascinating. They're a roadmap into someone's life, offering clues, remnants even, of how the person has lived. When they have a lot of laugh lines, you know how much they've smiled. When the crease between their eyebrows is deep, they've had worry. When they wear a full face of makeup, they're often hiding something they're afraid people will see."

"You know what's interesting to me," Everleigh said, reaching for the print, feeling the drips of the solution on the fronts of her sneakers, the wetness spreading across her toes. She clipped one side of the image up on the thick clothesline, then the other. "That a photograph freezes time. It doesn't matter if Marilyn found out a dear friend died a moment later or her face began to sag with age. In this photograph, she will forever be who she was when the photo was snapped. A carefree woman kicking her legs up on a wicker chair. She will always be this happy, this full of life, even though it's impossible to stay that way."

"Photographers stop time." The two women stood back from the print, now hanging, unable to really see it in the black light, but admiring the contrasting white and darkness of the actress's eyes.

"Yes!" Everleigh watched Starling climb up onto the tractor. "And in a photograph, nothing can hurt you."

"The frames are walls." Starling nodded.

"Yes." Everleigh thought that was true. Within the confines of a photograph, you controlled everything as the artist: the light, the mood, the pose. If you didn't want to see the truth, you didn't have to. An emptiness took over the barn as the words settled into the dust on the planked floors.

Starling climbed up to the enlarger to slip a different negative inside. Everleigh couldn't see her as much as she could hear her. "I have a picture I keep of my daughter in my wallet from when she was nine. We're on a carousel, our cheeks pressing against each other, her eyes bright as only a little girl's can be. We were so in love with the feeling of just being close to each other."

Starling was quiet a beat. "But little girls are so much easier than teenage daughters. And then they become women and blame you for all of their own shortcomings."

Everleigh looked into the darkness, hoping she'd say more. She heard only the sound of Starling making adjustments to the slide.

"My mother and I had an awful time in my teenage years, too," Everleigh said. "Actually, we still struggle."

Starling jumped down after turning the enlarger on and off. The next print was ready to go into the pool with the developing solution. "We all hate the ugly parts of ourselves we see in our mothers, and mothers hate the ugly parts of themselves they see in their girls. But we're so hard on each other, harder than mothers are on their sons, or daughters are on their fathers. My husband could do no wrong in her eyes, even with his myriad faults."

"But it's hard to make those generalizations," said Everleigh. "My mother is a depressive, and it's made me resent her, but not because I'm a depressive too. My entire childhood revolved around her mental state. Would it be a day she would feel well and take me to the park, or would she not have the energy to brush her teeth?"

Everleigh remembered what she'd read about Starling, how she'd left her husband and daughter to pursue her photography, and the judgment she'd felt reading that. "Do you talk to your daughter often?"

It would be several minutes before the picture of Nat King Cole began to show in the solution. Starling leaned over the pool to wait. "She and her father don't like me very much. If you stick with this"— Starling nodded toward the developing solution, the enlarger suspended in midair—"you'll see. Women are punished for making art."

Everleigh crossed her arms. "But not by your own family."

"Isn't that why I have to pick you up in the morning these days? Because your fiancé took away your car. Why did he take it away?" Starling looked over her thick black glasses at Everleigh, and it was then that she realized the photographer wanted her to answer, a teacher waiting on her pupil.

"I'm afraid he is punishing me lately."

"My dear, I hate to say it, but who wants to come home to a wife that's in the darkroom?"

"When we first met, he said he loved that I took pictures," Everleigh said. Roland always got a kick out of posing for her. He'd even brought her camera out from the city.

Starling ran her hand through the solution. "Let me tell you a little story. When I met my husband, I had a camera around my neck. I snapped all these wonderful pictures of the two of us as we were falling in love; it was his face that made me start studying other people's faces in my lens. I truly loved him." Her voice was distant, and she laughed, like she was lost in a memory, pulled backward in time and wanting to remain there a moment. The photograph was beginning to show its contours: Nat on the diving board, his feet dangling over the pool.

"Then I had Sally, and those tiny tulip lips of hers were too much to bear, and I couldn't take my eyes off her. I took pictures of her every single day, even printing them out and dating each one. The money I must have spent on film, and we didn't have that much money! My husband loved all of it. It was later, though, after he returned from the war, that my career seemed to be picking up. I was getting calls from photo editors. They were assigning me photo shoots that I had to board airplanes to get to. Suddenly, I was being offered more money than he made, and these assignments interfered with our home life and he ordered me to stop."

Everleigh wasn't certain if she'd continue working after this job. "So what happened?" She opened a can of ginger ale.

"I left. I couldn't take Sally with me. It was a horrific ending, to tell the truth, and she was so little. Twelve. But I thought I'd send for her later, once I was on my feet. It all happened so fast. I didn't anticipate that my daughter would hate me for walking out the door that night."

Something in the story brought out the pain of her own mother's trips in and out of the psychiatric hospital, a daughter watching her mother leave her behind.

Starling put the image of Nat King Cole into the stop-bath solution, then the fixer. "Once you have a little one, your ability to create, if you're a creative person, is hampered. It's very difficult to be an artist and a mother. It doesn't mean you can't, but it fights against the nature of the job. An artist lives in his own mind. A mother must live outside hers—she's always in the heads of her kids."

"I want a baby with Roland, I do, but I'm scared to have one for a different reason. I see the way my mother hurt me. What if I do that to my own child?"

"Parenting can be painful. It can be frustrating, even if it is often rewarding." Starling crouched to look closer at the print in the pool. "Children, no matter the age, take over your head, maybe similarly to the way mothers weigh on your decisions."

Everleigh hung the image on the clothesline. They were moving through the portraits faster than she thought they would. "My mother seems to breathe the air I breathe."

Starling sighed, like Everleigh was missing something. "I love my daughter and always have, but I love my work, too. I won't give it up. Some people didn't like that. She didn't like that. My husband and friends didn't like that. People feel threatened when you don't make the same choices as them. It's scary, I think, because if your life takes a different path, it makes other people wonder if their choices are wrong, too. Especially if there's something else they wish they were doing."

One night her mother had had too much to drink while on her medication and it had made her loopy, and she'd told Everleigh that she didn't love her father anymore. That she wanted to leave him. There was nothing to say at first, but then Everleigh had a glimmer of hope that if her mother left, she would be happy. That the trips into the mental institute would end, and her mother would be entirely hers. But her mother, who was snuggled in Everleigh's bed wearing her silk nightgown, had only shaken her head. "You think he'd let me leave? He'd ruin me."

"I don't know what I'd do if I left Roland." The words had slipped out, and she was surprised by them. Last night, after Curtis dropped her off, she'd sat near the living room window staring at the night sky, thinking about how she'd said she and Roland made sense in the city. But shouldn't they make sense everywhere?

"Are you considering it, leaving him?" Starling was waiting on a third print now: this one was of Marlon Brando.

"Not really. We already rented the wedding hall. We have a honeymoon planned for Niagara Falls, a house being decorated for us."

"That's not a very convincing argument, dear. I didn't ask what you have; I asked what you want."

They heard the flapping again, the whoosh of an animal flying overhead. It was a fruit bat living in the rafters. They'd woken it in the darkness, and after they'd chased after the animal with an old tennis racquet earlier, it went into hiding. Now it was swooping low again. Everleigh held the racquet up like she was on the tennis court, poised to swing. She felt a blur of air overhead, whacking the darkness and missing. Starling dove down every time they felt it flapping nearby.

Then the bat flew right at her face, and Everleigh screamed like she was being murdered. She slammed it, the animal careening wildly toward the wall. It fell to the floor, knocking over a canister of nails, causing Everleigh to shriek louder, shaking herself off like it had landed in her lap.

She felt terrible for hurting it, and yet, laughter bubbled up and out of her. "Oh my goodness. What if its fur is in the developing solution, or it fell on one of our prints?"

Starling moved to examine the pictures, howling. "Every shoot has a lemon moment, but this takes the cake. The photos look fine." She sat on a chair and unscrewed a metal thermos, guzzling one of her strange concoctions: spinach, lemon, maybe a whiff of apple. "Have you been drinking the drinks I bring you every day? I would say your block is lifting."

"I suppose," she said, not saying that the taste made her gag.

Starling was practically chewing the drink, it was so thick. "You need to call your mother, Everleigh. She misses you, I guarantee it. Talk to her about how you've been feeling, what's in your heart. She'll understand."

Everleigh sighed, leaning against a dusty box. "She'll make me come home, though, and I like it out here."

"Tell her that you're old enough to make your own decisions, and you don't need their money; you need their love."

It wasn't that easy, though, talking to her parents. It dredged up pain that no one but her could understand or even feel, layers of guilt and resentment interwoven with joy and happy memories. "I'll agree to call my mother if you agree to call your daughter. There has to be something you can say to win her back. . . ."

Starling stood then, returning to the film, making clear she wasn't interested in continuing the conversation. After she came down from the tractor, she said, "There's a cottage at the art colony. Someone is leaving—a sculptor is returning to New York. It's not much. Just one room with a bed and a drafting table, and it's only for a month. But you could use the darkroom and try this life out more seriously."

Everleigh had gotten a call from the *East Hampton Star* the day before; they were hiring her for another shoot. This time, she was scheduled to take pictures of some firefighters who had saved a family of ducklings from a sewer drain.

Starling picked up a corner of the print of Brando, then the other, and lifted it from the liquid. "It's ten dollars a week for room and board. Is it something you'd be interested in? Because I can talk to Lucca, who runs it. No one is going to interview you. They don't have anyone else lined up."

Everleigh's mind wandered to the neat row of white cottages at the art colony, the pebbly horseshoe driveway, the meadow where she'd lain down and closed her eyes that first day she'd met Starling. Sometimes she imagined what it would be like to live in one of those rustic cottages, to be one of the real artists, not someone pretending to be one, like herself. Everleigh imagined drilling a circle into the wall, any wall, and pushing it open and stepping into an entirely new life. She could do it. She could live there. She could keep taking assignments from the *Star*, work for Starling, maybe see Curtis again. Discover what it was like to be completely on her own.

It felt like the floor might suddenly give out under her feet. "Can I think about it?"

Starling smiled gently. "Of course. I'm rather partial to impulse, and it hasn't always served me well."

TWENTY-ONE

It was Thursday when she and Starling finally finished all eight prints for the show. Now the photographs were in the hands of the woodworker, who promised frames by Saturday. Exhausted from working dawn to dusk both days before, she and Starling agreed to take off the rest of the afternoon and tomorrow morning. Roland had already told her he'd be late tonight—something about a golf outing and dinner, although she didn't believe anything he said anymore, so he could be anywhere.

Still, knowing Roland was gone for certain, she'd arranged to take the photographs of the firemen for her second newspaper assignment at six. She introduced herself to the trio of handsome volunteers in their midtwenties as "Lee Farrows," and they made jolly conversation as they left the brick fire station to show her the drainage grate where they'd lifted out a family of trapped ducklings. She posed them looking into the drain, pointing, as if they were just seeing the tiny animals, then took a few more candid shots, avoiding the stereotypical arms-folded-across-the-chest pictures.

"That hotel fire in June was a bad one—did any of you fight it?" Everleigh asked, as they walked back to the fire station.

A crooked grin overtook Lafferty, a local who taught high school math during the school year; he was the most talkative. "We held those hoses all night and it didn't matter. It was like that hotel wanted to burn."

"You seem to think fires have a mind of their own," she said.

"In those big old houses in the summer colony, sure. They're built with timber. One match, and poof, the whole thing's in flames."

"Any idea how it started?"

He whistled, as if to say *it's complicated*. "It was definitely arson. I keep saying that whoever started that fire had to have been at the hotel that night; it went up too fast and furious for them to steal off."

Everleigh's eyebrow went up. "But you could hop the fence and run to the beach without anyone seeing you at all." She thought back to that night. While Roland snored in bed next to her, what had become of Stevie? He must have remained at the hotel, maybe checking into a room, because he was there in an instant, escorting people out of the burning building, throwing buckets of sand on the flames. But in what room had he slept? Had room twenty-three been occupied by him and the mysterious woman that he kissed in the phone booth? Had that been *Opal*?

Lafferty shook his head. "You misunderstand me, Miss. A person *could* race off, yes, but they wouldn't want to. A fire that big? Whoever started it wanted to enjoy the show."

"You really think?" she said, surprised.

He spat in the grass. "Most definitely. Arsonists like to watch."

Stevie popped into her head again, how he loved to make those big bonfires on the beach, how entranced he was by the flames. Roland had told her early on that Stevie had invested money in the hotel, that if Roland lost, he lost. But maybe him setting the fire had nothing to do with money. Roland may have done something to upset Stevie, but he also may have done nothing at all. Instead, Stevie might have set the fire to create hardship in Roland's life, just so he could swoop in and save him. She'd learned about this in psychology, how shared pain could glue people together.

Another fireman, a guy named Louis, broke into the conversation. "I got my money on Gordon, the caretaker."

"Excuse me?" Everleigh thought of the old man's wizened skin when she'd woken up in the cottage the morning after the fire. How put off his wife seemed, how the gentleman seemed as sad as Roland about the fire, like he'd lost something himself.

Louis wrinkled his bulbous red nose. "That guy was living in that place for ten years before that rich jerk came and kicked him out, making him beg for a job. I know it was his house, but that was class-A crummy."

The others murmured in agreement, and the conversation changed entirely then, something about a baseball game that weekend, and Everleigh said her goodbyes.

A bit rattled, trying to backtrack through the night, looking for clues to link Gordon to the fire, she found herself walking to the sweet Cape Cod building that was Southampton Children's Medicine. Stepping inside, the space smelled of rubbing alcohol and lemon.

"Curtis?" she called from the empty waiting room, where large alphabet letters were taped to the walls. He came out of a back room in blue scrubs, relieved when he realized it was Everleigh.

"I'm sorry that I didn't call you," he said, hands in his pockets. "But I didn't want to make any trouble."

"I've been at the barn every day with Starling anyway." A sudden bashfulness overcame her. Now that they'd kissed, it felt strange to stand here as friends.

"That's why you weren't at the gallery. I waited outside for you every morning this week around nine." He removed his lab coat. "Hold on. Let me change."

Everleigh nodded. She sat in the waiting room reading through the homemaking magazines. A recipe for French beans salad with mustard dressing. She yelled back to ask if she could rip it out. He said sure, but only if she cooked it for him.

"Of course," she said. "But only if you help with the dishes."

Minutes later, they were out on the bricked sidewalks, Curtis in khakis and a golf shirt, Converse on his feet. "Mom is making paella. Will you come eat with us?" Her heart pounded like she was running, her mind returning to the other night on the beach.

"Of course," she said. "But I'll need to buy your mother flowers."

The air was cooler than it had been an hour before. They were walking to his car when they ran into Ernest, who was parked next to Curtis. They said their hellos, Everleigh introducing Curtis as a friend.

"Have we met before?" Ernest said to him.

"I don't believe so. Unless you have kids. I'm the pediatrician in town."

Ernest reached his hand out to shake Curtis's; they were equally sized, although Curtis was twice as handsome.

"Are you doing some shopping?" Everleigh motioned to the bag he was holding; she was trying to play it cool but really she eyed him suspiciously, still uncertain if he was a good guy or a bad guy. "I thought that was Alice's job."

Ernest frowned dramatically. "She asked me to run out for a bottle of nail polish remover. Her nieces are visiting from Boston, and they're having a slumber party."

If Ernest noticed Everleigh's face fall, he didn't let on. Nail polish remover, also known as *acetone*. It was the chemical they'd found in room twenty-three, the accelerant that had started the fire. Was it possible that the hotel went up in flames because of something as simple as nail polish remover?

Ernest checked his watch again. "I best be getting back," he said. She nodded, relieved that Curtis was standing beside her, like he would offer her protection if she needed it. Because she was certain that if Alice was involved in the fire, then Ernest was, too.

"Good night." Everleigh waved. She wondered if the detective realized that acetone was in nail polish remover and that every woman—including her—had at least one bottle in their bathroom closet.

⸻H⸻

The Brightwells owned thirty acres in Bridgehampton, and she and Curtis turned onto the dirt road leading to their house, the wide-open fields green with lines of potato plants that stretched to the crash of the ocean. There was a simple white shack halfway up the dirt driveway where a few of the migrants, Black men who came up from the South for the summer, were packing up from a day's work.

They parked at a simple yellow farmhouse with black shutters, a small porch at the front, where a man and woman rocked in high-backed chairs. To the left of the house was a fenced garden; on the right was a field of sunflowers glowing yellow to the horizon. A wave of nerves washed over Everleigh as it did whenever she met someone new, but she reminded herself that his parents were farmers. She didn't have to put on airs. She just had to be herself.

As she and Curtis approached the porch, a man with light hair and freckles, wrinkles pulling away from his eyes, came to stand, holding a drink in his left hand. "Now, Curtis, you didn't say you were bringing company," the man said, adjusting his overall straps. "The name is Edward. I'm Curtis's father."

The air smelled of freshly turned soil, and she held out her hand, aware that it was red and raw from working with the photographs. "Everleigh Farrows of New York City." She'd been trained to sound formal during introductions, but Curtis's father looked at her like she was from outer space.

His father laughed, then said, "Edward Brightwell of the potato fields, by way of London, although my parents always said I was a smidge Scottish."

"There, there, don't torture our guest." A petite woman stepped forward, her long black hair tied in a ribbon at the nape of her neck. "I'm Julia, Curtis's mother, and you can forgive my husband's lack of grace." Everleigh could see why Curtis had such a distinct look: his mother seemed to be of Spanish origin, while his father's features were angular and English.

The farmer put his arm around his wife's shoulders. "She'll have you think I don't tell a good joke, but don't believe her. I'm as cheeky as you can get." He grinned, and Everleigh noticed a thin scar running the length of his left cheek.

Curtis hugged his father. "Hey, Pop," which she found endearing. Then, "Hola, Mama," he said, embracing her, too.

"Curtis," Julia said, concern gathering in her ample brows—they were long and wide and nearly touching. She glanced at Everleigh's ring finger. "You know I made paella. Is that okay with your guest? Because I can mix a fast salad from the garden, if you'd prefer it, Everleigh."

The setting sun invited gold specks into Curtis's eyes. "Don't worry, Mom—she's not scared of our food."

"I've been trying new things left and right this summer." Everleigh smiled.

"That sounds interesting." Julia placed her hand on Everleigh's back. "Since you're here, would you mind helping me in the kitchen?"

Curtis gave her an apologetic look, but she liked Julia Brightwell already, envious that Curtis had grown up with someone like her, a steady hand at his helm. A therapist once told Everleigh that she had to stop looking for mothers in the women she knew. She had to accept that she already had one, just an imperfect one. But she couldn't help it. Sometimes Everleigh met other families and thought, *How would I be different if I had grown up with all that stillness?*

Everleigh passed through a small living room with a moss-green velvet sofa with sagging cushions and a coffee table covered in plastic. They entered the kitchen through a swinging doorway, the area nothing more than a few cabinets, an icebox, and an antique white range. Wire baskets on the floor were filled with potatoes. On the burner was an enormous pot, yellow rice mixed with shrimp and mussels, clams, and peas.

Everleigh inhaled the most incredible smell. "Is that saffron?"

Curtis's mother stopped stirring. "You know it?"

"I've been experimenting lately," Everleigh said. "I never learned growing up, so I've been trying to teach myself, and there was a recipe in the Ladies Improvement cookbook—saffron chicken and rice. It wasn't nearly as fragrant, but it's familiar enough."

"What else are you making?" Julia asked, handing her a stack of napkins and a handful of silverware, leading her out the back door, where the family had fashioned a tarp like a tent, creating a shaded patio with views over the farm fields. The water was a sliver in the distance without a single tree to obscure the sight line. Everleigh chatted mindlessly about her failings with scrambled eggs and her love of simple tomato sandwiches while setting the scuffed square farm table.

They'd forgotten a tablecloth, and Everleigh was directed to the linen closet to fetch one. In the hallway were a dozen framed photographs of Curtis—riding a tricycle as a toddler, digging up potatoes as a boy. One picture showed him at his high school graduation, his arms around friends. One woman's chubby cheeks were familiar, making Everleigh squint. It looked like the woman from the hotel, Vivienne, the washerwoman. Only in the photo she was younger, by at least ten years. Perhaps they had grown up together.

There was a small brass bell attached to the back door, and Julia rang it twice. "It's meant to be heard from the fields, but it's how I always call them to dinner now." She smiled at Everleigh. Then she rushed to the table with steaming bowls of paella. Curtis and his father rounded the house, and Curtis winked at Everleigh, which made her smile.

"Curtis tells me you take photos for the paper," Edward said, tossing an empty mussel shell into a bowl.

"Yes, but I've only just started," Everleigh stared at the prawn in her rice; she'd only ever had shrimp cocktail, where the tentacles and eyes were deliberately removed, allowing you to forget the creature was ever alive.

Julia registered her hesitation, meeting Everleigh's eyes kindly and demonstrating wordlessly that you were to devein it, just like a typical shrimp.

"My family is from the Costa Brava, just outside Barcelona," Julia said. "My grandmother made paella every Friday night. We've tried to keep up the tradition."

Curtis tore a clam out of its shell, chewing and smiling. "When I was in med school in Boston, I begged Mom to drive up with a pot. You came, too, that one time."

His parents seemed charmed that he remembered. "That was the weekend," his father said, "that there was a nor'easter, flooded the fields. We lost half our yield."

Every bite reminded her of how new her life was beginning to feel. It was more spice than she was accustomed to, but that only made her like it more.

After dessert—a decadent caramel flan, also new to Everleigh and also delicious—she and Curtis went for a walk. He led her through the fields of sunflowers. "It's Mom's favorite flower, so Dad plants them every year."

"There must be a thousand of them," she said, twirling about. Everywhere you looked there were bees buzzing, the sunflowers standing in rows like people, their stalks at least five feet tall, their enormous petals and faces turned toward the lowering sun. The couple was halfway to the ocean when Curtis took her hand, a golden glow illuminating her smile.

"Your parents are lovely."

"Well, you know what it's like to be an only child. They have no one else to dote on."

Everleigh wished she could say the same for hers. "Have you ever brought a girl home before?"

He shook his head. "Nah," he said.

Her eyes grew to twice their normal size. "I'm the first girl you've brought home? But you've spent a total sum of ten hours with me."

A smile crept over his face. "Well, I didn't formally bring you home."

She felt herself blush. It was Everleigh who kept reminding him they were friends.

Their heels kicked up dusty dirt as they walked, their footsteps approaching a second abandoned white shack with open windows. Curtis ducked inside, pulling Everleigh in, the sun casting a small square across the plywood floor. He leaned in to kiss her, his hand running up the silk of her blouse. A mounting desire rose through her, but she hesitated, trying to decide if kissing him was worth the fallout if she was caught. But if someone walked by, they wouldn't even see them. She relented, and he kissed down her neck in an instant, her hair brushing against his cheeks. His mouth traveled to the second button of her shirt. She grabbed his face and raised it back to hers, wanting this to go farther but knowing it couldn't.

"Is there somewhere else we can go?" she asked. "To talk?"

They ran hand in hand through the dusty sunflower fields until another house appeared in the distance. This one was a white-shingled farmhouse with a porch, nearly identical to the one his parents had. He opened the front door, leading her quickly through the living room with its wooden planks on the floor and plumped couch. They ran up the stairs with its ornately carved newel post. His bedroom had views of the ocean in the distance, waves crashing along a sandbar. He laid her down softly on the navy quilt, and she thought how lovely life was with him. How predictable the path through the sunflowers was, how caring his mother had been, how Curtis had kissed her in the shed, and now they were inside his house, it was all too much to bear.

But she couldn't lose herself entirely in his kisses. She reminded herself that she had felt just as enamored with Roland the year before. She'd been convinced that they, too, were perfect for one another. Perhaps she fell for men too hard and too fast. Perhaps she looked to them to validate her place in the world, and when their adoration waned, she felt directionless. Even if she liked Curtis, even if she wanted to be with him tonight, she wasn't sure she'd ever give another man that power over her. She would need to slow this down.

Everleigh pulled away from him, gazed into his eyes, and ran her fingers through his hair. They lay facing one another on top of his covers, darkness closing in. She wanted to ask him if he'd had many girlfriends, why he wasn't married yet, if he wanted children.

Instead, she said, "There's an opening at the art colony where Starling is living. It's not much—a room and meals, a place to work on my photographs."

He didn't hesitate. "I hope you're going to take it."

"I want to, but there are bigger repercussions." Everleigh studied her fingernails, overcome with guilt. Living with artists? Kissing another man? If there was a hell, Everleigh was going. "Besides, I don't think I can break off the engagement. I'm not strong enough."

Curtis propped himself up on his elbows. "Maybe not. But building strength isn't only about walking away from something. It's about walking toward it. Do me a favor? Close your eyes."

She laughed, obliging him, her cheek resting on the pillowcase.

"Imagine you walk into a room, and it's pitch-black. Start filling up the space with things that make you happy. Think of the people you see, furniture, artwork, whatever. Okay, now switch on the light and take a look around."

Everleigh saw herself carrying a stack of freshly developed photographs into a sunny living room, Mango cat purring at her feet. She imagined Whitney and her mother sitting on the couch waiting for a pour of champagne, celebrating nothing other than life. Starling stepped into the frame.

She shot open her eyes.

"You see?" he said. "That is where you get your strength. Whatever you saw is what you should move toward. It's the life you want."

He was right, but Roland complicated matters. Despite his faults, she was promised to him. Of course she wanted what was in the room she envisioned, but not at the expense of her family. Not at the expense of forever losing the people she loved.

They walked back to Curtis's parents' house, the television illuminating the windows, and climbed into his car. On the ride home, they held hands. Curtis dropped her off a few minutes away from the cottage. She'd walk the rest of the way. Everleigh blew him a kiss, disappearing into the shadows of the looming hotel, back into the gloom.

TWENTY-TWO

To get to Whitney's luncheon, Everleigh left the gallery and rode her bike with her red heels in the front basket, her hair pulled into a French twist, shorts under her loveliest floral dress. Starling had wedged Everleigh's bicycle into her car trunk when she picked her up that morning, and now she was riding through the prettiest parts of East Hampton, the houses large and cedar shingled with lush sweeping lawns and well-tended roses and hydrangea bushes grown to the right height and perfect plumpness. Whitney's family's oceanfront compound had six bedrooms, tennis courts, and horse stables, the house itself sitting directly on the Atlantic. Everleigh dropped her bike near a row of polished cars parked by valets, and while hiding behind a shed, she shimmied off her shorts and approached the large oak door, ringing the bell.

A housekeeper in a black dress and white apron led her outside to the slate patio terrace where a dozen round tables were set with large bouquets of white hydrangeas at the center, the ocean breeze wreaking havoc on the tablecloths, held down with large smooth rocks.

There must have been four dozen women in attendance, eating off small cocktail napkins. The members of the Ladies Village Improvement Society of East Hampton were hardly a raucous bunch; they raised money to buy and plant flowers in the small East End villages each summer. One of Whitney's jobs was to create a master schedule of women volunteering to water and weed in the lovely downtowns.

Whitney saw Everleigh arrive, waving her over. It had been a while since she'd gone to one of these, and Everleigh was struck by how pristine the decor looked, with crisp white chairs, pots of overspilling tropical foliage, a view of the sea that was so perfect it seemed painted.

"You came!" Whitney hugged her. "This is my best friend, Lee. Lee, I want you to meet Mary and Kate." Everleigh smiled at two tall women sipping gin and tonics, their faces angular and made-up.

Whitney made small talk between them, about how they all got their hair coiffed by the glamorous Mr. Kenneth at Lilly Daché's hatmaking emporium on Fifty-Sixth. But the conversation stalled when Everleigh didn't share their enthusiasm for the star stylist's signature soft waves. Then Whitney asked Everleigh to follow her inside the house. She wanted to show her a new vase she bought, and for a moment, Everleigh thought her friend was going to tell her she was finally pregnant.

Instead, wrinkles creased Whitney's forehead as she clicked shut the French doors, whispering, "Lee, someone from the women's hospital in Westchester called me this morning, asking me to evaluate your character. He was asking me the weirdest questions. Had you made any irrational decisions lately? Are your moods predictable? Have you mentioned any hallucinations?"

The questions were immediately familiar; they were listed on the psychiatric intake form that her father filled out when her mother was having a spell. The answers went to the psychiatrist, and they determined her treatment. "Did he say why he was calling?"

Whitney squeezed her eyes shut, trying to remember. She continued to whisper. "No. I mean, yes. He said that they believed you'd benefit from inpatient treatment, but they needed to know where to place you. I was listed as a reference, and he asked that I remain discreet and not share the information, so that your placement is seamless."

Of course Everleigh's moods were unpredictable! No woman was so steady she didn't ripple, but that didn't mean she needed electrotherapy either. And no, she didn't have hallucinations. She wasn't even depressed. "But who called them? Why does anyone think I need the kind of help my mother does?"

"Well, I asked that, too, and the man said, 'You must know her fiancé, Roland Whittaker. He said she's been spiraling downward, and we're a little concerned. Her parents are, too.'"

Her parents! "Roland wouldn't even know that expression 'spiraling' if he hadn't heard me say that about my mother!"

Outside, women were still arriving—Everleigh saw Opal sway into the scene—and Whitney bit down on her lip. "I told him that you were perfectly fine, and he thanked me for my time. But I think you're in trouble, Lee. I don't know what Roland is telling your parents, but it doesn't sound good."

An image popped into her head: an ambulance pulling up to the cottage, men in uniforms with grave expressions walking toward her, her body being pulled outside in her nightgown, strapped onto the stretcher. "I'll talk to him tonight, if he ever comes home."

There was nothing wrong with her, so why was Roland doing this?

Everleigh calmed her breathing. "It's okay, let's go back outside. Nothing is certain anyway—maybe he's just exploring the idea."

Whitney nodded, moving back onto the terrace. "I need to make a quick announcement, but I'll find you after."

The world grew out of focus, and Everleigh moved through the clusters of women, barely able to feel her feet. After a brief hello to Opal, who didn't seem very interested in talking to her, Everleigh joined a group of acquaintances from the city who were complaining about their cleaning ladies. The topic, which could bond a circle of rich women in seconds, provided her a temporary distraction. Everleigh had been scrubbing her own toilet and sweeping her own house, giving her an entirely new appreciation of Nanny. It was silly to admit, but she'd been taken care of so closely for so many years, sometimes she forgot it was possible to open your top drawer and not find rows of perfectly folded underwear. These days Everleigh just dumped them in, even if Vivienne, the washerwoman, delivered them in neat stacks.

There was assigned seating, and she found her spot at a banquet table with Whitney and Alice and other women from the city who organized the Costume Institute Benefit, a fundraiser for the Metropolitan Museum of Art's Costume Institute. Everleigh wished she could change tables now that she was sitting directly across from Alice. A gentleman in a suit passed a platter of tea sandwiches around with a small set of tongs, and Everleigh opted for two small tomato sandwiches with bacon jam. Her version tasted so much better.

"Did you hear that Maybelle's is taking appointments for the latest collections from Paris?" said Ronnie Newton, a chubby girl in blue eyeshadow; her face drooped more than it should at thirty.

Whitney expressed aggravation that she had to travel downtown to find a decent dress.

The conversation turned to gossip about a woman—someone a few years older than them at Spence—who left her husband last year. Alice reported that when the gentleman didn't offer her child support, she'd been rendered penniless and forced to return to the Upper East Side apartment to live with him.

"How do you go back from that?" Geraldine Burrows said, putting her hand over her bow lips. "I mean, I'm not sure even *I'd* take her back." One of the women elbowed Geraldine's middle, reminding her she was being terrible, but she only snorted, a little too hog-like. "Well, she's a size four, double D. No man says no to that."

"We should be raising money to help her," Everleigh blurted, feeling the stares of the other women at the table. Whitney scolded her with her eyes, but she was undeterred. "Well, it's true. She's an unhappy woman who feels trapped. She deserves her freedom if she's courageous enough to ask for it." She thought of her mother, and how she'd admitted to Everleigh that she couldn't leave her father without trouble, and she imagined herself telling Roland that she was ending their engagement. What if he did something awful to her? Would the women at this table be gossiping about her at the next luncheon?

"Her freedom? She's not in prison, Lee." Whitney cleared her throat, making clear she found Everleigh's thinking extreme.

Everleigh crossed her legs, feeling the tight press where they met. "And how would we know, Whit? We're not living in their house, hearing what they say to each other. People don't need to be behind bars to feel locked away."

Geraldine folded her hands together over her plate. "Anyway. Can we move on?" The women at the table chuckled, even Alice.

"Come on, Lee," Alice said. "How many pet projects can you take on? You already have Roland." The other women grew interested in their lunch.

"The flowers near the bakehouse in town have been looking dreadful." Whitney recovered the conversation. "Who is responsible for the watering?" The conversation once again shifted, and Everleigh tried not to glance at Alice, wondering how she could sit here facing Everleigh, challenging her, if she'd been the one to light the hotel fire.

She refolded her cloth napkin on her lap, glaring at Alice. "I need to talk to you privately. But first—" And she looked about at the smug expressions of the other women at the table. "But first, I have an announcement. Starling Meade's art opening is this coming Monday night. Do all of you plan to go and support her?"

When they acted disinterested, Everleigh couldn't help but cast judgment. "You don't know Starling Meade? The famous photographer. Her photos will be at the Juniper Gallery in East Hampton. You should come, and try saying something nice for a change."

Everleigh couldn't take these women anymore, even Whitney, and the charade they all lived, as though catty women's chatter was all they were capable of. She could see now that it was women who sold themselves short. Didn't any of them want to be more than this?

"You should all go see her works," Whitney said, kicking Everleigh under the table, working to sound like her feathers weren't ruffled. "The portraits are intriguing."

Intriguing. Even that seemed a slight.

Everleigh led Alice to a corner of the lawn, where she twirled to face the petite woman who liked to brag she could cry on command. Would she cry now and feign innocence? Everleigh wouldn't ask her about the fire, not yet, wanting to collect as much evidence as possible against her first.

"At the hotel grand opening party, you made clear you knew Roland, and since then you've made clear you despise him. Why?"

A crow landed on a fence picket near them—a gloomy harbinger—and Everleigh ignored the urge to shoo it away.

Alice folded her arms. "You keep treating me like I'm the enemy, Lee. Believe it or not, I'm looking out for you. It's why Ernest came to warn you about the detective."

"But you led the detective directly to me, sharing those details of Elsa."

She wondered if Alice knew how neatly Everleigh had connected her and Ernest to the fire. Their voices at the pool, her threat to Opal at the bonfire, the missing locket.

"Lee, the detective asked if you've ever been questioned by police before. I couldn't lie."

"You didn't need to embellish either," she said, rolling her eyes.

"What I really want to know is why Roland is the enemy. Is this really about the fact that your parents don't want a hotel on Gin Lane?"

Alice glanced at the table where Whitney sat, then spoke conspiratorially, like they were two spies sharing secrets. "Well, maybe you need to know the real Roland. Because he gets away with everything."

Everleigh's voice shot out. "And Ernest. He said he'd go after Rolly if he saw you talking to him."

Surprise registered in Alice's brows. "Ernest misunderstands my preoccupation with Roland."

"Please tell me what he did."

She braced herself, knowing she couldn't wholly trust Alice, that if she had started the fire, this would be her chance to manipulate Everleigh into believing her innocence. Still, Everleigh was so desperate to learn the truth behind Roland's relationship with his father, the parts of himself that he kept hidden.

From the patio, friends called Alice's name; it was time for her to give a summer toast, but Everleigh suspected that they were merely trying to save her from the mad extremist who had dragged her away from the luncheon.

"Just take a drive to Mecox on the main drag in Amagansett," Alice said, "and you'll see Roland for who he really is."

"And what does that mean? What is Mecox?" It sounded like a hotel, maybe. She didn't want to go nose around Mecox. She only wanted to know what he had to do with Alice.

"It's a farm stand!" Alice yelled.

Everleigh pulled Alice by the arm deep into Whitney's house, bringing her to a sitting room with navy couches and a framed painting of a marlin. The air-conditioning made the sweat of her temples turn cold. "You keep saying you're looking out for me. So here's your chance. Enlighten me."

Alice's eyes flickered. In another room, there was the unmistakable sound of a housekeeper sweeping.

"Fine. It involves my cousin," Alice started, her voice quiet. She seemed surprised when Everleigh knew the details of the boating accident, that everyone expected Birdie and Roland to marry but Roland had broken her heart. "Maybe it doesn't sound criminal, Lee, but his family did egregious things to cover up the accident. They paid off the town to drop charges and they built a big new dock for boaters. They convinced two of Roland's friends to say they were on board, too, and that he hadn't been drinking. He got away with all of it, even though my cousin nearly died from a concussion."

"But she's okay, right? Her injuries weren't permanent?" The difference made this an issue of heartbreak versus irresponsibility.

Alice walked to the fireplace mantel, with its myriad framed portraits of Whitney and Truman on their wedding day. "Well, that leads me to the sticky part. Birdie was pregnant—she didn't know it then, of course—and Roland refused to ever see her again after the accident. His father protected him to the end, and the Whittaker family won't even acknowledge Sarabeth, and she's four now, with lots of questions about her daddy."

An image of a little girl with bouncing curls popped into Everleigh's mind, a Fair Isle sweater, a corduroy skirt, and shiny Mary Janes. The thought pierced her chest, needles poking through a photograph on a cork board. It was unfathomable that Roland had a child he ignored.

But Alice's story also succeeded in helping Everleigh understand why Alice despised him, why her family would try to stop his social climbing in the Hamptons. To them, he was nothing but a jerk getting a lot of undeserved attention. They were likely vindicated when the hotel burned down, and yet it seemed clear that they could still be behind it. It was easy revenge they could wipe their hands of.

"Maybe the child isn't Roland's—maybe . . ."

Alice shuddered in her sleeveless dress, reaching for her purse and pulling out a photograph of a little girl, the resemblance to Roland uncanny. Everleigh ran her finger over the child's round face, her pretty blue eyes, Roland's eyes. "Why wouldn't you tell me this?"

"I've been sworn to secrecy by my aunt. Birdie is engaged to another man, and everyone in town thinks her daughter's father was a navy man who died unexpectedly. If her fiancé finds out otherwise, he'll never forgive her."

Everleigh doubted anyone was that tight-lipped without having a stake in the silence themselves. Roland must have something over Alice, too. "And you? Are you innocent in all of this?"

Alice cocked her head. "I've watched my cousin suffer, Lee, and I won't let him trample anyone else's good name. That I promise."

Whitney rushed into the sitting room, taking a seat beside Everleigh, still staring at the picture. "That will be enough, Alice," Whitney scolded, glimpsing the photograph. "Lee doesn't need anything else from you, and frankly, neither do I. You can leave now."

Alice snatched the photograph from Everleigh's hands, returning it to her purse. "Well, the ladies are waiting."

They heard the door latch close, and Whitney held the back of her wrist to Everleigh's forehead. "You look faint. Are you okay?"

The news of Roland's child was crushing, she thought, but she didn't feel weak. Oddly, as she told Whitney what happened, she decided that knowing this put her on stronger footing—now she had leverage against Roland. Everleigh had already been having serious doubts about him, so what did this do except cement her feelings? It was just so sad that she'd chosen a man who could be so cavalier about having a child. Everleigh considered herself smart and insightful. How had she picked someone so lacking in morals? How had she not *seen* it in him?

"I'm just so disappointed in myself," she blubbered. Roland was so much less than she thought. Because he didn't just have troubles; he was troubled.

"Oh, Lee, we women are hopeless," Whitney said, hitting her playfully with a throw pillow. "It's your fiancé that ruined everything, and still you blame yourself. You are the most incredible person I know, and you've done only what you thought was right."

And wasn't that exactly what she needed to hear at this very moment? That Whitney didn't just believe she'd been wronged. That her friend trusted her judgment wholeheartedly, not just with men, but with every aspect of her life.

Everleigh wiped her cheeks, looking up at Whitney through watery eyes. She hugged her friend fiercely, remembering the diary they used to pass back and forth to each other in eighth grade, each writing a heartfelt or thought-provoking entry before bed. How when her mother was in the hospital, Whitney would come over to study with her or eat dinner with her and her father. How Whitney had stood at her college graduation, insisting on moving her own celebration so she could see Everleigh collect her diploma.

They took a moment to fully appreciate the love they had for each other, even as voices from the party drifted in through the open door in a distant room.

TWENTY-THREE

❧

There was a crew in the gallery when she returned, a few artsy men of various ages that Starling invited from the art colony to help hang the finished portraits. As they hammered and Starling measured and directed, Everleigh studied the pores and lip lines and pupils of the Hollywood stars in the photographs, their expressions leaping from the walls and stirring her emotions. She dreaded coming face-to-face with Roland tonight, confronting him about the call Whitney had received. There had been an unspoken trust that they'd stand by each other after getting engaged. But for him, like her, the schism had grown deep. Whatever he saw in her when they'd met had changed, the spark diminishing, just like her alleged mental capacity. Was it that he saw her as weak, or too strong? Her contrarian views about work so dangerous that he was willing to lock her into a psychiatric hospital to "save" her.

On the drive home that night, Everleigh was quiet in the station wagon, but if Starling noticed, she didn't say so. They turned onto Gin Lane to the smell of barbecue chicken, which is what she planned to make, too.

"Have you considered the room at the art colony?" Starling asked, pulling into the cottage driveway.

There were too many decisions to make right now. Across the

lawn, she saw Rolly sitting in an Adirondack chair by the lackluster pool, now drained of water and lined with muck collected from rainwater and debris. A few workers had lined up for payday, and she watched Stevie hand them envelopes of cash; she could see the men counting the bills. "I need one more day, just to figure things out," she said, and Starling glanced in the direction she was looking.

Her tender expression communicated understanding. "I'll tell them to hold it a bit longer."

Inside, Everleigh dumped chicken legs into a bowl of barbecue sauce she'd made, chopping fresh parsley and onions from the local farm stand and mixing it into the marinade; she'd planned this summer dinner all week, and now nothing seemed more unappetizing. She slumped into the kitchen chair, hunching over a blank piece of paper with a pen.

Something happened when we moved out here six weeks ago. I began to discover that there are parts of me I didn't even know existed. Maybe there were things I wanted to do with my life beyond getting married. None of this is your fault. It's simply that I've had time to think, and I know some things that I didn't before.

Things are not right between us, and you must sense that. I don't want to walk down the aisle like this, and until we work things out, I think we should call off the wedding . . .

After leaning the letter against the fruit bowl, she fetched a pot to boil water for corn. She wouldn't accuse him of an affair, and she wouldn't mention the bit about the mental hospital. The goal was to have an amicable conversation, no matter how betrayed she felt. It would be easier. She watched Roland through the window, still near the pool, drinking a cocktail. Finally, about thirty minutes later, with skies a Palm Beach–blue, she heard his footsteps. Then he was hugging her from behind, slipping his hand down the front of her capri pants.

"Roland!" she scolded, the sweet smell of corn bubbling up from the pot. He hadn't been this amorous in a month, and it felt unwelcome. A sour taste balled in her mouth, the memory of George Sheetz.

He waved his clipboard. "I just got an infusion of money, and we can have ten more workmen here tomorrow. We may be able to finish by September." She was relieved his mood was bright; it would make what she was about to say more palatable.

She grabbed the letter she'd tucked in an envelope and went outside to dump charcoal in the grill. "Did your father come through with a check?" She knew it was Stevie's money; she'd seen him paying workers two weeks in a row now.

"Hardly." He watched her squirt lighter fluid, his chambray shirt untucked and open to his chest. "Isn't this my job?"

"When the hotel reopens, don't name it after me again, okay?" Her tone was snappish, hardly the calm she wanted to project. She handed him the matches, tucking the letter into her shorts pocket. She wouldn't give it to him; she'd tell him how she felt instead, right this minute.

The flames shot upward, toxins swirling into the air. "You don't rebuild and rename. It will be the triumphant return of the Everleigh, rising from the ashes." His arm slipped around her, and he tried to kiss her neck, but his lips felt wet and sloppy. She ducked out of his embrace.

"What is this?" He'd somehow snatched the letter from her pocket.

"Can you just light the grill?" She jumped up to retrieve the envelope, but he held it higher, and she felt like a cat then, standing on hind legs, swiping at yarn.

"I must read this." He tore open the seal.

"Roland, stop. You need to give it back—"

"It has my name on it." She smacked him across his cheek.

He rubbed the spot where she'd hit his face. "What the hell, Lee?"

The tears were already coming. "I know about the baby."

"What baby?"

"The child, your daughter, with Alice's cousin. Don't lie, Rolly. You've done enough of that already. It wasn't just a boating accident, was it?"

"I was going to tell you about these crazy ideas she has, I swear it, but then time marched on, and I figured I'd tell you after the wedding." Roland reacted to the news like he did to the arson. It was easier to deny the truth if you could invent a better one. According to Roland, the detective was exaggerating the arson, and Alice's cousin was pretending the child was his.

"She looks just like you, Roland."

He unfolded the paper from the envelope. Not wanting to see his face as he read the letter, she rushed inside and drained the corn in a colander. Every sound was magnified, and she heard it the way a fox would: the fluttering of the page in his hand, his noisy swallow. With her back to the door, she listened for the creak of the screen, and when it came, she pulled two plates from the dish cabinet, putting a cob on each, slathering them with butter, sprinkling salt. What a waste it was cooking this knowing she'd never bite into the sweet white kernels, that she'd be too sick to her stomach to swallow.

His voice lashed out behind her. "You can't leave me, Lee. Your parents put me in charge of you."

Everleigh whipped around. How smug he was. Had he always spoken to her like she was stupid? "I think you've misunderstood. You're not watching over me."

The steam from the corn rose up her blouse, but she was already filled with heat.

"Well, then I'm protecting you, Lee, from these radical people you spend time with, these ideas they've put into your head." Ripping open the fridge, Roland pulled a bottle of Ballantine and popped off the cap.

"Protecting me? From who, an old woman who takes photographs?! Why does that scare you? Why is that so frightening, Rolly?" Her voice was screeching, manic sounding. "Whitney told me you called the women's ward, that you're trying to find me a bed."

He took a swig, his face arrogant. "Call your mother, Everleigh. Go ahead, dial her. I've been in touch quite frequently, and she's worried, too. Worried that all of this talk about taking pictures is distracting you."

"Distracting me from what? You?"

"Your mother said, 'I didn't raise her for these wasted days with a camera around her neck.'"

"You're lying. You lie about everything."

Roland put down the beer, his eyes finding hers, drawing near. "Honestly, I think the doctors will be good for you, Lee. They'll help you see what's really important."

She punched his torso hard with her fists, although he was thick and solid and didn't move an inch. "I'm not sick, and you know it."

An old fear lodged in her throat. She'd always been scared to lose her mother, but she was even more scared of becoming her mother.

He put his hands on her shoulders, steadying her. "You're not fine. You leave every morning, and you don't clean up the cottage, you don't care what I'm doing, you don't care about going out to parties or playing mah-jongg. You don't care about anything anymore. Except that gallery and *whatever* goes on inside."

She rolled her eyes so he could see. "Is your ego so fragile that my waning interest in you must be tied to psychological distress?"

He found that funny, smiling at a blank wall. "So what is it then?

You take one picture for the provincial little paper here, and you're going to get a job, get your own place. Well, no one is going to hire a rich girl whose only artistic accomplishment is painting her nails."

He was so condescending, so dismissive, it enraged her. "I don't even paint my nails, Rolly, but you wouldn't know that. Because you don't see me. You don't see anything but the end of your own nose."

"You mean *your* nose." He laughed. He knew she was self-conscious about her nose, and she hated him more now. "Oh, right, Lee. You barely keep up with your looks these days. I forgot to tell your parents *that part.*"

Was he implying that she let herself go? After all those nights she'd stood at the stove in heels. Everleigh reached for one of the cobs, lobbing it at him. She missed, and the corn splattered against the kitchen table. She stormed off into her bedroom, where, Mango sat up on the bed, watching her as she pulled her suitcase out of the closet, stuffing her clean, folded laundry inside.

"You have a child."

He paused in the doorway, heat rising up his neck to his cheeks. "I told you, we all have pasts that haunt us."

"So you admit it then. She's your daughter."

"She was a mistake." He stormed out, the back door squeaking open and shut, and through the window she saw him slam his foot into the grass, shaking his head with disgust, or was it shame? No, it was an arrogant smirk reshaping his charming features. He was calculating what lie he would tell next to keep her in this cottage with him. Everleigh packed her cold cream, her cream rinse. She was collecting her brush rollers when he stepped back into her bedroom.

He gently closed her suitcase. "C'mon, pet, I don't want you to leave." A wariness in the way his lips parted, a clamminess in his touch. "Can't you see? This summer is ruining us, everything we had. You're throwing it away over this woman, this militant. . . ."

Even with all her anger, Everleigh decided that she felt sorry for him, because she imagined how his father must have lashed out at him after the boating accident. The pregnancy. The humiliation he had to endure, assuming that was why they were estranged.

She kept her eyes at her feet, wishing she'd simply collected her belongings and walked out. A confrontation was what she wanted to avoid. "Why are you talking to my parents?"

Roland petted Mango as she paraded on the bed near his hand. "Because I wanted them on my side. Because I was scared that you'd do exactly this: wake up one day and decide to leave." He dropped his head in his hands, shaking it. "It's been messy. I've been messy. I'm sorry, but . . ."

Everleigh squeezed her eyes shut. He wouldn't change. He never would. And she was struck by the thought that humans were incredibly disappointing. They could crush you with their words and actions over and over again, and, still, you expected more of them. You believed in them, the possibility of their transformation, because if you didn't, what *did* you believe in? That promises were empty, that people were set like a clock. If she didn't leave him, there would be a lifetime of these same conversations in front of her, the same accusations and denials. The back of her throat burned as she whispered, "But you don't need me, Rolly—I know there is someone else. The grapevine has told me everything other than her name."

He coughed, clearing his throat. "That's long over. It's you I want. It's you I love."

Suddenly, he was talking as though he couldn't live without Everleigh, and yet there was this other woman, the detective had even confirmed it, and she had meant something to him. Did men rank the women they were with: one was good enough to sleep with, but another better for marriage?

He leaned in to kiss her damp cheek, and she turned away. "You shut me out, pet. Maybe it started the moment I brought you here. Maybe I shouldn't have built this damn hotel."

"But even after that," she said, her eye catching the line on the wall where it was half-lilac, half-white. "You didn't even finish painting our bedroom, Rolly. What was our bedroom."

Everleigh snapped shut the leather case of her camera. If she was looking into the viewfinder, she could see Roland so clearly. He was disappointed in the person he fell in love with, but so was she; he wasn't who he promised to be either, and it made the moment even more impossible. "I waited for you every day in this cottage, cooking for you, asking if you would walk with me on the beach. It wasn't me that wasn't interested, Rolly; it was you. That much I'm certain of."

It was as though he bit into a lemon. "But the hotel needed my focus. There's so much to manage, and maybe I lost sight of you, of us." He opened the linen closet in the hall, pulling out the can of lilac paint, grinning at her. "I'll finish our bedroom right now, if it matters that much to you."

She wondered if she could do this, leave a man she loved, because even with all that Roland had done, she knew she cared for him. It was like her former self existed on a different plane, and she could envision herself laughing on Roland's arm, planting a garden at their beautiful home, sitting beside the Christmas tree with hot toddies, nodding in agreement that life was swell. Yet, when she looked closer at those pictures, it was her mother in the frame. Her weak smile, her longing to be somewhere else. Her pretty dress and fashionable shoes merely a distraction for how broken she was. Photography would save her from all that because it had given Everleigh purpose, an excuse to go out into the world and make it hers.

"I've stood by you this whole summer, Rolly. This hotel. This secret about your family that you won't tell me. This reason why you've asked every other person you know for money except for your father."

The tears started to come again, and it killed her that he knew she was upset. She wished he thought her made of stone. Hauling her bag into the living room, she grabbed a notebook and a dozen canisters of film.

He blocked her way into the kitchen, raising his voice. "I told your parents that you talk to yourself, that you write down who knows what in that notebook of yours. That you suffer from delusions, thinking you're some bohemian."

She pushed past him. "Well, good for you." Roland's views would never change, just like her father's wouldn't; people could ease into difference, but in this fight, neither one had incentive to change. Roland would say he loved her again and again, but nothing would be different. There would be more women—even she knew that. And whether or not Everleigh left had little bearing on Roland's ability to go after what he wanted in life. But if she went through with this wedding, knowing what he expected of her, she wouldn't get another chance.

Roland hulked near her, his voice in her ear no matter where she moved in the house. "You realize I've been holding off your parents. They were insisting on hauling you back to the city, but I told them that you're seeing a doctor, one that is managing a regimen of lithium for you. Your mother is so thankful. I'm starting to think your parents trust me more than they trust you."

"You'd tell my parents anything to get what you want. Right now I'm not sure if that's money or me."

Roland snickered. "You'd be surprised by how little you're worth to them. The amount your father offered to help with the hospital fees was a pittance."

She nearly threw her engagement ring at him, but then she remembered she could sell it. It was worth at least a thousand dollars. That could get her by for a while.

"Mango," she called sweetly. She bundled the cat in her arms and barged out the back door. "So the reason you're still with me is because you've been holding out for a check from my father. Why don't you just ask him to sign my inheritance over to you?"

He rubbed hard the back of his head, missing her sarcasm. "I don't need your money, Lee. Lest you forget, I'm a Whittaker."

"But—" He didn't have the Whittaker money, and why? It must be because of the crash, the child. If anyone needed her inheritance, it was him.

Roland pushed his hands into his shorts pockets. "Your family is worthless to me."

She sucked in a breath, gut-punched, picking up her purse and camera bag, then her suitcase by the handle. This was it. This was goodbye. She believed in transformations; she'd seen it happen to others while taking their pictures. Now she wished she could snap a photograph of herself at this moment, even though her eyes had red rings and her cheeks were puffy, because this was life. The pain that came with making tough choices. The hope that lingered when you knew you were doing what was right.

Nothing could have kept her at the cottage now, and with Mango tucked under her arm, she hurried off down the road carrying her suitcase.

He ran after her for a minute, then stopped and yelled, "You'll never make it on your own. You need me."

Her bags were heavy, and her head was hot, making her dizzy. Roland was out of sight when she finally stopped to catch her breath, and Mango jumped out of her arms onto the curb with a *meow* while Everleigh crouched and vomited.

Close your eyes, imagine what in the room would make you happy.

When she fluttered open her eyes, the sky was turning pink. She pushed on, trudging past the mansions with their grand awnings and regal house numbers, until she stepped onto the bricked sidewalks of the village of Southampton. There, she'd find a pay phone and make a call.

Someone would pick her up, anyone besides Roland.

It was dusk when Starling pulled up in her Mercedes station wagon. Standing at the pay phone in town, Everleigh had used two nickels to call Whitney, but she wasn't home. She wouldn't call Curtis, not to mend her broken heart.

As soon as Everleigh collapsed into the passenger seat, the car smelling metallic like an open canister of film, Starling said, "The breakup went well, did it?"

Everleigh laughed, despite her puffy eyes, having thrown her stuff into the backseat in a heap, Mango climbing on her lap. "He's been telling my parents I'm mentally unstable. So that was a highlight."

Starling's lips tensed, a dozen threadlike worry lines pushing up around them. "I told you that art scares people. Are there any records, anything they can hold against you? They can take you against your will."

Everleigh put her bare feet on the dashboard, burying her face in her knees. "I've talked to analysts over the years, but about my mother. Not about anything to do with me. I need to call my parents. I don't know what else he's been telling them."

Starling did a double take. "But they would trust you over him, correct?"

"I would hope." Through her legs, Everleigh saw a half-empty bottle of absinthe on the floor mat.

"Well, don't let them force you into the looney bin," Starling said. "Don't let them convince you that you need fixing." They came to a stop sign, Starling peeling out after.

"What is it about me—" A well burst open inside Everleigh, flooding her face with tears. She tried to catch her breath, hiccupping instead. "What is it about me that I keep disappointing everyone around me? I'm not who my parents want me to be. I'm not even who Roland wants."

For a moment, Starling didn't have anything to say. She handed her a handkerchief.

"But you are still becoming you, Lee—there's no rule that you have to know yourself by a certain age, and this hurts, this hurts because you're trying not to disappoint yourself. You're holding yourself to a greater standard than any of the other people in your life ever have, and they're not prepared for it." Starling's snowy hair blew back off her lined forehead, silvery white wisps framing her oval-shaped face, her translucent skin, a blue vein snaking near her temple.

Everleigh sniffled. "Maybe I'm not prepared for it either."

The car engine rattled as it drove, and rather than turning off toward the artist colony when they reached Bridgehampton, the artist glanced at Everleigh, smiling. "Let's take a drive. To Montauk. Salt air clears the head."

Everleigh nodded. She hadn't made it as far east as the oceanside town of Montauk, but it was as far as Long Island went. After that, there was nothing but open ocean until England.

They passed a series of potato farms and the familiar windmill of East Hampton, then a few shopfronts in the even smaller farming community of Amagansett. From here, the road dipped down to a narrow spit of land, the ocean on one side and the bay on the other. There wasn't a tree in sight, just wide stretches of sand with the Atlantic Ocean pounding. At this time of night, the water shimmered, the sun making its final descent over the giant billboards announcing fishing tours and seafood shanties.

The car zoomed by Hither Hills State Park, where grassy dunes rose in natural humps, suddenly obstructing the view of endless blue.

Everleigh stared out the window, Roland's angry words and Starling's calming ones circling her head like a dog chasing its tail.

Montauk had a single bar, a few roadside motels, and a row of ramshackle fish houses. They parked at a clam bar and shared a cardboard container of steamed clams at a picnic table. Typically, Everleigh was the one who initiated conversation between them, but tonight she didn't care much for talking. She was trying to figure out how to tell her parents about her decision to split from Rolly and move into the artist colony.

Starling eyed her. "You're not eating much."

"How can I?" Everleigh tucked her hands under her thighs.

The photographer tipped her head down, looking over her glasses. "Because you're hungry?"

Everleigh said, "I will never come back from this. How will I ever come back from this? My parents won't forgive me for calling off this wedding, and they already think I'm certifiable." She could see Starling's mind working, but Everleigh couldn't stop hers from unraveling, even if they were sitting at a picnic table in Montauk surrounded by fishermen and tourists.

Starling smacked the splintered wood of the tabletop with her palm, a mother frustrated that she wasn't getting through to her child. "Because life will go on, Everleigh. Today, your heart is mangled, but tomorrow . . . well, tomorrow is going to feel incredible."

Everleigh shook her head, wiping at the glob running out of her nose—the nose Rolly had just mocked.

"You're going to love tomorrow," Starling said. "Because you're going to wake up in cottage number nine. You're going to look at those wonderfully blank walls. You're going to hear the other artists shuffling about in their cabins getting ready to work, emerging into the early-morning sun, and you're going to think to yourself: *What will I make today? What will I make, Lee?* All that has encumbered you will be gone. You can create."

The pressure in her chest loosened because Everleigh hadn't thought about tomorrow or the next day or even the possibility of a happy ending, at least not since she walked out of the cottage today.

"You have such belief in me," Everleigh sighed, grateful for it. At the next table, two men were cracking cooked lobsters, pulling the stringy meat out of the shells. She felt just as torn open.

"Every day, even if shitty things are going on in my life, Lee, I wake up and think to myself: *What will I put out into the world?* When you're a creative, you can't help but get those ideas out of you, onto paper, a canvas, a typewriter. It's like breathing, and until you give your-self the space to do it, you're going to feel like you're all cooped up."

Everleigh kept notebooks of ideas. Sometimes she walked down the city street, clicking an invisible camera in her mind. She could be moved by the flow of a woman's hem, a crack in the sidewalk catching the light. She supposed Starling was right. Everleigh was born into a household where no one made art, so it felt wrong, almost like a crime, to choose it. But all those ideas of hers were fighting for prom-inence, they were trying to find a way out of her, and if she only had the time, and a place where it was safe to create, then maybe those ideas would emerge.

Everleigh dunked a clam in butter, the salty brine soothing her throat. "Nine is my lucky number, you know. I was born on April ninth. Are you sure I can stay there, in the cottage, tonight?"

"It's empty, isn't it?" Starling smiled at her. "Anyway, you'll be in good company at the art colony—we all have something keeping us up at night."

Everleigh watched as the artist pulled the bottle of absinthe out of her purse, pouring it into her empty water cup. "That stuff smells terrible."

Starling swigged it down, sucking her cheeks in when it stung. "Well, it doesn't make me feel terrible. I have a lot riding on this show." She offered Everleigh a shot, and she gulped one back, gagging. "I begged to get this gallery viewing, and even then, they're making me pay to rent the space. An artist paying to hang her photographs. Can you imagine? You think Jackson Pollock ever paid to have his pictures displayed?"

Starling Meade's photographs regularly appeared in glossy magazines. She'd taken pictures of fashion models for cosmetic brands. "I don't understand," Everleigh said.

"You think you're the only one fighting, dear. Well, you listen to me, you're gonna be fighting your whole life to get people to pay attention to your work. So you're gonna have to toughen up, and fast." Starling took her hair out of the ponytail at the nape of her neck, letting it fall around her shoulders. It turned her presence ghostly, like she might start floating. She tucked a piece behind her ear, and Everleigh could see her then, twenty-four with bright eyes, starting out in her career at a time when women didn't dare do a man's job.

"The prints are going to sell, Starling. Everyone will be talking about the show."

The artist rested her cheek in her hand. "My agent said I need to sell at least half."

"Or what?"

"Or I'll never get in a city gallery. What I'm doing with their faces, Everleigh—it's new. It could fail. It could be the end of me. I've already been written off as a has-been by young photo editors."

It was hard to fathom, and she thought Starling wrong. She was at the pinnacle of her career. "But everyone wants to see what you do next. These photos of Nat King Cole and Lucille Ball—they're going to blow people away."

"In this business, you're only as good as your last photograph."

Starling tapped her fingers against the table, smiling, vulnerability betraying her.

"We will do this together." Everleigh patted Starling's back, her spine curved and hardened with age. She knew the patrons coming to the art show, and Everleigh would be sure that the prints sold. Starling had spent the summer boosting her up, and she would return the favor.

Out of the corner of her eye, Everleigh spotted a girl in a bathing suit, maybe twelve, with wild blond hair, long skinny legs, and bare feet, licking a dripping ice cream cone; in the negative space just behind her an older couple were slurping oysters, the light streaking across the picnic table, the colors blurring and popping at once.

"Oh, Lee." Starling clapped her hands at her heart. She was looking in the same direction as Everleigh, at the girl. "The most important thing you can do as a young photographer is learn how to see, and you can see everything about that girl, too, can't you? Capture it, Lee. Go and get it."

Everleigh ran to the car, reaching for her camera from the backseat. She imagined the close-up color photograph instantly, a symbol of summer, and not the buttoned-up version she'd captured on the sidewalks of East Hampton. In this version, in this girl, she would frame summer as authentic, carefree, fleeting; you couldn't help but smile when you looked at it. Rushing back to the child, she asked if she could take her picture. There was no posing, no putting on. A clean, honest click, with the right light, the right story.

After exhausting her roll of film, Everleigh returned to the picnic table to a beaming Starling. "You see now. A camera is only a tool to capture an image. But it's you that needs to compose, Lee. And if you can compose a picture like that, you can compose your entire life."

She smiled, finally taking another bite of food.

It was Everleigh that drove them home, Starling snoring in the passenger seat. They were an odd couple, weren't they, Everleigh thought, but they made a good team. The car nearly blew by Mecox Farm, which she hadn't noticed on the way to Montauk. When she spied the strawberry-shaped sign clearly, she slammed on her brakes. The car bounced into a pothole in the dirt parking lot. Alice's words replayed in her head: *Just take a drive to Mecox on the main drag in Amagansett and you'll see Roland for who he really is.*

The headlights shone onto the cornfields thick with four-foot stalks. A few hundred feet back from the road was a simple ranch house with one light on, a truck parked in the driveway. Everleigh parked and walked over to what looked like a wall-less shed with empty shelves, a chair where an attendant normally sat, and an empty cash box. A few pictures were tacked up, and Everleigh tore one off and held the image up to her taillight. There were four young women smiling, posing together in front of the stand. She recognized one immediately: Vivienne, who did her laundry, her long hair parted on both sides of her head, her dimples deep and cheerful.

Starling popped her head out the window, blinking her heavy eyelids twice and looking around, noting the Mecox Farm sign. "They sell opium," she announced.

"Huh?"

Starling closed her eyes sleepily. "Speed. Weed. Take your pick. All of Gin Lane comes out here. Your friend Stevie runs this place."

Making casual deliveries around town was risky enough, but having a designated spot for an illicit drug business? "How does he get away with it?"

Starling shrugged. "Friends in high places."

A pair of headlights blinded Everleigh's eyes, and she covered her face as a car pulled into the lot beside Starling's wagon. Two women laughed in the backseat, rock and roll blaring out the front windows. The driver got out, a preppy gentleman with narrow-set eyes whom she recognized from the Meadow Club. One of the men who cycled through tennis with Roland.

He looked at the darkened farm stand, then back at Everleigh, raising an eyebrow. "Are you the one with the stuff?"

"Oh no, you misunderstand, I'm here because—"

He sniffed. "You're Roland's girl, right? He sent me here, said this is where I could get the goods."

"Oh. I'm sorry. The farm is closed up for the night."

The man gave her a strange look. "What a colossal waste of time." He bit at his fingernail, then spat. "Dirty bastard."

The women in the car heckled him to get booze instead, and the man turned away from Everleigh and got back in the car.

"Wait," she said, following him to his car window. Starling said it was Stevie's place, but maybe it wasn't. Maybe it was Roland's. "I thought he was at a bar. He told you to come here to meet him?"

Even with her pleading look, the gentleman shrugged, like he didn't care much. "No, he said his buddy would be here. The carrottop." *Stevie*, just as Starling said. He backed up, then shifted the gear, and Everleigh exhaled. But just before he pulled onto the main road, he stopped the car again and snickered. "He must get a cut of the returns though."

"What did you say?" she said.

The streetlight illuminated the passengers in the car. "Roland. He must get a kickback, right, or he wouldn't always be telling us suckers at the club to make the drive out here from Southampton. Very persuasive, your fiancé, telling me they had the cleanest grass on the whole East End."

Everleigh forced a phony smile. That's what Roland was. Phony. He put on as a society darling, but really he was covered in muck, she thought as she returned to the car.

Driving the East End roads at night was like pushing through a maze in the dark. Starling had to remind her of each turn to get back to the art colony. Everleigh's thoughts churned. Roland wasn't necessarily doing anything illegal if he was sending people to the farm stand, and yet, he was complicit in Stevie's illegal dealings. And what was in it for him? She thought the gentleman must be right; Roland must get a fraction of the profits. The hotel renovation happened in fits and starts, like it depended on this kind of unreliable financial well. Perhaps Opal had only given him an initial chunk of cash, and Roland was actually funding the renovation of the hotel with a cut of money from the farm stand. She hadn't thought much before about why they paid all the construction workers with cash, but maybe this was it.

The twin bed in cottage nine at the art colony was springy and uncomfortable, squeaking when you moved from left to right, but she wouldn't have slept well anyway. By the time she heard others rustling in their cottages, she'd been up for hours, Mango purring beside her. As grateful as she was to be in one of these cottages, she also knew she wasn't quite as contrarian as Starling and the others here. Unlike them, she didn't believe conformity was a sin. The idea of getting married and having a child was still something she wanted. It just wasn't mutually exclusive with art.

But something else was bothering her, her mind restless from the events of the day before. It was Roland she was thinking of. Which was funny because even if Roland had disappointed her once again, she had to admit that his illegal dealings were also delivering relief. She'd certainly made the right choice in breaking things off with him, even her parents would be able to see that. But she was bothered by something else, the sense that she had a moral obligation to call the detective and share the disturbing news she'd discovered about Roland's role at the farm stand. It was a piece of the puzzle he needed, and yet, Everleigh couldn't bring herself to turn him in. She might not be in love with Roland anymore, but she didn't want to destroy him either.

Another thought nagged, too. Everleigh was curious why Alice, who knew what was going on at Mecox, didn't report the illegal business to the detective herself. With all the disdain Alice had for Roland, why had she continued to protect him? He would have been taken away in handcuffs, the hotel left to die half-finished, and Roland might have even gone to prison. The perfect revenge. Everleigh's eyes widened, and she sat up fast in bed, startling Mango, who lifted her head before dropping it back onto the pillow. Suddenly, Alice's motives seemed so certain. If Alice reported Roland's farm stand, the detective might wonder what Alice had against him, and that could deepen his investigation of her role into the arson. Perhaps, Alice feared that one wrong move would lead the detective straight back to her. Or maybe, after setting the hotel fire, she didn't feel the need to twist the knife any deeper.

After washing up, Everleigh and Starling drove together to the gallery, the radio playing classical music, unnerving her with its erratic notes. It was Saturday; the art show opened in two nights.

Details of the previous day—the trip to Montauk, the bottle of absinthe, Everleigh turning her life upside down, Starling's admission that the show might fail—faded as the workmen hung the last few prints. They both sipped black coffee, examining the portraits and making adjustments.

"Lee, did you hear me?" Starling said.

She snapped out of her daze. "I'm sorry. What did you say?"

They would use a hot glue gun to place the title labels to the right of each photograph.

Everleigh nodded and got to work while Starling played with the lighting. But her mind wandered to her mother. She had to know that her daughter was stronger than how Roland described her, that she wasn't wired the same way. They finished working around six, the air smelling of cotton candy thanks to a children's carnival being set up on the sidewalks.

Everleigh reached for her purse, poised to leave. "I have to go home tonight. To the city."

The wrinkles around Starling's mouth deepened even though her eyes brightened. "I know you do. How will you get there? There aren't any trains this late."

Everleigh took in the enormous photographs. Seeing the faces this big was overwhelming, powerful. "I'll drive."

The woman nodded, surprising Everleigh with an embrace. "Whatever you say to your mother and your father, whatever ugliness transpires between you, just make sure—before you walk out the door to come back here—that your mother knows you love her."

Moisture balled in the corners of Everleigh's eyes. "I'll be back before the opening, I promise."

Whitney had agreed to let her borrow her car. She would leave the keys on the driver's seat, and as Everleigh left Southampton, she decided to make a stop before merging onto Sunrise Highway toward Manhattan. Parking in front of Curtis's medical office, she slipped a letter into the mail slot, knowing he wouldn't get it until Monday morning.

"I loved your family. Went to the city to work some things out with my own, but I'll be right back. Staying at the art colony. Will you be my date to Starling's art opening Monday night? xo Lee."

TWENTY-FOUR

It was louder in the city than Everleigh remembered, the rising deci-bels a comfort as she pulled onto Central Park South, nearing the Plaza. Goodness, how she missed New York. If she could train her camera on the sidewalks right now, she would cram so much into the frame: women in evening skirts and men in summer fedoras, yellow taxi cabs blaring their horns, outdoor café tables crowded with diners, the blinking lights of a corner pizza joint. She inhaled the scent of laundry, dryer steam wafting from basement windows. It was a city you didn't realize you loved until you left.

After parking in a nearby garage, Everleigh walked to the Plaza's entrance. The doorman grinned when he saw her; he was the one that she'd paid to teach her to drive a few years back. "I'll be damned," he said, nodding at the car keys in her hand. "Your parents finally got you a set of wheels, Miss Farrows." This made Everleigh smile.

"Something like that," she said. Pasquale, a second doorman, opened the front door for her, a silver tooth inside his mouth.

"Miss Farrows. Where have you been? I have no one to win money from on the Yankees."

She laughed, forgetting that the help treated her like a princess.

The lift operator made small talk with her, too, complaining of the crowds at Coney Island while pressing the button for the fourth floor. It felt like someone was tickling the insides of her stomach. He lifted the crank of the elevator, and as the doors slid open, Everleigh sucked in a breath. Her parent's mauve front door was the second on the right, and she nearly knocked, but then she remembered these were her parents.

After turning her key in the lock, Everleigh kicked off her shoes and stepped onto the plush beige carpet. How soft it was compared to the sandy wood floors of the cottage!

The round, freshly waxed mahogany entry table had a bouquet of late-summer pink dahlias at the center, and a crystal chandelier hung overhead. She strode down the long hallway in the apartment calling, "Hello." Her father was in the next room watching television.

"Who's there?" he said, a blind man struggling to see.

"It's me, Daddy," she said. "Lee."

Her father stood to turn off the TV when he saw her in the living room. His arms were crossed, like his eyebrows. "Are you done with your little vacation?"

She clenched her hands into fists at her sides. How easy it was for Curtis to hug his father, and now here she was facing her daddy, feeling frozen, unable to say that she'd missed him despite everything. "Where's Mommy?"

Her father sat and stretched his arm along the back of the yellow brocade sofa, the paisley swirls busy and raised, the pattern so strong it could make your head spin. Or maybe her head was spinning.

"She's taken to knitting again," he said.

That was a good sign, proof that Mommy was still doing all right.

"She's been in a good place," she said. Everleigh sat on a chair opposite her father. She folded and unfolded her hands, her eyes traveling to the family photos on the wall: a pudgy Everleigh learning how to walk in Central Park, her parents in a canoe on their honeymoon Upstate. She'd rehearsed what she would say the entire drive, but now, surrounded by the familiar ceramic curios in the glass cabinet, statuettes of children dancing carefree, she was reduced to silence.

Her father cleared his throat. "I've cut back on Nanny's hours. We don't need her as much. Mommy is cooking these days."

"Me too," she said brightly, feeling like they'd found common ground, but then regretting it. Her father wasn't interested in her forays into the kitchen.

Everleigh locked her hands in front of her left knee, taking in the room like she'd never been there, like she hadn't spent every heartache crying into these pillows under the Pierre-Auguste Renoir. The piece was nothing but an eight-by-eight sketch, but it was the beginning of the painter's famous painting "Luncheon of the Boating Party." Maybe this conversation was the beginning of something, too.

It was Everleigh's turn to say something, but her father wasn't angry, and that was confusing her. The quiet unnerved her; how easy it was for him to wait. The ocean felt so far away here. Without the sounds of birds or crashing waves, the voices of kids riding by on bikes, you could forget it was summer altogether. Finally, she spoke up.

"You can't make me stay here to take care of Mommy. It's not my responsibility to hold her together like glue. I deserve a life."

Her father was dressed like the men at the Beach Club in their belted khakis and golf shirts. His limbs were thick and doughy, and he was the kind of man whose flesh seemed to spread in armchairs, growing wider as he sat. That had intimidated her when she was a child, how large he appeared, but now, his stature wasn't so formidable. If she saw him at the club, she would have written him off as a middle-aged bore with a bulbous stomach from eating too many medium-rare steaks.

He cracked his knuckles. "No one is holding you hostage. You know that's not what this is about."

"Admit it. You cut off my trust because I didn't come home for Mommy."

He opened his cigar box, then bit off the end of his Cuban. "Nonsense. I cut off your trust because I didn't have faith in Roland. He's a marauder."

She shot her eyes to him, shocked. "But Daddy, how did you know? I thought you and he were on the same side?"

"Well, not for long," he quipped.

She lowered her eyes to the tips of her ballet flats. "He's been telling you things, terrible things about me. Like I share the same delusions as Mommy, but you know I'm not like her. You don't need to pay my fiancé to watch over me. I'm strong, Daddy. I'm healthy, and I'm—"

Her father cut her off. "I haven't given him a dime since the fire, although he's tried." Lighting his cigar, he inhaled three times before blowing out a plume of smoke. When he returned to his position on the couch, Everleigh edged closer to him.

"I'm leaving Roland, Daddy. Maybe that will crush Mommy, or maybe it won't. But I can't make decisions about my life to keep her from falling apart."

In another room she heard the shuffling of feet, her mother moving about. Her father watched the doorway, waiting for her to appear, while exhaling smoke rings. "You know, Everleigh, when we had you as a baby, we couldn't stop holding you, dangling toys over your crib for you to coo at. You were ours, and we could keep you forever."

He turned his face away, his nose imposing from the side, blowing the cigar smell in the direction of the open window. "But when your mother got sick, I couldn't do it. I couldn't raise you on my own. But I've had time to think since you were gone, and maybe I've been unfair. Maybe I put too much on you over the years."

Everleigh felt her face scrunch up and her lip quiver. If Starling were taking his picture, if she blew up his face like one of the images in the gallery, Everleigh would have seen much sooner the way her father held his bulldog jaw, how the tiny muscles in his mouth tensed, how he rarely let his jaw slack, a perpetual teeth grinder. But in the photograph above his head, the one of him and her mother on the canoe, his jaw wasn't his most prominent feature at all; it was his blue crinkling eyes, soft and open, turned up with joy. His face had changed over time, but then again, so had his life. So had his wife.

Before Everleigh got a word out, her mother swooped in like a hawk, reaching for her daughter fast and hard, a pink cashmere shawl wrapped around her shoulders.

"Lee! I thought that was you. Oh, sweetheart, why are you crying?"

She fell into her mother's embrace, her warm chest pressed against her own. "I'm sorry I haven't called, Mommy. I've been so—"

"Distracted." Her father had moved into the corner of the couch, his stockinged feet up on the walnut coffee table.

Everleigh raised her eyes to her mother's. "No, Mommy, I've been so happy."

Her mother hugged her tight, and it felt like she had more than two arms, like she was holding her from every angle. "But Roland, he said you haven't been able to get out of bed some days. That you're hysterical. Daddy and I were going to drive out last weekend to pick you up, but Roland swore he had it under control. He said you refused to speak to us."

She'd learned in biology that there were thirty-three bones in your spinal column. Everleigh felt each one stiffen. "You mean, you thought Roland had *me* under control?"

Everleigh stood, watching her mother's eyes pooling with tears. She was taken back to that day at the Plaza, walking onto the cold tile in the bathroom with her mother in the bathtub, her wrists sliced open to red streaks, the water pink. Oh, how she'd screamed!

Everleigh caught hold of her temper, and on instinct, she sat beside her mother, reaching for her hands, rubbing her thumbs against the scars on her wrists. "Here's what's really happening. But you need to promise you'll listen. No interruptions. You too, Daddy."

Her mother wiped at the faint creases in the corners of her eyes; she was younger than Starling, by at least ten years, and it showed in her smooth face. "Go on."

As the room grew thick with her father's cigar smoke, the smell of maple and grit, Everleigh told them that she hadn't been happy at the hotel from the moment they arrived. How the fire detective was certain someone had burned it down, but they still didn't know who. How she suspected Roland was up to something no good with the farm stand, how she knew there was another woman. She told them about the Juniper Gallery and Starling, and how she already had another photograph in the paper. Now the paper had assigned her a third project.

"I know you never liked the ocean, Daddy, but I love the sea air," Everleigh said, feeling herself brighten inside. "And there's a cottage there. It's simple but perfect, and a friend is letting me stay while I figure out where I'm going to live." She left out the part about the artist colony—they already thought her work with Starling too extreme.

"Dear God," her mother said as Everleigh's voice trailed off. Her father ashed his cigar in the silver tray, and she tried to read his blank expression. On the corner card table, there were stacks of wedding invitations, at least three hundred, and she was certain they were already addressed. There was the matter of the venue deposits, the humiliation that her parents would feel having to explain why yet another engagement had been called off.

"Cripe." Albie stormed out of the living room, then returned immediately with a thick white envelope. He dabbed his forehead with a handkerchief. "I didn't tell either one of you before, but I did some digging about Roland over the last few weeks since he kept asking us for cash."

He dropped it on the coffee table.

Everleigh opened the seal and pulled out a black-and-white photograph of Roland dated 1953, four years ago. He was holding a beach ball, a young woman beside him in a modest bathing suit, a lake behind them. She put the snapshot flat on the table, pulling out the report, ten double-spaced pages marked "Private Detective Report."

She wasn't sure she wanted to read it.

Her father leaned back, placing his hands behind his head. "Unfortunately, our Roland has gotten himself into trouble before. He's forbidden at the Whittaker house in Detroit. In fact, he's not even supposed to use the family name."

Her mother smacked the couch, although Everleigh wasn't sure who she was mad at, Roland or her father for keeping this secret. "Oh, Albie. Why didn't you tell me?" Her parents quarreled, her mother's words high-pitched and shrill, but Everleigh kept reading the dossier, her mouth falling open.

Roland's refusal to call his father made perfect sense now. He kept saying how his father would be angry at him for the fire, that it was one more thing he'd messed up. He loved to hear stories of people disowned by their family, later earning their way back into the fold. Because it was what he was trying to do, earn back his father's good graces.

Fear choked her when she realized there were several more pages; what else had he done? "Why can't he use the family name?"

Her father picked a piece of fuzz off his pants, flicking it. "He has a few disorderlies on his record, but it seems like his father lost patience for his antics after he crashed a boat, nearly killing his girlfriend at the time. She was pregnant."

"Do you want tea? I think we all need tea," her mother said, rising.

With her mother in the kitchen, Everleigh continued reading through the file. After paying to replace the community dock and getting him off in court, as Alice had said, Roland's father had him arrested a month later for breaking into the family home. The next part of the report was hazy, but the investigator said there was a family disturbance four months later. The cops were called again, and the father was taken to the hospital after suffering a heart attack. When he was released, he told Roland that he'd entered a trust in his name and signed over the deed to the Southampton house. Roland should attend college and do something productive with his life, but he never wanted to see him again.

Everleigh lowered the report to her lap. "So when the hotel burned down, Roland really did lose all of his money. Because that was the only asset his father had given him."

Her father nodded. "This may be hard to hear, Everleigh, but I think he chose you, in part, because of your trust. Our family name carries weight in this town, and if he couldn't be a Whittaker, he might as well be a Farrows."

But he never shed the Whittaker name. He went out of his way to alert people to it. Still, her trust did explain why he was hanging on to her, even as they drifted apart.

Everleigh's mother carried in a tray with a red ceramic teapot and three matching cups in the shape of tulips. She poured each of them Earl Gray, Everleigh grateful for it.

Roland. His longing for his father to come see his shiny new hotel was a longing to see him. The need to prove something, to demonstrate that he could run a viable business. It was because he'd been cast aside. Roland had seduced her with his good looks and charm, but she wondered now who he truly was. How did he get up each morning and look in the mirror, keeping these secrets from her? At some point, the Detroit gossip would have landed in her lap.

Into her tea went a honey stick. So far, they'd only talked about Roland. But she still hadn't said what she'd come to say, and that is where it would get difficult. She was leaving Roland, but she was also leaving her parents.

Her voice sailed out over the quiet living room. "I came here to tell you that I'm moving to Southampton."

Her father abruptly stood and began to pace, shuffling back and forth from one arm of the couch to the other.

"Oh, Lee, honey. Don't speak that way." Her mother lifted her teacup to her mouth.

"But, Mommy, I don't need to be married to leave home."

Her father stopped pacing, lolling his head, like she was physically exhausting him. "What do you think you're going to do out there? Farm?"

Thoughts of the gallery, the firemen she'd taken pictures of, and all that ocean flooded through her. The tidy sidewalks, the child with the dripping ice cream at the clam shack, the green meadows, the vast potato fields.

"Probably not," Everleigh said, sliding her purse up onto her shoulder. "Maybe I'll get a job at the paper. And maybe I'll fall flat on my face. But I just want to try, Daddy."

Her father returned to the sofa, fixing his eyes on her. "I won't reopen your trust, Lee."

"You know, I'm doing okay without it." She kept the corners of her mouth from turning up; she was proud of herself for getting here, for being in a position where she didn't need her trust.

Her mother rushed beside her, cradling her face with her palms and kissing both cheeks. "I'm not okay with this idea, not even one bit."

It was her father's reaction she was waiting for though, the thunder of his voice, an unanticipated summer storm poised to drench her. But his voice turned meek, like he was tired of fighting this battle, like his eyes had opened to something he hadn't seen before. "Lee, women don't leave home without—"

Everleigh cut him off before he could make a threat or give her an ultimatum. "I know, Daddy. Women don't leave home without saying goodbye." Everleigh sprang into her father's soft arms, hugging his middle with all her might. He took her in, the way she hoped he would, even if his face was still a scowl.

Her mother moved to join the embrace, and there they were, the three of them, their arms linked, trying to find balance and connection in their weary hearts. Her mother's eyes glistened as she stroked Everleigh's hair, like she had since she was a child.

"I will come visit you, Lee. Can I do that? I'll take the railroad. I miss you too much, bunny."

"Of course. I love you both," Everleigh said, feeling like she'd landed on her feet, maybe for the first time since Roland took her out to the hotel. Because she would drive out of New York knowing that she had their support, even if they were reluctant to give it.

"Don't drive back tonight," her mother said, crying and laughing. "We can stay up talking, and I'll make you milk toast in the morning."

"Oh, Mommy, yes. And we can drizzle honey on slices of fresh cantaloupe. I've been eating it for breakfast, and it's the most delicious thing I've ever tasted. Except for tomato sandwiches. Oh, and garlic butter clams."

Later, as she lay down in her childhood bedroom, Everleigh

thought her parents' reaction too good to be true. She woke with a nightmare in the early morning: her father instructing an orderly to strap her down to a gurney and carry her out of the Plaza, only to lock her in the back of an ambulance. Sirens blaring.

She left at dawn, before either one of her parents could change their mind.

TWENTY-FIVE

Bottles of champagne chilled in silver ice buckets with neat rows of skinny crystal flutes lined up beside them. A crowd mingled in the Juniper Gallery, the air growing stuffy with people, even with the Dutch door open. Starling stood in the center holding rapt the attention of art enthusiasts, a circle of men still dressed in black suits and shiny dress shoes worn there on the train. Their wives circled the room. Glasses clinked.

Whitney breezed inside during the first hour, kissing both of Everleigh's cheeks, telling her straightaway how fabulous the prints were. "How did it go in the city?"

Everleigh hadn't seen her when she'd returned the car earlier. "It was upsetting, but wonderful, too. I'll fill you in later, but I think my parents and I are finally on the same page."

"I'm so relieved—that phone call scared me." Whitney pointed at the photographs in awe. "I can't believe you worked on these."

After that, the two friends moved through each portrait, Everleigh giving Whitney an insider's take on the show. It was in front of Lucille Ball that Everleigh introduced Whitney to Starling, and it felt like the cosmic meeting of two entirely different planets. The women shook hands, and the artist, with her thick glasses and black silk Oxford blouse, offered insight into how she got the comedienne to pose. Then she motioned toward Everleigh.

"Your friend has real talent," Starling told Whitney, the quiet voices of patrons talking all around them. "You should ask to see some of her artwork."

"Thank you." Everleigh blushed. "Whitney was one of my first subjects."

The memory amused Whitney. "She'd make me pose in the city streets in prom dresses, cabbies honking at us."

"I believe it. When Lee sets her mind to something, she doesn't let up."

A warmth spread through Everleigh, her chin tilting with satisfaction. She had never felt so seen.

When Starling went off to greet another visitor, Whitney gushed. "I've never met anyone so captivating." She pressed her thumbs into Everleigh's palms. "I see why you love it here, Lee. I'm sorry for being so daft."

"It's okay." It was a seal of approval she shouldn't need or want, and still, hearing Whitney say that had made her happy.

Whitney went off to mingle with a friend from the Maidstone, and Everleigh lost track of her while showing around guests who had checkbooks ready. Later, before Whitney left, she found Everleigh once more and handed her a hundred-dollar deposit for the portrait of Lucille Ball. She *just had to have it* for her Bronxville family room, she said, but Everleigh suspected she bought the picture as much for her house as she did to support her work at the gallery. It was a reminder that while their worlds might drift apart, they'd always figure out how to meet each other halfway.

The crowd grew thick, with enough people squeezed inside the gallery that some spilled onto the sidewalks. Everleigh was taking around a woman from the Meadow Club, talking up Starling's work, when she saw Curtis step inside. Their eyes met from afar, and Everleigh smiled at him. Curtis grinned back, making Everleigh return her attention to the aging woman in the emerald-green suit.

Curtis was with someone, a woman she couldn't see well, and Everleigh assumed it was his mother. Then her face came into view, and she realized it was a different petite brunette.

After she finished up with her client, Everleigh clicked her heels over to Curtis. He pecked her on the cheek, remarking, "These photographs, Lee!"

"Thank you for coming." Everleigh smiled at him, turning to the woman. "Vivienne, hello."

The young woman looked as she always did, her hair parted down the middle with two runways of glossy hair resting on each shoulder, long plaits held in place with barrettes lined with pearls. "Hello," she said.

"I was nervous walking in here on my own." He laughed.

Vivienne's tangerine halter playsuit was much too short to be worn as anything other than a beach coverup. It was particularly tight around her middle, where a small bump protruded. When she realized Everleigh was sizing up her hemline, Vivienne turned apologetic. "I was fetching eggs when Curtis and I ran into each other outside Bohack's Market. He talked me into coming here, but I feel a fish out of water."

"Don't be silly. Art is for everyone." Everleigh believed it to be true, too—beauty wasn't only for the people who could afford to buy it framed and matted.

"I haven't seen Vivienne since she returned from the city, but we grew up together." Curtis looked back and forth between the two women. "Wait, how do you two know each other?"

"Vivienne does my laundry." A film of jealousy had developed after seeing Vivienne with Curtis, and her cheeks burned because she knew it was transparent that she was threatened by this cute-as-pie woman.

Out came Vivienne's dimples from her baby face. "Guilty."

"You're working for your mom again?" Curtis seemed concerned, and Vivienne shrugged.

"It's been okay so far."

Curtis made a face that said, *we'll talk more later.* Then he pointed at the photograph of Nat King Cole. "Lee! How did you do this?"

"Well, I didn't. But I helped Starling. You should have seen us developing these prints in baby pools in a barn. There was a fruit bat flying around our heads, and we kept having to duck. But she knew what she was doing. Her instincts are so good."

She sensed Vivienne inching closer, and Everleigh took a subtle step backward. They continued to chat about the art. Curtis was interested in why the other photographs hadn't made the show, what had edged them out. As she answered, she caught Vivienne staring at her side profile, her gaze steady, her lips parting. Everleigh glanced over, but the woman darted her eyes away, her pupils so black they were nearly violet. Even when Curtis asked how her first night in the art colony was and Everleigh answered, she knew that Vivienne was studying her. But she felt a stronger sensation, too, an energy coming from her, something closer to attraction. Like she wouldn't have been surprised if the woman recited details of Everleigh's life back to her, or tried to kiss her, and the thought of it caused the small hairs on her neck to prickle. Had Vivienne been so interested in her the last time they met? She didn't remember. She associated the young woman with nothing more than an impeccably folded stack of laundry.

Everleigh felt a gentle tap at her elbow and jumped from the touch. There was Starling, her long white hair brushing against Everleigh's arm, whispering and pointing across the room. "I get the sense that a serious art collector has arrived. A friend of yours, I believe. Will you tell her about the photographs?"

"Of course." Everleigh excused herself, relieved to put distance between her and Vivienne, wishing she would leave. "I have to help Starling with something. Curtis, I hope you'll stay. Please get some champagne and wait for me."

He adjusted his seersucker bow tie, the corner of his mouth turning up. "Of course, I'll wait for you."

"Nice to see you, Vivienne," Everleigh said, wondering if she'd been too obvious that she wanted Vivienne to leave—or not obvious enough? She forced the weirdness of the incident out of her mind as she crossed the room to the front of the gallery where there was a grande dame in a royal-blue dress with a wide-brimmed hat. Everleigh thought that she was the collector until the woman stepped out of the way, and there she found Alice. Alice, the epitome of style in a satin pencil skirt with a spaghetti strap blouse, her hair curled into ringlets and pinned back with rhinestone barrettes. She was wearing *the locket*, too, the simple gold heart dangling from her wrist.

Alice raised her glass. "Look at you, running about like you own the place."

Kicking herself for extending an invitation to her at Whitney's luncheon, Everleigh asked Alice if she was a collector of artistic photographs. Ernest stepped beside her. "We are beginners, but we are interested in getting more serious." He handed his fiancée champagne.

Just like she did with every other viewer in the gallery, Everleigh walked them from one oversized frame to the next, telling an anecdote or two about each celebrity depicted. For Marilyn, it was how the picture was taken a month before she stood outside of her Beverly Hills home and announced her divorce to Joe DiMaggio for "mental cruelty." For Nat King Cole, it was that his young daughter, Natalie, was making faces from the sidelines, which was why he was laughing so hard. They were on the third picture—the one of Lucille Ball selected by Whitney—when Alice folded her arms and took a step back.

"This one is already sold," Everleigh said, not wanting her to get her hopes up. Alice snapped her mouth shut. A friend called her name, and Alice shimmied off.

Everleigh walked Ernest in front of Paul Newman, standing in front of his undeniably chiseled face, when he leaned into her. "Lee, we're not really here for the art."

"Oh?" She felt her lips tighten.

Ernest looked right and left, like he was about to cross the street, pausing as an elderly woman came to examine the photo. When she left, he said. "We're about to leave town. Our wedding is in the city in a few weeks, and then we're off to Saint-Tropez for our honeymoon. But I needed to tell you something."

"I already know about Roland's father disowning him. Alice told me most of it already."

Ernest cleared his throat. "I'm not here about Roland, at least not directly." They stood side by side, facing the photograph rather than each other.

Everleigh turned in the direction of the growing crowd; even if she was curious, he was wasting precious time that could be spent showing people around. "I must be getting back to the show—"

"Bear with me, just for a moment." He wiped his forehead with a handkerchief. "The night of the fire, you saw Alice and me at the pool, having a row."

Everleigh nodded. Near the front door, she saw Starling talking to Curtis, and she wondered what they were saying. "Yes."

"That is true, we were in a row, and I told the detective that. But as you may know, the detective thinks I may be connected to the fire, which I am not, and I find his persistence frustrating. It's my good name on the line. So I started doing a little detective work of my own, and I've found something."

If her senses were radio dials, Everleigh tuned them for clarity. She tried to predict what Ernest would say next, but she couldn't. Had he kept something hidden all along and now he was pretending to reveal it to her?

"Remember, Alice left the party and returned to the city, while I passed out at the pool." A burst of college kids stepped inside with boisterous voices.

It was how Everleigh remembered the night, too. She'd gone to sleep after watching the staff mopping the conservatory, and she'd startled awake to the fire alarm. "It spread so quickly," Everleigh said.

Two beatniks examined the photographs, their expressions as severe as their outfits, mumbling something about how the photos were too soft. "I must have woken up at some point before the fire, though, because there was a housekeeper standing over me, a woman who brought me a blanket. As the investigator began questioning me more seriously, I knew I needed to find this housekeeper, to see what she knew because she was there as late as I was. Her name is Sara Nowak, she's a local woman, and I'll pass this on to the detective, but, Everleigh, Sara knows who was in room twenty-three on the night of the fire."

Sara was the woman who had snickered about Everleigh on her first day in the hotel, calling her a princess. "Why wouldn't the detective already know this? He spoke to everyone who worked at the hotel."

Ernest shook his head, pulling on the fabric of his shirt, shaking it to fan himself. "Well, that's what he said, but the detective's reach isn't as extensive as he's led everyone to believe."

The prospect of a mysterious housekeeper appearing out of the shadows seemed fairly convenient for Ernest, especially if the detectives were closing in on Alice and Ernest as the arsonists. "Why wouldn't she have come forward before this?"

Ernest tapped his foot. "Because she wasn't aware of the details of the investigation—she didn't know anyone was even looking for a hotel guest ledger. She's busy waitressing at a clam bar on the Napeague

Stretch with a toddler at home. She didn't even know that anyone wanted to know who was in room twenty-three. And I'm sorry, but there's something about Roland. Would you like to sit down?"

"No, I'm fine." Everleigh's throat tightened with fear. She'd distrusted Alice and Ernest all along; the clues she'd discovered suggested their involvement. But Everleigh also had to admit that Alice had been honest with her about Roland. Maybe there was something to this emerging detail. "Well, Roland was in bed with me, so I know it wasn't him. So who was it?"

Ernest hedged. "Well, I've only seen a picture of her, but she's local, too, her name is—" At that, the color drained from Ernest's face, and his eyes glared with extreme interest in the direction of Curtis, who was standing in the corner of the room sipping a flute of champagne. Next to Vivienne. Her long brown hair was divided into two plaits, each lying on one shoulder. Like no matter how she styled it, it would divide at the center and be held in place with those pearl barrettes. Everleigh struggled for air in her larynx.

"It's her," she said, pointing.

"Yes, Vivienne."

Vivienne with her pregnant belly. Vivienne who had stared creepily at Everleigh tonight. *Vivienne. Vivienne. Vivienne.*

Everleigh could no longer hear the voices of everyone at the party, their movements slowing, as though she'd just taken a photograph, freezing everyone in expression and gesture. She imagined her face— surprise, shock, realization—as she locked eyes with Vivienne and took in her expression—cowering, fear, denial. As if Vivienne was aware that someone knew she'd started the fire.

That Ernest knew. And now Everleigh did, too.

Gauging the speed of Everleigh's footsteps, the strain of her jaw, Vivienne's smile fell. She put her hand on Curtis's back a moment, saying something in his ear, and dashed out the Dutch door.

Everleigh ran out to the sidewalk, dusk only just settling in, looking for Vivienne's bright orange romper. The young woman was rushing in the direction of the windmill, back toward Bohack's Market. With the show in full swing, Everleigh couldn't leave the art gallery. She certainly wasn't going to call the police and disrupt Starling's grand opening.

Ernest stepped out onto the sidewalk, catching sight of Vivienne disappearing into the shadows. "That is her, I'm certain."

"She used to work at the front desk at the hotel. But why would she burn it down?" Everleigh said. Maybe she'd been wrong about Ernest and Alice. She'd been wrong about Stevie.

"I haven't figured that out yet. But it's something to do with Roland, Lee. He had a relationship with her. The entire staff knew that part, the housekeeper told me as much."

Everleigh's mind reeled. Vivienne batting her long eyelashes at Roland from behind the reception desk. Vivienne running down the stairs and banging into her the night of the fire. *Most likely, from room twenty-three.* Vivienne crying hysterically outside the blaze, like she was somehow responsible, while Everleigh consoled her. Vivienne picking up laundry the first time, flirting with Roland when she thought Everleigh couldn't hear.

And Vivienne tonight, clearly pregnant. Her small bump filling out her romper more than it should.

It was Stevie who ran the drug farm, but Vivienne obviously worked there based on the photograph tacked up at the stand. Roland pretended to run into Vivienne at the gas station, but perhaps he'd been seeing her all along. They were all certainly connected more than Roland let on; it was clear in how Vivienne looked at her tonight, possessed with envy, like she wanted to inhabit Everleigh, like she wanted to be her.

Ernest motioned to Alice, who was still inside, and he kissed

Everleigh goodbye on both cheeks. "I'll call the police and tell them what I know."

"Have a lovely wedding," Everleigh said, knowing despite this distraction, she still had to go in and work. "Ernest," she said, waiting for him to turn back. "Thank you."

Everleigh once again joined the exuberant voices carrying on inside the gallery, willing herself to focus and help Starling sell more prints. She walked more guests about, all while trying to connect the dots in her head.

Vivienne. Her too-small romper. Her rounded, bulging belly. The laundress was either the most cunning woman she'd ever met, or she was an innocent, wrapped up in something illegal that she no longer had control over.

The last patron left the art gallery around ten, three of the eight photographs sold and two others reserved for individuals who said they'd return the following day with their checkbooks. It wasn't a guarantee, but she and Starling were running on adrenaline, calling the night a huge success. Of course, they still had to see how the reviews came in; Sandy Slidings from the *New York Times* had walked the exhibit without expression for an hour, without even saying hello to Starling. Igor Cassini had kissed Starling on both cheeks before saying he would tell the world to come in Friday's Cholly Knickerbocker column.

Curtis came in holding a cheese pizza after fetching it for the women, who'd announced they were starving. They sat around a table littered with discarded champagne glasses and ate greasy slices off paper plates, comparing notes about the eclectic mix of attendees.

"I best be off." Starling put her plate in the trash. Friends from the art colony, people Everleigh was only just meeting, were throwing an afterparty on the beach. "It's just an excuse for them to drink heavily, but I suppose I better show up," Starling said, gathering her purse and two leftover bottles of champagne. "Will you two clean up when you're done? Then lock the gallery."

When Everleigh and Curtis were finally alone together, Everleigh became aware of her body, the breath rising inside her. The door had barely clicked shut when Curtis crawled closer to her, kissing her so softly on the lips she thought she was slipping into a pool of cotton.

"Thank you for coming." She grew trembly, thinking of Vivienne, even as she returned his kisses. She pulled away gently, not wanting him to think she wasn't interested. "Shall we tidy up first?"

Curtis put Elvis on the turntable, while Everleigh soaped the crystal flutes one at a time in the sink in the back of the gallery. Curtis carried in the glasses. She told him that she'd broken things off with Roland, that she'd made peace for now with her parents in the city. Then she turned the conversation toward what was really on her mind.

"Curtis," she said. "Tell me about Vivienne."

"What do you want to know?"

When she said, "Everything," he sighed.

"She's had a tough go of it. Her father ran out on them when Vivi was seven, and her mother . . . she started that laundry business, but she wasn't much of a mother. Laid a hand on her daughter one too many times."

The suds were vanishing, so she squeezed in more Lux dish detergent. "How awful. Did she come out okay?"

"Well, some of us tried to help, buying Vivi shoes or delivering hand-me-downs. She lived with us for a year, and my mother really tried, but she missed home, and ultimately, Vivi went back to her mother. A few years later, I heard she was living in the city, attending secretarial school. I didn't think she'd come back, and then here she was."

"Was there ever any . . ." Everleigh arranged the wet glasses on a cloth towel. "Well, was there ever any trouble with her?"

Curtis stopped drying and looked up. "You don't think she has something to do with the fire?"

Everleigh shared what the housekeeper told Ernest about Vivienne. How she was on the second floor, possibly in room twenty-three, where the fire originated. "It doesn't mean it's her, but Vivienne was there that night, and she's remained connected to our lives. Did you notice that she was pregnant?"

"I wasn't sure she was ready to say anything." He turned his back to the overturned champagne flutes, crumpling his face in thought. "Vivienne is the kind of person you always worry about. For years in high school, whenever I heard an ambulance, I wondered if it was her on the other side. I heard rumors she was mixed up in something bad."

Everleigh shook off a chill. Had Vivienne actually come to see Everleigh tonight? All night, she'd been studying her with that enamored expression. She'd tracked her movement in the gallery, looking away each time Everleigh caught her. Something about the interaction had felt threatening. It was why Everleigh had wanted her to leave.

"Has she ever hurt anyone?" she asked Curtis, who closed his eyes to think.

She soaped another glass, the water running through her fingers.

"There was some trouble." He dried the glass with a dish rag. "When she lived with us, my mother caught her with matches in one of the barns. She liked to light and blow them out, but then she set her fingers on fire. Mother found her one day, screaming while watching them burn, and we rushed her to the hospital. After that, I remember Mother hiding all of the matches on the highest shelf in the kitchen."

The puffy scarring on Vivienne's fingers; she'd noticed it when she'd picked up the laundry.

"That's beyond awful." Everleigh turned off the faucet. "Is she a depressive?"

He dried the final glass. "She'd get real low sometimes, sure."

So Vivienne was sick like Everleigh's mother was sick. A sadness that could overtake you, make you desperate enough to take your own life. Or start a destructive fire. Earlier tonight, Vivienne had said she and Curtis ran into each other outside Bohack's—that she was buying eggs—but she wasn't even holding a grocery bag. Maybe she put it in the car? Or was she trying to run into Curtis, using him as an excuse to get into the show?

When speaking to Ernest earlier, with Vivienne still across the room, it was as though Vivienne knew Everleigh would ask her about the fire. Vivienne had seen her pushing through the gallery crowd toward her, and she'd run. Had she fled to Roland? Everleigh knew he was having an affair, and why else would Vivienne be so interested in Everleigh? The day she'd picked up the laundry, Vivienne had flirted openly with Roland, and the energy that passed between them was palpable. Everleigh had known they were together, hadn't she, when she'd overheard them talking? But she'd ignored it, like she'd ignored many things.

Roland was good at picking up strays—they were always so impressed by his good looks, his important name. In his orbit, they had purpose. Stevie was a prime example. But it was embarrassing to Everleigh that she'd fallen into the same trap. She'd been so clouded by how perfectly put together his face was, how proud her parents were of their daughter's impressive catch. He got her at a weak moment, just as her mother went into the hospital, just when she needed someone to take care of her. He'd seen that, and he'd taken advantage of her the way he'd taken advantage of everyone else.

Maybe despite how different her and Vivienne's backgrounds were, they weren't all that different. They were two women looking for a man to make them feel wanted. To give them a place in this world.

Curtis took a step closer. "I don't think you should be alone tonight. Come stay with me, and we'll talk this through."

The invitation was a relief; she was a bit shaken up to go home to an empty cottage at the art colony. "I'll sleep on the couch."

His eyes crinkled. "Of course."

Everleigh dried her hands on the dish towel, then pulled Curtis to her by the waist. "Curtis, I need to talk to Vivienne—can you tell me where she lives? I'll go see her in the morning."

Curtis kissed one of her cheeks, then the other, then her lips. His were soft and warm, and in between he said, "She's on the main road, lives in a rancher house in Amagansett. Right behind Mecox Farm."

TWENTY-SIX

They went back to his house in the potato fields, passing one of the two barns that were dug partially underground to keep the crops cool. His car bounced along the dirt road in the dark, the night so still that after they parked, the slam of her car door sounded amplified. She imagined the scurry of every animal in earshot.

The porch light was off, and so was every lamp inside, so he told her to wait outside while he flicked on the lights. A small pond near the house was ringed with cattails and water lilies, the silence interrupted by a bullfrog serenading another with his rhythmic call.

"That's Norman." Curtis smiled when he popped his head out into the warm summer night. "You should see the size of him."

She imagined Curtis sitting near the pond and watching the frog, and she decided she would be content doing that with him, simply studying nature. "He's quite persistent." She laughed.

The farmhouse smelled of citrus, from the oranges on his kitchen table, and the brine of the sea, from the air blowing in through two open windows. There were tiny rosebuds on the kitchen wallpaper, and in the living room, a fireplace was bricked with a shelf across the mantel, lined with history books. Curtis mixed them both gin and tonics and they sat together on the navy couch, the curtains billowing with the wind, and they remained that way, talking and laughing, Everleigh feeling as content as she'd ever been. She snuggled into the crook of his arm, watching his fingers dangle just above her chest, sending a tingling through her blouse. She imagined what it would be like to live with him, how different it would be from living with Roland. Curtis took care of his house; he was a man who did his dishes and swept his floors.

"Will you go on a proper dinner date with me?" He threaded his fingers through hers against the couch.

She laughed because it was true; they'd spent time together but none of it included sitting across from one another at a restaurant. "Most certainly. I know this great clam bar in Montauk."

The corners of his mouth turned up. "Now you sound like a local girl."

At some point later, they fell asleep together on the couch, and she slept deeply, the comfort of his warmth under her. She dreamed of the sunflowers outside his windows, how lovely it would be to get lost in one of those fields with him, a placid smile overtaking her sleep.

But her conscious mind came to slowly, something pulling her awake. It was a voice, someone calling to her.

Everleigh.

The "leigh" dragged out with an *eee*, and Everleigh reached for the sunflowers, but the thick stalks disappeared, and she fell through the air, plunging downward. Another whisper.

Everleigh.

She snapped open her eyes, giving them time to adjust to Curtis's dark living room. A clock on the mantel ticked one. The curtains billowed like ghosts dancing in the room. The couch cushions beside her were empty.

"Everleigh." This time it was real. A voice, sounding just outside the window. She whipped her head around, thinking she saw the retreat of a shadow, but it was too hard to see anything in the blackness.

"Curtis," she called, waiting for a response. She could hear the rise and fall of her breath, too scared to look outside because she was certain she'd find a shadowy silhouette in the window frame. An enraged Roland, she thought. He was on the other side of these walls, hunting the grounds for her. But it couldn't be. It was a woman's voice.

The front door clicked open, and her chest thumped with fear. Everleigh braced herself, a deer in headlights. Curtis came in with a shotgun at his side. He balanced it upright in a corner in the hallway, his brows angled with concern.

"I'm sorry," he said. "I didn't want to wake you. I heard something, raccoons."

"Someone was calling my name. A woman." Everleigh started to cry. He wouldn't carry a gun for a raccoon.

He rubbed her back. "No, no. I was right outside. There's no one."

A floorboard on the porch creaked, and he shot up, listening. When he sat down, she said, "She was calling my name, just outside the windows. It's Vivienne. I just know it is." Roland had his faults, but she knew he wouldn't hurt her. But Vivienne, the way she'd sized her up at the gallery, the way she'd run out when Everleigh approached her, she might be scared that she had discovered her secret. She might have come to silence Everleigh.

His eyes darkened. "She wouldn't hurt anyone."

"So you say. But Curtis, we have to call the police," she whispered. "We shouldn't have waited. . . ."

There were sirens, the loud wailing sirens of fire trucks, racing somewhere closer to the main road, the lights ripping through the dark, a red strobe flashing through the potato fields. They ran to the windows, thinking somehow the firefighters were heading there, but they faded into the distance. A minute later Curtis's phone rang, the police alerting him there was a fire at Mecox Farm; he should remain on call.

After hanging up, he told Everleigh about the fire at the farm stand. "What if Vivienne set the fire?" he said. Curtis grabbed his keys to drive to Vivienne's house, Everleigh following, both of them running in a burst out the front door and onto the porch. *What if she'd done something to hurt herself?*

Out of the darkness came a voice. "He made me do it."

Everleigh's head smacked into Curtis's back, their bodies jumping at the sound of a woman's voice.

"Jesus, Vivienne."

Vivienne sat in a rocking chair, her cherubic face illuminated by the porch light. "I'm sorry I startled you. I was trying to talk to Lee. I can't leave town without her knowing Roland's part. That this was his doing."

Curtis glanced at the screen door, no doubt regretting that he couldn't get inside to his gun, not without being obvious.

"No one can make people do things, Vivienne, especially terrible things." The gall of this woman to come here, to come looking for her as though Everleigh was the one who did something wrong. "You lit the fire," said Everleigh. "The fire that tortured Roland, and you could have killed people. You could have killed me."

"And I followed you again tonight." Vivienne held her gaze, her cheeks dimpling with nerves, glossing her lips with her tongue, waiting for Everleigh to understand. Everleigh remembered the voice she heard tonight, the reality that someone was watching her—had been watching her all summer. She shuddered, her fingertips trembling. *Had Everleigh herself been the target all along?*

"You were trying to hurt me?"

All this time, Everleigh had assumed the arsonist was delivering revenge to Roland. But punishing Everleigh would punish him, too. The fire might take his hotel and his fiancée. Maybe even him.

Vivienne crossed her arms. "You have to understand my predicament. I was so angry."

Something in Curtis shifted, his posture stiffening. "Vivi, what is going on? Don't misplace your anger on Lee. She didn't do anything."

"Don't worry." Vivienne patronized him like an older sister. "I'm not going to hurt your little girlfriend."

That she even said she wouldn't hurt Everleigh was unsettling though, like it was up for discussion.

Curtis took a step closer. "Vivi! You and I, we're like family."

The woman nodded like she'd heard it all before, and her shoulders collapsed. She wiped the corners of her eyes. "I'm sorry, Curtis. Things are just so complicated."

They listened to her soft sniffles, plotting what to say next. Even though she was frightened, Everleigh sensed the woman needed care, that she was walking a tightrope and might jump at any minute. "Vivienne, I'm sorry for whatever he did to you." Her eyes went to the woman's stomach, where her belly rounded. "He's done it before."

Vivienne ignored her, talking as though she'd rehearsed this conversation for days, like someone wound her up and she wouldn't stop until everything was out. She reached into her pocket and pulled out a seahorse with the number twenty-three on it, a key dangling from the ring.

"Room twenty-three was our room. We'd meet there and daydream about what our life could be like together. We liked to talk about the future, Roland and me, ever since we met on a park bench in Central Park."

Everleigh glanced at Curtis, and he read her expression, turning his lips down in an apology. "You knew him in New York? When?"

"He broke things off with me after the two of you met. The biggest heartache of my life. But he came back one night saying that he missed me. That he needed to marry you, but when the time was right, he would return to me."

"The liar." The realization stung, even if Everleigh was done with Roland.

"I found out I was pregnant the day before the hotel fire. As a woman, you have to understand. . . . I loved him, and I came to tell him about the baby. He said he had to be with *you, you, you,* even if he cared for me. He said he wouldn't help me with the child. He'd drive me to a friend in the city who could take care of it. Well, I wouldn't."

A second child. A second woman he was willing to abandon. "I'm sorry, Vivienne," Everleigh said. "I didn't know—"

The woman scrunched her face into a wrinkled ball. "I waited for him in the room after the hotel party. He said he'd come once you were asleep, but then he didn't, and I sat there in my dress thinking how if I took you away, he would come back to me. So I lit that stupid match. But as the flames shot up, he never even came to check on me. It got too hot and I ran outside, and you consoled me on the lawn, and he ignored me still. I realized that I'd done something unthinkable." Vivienne tried to catch her breath, her chest heaving with upset. "You see, then, how he made me do it."

"But Vivienne," Everleigh started, locking worried eyes with Curtis. "Does he know it was you?"

"Of course he doesn't. He wouldn't have kept coming to the farm stand to see me. He'd take me for a walk, and we'd go into the laundry, and he'd bring me presents, like these." She twirled at her shiny earrings. "Two weeks before the fire, he gave me a locket with an *A* engraving, for *Amour,* his nickname for me. He changed his attitude, seemed to accept the baby was coming, promising to provide for me with a monthly allowance. Then just last week he told me he never wanted to see me again. For no reason at all."

The *A* on the locket; it didn't stand for Alice. It was why Everleigh couldn't find it on anyone's neck in the pictures from the party; she didn't take pictures of the help, which Vivienne had been.

There was so much to despise about this woman. There was a chance she'd been in the cottage while Everleigh was at the gallery. She might have had relations with her fiancé in *her bed*. She'd set the hotel fire hoping Everleigh would perish. And still, Everleigh's anger was directed at Roland. She pitied Vivienne, a couple of years younger than Everleigh, who was now facing an uncertain future.

She thought of her and Roland's big fight, how Everleigh had left Roland standing at the cottage. Perhaps he swore off extramarital affairs then, hoping to win back Everleigh's affections. Why else would he break things off with Vivienne, just as Everleigh was setting him free?

"Curtis and I, we will help you. We'll come up with a plan. . . . I won't let Roland get away with this."

Vivienne came to a stand, the rocking chair swaying behind her. "You rich people are all the same, thinking everything can be solved with money. I loved him, Everleigh." In the distance, another fire truck blared, and the sound of it made her smile. She thrust her shoulders back, inhaling deeply and wiping her eyes. "Anyway, he's getting his, and I must be going. Far, far from this awful place."

Curtis followed her off the porch steps, putting a hand on her shoulder. "Vivi, you don't have anything to do with those sirens, do you?"

She shrugged, smiling, her dimples masking her wicked expression. "Don't you worry about me. All that money he and Stevie were hiding, those stacks of twenties from the farm stand they'd been using to fund the hotel's renovation, they left it in Mama's old horse corral. Well, now it's in the trunk of my car. I took everything from him. I'm only sorry that I won't pay you back your share."

My share, Everleigh thought. "So they used that money I gave Roland to start the drug business at the farm?"

"They can be quite crafty together, Stevie and Roland, but the police have caught up with them. Did you hear that Roland was arrested yesterday? On an anonymous tip." Vivienne grinned. "They certainly underestimated me."

Vivienne took off running down the path through the sunflowers, while Everleigh fell backward into the rocking chair. With her gone, the darkness no longer felt like a threat, and Everleigh considered what Vivienne had said, about how long she and Roland had known each other, that Roland and Stevie had used Everleigh's father's money to fund their illegal dealings. It was as though she had never known Roland at all. "Every time he left the house, every single thing he said to me. I had no idea how many lies he was telling."

"Just remember that he can't hurt you anymore." Curtis cradled her cheek with his hand, and she turned her face to kiss his palm. She closed her eyes. If Roland had been with Vivienne before meeting Everleigh, he'd never stopped loving the local woman. Which meant he'd never fully loved Everleigh. When she opened her eyes, Curtis smiled.

"I'm still here," he said. They sat on the couch for an hour in the dark, still in shock, working to understand, through a series of yawns, what had propelled Vivienne to do it. The desperation she must have felt.

Light slipped over the horizon.

They trudged up the stairs holding hands. Everleigh would call the detective in the morning, or maybe she wouldn't call him at all. Telling on Vivienne meant she might be captured, that her baby would be taken from her. Everleigh couldn't decide if the woman deserved her freedom or not. Vivienne had so clearly been wronged. But even after learning Vivienne had set the fire, Everleigh knew she wasn't entirely crazy. Vivienne was a woman trapped. A woman who felt like she didn't have any options. Then again, she'd done the unthinkable, nearly killing an entire hotel full of people.

"We need to turn her in, but we'll give her a head start." Curtis's head had already hit the navy-blue pillowcase, and Everleigh nodded. "Let's fall asleep holding each other," he said.

The sweetness of his gesture momentarily pulled her away from what Roland had done to her, what Vivienne had done to the hotel. She remembered the art opening, the days developing photographs with Starling, how Curtis looked when she found him that first day in her viewfinder, the pride she felt when she saw her photograph in the newspaper. The realization that you could find happiness in the hardest of times. Which is what her mother had inadvertently taught her. That resilience had a face.

SEPTEMBER

TWENTY-SEVEN

Promptly at five, Everleigh emerged from the Juniper Gallery into the humid summer air to find Curtis, his race car parked on the street. Tourists slowed as they walked down the sidewalk, shopping bags in hand. Not entirely gawking, but rather curious about where this flashy yellow car had come from. Curtis leaned up against the passenger door, where the number ninety-nine shined in metallic paint, draping one arm across the length of the open window. He'd won the Bridgehampton Sports Car Races two weeks before, a large golden trophy now sitting on the mantel of his fireplace.

"Are you posing for me?" She twisted her hair up into a bun, her neck hot with sweat.

"I thought you might want to go for a drive." He had this way of tipping his chin down and looking up at her that was flirty, but it also gave her the impression that she was the only thing he could see, no matter how many lives unfolded around them.

"Only if I'm in the driver's seat. You're not the only one who likes to drive fast cars, you know."

"Oh, I know." He winked at her, and she chuckled, because who winked anymore besides cheesy dads on television shows, or small-town pediatricians?

Starling had been giving her a ride to and from the gallery every day, but the show was coming to an end this first week in September. Then Everleigh had to find her own way. She'd been hired to man the desk at the gallery for the next show, a collection of watercolor paintings by a local painter. The gallery's owner had recently boarded the *Queen Mary* destined for London and needed someone to answer the phones. For fifty dollars a week, Everleigh jumped at the position. One block from the bay she'd found a small cottage, which Whitney had helped her and Mango move into last week, a space of her own with heat, unlike the art colony, where she couldn't stay once the weather turned cool. She and Curtis had spent nary a day apart, but she didn't want to rush into another relationship either. She'd been in touch with her parents to secure a small loan. She would pay them back in monthly increments, but she needed to buy her own car to go back and forth to work.

The radio blared from the car windows, loud enough to hear it from the pavement, and it was playing the first acoustic riffs of "Bye Bye Love." The Everly Brothers' hit was her favorite song of the summer—it might have been in everyone's top three—and every time it came on the transistor in the kitchen, Everleigh turned it up so loud, the speaker crackled enough to make her turn it down a smidge.

Curtis reached into the car and turned it up even louder. Tourists stopped to see what was happening, if the sudden increase in volume signaled that the gentleman was about to make a grand announcement. Curtis started to sing along to the song, quietly at first, but then, realizing he had an audience, he pretended to hold a microphone, sliding to the right as if he were gliding on air. Then he started belting out the song along with the music.

There goes my baby with someone new. She sure looks happy. I sure am blue. She was my baby . . .

"Isn't that Doc Brightwell?" a woman holding a toddler said.

"Hey, Doc." A matronly type in a red-skirted suit grinned. "Don't you have patients?"

He waved, then refocused on Everleigh, who found herself rocking to the beat in her blush skirt and navy blouse, embarrassed that anyone was looking at them at all. That Starling might see her through the window acting a fool in love.

Starling. That is who she cared most about, and the artist was leaving tomorrow to return to the city. Everleigh couldn't bear it.

Bye bye love. Bye bye happiness. Hello loneliness. I think I'm going to cry.

Curtis spun on the pads of his feet, taking her hand and pulling her close, like they were back on the dance floor at the hotel's grand opening. Her espadrilles kept in line with his rhythmic footwork, and she let herself go in his arms, singing along to the song and spinning in and out of his embrace as he led her. To be led. It felt wonderful to feel his body suggest a movement to her, and then there she'd go, because she wanted to, not because she had to.

The detective had called her a few days after the gallery opening to alert her that Roland and Stevie would be held indefinitely for their drug business; apparently, he'd been investigating the pair as closely as he had been the fire. It was reported in the Cholly Knickerbocker column soon after that Mr. Whittaker Sr. had flown in from Detroit with his lawyer to bail Roland out, at least temporarily, and she still hadn't heard what happened to Stevie.

Everleigh ran into Roland only once, at the grocery market, of all places. It was awkward in the way that it's always awkward when you're thrust into conversation with someone you've fallen out of love with. Roland was clean-shaven as always, smelling of his cedar cologne, and she didn't tell him that Vivienne had come to the farmhouse, that she'd admitted to setting the fire, even if police still hadn't found her. She knew he'd seen it in the papers, the main suspect leaked to reporters by an unnamed source. Instead, she'd asked after the hotel, and he'd said he found a better property in Boca Raton and would be leaving town as soon as he found a buyer for Gin Lane. They'd said a pleasant good-bye. It was strange leaving so much unresolved between them, and yet the conversation they could have had would have been so big, so mentally draining, that she'd decided it would be best simply not to have it.

The song wasn't over, but the crowd applauded as if they were winning something, and she supposed dancing in the street at five o'clock on a weekday was like winning at life. Because when else would you ever do this? She pulled away from him for a moment, forcing her stiff rich-girl shoulders to loosen, and she fluttered her eyes open, grinning and laughing.

It was disingenuous to say that Curtis had made her this happy. She wouldn't give a man credit for freeing this spirit inside of her. It was living on the beach and working for Starling. It was how seriously Starling took her opinion, the fact that Starling had given her that first assignment. Maybe it was hokey, but it was those mornings making eggs at the stove. The sense that she was taking care of herself. But Curtis, he'd helped, too. Because he encouraged her; he loved her this way, this new way she felt.

"Why did you ask me to dance that night? At the hotel opening," she asked him. He'd seemed to pluck her out of the crowd, and she wondered if she hadn't seen him again at the party, whether they would even be together.

Curtis twirled her around beside the car. "It was your height."

She burst into laughter, disappointed with the answer. "Oh right. The giraffe on the dance floor."

He was blushing, and she sensed that there was something else he wanted to say. "Well, your height is what made me notice you. But I asked you to dance because you looked so strong standing there, like you knew exactly who you were."

But she hadn't known then. She was only still learning about herself out here in her cottage near the sea. She locked her arms around his neck with a coquettish grin. "Well, you did say I was a 'windmill girl.'"

"My windmill girl," he said. And then he kissed her.

The trunk of Starling's station wagon was loaded with a large green duffel and several camera bags as well as photo lights and reflective screens. Everleigh pushed in a box of files Starling had been keeping in the gallery, a record of any sales they'd made, a catalog of the portraits they'd created, many of them taken out of the frames and filed in between slices of tissue paper to keep the pictures from sticking.

"Let's sit outside with our green juice," Starling said, her spirits more chipper than Everleigh's that morning. Everleigh didn't want her to go. They were friends, but more than that, Starling had been a teacher and Lee her pupil. There was still so much she wanted to learn, and not just about photography.

In the back of the gallery, Starling split the thick concoction she'd brought into two paper cups, then handed Everleigh one, keeping the other. When they were sitting on the park bench out front, Starling held up her cup in a toast. "To no longer being blocked."

"Oh yes, cheers," Everleigh said, drinking a gulp and gagging. "Oh, Starling, I try, but I don't know how you drink this stuff."

Starling laughed. "It keeps me going. It's kept you going."

No, you kept me going. A bus puttered by, the faces of people in the windows looking out at them. It popped and hissed as it started and slowed.

"What will I do now?" Everleigh asked. She didn't really expect an answer, and yet Starling had walked her through every other big decision she'd made this summer. A lifetime stretched out before her, a vast unknowingness that thrilled but also scared her. The artist turned her head, her glasses straight on her nose, a crinkle in her eyes.

"You will live, Everleigh. You will live like you never have before. And you will send your pictures to me as you develop them. Won't you? So we can talk about them and make them better. Because you will get better."

Everleigh remembered the day she'd asked Starling for the job, how she'd hugged her, and the woman had been awkward, her arms hanging limp by her sides. She wanted to hug her now. "And what will you do?"

This close, Starling's face was nearly translucent, her skin so fine, a labyrinth of faint blue veins crossing her cheeks. "Oh, what I always do. Wait for the phone to ring. Dinners at Sardi's. Go off to my next assignment."

Everleigh turned sideways on the bench, crossing her legs. "I have an idea, you know." She explained about Whitney's mother being on the board of a publishing house, how Whitney had talked endlessly about Starling's pictures to her, how they were interested in turning Starling's works into an art book. "Wouldn't that be grand? I gave them your phone number back in New York."

Starling took her hand, just as her mother would have, squeezing it. "You're a good girl, Lee. A really good girl."

Her chest burned with heartache while glowing with pride. "I'll never forget you," Everleigh managed, smiling. "I feel like we need a yearbook to sign. You know, where you write 'Friends forever.'"

Starling beamed, throwing her head back in a belly laugh. "Oh, those girls, and those awful empty lines."

With her hands back in her lap, Everleigh watched as Starling stood and lifted her glasses to dab at her eyes with the sides of her thumbs. "Guess who I'm having lunch with next week?"

Everleigh followed Starling to her car. She raised an eyebrow. "Who?"

"My daughter. I'm going to Virginia to see her and my grand-daughter."

Everleigh jumped up and down, clapping. "That's wonderful. Really."

"You reminded me, doll, just how much we girls need each other." Starling turned over the engine. "So thank you, Everleigh."

The moment seemed full and long, everlasting, until the artist put the car in drive.

"Starling, wait." How could she have forgotten? Everleigh dashed inside and pulled something out of her purse, a photograph she'd taken the night of the gallery opening. She ran outside with it, then handed it to Starling through her open car window.

"What is this?" Starling said. Everleigh watched her friend take it. It was Starling, standing catty-corner to the portrait of Nat King Cole, her face radiating as she grinned at someone off camera. Everleigh had developed it in black and white.

Everleigh pressed her lips together. She loved this picture, and she hoped Starling did, too. "I shot it from the hip."

Starling adjusted her glasses. "You got lucky, didn't you? I like the contrast with Nat behind me, sure. You framed me well, too, got my back at the right angle, even the buttons of my blouse are in line with the seam of the wall behind me. It's very interesting." The photographer tucked it into her purse on the passenger seat.

"It's your happy face." Everleigh couldn't help it now; she had to hug her. She ducked into the car window, embracing the artist, who smelled of developing solution; after all these years in the darkroom, the acrid scent must have seeped into her skin like perfume. She didn't care if Starling didn't hug her back.

But then she felt Starling squeezing her. After a few seconds, they let go, the two of them smiling at each other.

"We had good times, didn't we?" Starling waved, her hands

sheathed in white leather driving gloves, her hair tied back with a gingham scarf. "Okay, dear. See you in the city."

"I'll send you my photos," Everleigh yelled as the car pulled off.

Everleigh had wondered all along what she'd see when she looked at Starling through the camera lens. She'd never tried to take her picture, knowing the artist would have said no. But at the art opening, it had been easy. Everyone was taking photographs that night. She might have taken the picture she'd given her from the hip, but Everleigh had taken many others looking into her viewfinder. Photographs where she raised her camera, adjusted the focus, and snapped.

Even now, Everleigh was surprised at the woman she found on the other side of the lens. Because when she looked at Starling, she saw herself.

Everleigh turned on her heels, facing the quaint white building with the dentil molding around the trim. She stepped inside the blue Dutch door, sat behind the desk, and put her feet up on it. She glanced around the empty space in the bright morning sunlight.

A film of confidence washed over her. She found herself grinning, even though there wasn't anyone to smile at. Because this was her life, and it was hers to keep.

ACKNOWLEDGMENTS

Novels are inspired by myriad experiences, people, and moments, but the beginning of this story can be traced back to an article I read while researching *Summer Darlings*. I came across a story about the fascinating marriage of prominent Chicago businessman Potter Palmer and his young socialite wife, Bertha Honore. In 1871 Potter surprised his new wife with an extravagant gift: the glamorous Palmer House hotel on the Chicago Loop. Thirteen days after its grand opening, the hotel burned to the ground in the Great Chicago Fire. The stunning Palmer House that is known today was rebuilt on a $1.7 million loan, and at its completion, the hotel's luxury amenities rivaled the fanciest hotels in the nation. (The floor of the Palmer House's barber shop was said to have been tiled in silver dollars.)

After reading this snippet, my imagination began to reel—the idea that Bertha's fiancé gifted her a hotel, that it burned to the ground thirteen days later, that their relationship weathered such a tragic beginning. I immediately imagined a young, wealthy engaged couple in Manhattan in the 1950s. My heroine's fiancé would give her a similar unforgettable gift: in my novel, a Southampton luxury hotel. While I haven't stepped foot in the Palmer House, the beginnings of the famed hotel gave me a fascinating plot to hang a novel on.

368

ACKNOWLEDGMENTS

I grew up near Southampton on eastern Long Island's north shore, and multiple times each summer, my parents would pile us into the car and make the one-hour journey out to Montauk to spend time with my aunts and uncles and cousins who lived or summered there. Old timers in the Hamptons like to lament what it used to be like (rather than the busy, heavily trafficked, but still beautiful locale it is today), so I thought to myself: *What was it really like back then?* For my research, I relied on local historians, interviews with long-time summer and year-round residents, and the digital archives of papers like the *East Hampton Star*.

For help in filling out details of the time, thank you to Dan Rattiner, editor-in-chief of *Dan's Papers*, who spent hours with me on Zoom during COVID times letting me mine his knowledge of the area at midcentury; Emily Guerrero, a local history librarian at Southampton's Rogers Memorial Library; Mary Cummings, historian at the Southampton History Museum; Laura Donnelly, a food critic at the *East Hampton Star* who regaled me with stories of her East Hampton summers with her famed grandparents Gerald and Sara Murphy; Howard Katz (thank you, Zibby Owens), whose accounts of summering in Southampton in his twenties helped illuminate the times; Laurie Carson, whose family has been in Southampton for five generations, painted a vivid picture of the 1950s and 1960s; Andrea Meyer, archivist at the East Hampton Library, who helped with very specific questions of the time period; and *New York Times* writer Julie Satow, whose book *The Plaza: The Secret Life of America's Most Famous Hotel* answered most of my questions about Everleigh's home at the iconic New York hotel. The following books also offered helpful portraits: *Hamptons Bohemia: Two Centuries of Artists and Writers on the Beach*, *Ninth Street Women: Five Painters and the Movement That Changed Modern Art*, the writings of Patricia Highsmith, the words and pictures of photographers like Richard Avedon and Diane Arbus, who inspired a character like Starling.

When the team at Gallery acquired my first novel, I didn't realize I was being invited into a superstar team of publicity, editorial, and design professionals. Now I've been blessed to work with them a second time. Marketing whiz Abby Zidle, your kindness is something I'll always be grateful for; thank you for all your hard work and support. To Lauren Truskowski, thank you for your publicity genius (and all your patience when I asked a million questions!). To publisher Jen Bergstrom for trusting in my novels and giving them a true home, and to the design team—the BEST out there—who created this stunning cover (and the last one, too). My wonderful acquiring editor, Kate Dresser, got this story from the start, and the insightful Maggie Loughran didn't just pick up where she left off; she pushed the story to new heights. Maggie: You were an unexpected gift. Without your careful attention, this novel would not be as fast-moving or compelling. To my agent, Rebecca Scherer: Somehow you are always able to see what I'm trying to do in my stories long before I accomplish it. Thank you for the endless readings and your ability to get me where I'm trying to go.

To Nancy Fann-Im for your time, especially when you have so little of it: You helped me shape this novel in its midlife. Laura Bower: Your cheerleading and editorial advice are something I've come to depend on. Meredith Mialkowski: Thank you for loving (and critiquing) everything I give you to read. Mom: Thank you for gifting me your stories of Montauk in the sixties—such fun. Fellow writers Jean Huff and Carolyn Lyall, and my teachers Pat Dunn and Jimin Han: Those days we showed up for class on Zoom during lockdown sustained me in those dark days. So did your belief in my story.

To Harper, your endless desire to create is awe inspiring. Thank you for being quite possibly the only twelve-year-old boy on the planet who wants to talk through novel ideas and character development with his mother. And to Emerson, my seven-year-old extraordinaire, whose wisdom, generosity, and effervescent personality cast a brilliance on everything you do. The two of you are my finest creations.

To John. Thank goodness you walked into Math 110 with that long hair and ridiculous necklace all those years ago. I fell in love in an instant, and that love is what keeps me going. It's me and you forever.